The Wilderwomen

ALSO BY RUTH EMMIE LANG

Beasts of Extraordinary Circumstance

The Wilderwomen

Ruth Emmie Lang

ST. MARTIN'S PRESS
NEW YORK

This is a work of fiction. All of the characters, organizations, and events portrayed in this novel are either products of the author's imagination or are used fictitiously.

First published in the United States by St. Martin's Press, an imprint of St. Martin's Publishing Group

Printed in the United States of America. For information, address St. Martin's Publishing Group, 120 Broadway, New York, NY 10271.

Designed and illustrated by Gabriel Guma

ISBN 9781250246912

To my parents, Norma and Jas,
who made us a home despite missing theirs

The Wilderwomen

BEFORE

Nora Wilder was supposed to be a bird. At least that's what she thought when she looked at herself in the mirror and saw arms where wings should be. The closest she actually came to flying was when her younger daughter, Finn, slipped from her grasp and sprinted toward a busy street. Nora swooped down on the toddler, and Finn's tiny body began to tremble in her arms. As her daughter anxiously kneaded her chest, Nora stroked her soft-spun curls and wished she didn't have to scare her baby to keep her safe.

Although her wings were imaginary, Nora felt an almost continuous desire to stretch them, to unclench the knot in her back that tied them down and with one powerful flap, lift off into a cloudless sky. Their being imaginary also didn't mean that her wings weren't so blue they were almost black, the kind of blue you wade into and disappear. That's what Nora saw when she walked out her front door for the last time: the tips of two ink-blue wings fanning her peripherals, one for each of the daughters she would leave behind.

Nora's elder daughter, Zadie, must have been part bird because she knew how to squawk. When Zadie was a baby, Nora was convinced that she must have swallowed bagpipes filled with broken glass, because that was the sound that came out of her mouth every time she cried. It sometimes lasted for hours at a time, and Nora did everything she could think of to get her to stop. She would try rocking her, feeding her, changing her. When all else failed, she'd play one of her favorite cassettes in hopes it would soothe her daughter to sleep.

It wouldn't. Zadie would only wail harder. Nora would look at the phone on the wall and wish she had someone she could call, someone who'd rush over and recommend a kooky home remedy like rubbing smashed bananas on her baby's chest while counting to one hundred. That wouldn't work, either, but at least she'd have someone to talk to and hug when she started crying, too.

She was alone in a town she barely knew with a screaming baby who had terrible taste in music, but something outside of herself was telling her this was the place she was supposed to be.

One morning, after a sleepless night and four Tom Waits albums, Zadie was particularly ornery. "Hey! I don't make fun of *your* music," Nora joked feebly and stopped the tape.

Out of ideas, Nora crossed the room and opened a window to let in some fresh air. "Feel that breeze?" she said to the writhing, red-faced creature in her arms. "Isn't it nice?" Zadie's bleating abated a little and she cautiously cracked open a pair of eyelids that until now appeared to have been swollen shut. Nora tracked her child's gaze to something in the walnut tree outside the window: a thrush. It puffed out its spotted chest, tilted its head back, and sang four lilting notes with a trill at the end, and just like that, Zadie's crying stopped. Nora was so relieved she started laughing. "So you like birds, too, huh? Well, at least we have *something* in common."

That afternoon Nora bought a bird feeder at the hardware store, filled it with birdseed, and hung it on the tree outside Zadie's bedroom window. When it was time to put her down for the night, Nora opened the window, and the room filled with the sounds of whippoorwills, mockingbirds, robins, and thrushes. Zadie's eyes opened wide; then slowly they began to loll. As the birdsong turned to crickets, the arms that cradled Nora's baby grew feathers the color of the night sky, and Nora sang a song about a little bird who was both very near and very far from home.

AFTER

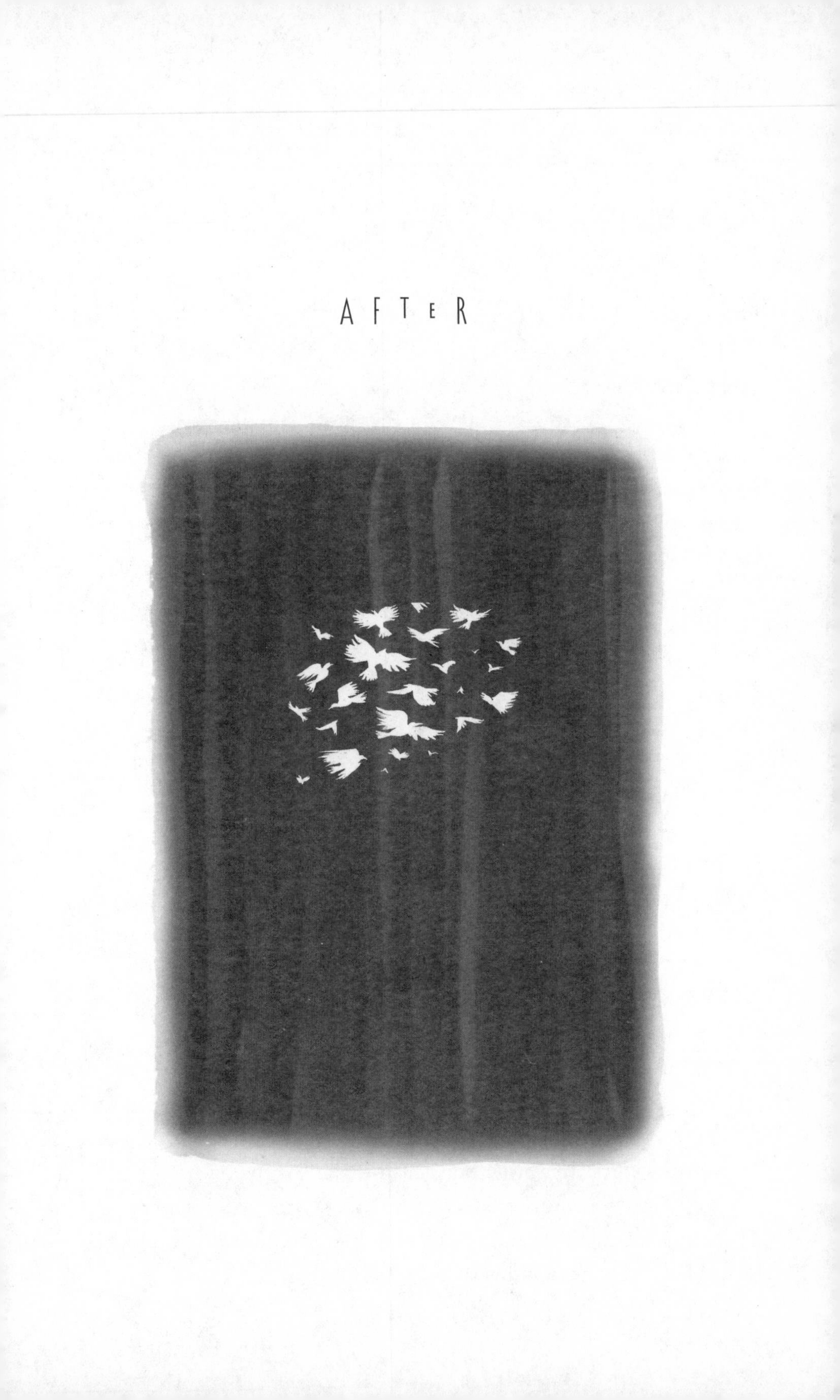

ONE

THOUGHTS ON SUN HATS

Zadie Wilder owned six sweaters, four pairs of leggings, and one extra-large beach towel. The reason she knew she had exactly six sweaters, four pairs of leggings, and one extra-large beach towel was that she was attempting to cram all of them inside an already bursting suitcase. She had to work fast. Her ex, Dustin, would be clocking out in a few minutes, and she hadn't even packed any of her cassettes yet. Out of all her worldly possessions, her cassette collection was the one thing she couldn't bear seeing smashed on the pavement below their—okay, *his* third-story apartment window.

Dustin was never quite able to grasp why she cared so much about them. "They were my mom's," Zadie had said.

"Yeah, but didn't your mom, like, *leave* you?" Callous, maybe, but not untrue. To this day, Zadie still wondered why Nora hadn't taken any of her cassettes with her. Her mom's '97 RAV4 might have had a hole in the floor and sounded like a go-kart when it accelerated, but at least it had had a working tape deck. The day Zadie got her driver's license, Nora had tossed her the keys and they drove around town for hours listening to the tapes Nora kept in the glove compartment. That's how Zadie discovered Blondie, the Indigo Girls, and Prince. When Nora left two years later, she took the car, but Blondie and the rest of her musical idols stayed behind. *It's not like her,* Zadie, still in shock, had thought at the time. *She never goes anywhere without her music*. In a way, it was more surprising than the disappearance itself.

Now it was Zadie's turn to disappear. Dustin had asked that she "leave no trace" of ever having been in his apartment. As Zadie rinsed a lipstick smudge off one of his glass tumblers, she felt more like she was covering up a crime scene than surrendering the title of Dustin's part-time live-in girlfriend. Soon she would go back to her own apartment, unpack her things, and decide how sad she really was about the breakup. Right now she didn't feel much of anything, except maybe a little nauseous.

It's not like she was totally alone. If she got lonely, she could talk to the Ladybug. According to the various mommy blogs, Zadie's baby was the size of a sweet pea, but she found the whole food-to-child analogy creepy. It made it sound like her baby was something to be harvested when ripe, then stuffed in a cornucopia on Thanksgiving with some gourds and ears of corn. So instead she decided to measure the size of her child against other living things. At six weeks, her baby was approximately a quarter of an inch long, the size of a ladybug. In two weeks, it would be the size of a honeybee. Eventually it would be big enough that she could start comparing it to cuter animals: a chipmunk, maybe, or a kitten, but for now she'd have to settle for ones with exoskeletons.

"You were kind of his idea, you know." Zadie addressed her midsection as she placed the clean glass in the dish rack. Dustin had broached the subject of kids a few months earlier during a trip to the animal shelter. As they browsed crates of underexercised dogs, he said, "You know what would be even cooler than a dog?"

Zadie thought he was going to suggest they adopt a snake or an iguana, some gross bachelor-pad animal that would require keeping tubs of crickets in their freezer. She opened her mouth to protest when he blurted, "A kid!"

The next day, in true Dustin fashion, he forgot he had even made the suggestion. Then several months later, in an ironic twist of fate, Zadie found herself pregnant anyway—a fact that she had still not yet shared with anyone, including Dustin. She should have seen it coming, and not just because she had terrible luck, but because she could literally *see things coming.*

She was seven years old when she first realized there was something different about her. That day she was "helping" her mom in the yard by detonating the piles of leaves that Nora had spent all morning raking. Through the leaves that tumbled in front of her, she saw Clarence, Finn's father, smiling at her from atop a ladder that was leaning against the side of the house. He pulled a wet bundle of leaves out of the gutter, held them up for her to see, and made a stink face. Zadie took this as a challenge. She reached into one of her mom's piles, held up her own bundle of leaves, then tossed them into the air like confetti. Clarence tried tossing his leaves, too, but they clumped together and landed on the driveway with a splat. Zadie giggled.

As Clarence turned his attention back to the task at hand, Zadie was struck by an uneasy sensation. To her seven-year-old brain, it was much like the feeling she experienced when she went too high on the swings and her stomach felt like it was floating. It was soon followed by a single scary thought: *Clarence is going to fall like the leaves.* Confused and frightened, she turned to her mom, who was in the middle of bagging the leaves she'd collected. Before Zadie could utter a word, she heard a crashing sound behind her. She whipped around and saw Clarence on the ground, clutching his left leg. It looked funny, like her dolls' legs did after she'd turned them around the wrong way.

Then the screaming started. Zadie had never heard a grown man make a noise like that before. It was the scariest thing she had ever heard. Nora rushed over to him as Zadie fled into the house and up the stairs to her bedroom. She hid under the covers and cried until she heard the wail of the ambulance.

It had taken Zadie several days to work up the courage to tell her mom what had happened to her that day. By that time, Clarence was camped out on the couch and using a wire clothes hanger to scratch under his cast. Zadie made sure the door to the living room was closed before she said, "It's my fault."

"What's your fault, hon?" Nora's tone was gentle, understanding. Zadie artfully dodged her mother's gaze as she shared the phrase that had entered her head moments before Clarence fell. That was the day she learned what a psychic was and that maybe she was one. It was also the day she decided that a psychic was something she'd rather not be.

Unfortunately for Zadie, she didn't have much say in the matter. Like an outdoor cat, her premonitions came and went as they pleased, filling her head with strange and often cryptic phrases that she had no idea how to interpret. Thankfully, she never had visions. Her sight was her own. It was her mind that sometimes felt like it belonged to someone else.

If she felt one of these unwanted thoughts coming on, she'd stick her fingers in her ears, close her eyes, and hum a song. Sometimes that was enough to quiet her mind, at least for a while.

Her attitude shifted as she entered her teen years, however, and she taught herself how to harness her gift to her advantage. Her primary objective was no more complicated than that of other kids her age: to impress her friends. And it worked for the most part. When she won six free concert tickets from an unsuspecting DJ by predicting what song would come on the radio next, she invited the five cutest boys in her class to go with her. She got her first kiss that night.

But even as she cheated radio stations and dumped boys hours before they'd planned to dump her, she had one steadfast rule: never use her ability for anything of consequence. She preferred it that way. The last thing she wanted was to be that person in a disaster movie whom everyone thinks is crazy for predicting the apocalypse. Then when it turns out she was right all along, everyone looks to her to fix it. Zadie didn't want that kind of responsibility. It was hard enough just getting to work on time every day without neighbors bugging you about when the rapture was coming.

Or at least that's what she told herself to help her sleep at night.

A half-baked practical argument was easier to stomach than the true reason she'd stopped using her gift completely: that one awful moment she'd spent a thousand wishes trying to undo.

Before her mind had time to go down that particular rabbit hole, Zadie heard a faint *ding* in the other room. Someone had texted her. Either it was a message from Dustin reminding her to remove "that slimy seed goo" (i.e., chia seed pudding) from his fridge, or it was her little sister, Finn. Her high school graduation party was tomorrow, and Zadie was dreading it. She would have to drive an hour each way from her apartment in Austin to the exurbs of San Antonio just to make awkward small talk with Finn's foster family, the Andersons. They were nice enough, but Zadie got the distinct impression that they didn't like her. She couldn't blame them, really. For the entire first year Finn was living with them, Zadie, who was eighteen at the time, did whatever she could to get her sister back.

With Clarence long out of the picture—he'd left when Finn was three and was rumored to be living in South Africa with his new wife and baby—Zadie was Finn's next of kin. The case officer at Child Protective Services told Zadie that she needed to provide proof of stable full-time employment before they would even consider granting her legal guardianship. "But she's my sister!" Zadie had protested.

"I know," the woman said patiently—or patronizingly, as Zadie remembered it—"but we have to think about what's best for Finn."

If Zadie had been a year younger when their mom left, someone would have helped her decide what was *best* for her, too, but because she was technically an adult, she had to figure that out on her own. Five years later, she was still working on it.

Zadie was on her way to the bedroom to get her phone when a wave of severe nausea overtook her. She sprinted to the bathroom and surrendered the contents of her stomach into the toilet bowl. This was just one of the many perks of her first trimester that Zadie wished she could predict on command. If only she could have premonitions that would allow her to slip away discreetly and arrive at the bathroom with time to spare, not crash into a stall like a college student on a bar crawl. Sadly, the premonitions that managed to sneak by the wall she'd put up were rarely that accommodating.

Her phone dinged again. Zadie gargled some mouthwash, then went to the living room and picked it up. She was surprised to find that both texts were from Finn (she usually forgot to text Zadie back). The first one read:

SWIMSUIT SHOPPING NOW. WHAT ARE YOUR THOUGHTS ON SUN HATS?

LIKE, DO PEOPLE REALLY WEAR THEM OR ONLY IN MOVIES?

Then, three minutes later:

TOO LATE. I BOUGHT THE BIGGEST ONE IN THE STORE AND I LOVE IT.

Zadie had no strong feelings either way about sun hats, but she was looking forward to the trip Finn and she had planned. They were going to drive down to Galveston and spend a week drinking sweet tea and reading on the beach. Zadie had already gone to the library and checked out an embarrassingly large stack of romance novels.

For Zadie, it was a chance for her sister and her to reconnect. When Zadie still lived in their old neighborhood just north of San Antonio, she would take Finn out every Friday for frozen yogurt, but after she moved to Austin a year later, it wasn't long before their weekly ritual became a monthly one. Now, if she was lucky, they saw each other a few times a year.

It's not like either sister had overtly decided to cut ties with the other. Over time, they had just sort of drifted apart like unmanned canoes, or rather, Zadie had drifted while Finn stayed safely tied to the dock. Recently, Zadie had felt like she couldn't even see the shore anymore. Her family was somewhere in the salty haze, so obscured that she sometimes doubted its very existence. It was during one of these moments of existential panic that she called up Finn and asked if she wanted to take a post-graduation trip with her.

In four days, she would have her family back (or what was left of it). They might not have been as close as they once were, but Finn belonged with her, not Steve or Kathy or anyone else.

Not even their mother.

Nora Wilder was a ghost to Zadie, and ghosts don't exist.

Zadie unlocked her phone and texted Finn back:

HOW BIG ARE WE TALKING ON A SCALE OF FEDORA TO SOMBRERO?

Three typing bubbles came up on the screen, followed by a GIF of a shirtless, presumably inebriated man balancing a kiddie pool on his head.

CLASSY, she texted, then checked the time. It was almost five-thirty. Dustin would be home any minute. Zadie dragged her misshapen suitcase to the front door, then went back for her box of cassettes. As she picked it up, she felt a premonition rising in her gut. "Noooooo. Not now," she groaned as the feeling intensified.

Zadie shut her eyes and hummed the first song that popped into her head: "Everybody Wants to Rule the World" by Tears for Fears. By the time she'd reached the second verse, the feeling had passed and she heaved a sigh of relief. The last thing she wanted to know about right now was the future. She needed to get through the present first.

Look on the bright side. People were always peddling silver linings to her, ever since she was a kid. She'd said, "But I don't have a dad."

They'd said, *At least you have a mom.*

After her mom left, she'd said, "I don't have a mom."

They'd said, *At least you have a sister.*

And when she told Dustin that she felt like Finn was slipping away, he just shrugged and said, "At least you have me." That was the moment she knew she had to end things with him: because his expression of commitment, albeit flippant, was not enough to console her, and never could be.

Dustin's cat, Gus, rubbed up against her leg. She gave him one last scratch under the chin before pulling Dustin's house key off her key ring and setting it on the novelty notepad on the foyer table. She paused for a moment and wondered if she should leave him a note. She could think of only one thing she wanted to say to him, but that was too important to scribble on a piece of paper shaped like a Space Invader. She would tell him in person, but not today. Today she had to disappear.

Finn Wilder donned her new sun hat as she stepped barefoot into the soft spring grass. She loved being barefoot so much that she regularly left the house without shoes, even in the blazing Texas summers that baked the concrete and turned lawns to straw. Her foster dad, Steve, joked that the soles of her feet were thicker than his beagle, Milly's, paws. Finn tested this theory once by walking Milly barefoot down the gravel driveway that led from the house to the barn. When Finn limped back into the house five minutes later, Steve chuckled and said, "I stand corrected."

Finn jogged across the backyard, keeping one hand on her head to prevent her hat from flying off. Milly followed closely on her heels, nearly running into Finn as she came to an abrupt stop next to the bird loft. She and Steve had spent an entire weekend building it out of scrap wood and chicken wire. As they worked, they drank Crystal Light and listened to music and stopped only long enough to wipe the sweat off their brows with the backs of their arms. It was the kind of project she would have done with her own dad had he stuck around long enough to teach her how to hold a hammer. No, her mom had taught her that. Everything she knew came from her mom.

Finn lifted a bag of birdseed out of a wooden storage bin and opened the miniature screen door. "Here you go, Chris Five. Don't eat it all at once or you'll spoil your dinner," Finn said as she filled the bird's dish with feed. The white pigeon gawked at her with a vacant expression befitting his brain size, then proceeded to peck away at the mound of multicolored seeds with every intention of cleaning its plate.

Finn had bought the first Chris from a lady who bred doves for wedding ceremonies and made her own yogurt. With her purchase, she also received a complimentary cup of yogurt that tasted like the birds had had some hand in making it. Only two days later, as Finn was cleaning the enclosure, the bird slipped past her and disappeared over the fence.

Chris One never came back. Neither did Chrises Two or Three after they made their escapes. Chris Four stuck around for over a month only to make its getaway when Finn pulled it out of the loft to show her friend, Kristen. Kristen made a noise that to human ears sounded like a squeal of delight, but to bird ears probably sounded like a hawk screech, because Chris was airborne before the last vowel left her mouth.

In an attempt to assuage her guilt, Finn fantasized that the birds had flown all the way to Hollywood to live closer to their eponym, Christopher Walken, but realistically, she knew they were probably just aimlessly flying around town, looking for food and hiding from cats. She thought about putting up flyers, but she didn't think her foster parents would appreciate random strangers turning up at their door with stray birds. One stray kid was enough.

Finn plopped down on the grass next to Milly, who was scratching an itch by wriggling furiously on her back. When she finally flopped back onto her side, one of her ears was flipped inside out. Finn flipped it back, then looked toward the house, where her foster mother was having an animated discussion with the party planner on the back deck. Even from fifty yards away, Finn could hear every word. Kathy wasn't shouting, exactly. Her voice just carried well, possibly *too* well, or as she liked to say, *I'm not loud. Y'all just need to turn your hearing aids down!*

"I guess we're all set for tomorrow then, except . . ." Kathy paused. "I don't know about the hay."

The woman, an anxious-looking creature with dark circles under her eyes, frowned. "You want to cancel the hayride?"

"No. Just the hay."

"I don't follow."

The hayride had been a favorite part of Finn's trips to the zoological gardens as a kid. She and her mom would ride it four, sometimes five times in a row before heading over to the aviary to feed the birds. Finn must have shared this story with Kathy, because when it came time to plan her graduation party, she was the one who suggested the gardens. Finn didn't have the heart to tell her that she'd outgrown hayrides and petting zoos and just about every other activity she'd booked for the weekend.

Kathy continued, "Don't you think it's kind of scratchy?"

"Yeah. It's hay," the planner answered flatly.

"It's just . . . you know, it's summer and folks will be wearing shorts, and I don't want their legs to get all scratched up. What about folding chairs?"

"*Folding chairs?*"

Incredulous. Finn had learned the meaning of that word while studying for the SATs. She said it softly to herself as she watched the woman hurriedly scrawl something in her notebook. Kathy seemed oblivious to the woman's frustration, which was evident to Finn from half a football field's distance away.

This wasn't the first party Kathy had hosted. She threw one for just about every major holiday. Finn could feel the memories of those days all around her: apple bobbing on Halloween, grilling on July Fourth, more apple bobbing on her birthday just because she liked apple bobbing. To be clear, none of these memories were hers. She wasn't the one who ate a bad egg salad sandwich and got sick in the pool. That memory and many others had been left behind by Kathy's friends, like a guest book of sorts that only Finn could read.

It started when Finn was eight years old. She was in her room, braiding a bracelet in front of the TV, when her field of vision began to shrink and the cartoon she'd been watching sounded muffled and distant. Terrified, Finn frantically grabbed for something to steady herself, but found that she had lost all sensation in her hands. As her own senses melted away, a new sound filled the void. Two voices. One male, one female. From their tone, they seemed to be arguing. About what, Finn wasn't sure, but somehow, she was able to discern that the conversation she was hearing had happened in the past, well before her or Zadie or her mom ever stepped foot inside the house.

Moments later, her senses returned to normal, but Finn was left in a state of shock. She spent the next hour sitting on her favorite beanbag chair, afraid to move in case the feeling came back. It was Zadie who finally found her. "Finn? What are you doing?"

"Something weird happened."

"Weird? How?"

She attempted to explain what she'd heard, keeping her voice low and her body still. "You know, um, when someone shouts in a cave? And you hear it a bunch of times?"

"An echo."

"An echo, yeah," she said, her voice tight. "It was like that."

"What was like that?"

"The memory I had. It didn't happen to me, but I remembered it."

"Are you saying you can read other people's minds?"

"No."

"No?"

"I don't think the memory is in their head anymore."

"Where is it then?"

"Just . . . around."

Zadie squinted, trying to understand. "So someone left their memory behind and you found it?"

"I guess."

"Huh."

"Yeah."

Finn's first instinct turned out to be right. From that day on, she could feel memories everywhere she went. At school, on the playground, between the dim library stacks. Bathrooms in particular were a hot spot for bad memories. It's where people came for privacy when they needed to cry. Finn couldn't walk into a stall without feeling like Moaning Myrtle was in there with her. Zadie assumed she didn't like bathrooms because of the decades' worth of smells, which is why she sometimes called Finn's gift "Smell-O-Vision."

During the years that followed, Finn got used to the "echoes." They weren't usually complete memories, just sensory fragments: the sound of a doorbell, the drag of water running through hair, the sour scent of newly laid mulch. Most of the time, Finn had no idea whom the echoes belonged to. But sometimes, if she held the echo in her mind long enough, she could pull on the thread and glean a little more information about the original owner. It wasn't something she did often, because she sometimes discovered things she would have preferred not knowing. It was for this reason that she linked her pinkie finger around her sister's and repeated after her, "I promise to never use my ability on you." To this day, she'd held true to that promise. They both had.

Finn . . . Kathy was calling her name, but her voice was mostly drowned out by the sound of firecrackers from last year's Labor Day picnic.

Hey, Finn! Kathy was now looking directly at her. Finn hadn't yet told her foster family about her echoes. It wasn't that she didn't trust them. She just couldn't imagine a universe in which they took her at her word and didn't ask a million probing questions and didn't spend an hour on the phone with their psychologist friend, Greg, who didn't set up an appointment for her with Greg's colleague, Jill.

No. They couldn't know. For now, at least, she would continue to let them believe she was just a spacey kid whose attention sometimes required a loud dog whistle.

Finn inhaled a deep pocket of air and let it out slowly. As she did, the firecracker pops faded away and were replaced with a sound equally as jarring. "Finn!" Kathy shouted. "What do you think? Folding chairs or hay?"

Finn thought for a moment. "Why don't you just put blankets on top of the hay?"

Kathy made a clucking sound with her tongue and fired a finger pistol at her. "That's why you're the high school graduate!" Then she turned back to the planner and said earnestly, "We're so proud of her."

Finn felt a pang of sadness. She loved her foster parents and wanted to make them proud, but implicit in their pride was the absence of her real mom. Nora was the one who should have been throwing her a graduation party. It probably wouldn't have had a caterer or a hayride or more than twelve people in attendance, but it wouldn't have mattered. They would have ordered pizza with extra cheese and hogged the karaoke machine until their guests got bored and left. That's what they did for all of her birthdays growing up, and she would expect no less—or more—to celebrate her graduation.

For the last few weeks leading up to the party, Finn had fantasized that her mom would show up unannounced. Before she'd disappeared, they'd often talked about the things they would do once Finn turned eighteen: the trips they would take, the exotic food they would eat, the men they would trick into thinking they were wealthy socialites. It would be fitting that Nora would reemerge only weeks before her eighteenth birthday and whisk her away on some grand adventure.

In these fantasies, Finn imagined her mom showing up to her party wearing a hilarious disguise. Although she had a hard time picturing what Nora looked like under the neon wig and rhinestone sunglasses. Finn worried that her memory of her mother was beginning to fade. Did she take her coffee with milk or sugar, or milk *and* sugar? Was her hair naturally auburn or did she dye it that way? Was she tall or did she just wear heels a lot? What did her laugh sound like? What about her voice? Would she even recognize her mom if she called her right now? *Probably not*, she thought. Finn was scared that what memories of her mom she had left, she'd made up to make herself feel better. Sad kids have some of the best imaginations.

"Thanks for the help, Finny." Kathy sidled up to her and squeezed her around the shoulders. Milly's tail thumped on the grass.

"No problem. Just don't use my comforter. I don't want hay in my bed."

"I would never. I'll use Steve's sleeping bags."

"That'll be a fun surprise for him the next time he goes camping."

"He probably won't even notice. You know, I once found a pinecone in there. Flat as a flapjack, like he'd slept on it all night. Can you believe that? A *pinecone*."

"Nope." Although Finn had seen Steve sleeping on a pizza box once, so maybe she could.

Kathy gasped and touched the brim of Finn's sun hat as if she had just noticed its presence (even though she had ducked under it to give Finn a hug). "Love the hat, by the way. Very Coco Chanel. Did you get it for the party?"

Finn wasn't exactly sure what Coco Chanel was, but it sounded fancy. She flashed a smile and said, "No, it's for the trip."

Kathy's tone flattened a little. "Ah. Right. The beach."

Finn knew her foster parents weren't thrilled with the idea of her taking a trip with Zadie. For reasons she didn't completely understand, the three of them had never gotten along, so it had taken some convincing to get her foster parents to agree to it. They said yes on the condition that Finn text them every day and call them immediately if Zadie tries to offer her any "age-inappropriate substances." Finn had to bite her lip to stop herself from laughing. She opted not to share the fact that she'd already partaken in such substances without Zadie there to offer them to her.

"Well, you look just like Audrey Hepburn," Kathy said, shrugging one shoulder to her chin like a starlet from old Hollywood. Finn doubted the accuracy of that statement, mainly because Audrey would never pair her hats with Hawaiian-print board shorts.

"Well, I should probably go get those sleeping bags." Kathy gave Finn another quick squeeze. "Hey. Before I go . . . have you given any more thought to our offer?"

Finn stiffened. She'd thought about it a lot, but she hadn't made a decision yet. On the one hand, she'd be lucky to have adoptive parents like Steve and Kathy. From day one, they never treated her any differently from their own son. On the other hand, she was still holding out hope that Nora was out there somewhere, making plans to return to her. The memory of her mom may have faded with time, but if there was one thing she was certain of, it was that her mom would never have left her daughters on purpose.

"I'm still thinking about it. Is it okay if I let you know when Zadie and I get back?"

Her foster mom gave her a muted smile. "Of course. And no matter what you decide, we love you."

"Love you guys, too. And I think I *will* wear the sun hat to the party."

Kathy brightened a little. "It would look great with your dress." She winked at her, then headed toward the house.

Finn turned back to Chris Five, who was now sitting on his perch. With his wings pressed against his body and his feet hidden beneath his round bird belly, he looked like an egg someone had hidden for Easter. "What do you think I should do, Chris?" Finn asked. Indifferent to her quandary, the bird closed his eyes.

Then, more to herself than to him, "Don't tell Zadie."

Two

Time for Cake

Zadie was late as usual. You'd think a psychic would always be one step ahead, but she wasn't like most psychics. Actually, Zadie had no idea what most psychics were like because she'd never met another.

When she opened the double doors to the zoological gardens' party pavilion, not one of the bustling partygoers looked in her direction. She wasn't particularly surprised that no one noticed her. Zadie's and Finn's lives didn't overlap much. If she were to illustrate it using a Venn diagram, there would be a small sliver where their circles intersected with their mom's name written on it along with Cowgirl, their childhood cat.

Clutching a poorly wrapped graduation gift in her arms, Zadie took a deep breath and crossed into Finn's circle. She awkwardly shuffled through the sea of family friends, classmates, and teammates dressed in various hues of sidewalk chalk. She felt utterly out of place in her distressed skinny jeans and neon yellow bomber jacket.

Eventually she spotted the gifts table by a window that overlooked a colorful wildflower garden and made a beeline for it. Hers was by far the shabbiest of all the presents—she hadn't even thought to stick a bow on it—so she hid it behind a giant gift basket filled with expensive beauty products. Clearly, whoever had bought that gift didn't know Finn at all. She never even wore mascara.

Or maybe she did. Zadie hadn't seen her sister in months. She could have gotten a nose job for all she knew.

She discreetly slipped a perfume bottle from the basket and spritzed a small amount on her wrist. As she placed the bottle back in its shredded paper nest, she heard a voice say, "Hi, Zadie."

Zadie jumped and turned to see Finn's foster mom, Kathy, standing behind her, smiling with all the enthusiasm of someone asking if they have something in their teeth. She was wearing what Zadie thought of as a *momcho*: a silky poncho with a colorful print and often some kind of rhinestone brooch pinned to the shoulder. Kathy's was a jewel-toned paisley number that accentuated her inner Blanche Devereaux—a compliment coming from Zadie, as Blanche was by far her favorite Golden Girl.

Kathy's eyes flicked over to the gift basket, her subtle way of letting Zadie know she was watching her. "Finn is excited to see you. She can't stop talking about your trip."

Zadie tried to mask her discomfort under what she hoped was a smile. "Yeah, it should be fun."

"I love the beach. Steve and I try to make it down to the Gulf at least once a year. It's where I got that." She pointed to a corkboard display decorated with photos of Finn. On it hung a whitewashed frame that read LIFE IS BETTER AT THE BEACH with a picture of the whole family—Kathy, Steve, their adult son, Daniel, and Finn—taken on one such trip to the beach. The shot captured the four of them mid-jump, all with cheesy grins on their faces.

Zadie searched for something to say. "Cool" was all that came out.

"We've been talking about moving down there when Steve retires in a couple of years. Finn already has a place picked out for us. She says she's going to take the master." Kathy started to laugh but stopped abruptly. She must have seen the expression on Zadie's face. The one that looked like a flower whose last petal had just been plucked.

"Z!" Finn lurched out of a scrum of red-and-white varsity jackets and tackled her sister in a hug. "You're here!"

Zadie stumbled back a step. She wasn't much of a hugger, never mind a surprise hugger. Finn was the opposite. When she was a kid, Zadie remembered her regularly hugging strangers at the park or at the library. In that way, Finn was a lot like their mom: sweet, bright, citrus. She even looked like her from certain angles; they both did, despite looking nothing like each other. Finn was tall and dark, with glossy black curls. Zadie, although five years older, was three inches shorter, with the complexion of a shortbread cookie. Most people had no idea they were related.

Finn pulled away and struck a pose. "What do you think?" It took a second for Zadie to realize she was talking about the straw UFO on her head.

"It definitely makes a statement."

"I think you look *gorgeous*," Kathy said emphatically. "Doesn't she, Steve?"

Steve was on his way to the buffet to load up his paper plate for a third time when his wife corralled him into the conversation. He had grown out and waxed his mustache since the last time Zadie had seen him and, like many of the men over the age of fifty in the room, was sporting a bolo tie. "What was that, honey?"

"I said, 'Isn't Finn pretty?'"

"Oh, yes. Very handsome."

Kathy's jaw dropped. "Steve, you don't call a lady handsome!"

"Why not? Handsome was commonly used for both men *and* women at the turn of the last century."

Kathy turned to Zadie. "He reads one Jane Austen novel, and now he's using words like *incorrigible*."

"She hears that one a lot." Steve winked at the girls, then jumped out of Kathy's reach as she attempted to swat him. "If you need me, I'll be with the meat," he said and hurried away.

"I should probably check in with the caterers about the cake." Kathy nodded politely at Zadie. "It was nice to see you."

"You too."

"All right. Well, you two have fun!" Kathy waved goodbye, then sashayed into the crowd.

Finn turned to her sister and smiled. Several awkward seconds later, Zadie broke the silence. "Kathy went all out with this party. I've been to carnivals with fewer attractions." She glanced out the window at a bouncy castle overflowing with teenagers which was next to a pen that contained several mini horses. From the outside, it looked more like an eight-year-old's birthday than a graduation party.

"It's *a lot,* isn't it?" Finn half-grimaced. "I said I didn't want to make a big deal out of my graduation, but I guess she didn't hear that part. I mean . . . I haven't even met half of these people. A guy I've never seen before actually asked me what the graduate's name was so he could write it on a card."

"I hope you didn't give him your real name."

"Nope. I told him her name was Chrisantha Applebees."

"Like the restaurant chain?"

"Yup. I was sure he would know I was messing with him, but he actually wrote it down! I feel kind of bad about it now."

"If he wrote her a big check, you might have to change your name to Chrisantha."

Finn laughed. "I hadn't thought about it that way."

The conversation settled into awkward silence once more. *What happened to us?* Zadie thought. They used to tell each other everything, often staying up well past Finn's bedtime to share their dreams for the future as well as their fears. Their dreams changed almost weekly, but their fears stayed mostly the same. In those days, Zadie never would have imagined that she'd look into her sister's face and see the wandering gaze of someone searching for something to say. Zadie almost blurted out the news of her pregnancy just to fill the void.

Thankfully Finn spoke first. She stepped closer to Zadie and spoke in a low voice. "Hey . . . you haven't seen . . ." She trailed off.

"Seen what?"

Finn screwed her mouth to the side. Something she did when she felt embarrassed. "Never mind. It's stupid."

"You can tell me."

"No. Forget I asked."

Just then a female friend of Finn's came running up. "Finn! You've gotta come with me. Jack wrote a song for your graduation, and it's *terrible,* but in, like, a funny way."

In an instant, Finn's whole demeanor changed. "Seriously?" she squealed, then turned back to Zadie. "I'm gonna go check this out, but let's catch up later, okay? We can talk vacation plans."

"Yep. Totally. See you later," Zadie said and watched her sister disappear into a swarm of laughing teenagers. She could feel a clot of envy forming in her chest. It wasn't that she wanted Finn's life, exactly; it was that Finn appeared happy in a way that Zadie herself hadn't been in a very long time. Finn had a family who threw her parties and friends who wrote songs for her. Even people who didn't know her gave her cards and fancy perfume.

Zadie had Finn. Or at least she used to.

She needed fresh air. Zadie stepped out onto the deck, which was possibly even more crowded than the room she had just come from. She counted five extra-large coolers, all of which were also doubling as seating. "Excuse me," she said as she reached down to open one of them. The man sitting on it sighed to make sure she knew she had inconvenienced him before standing up. To get back at him, Zadie took her sweet time before finally digging a flavored seltzer water out of the ice.

She cracked open her can and surveyed the grounds, looking for a place where she could be alone for a few minutes. Behind the petting zoo, she spotted a tractor-trailer filled with hay and made her way toward it. Zadie pulled herself up onto one of the hay bales that was covered with an unzipped sleeping bag. Maybe it was the pregnancy or maybe it was just the stress of being an introvert in a house full of strangers, but she suddenly felt exhausted. She lay flat on her back and closed her eyes, feeling the warm sunlight on the backs of her eyelids.

Zadie must have fallen asleep, because when she opened her eyes, the trailer was moving. She sat up groggily and realized she was not the only passenger. Two parents and their three young children sat across from her, along with a small posse of moody-looking teenagers who must have boarded the hayride for the irony of it but were probably secretly enjoying themselves.

"Ah. You're awake!" said the person sitting next to her. Zadie turned and saw that it was Daniel, Finn's older foster brother as well as a guy who kept a ukulele in his car just in case of "emergencies." Zadie hadn't asked him what he meant by this, because she was afraid he'd say something corny like, "*Fun*mergencies!" To be fair, Daniel was a kindergarten teacher, so he probably had more use for a ukulele than most. He was clearly on the hayride by himself, which Zadie found kind of odd but not that surprising. Daniel didn't strike her as the kind of guy who cared much about what other people thought of him.

"Welcome to the party, or should I say part-*hay*."

That joke was particularly bad, even for him. "Hey, Daniel," Zadie said as she looked around for the event pavilion and saw only an exhibit about local flora.

"I would have woken you, but you looked so comfortable."

"I don't usually fall asleep in public, but I didn't sleep great last night."

"Don't worry about it. I'm used to people sleeping in weird places. I once found one of my students asleep under the sink hugging a bag of guinea pig food like it was a teddy bear."

"That's cute."

"Oh, it was precious," he said earnestly. "We did have to call his parents, though, 'cause it turned out he'd been eating the guinea pig food for weeks."

Not cute. What if her kid ate pet food? Or paste? *Do kids still eat paste?* she wondered.

"I moved the food to another cabinet, but he's a smart kid. At recess, I found him hiding out in the tube slide, munching on those pellets like they were candy." Daniel laughed and sighed fondly. Zadie cringed.

"So how have you been?" he continued. "I haven't seen you in forever."

"Oh. Uhh . . ." Zadie was unprepared for this line of questioning, so she decided to keep it vague. "I'm . . . good."

"How's Dustin?"

Zadie was surprised he remembered her ex's name. They'd met only once at an awkward run-in at Costco. "He's, uh . . . good, too."

"Glad to hear it."

Zadie glimpsed the pavilion in the distance. Was it just her, or were they getting farther away?

Everywhere Finn looked, she thought she saw her mother. She stopped in her tracks beside every woman with long auburn hair, every vaguely familiar laugh, every sarcastic remark. Her party had become a hall of mirrors, only instead of her own reflection staring back at her, it was her mom's.

Finn spotted a group of women huddled together on the deck's gazebo. She recognized several of them from the halls of her high school, teachers mostly, but there was one woman with her back turned that she couldn't identify. She wore an anklet similar to the one Finn was currently wearing on her ankle, silver with two tiny charms, an *F* for Finn and a *Z* for Zadie. It had been her mother's. The day Nora disappeared, Finn had found it lying on their driveway. She'd barely taken it off since.

Finn approached the woman, who then looked over her shoulder at her. "Oh, hi, Finn! Congratulations on graduating." Finn's heart dipped. It was Mrs. Kirby, the freshman English teacher whom many of the younger students called "Mrs. Coleslaw" for reasons unbeknownst to Finn. Finn could only assume the nickname had originated during one of her regular shifts as cafeteria monitor.

Finn tried to hide her disappointment. "Thanks, Mrs. Kirby."

"Do you know what you're going to study in college yet?"

She had been asked this question a lot and already had an answer prepared. "Ornithology."

The teachers looked at one another, impressed by her specificity. She wasn't actually planning on studying ornithology. She had no idea what she wanted to do with her life, but that response was too mirthless for a party. Before she could get roped into a lengthier conversation about her hopes and dreams, Finn felt a sharp pain in her foot and gasped. She looked down and realized that she had stood on someone's discarded disposable fork. The weight of her body had cracked the plastic, and a piece of it was wedged in the sole of her foot.

"Excuse me," she gasped, and limped in the direction of the bathroom.

She was halfway across the deck when she heard a voice say, "Hey, Finn." She turned and saw Jonathan, anchor of the four-by-four and former crush of Finn's, standing with a group of guys from the track team. He had eyes that could look either brown or green depending on the light. Today they looked green.

"Oh, hey, Jonathan," she said, half grimacing and shifting her weight to her uninjured foot.

He glanced from Finn to the bouncy castle, which was now overrun by a group of Steve's colleagues' children and a traumatized-looking Labrador retriever who couldn't keep its footing on the inflatable rubber floor. "Cool party."

Her cheeks grew hot. "Thanks." Okay, maybe Jonathan was more of a current crush than a former one. Technically, they didn't know each other that well, but Finn had felt a special connection with him ever since she'd taken over his old locker at the beginning of last school year. Every time she opened it, she would get a whiff of one of his old memories: a friend clapping him on the back, the song he was listening to, a test marked with a red D that he'd crumpled up and tossed behind a pile of dirty gym clothes. Jonathan didn't really know her, but she knew him (in a skulking, unrequited-love sort of way).

"Got any big plans for the summer?" he asked.

"My sister and I are going to the beach for a week. How about you?"

"Just chillin'," he replied. The guys he was standing with all nodded in agreement. Chillin' was by far the most popular activity among the suburban teen population. In contrast, Finn could think of nothing more boring than hanging out in her basement all summer watching Netflix. "That sounds . . . fun."

Jonathan nodded slowly, *chill-ly*. His gaze drifted to the ground and a disgusted look came over his face. "Is your foot bleeding?"

Finn looked down and noticed a smear of blood on the deck. She shrugged and tried to play it cool. "It's no big deal. It happens all the time."

"Maybe you should start wearing shoes, then." There was no humor in Jonathan's voice. He didn't joke about feet. After all, he had a scholarship riding on his.

"Yeah, you're probably right. I'd get fewer forks stuck in my foot, that's for sure!" She snorted.

Jonathan grimaced. The more Finn liked a guy, the flatter her jokes fell, she'd noticed.

"I should go grab a Band-Aid. See you later!" She hobbled as fast as she could into the pavilion and locked herself in the women's bathroom. "Smooth, Finn," she muttered to her reflection in the mirror, then lifted her injured foot into the sink. She examined the cut. It didn't look particularly deep, nothing she'd need stitches for. She ran water over it and grabbed a bandage from her purse. As she was peeling off the paper backing, she heard a knock at the door.

"Finn?" It was her foster dad. "Your mo— Kathy told me to tell you it's almost time for cake."

"Thanks. I'll be out in a minute."

"Is everything okay? I saw you limping."

"I stepped on a fork." Finn smoothed the bandage over the wound and gingerly placed her foot back down on the floor.

"At least it wasn't a knife."

Finn opened the door and Steve handed her a pair of flip-flops. "For your own safety."

"Thanks." Finn took the flip-flops without protest and slid her feet into them.

"I'd like to say you learned your lesson, but I know you better than that," he said, amused.

Finn smiled. It was true. Steve knew her better than almost anyone. She didn't remember much about her biological father, and based on the things she'd heard about him, she never really cared to. Steve was the only person she would ever dream of calling Dad.

"Well," he continued, "I'm going to go find a strategic spot next to the cake so I'm first in line. Unless there's something else on your mind?"

Finn hesitated. Sometimes she wondered if Steve had a special gift like Zadie and she did—he was that good at reading people. "No. I'll see you out there."

"Okay. Cake's in five," he said, holding up as many fingers.

The guests began to filter out onto the back deck, where a large dessert table had been set up. In the middle of it sat a huge sheet cake decorated to look like a mortarboard. A few weeks ago, Kathy had asked Finn what flavor she wanted her cake to be. Finn had changed her mind several times before deciding on strawberry with vanilla frosting.

"There she is! Finn, come here," Kathy flagged Finn down as she stepped out onto the deck. Her senses were suddenly flooded: coffee-singed tongues, static cling, itches that could not be scratched because they weren't really hers. Most of her echoes were mundane like this. Finn guessed that it was because those memories existed on the surface of peoples' consciousness. They were looser, more likely to flake off and catch wind. The memories that really mattered, they lived somewhere deeper, somewhere that had to be mined to get to them. That's where the good stuff was: the diamonds and the coal.

Finn shooed away the echoes as though they were a cloud of gnats and smiled back at Kathy. "If I come over there, do I get cake?"

"Better," Kathy replied. "You get a heartfelt speech."

Finn performed an exaggerated eye roll for the crowd, then crossed the deck, flip-flops slapping against her heels as she walked. She joined Kathy and Steve by the cake table and braced herself for an embarrassing display of parental affection.

"Finn. It seems like only yesterday—" Kathy's voice croaked. Finn was surprised. She usually got at least three or four sentences out before the tears started. Kathy took a deep breath and continued, "It seems like only yesterday that you came to live with us. Over these past five years, we've seen you grow from a little girl into a woman."

Kathy's speech was starting to sound like the puberty talk she'd given Finn in the seventh grade. She shifted uncomfortably and looked away so that she didn't meet the gaze of any of her friends. Then she felt something inside her shift, like a dip in barometric pressure before a storm.

This echo wasn't like the ones she was used to. What she was experiencing wasn't a specific sound or smell or taste. It was a feeling, a feeling of familiarity, like she was remembering something from her own life. Finn needed to know more. As discreetly as she could, she pulled at the thread of the memory. She felt it start to unravel, felt the stitches drop one by one, row by row.

The tractor hadn't yet come to a complete stop when Zadie jumped out of the hayride. "*Some*body's excited for cake!" Daniel joked.

Zadie laughed halfheartedly. "Yep. Can't get enough of the stuff." She didn't even like cake, but Daniel had given her an out and she wasn't going to waste it. "See ya later, Dan."

All of Finn's guests were either squeezed onto the pavilion deck or had spilled out into the surrounding wildflower garden. Zadie didn't see her sister, but she did hear what sounded like a parrot saying Finn's name. *Speech time,* she thought, grimacing at the memory of the last of Kathy's speeches she'd had to sit through. It was at Finn's end-of-the-season cross-country banquet. After Finn was presented with the MVP Award, Kathy had practically shoved the coach aside to get to the microphone. Her sister had looked mortified by the whole display and couldn't get off the stage fast enough.

Zadie couldn't see anything from down on the lawn, so she circled around the building and went in through the front door. The deck was so packed that Zadie had to stand half in, half out of the sliding patio door. To not waste precious AC, she closed it as much as she could without squishing herself. It gave her the appearance of someone who had made a run for an elevator and got there a second too late.

As Daniel had predicted, the object that had drawn the party guests to it like bees to a punch bowl was indeed a cake. Finn stood patiently beside it, smiling mildly. Zadie tried waving at Finn, but succeeded only in drawing the attention of Kathy, who was in the middle of delivering her Proud Mom speech: "—of her accomplishments: star track athlete, magna cum laude, just to name a few." From the bravado in Kathy's tone, you'd think *she* had done all of those things herself, not Finn. Zadie had always suspected that Kathy was the kind of woman who lived vicariously through her children, and now she was surer of it than ever. *I promise not to do that to you,* Zadie told the Ladybug inside her.

All of a sudden, her gut did a somersault. She didn't have time to close her eyes or hum a song. The premonition came at her with such force she felt momentarily dizzy.

THE SKY IS FULL OF BIRDS.

Each word was a boulder. The heft of them made her sway, made her brace herself against the doorframe and look to the sky, half expecting birds to start falling to the earth, biblical style. But Zadie didn't see even a single sparrow.

THE SKY IS FULL OF BIRDS.

As with most of her premonitions, the message was so obtuse it was functionally useless. She shook her head, trying to knock the words loose so she could flush them from her system, but they stuck to her brain like a bur.

THE SKY—

Zadie was moments away from leaving the party before the cake was even served when the premonition finally lifted, one word at a time: *birds . . . of . . . full . . . is . . . sky . . . the . . .* Each one evaporating like mist into the blue sky.

Finn tried to move but discovered that she was frozen in place. The only muscle she could feel was her heart thumping against the wall of her chest, and the familiar feeling that had comforted her only moments before had taken on a wistfulness that made her want to cry. She searched the faces of her guests. Did the memory belong to one of them? If so, she saw no sign of it in their smiling faces.

One by one, the sounds of the party began to peel away until all that was left was the rhythm of Finn's own breath. Then a voice cut through the silence. A woman's voice. Humming a song she recognized.

A song about a bird.

No one else saw it when it happened, but Zadie did: Finn's unfixed gaze, the subtle clenching of her jaw, the twitch in her right index finger. She'd seen her sister like this before, but not since she was a kid, back when she had less control over her gift. Zadie had to get to her sister before someone noticed and decided she was having a seizure.

"Excuse me," she said to no one in particular as she squeezed through the crowd. Jostled strangers flashed her dirty looks as their lemonades sloshed over the lips of their plastic cups, but Zadie plowed ahead. Her progress was stalled, however, when she ran into the railing that separated the upper and lower levels of the deck. Zadie looked down and realized there was no way of getting down to the first level from where she was without climbing on someone's shoulders.

She turned her attention back to Finn and saw her sway on her feet. But rather than fall, her sister pivoted sharply on her heels and broke into a sprint that sent her flying down the deck stairs and along the brick path that led to the rhododendron garden. While Kathy and the guests stared after her in stunned silence, Zadie wasted no time in squeezing back through the crowd toward the pavilion. When she came out the other side, she started running. It had been years since she'd last been to the zoological gardens with her mom and sister, but she still knew the place by heart. And she was pretty sure she knew where Finn was headed.

Three

Twelve Months

(until Nora Wilder's disappearance)

That's because I have eyes in the back of my head." Nora had her back turned to the girls, her hands submerged in soapy water, blindly feeling the bottom of the apron sink for forks like a diver searching for sunken treasure. Being careful not to move her head too much, she sneaked a peek at Finn's skeptical reflection in the kitchen window. Her daughter was so cute when she was suspicious.

"You haven't touched your potatoes," Nora said without turning around.

Finn looked down at her plate. It was true. She had eaten her chicken and broccoli, but the lump of mashed potatoes still sat there like a half-melted snowman.

"She's messing with us," Zadie said, stealing a bite of Finn's potatoes. "If she really had eyes in the back of her head, she'd see this." Zadie strategically held up her middle finger in what she guessed was her mom's blind spot.

"I don't need to see behind me to know what you're doing right now," Nora said, resisting the urge to flip a bird back at Zadie. Finn was still too young to see that side of her yet, but she was looking forward to the day when her almost-teenager dropped her first f-bomb. When a seven-year-old Zadie came home from school one day and told her that baths were "bullshit," she'd laughed so hard she'd cried.

"If you have eyes back there, then why don't your hats have holes in them?" Finn smiled smugly and crossed her arms.

"That's a great point, Noodle. I *should* cut holes in them. Now, are you going to eat those potatoes or not?"

"Do I have to?" Finn asked.

This was the first Nora had heard of Finn's not liking potatoes. It was the first she'd heard of *anyone* not liking potatoes. "No, you don't have to, but if you're not going to eat them, will you scrape them into the trash?"

Finn hopped to her feet and carried her plate to the trash can, but instead of throwing away her potatoes, she held her body stiff the way people do right before they sneeze. Nora took note of her stillness and asked, "What is it this time?"

"Coyotes."

Zadie piped up. "Again?"

A second later, Finn's body relaxed and she pushed potato into the trash can with her knife. "Yeah. It's okay, though. I like coyotes."

There was a pack of coyotes that lived in their neighborhood. Nora would sometimes hear them yipping in the evenings, but tonight all she could hear were crickets. Nora was grateful that Finn's echoes—as they'd come to call them—didn't seem to bother her. She was already an exceptionally empathetic person, so Nora worried that taking on the burden of other peoples' memories would be too much for her, but so far her daughter had handled it with grace.

"Finn, hand me your plate and go brush your teeth, please." As usual, Finn did as she was told and padded down the hallway to the bathroom. While Nora was wiping her wet hands on a dish towel, she felt her seventeen-year-old staring at her. She turned around and saw the same leery expression on Zadie's face that she'd caught glimpses of all week. Tonight, however, Zadie didn't try to sneak it away. She wanted Nora to see it.

"What is it, Zadie? I know something's up."

Zadie paused, the bated breath before a cork is popped. "Why won't you tell us what your gift is?"

"I just did," Nora replied glibly.

Zadie's eyes narrowed. "I'm not a kid. You can't fool me."

She was right. Her daughter was no fool. She was sharp and cunning and rigged with booby traps.

"We've been over this. I don't have a gift." It felt like the truth. At least, from what she could remember, and there was a lot about her life that she did not remember.

"How is that possible if both your daughters do?"

Nora sighed. "I don't know, Zadie. I don't know how it works. Either you can believe that I'm just a normal person, or you can believe that I have eyes in the back of my head. Your choice."

Zadie held Nora's gaze for a moment longer before abruptly standing up from the table. "I'm reading Finn her bedtime story, then I'm going to cut holes in all of your hats," she said with an impish grin.

Zadie was probably just bluffing, but Nora decided it would be best to hide her favorite hats just in case. But first she drained the water from the sink, headed to the living room, and switched on the TV (*Law & Order* was starting in ten minutes). Then she climbed the stairs to her bedroom.

Only she never made it to the top.

"It's what I deserve,' said Magnus aloud."

Zadie was sitting cross-legged on Finn's bed, the chapter book they'd spent the last few weeks reading open on her lap. Finn lay beside her sister, a starburst of black curls splayed across her pillow, her blanket so tightly tucked that she looked like a butterfly in a polka-dot chrysalis. Zadie imagined her emerging from it in the morning with huge spotted pink wings.

"'After all, had he not chosen this life?'" she continued softly. "'Growing up, he had always been a boy with his head in the clouds, so it was only fitting that he should end up here, a mile above civilization, invisible to everyone and yet unable to hide from the one person he truly despised: himself.'"

Finn whimpered in sympathy. Zadie turned to her sister, surprised. "You feel sorry for him?"

"He's all alone up there on that mountain. He has no friends."

"Yeah. Because he *betrayed* all of them."

Finn shrugged, loosening the blanket around her shoulders. "I still feel bad for him."

Zadie was continually impressed by her sister's capacity for empathy. Not even a murderous wizard was beyond absolution in her eyes. "That's the end of the chapter. Do you want me to keep reading?"

"Nope," Finn said, her *p* popping like a corn kernel. "I'm tired."

"Okay. We'll pick it up again tomorrow." Zadie closed the book and sat it on Finn's nightstand next to her fuzzy alarm clock.

"Hey, Zadie?"

"Yeah?"

"Do you think Mom is happy?"

The remark would have caught Zadie off guard if she hadn't also been wondering this herself. Their mom hadn't been smiling much lately, and when she did, it looked like wallpaper peeling at the edges. "Why? Do you think she's not?"

Finn paused as if reconsidering. "Not *un*happy, just . . . lonely, maybe. I dunno . . ."

"She's not lonely," Zadie said in a tone she hoped was reassuring. "She's got us."

"But what about the rest of her family?"

Nora never talked about her parents. Zadie didn't even know if she had siblings or not. Their mother's past was kept behind a locked door, and no matter how hard Zadie squinted, she had never been able to see anything but the vaguest of shadows through the keyhole. "I'm sure she's fine."

"Yeah . . ." The petals of Finn's eyelids closed. "You're probably right."

Zadie waited until she felt her sister's breath nestle into a slow, hibernating rhythm before carefully climbing off the bed and slipping into the hallway.

The lights were on in the living room at the end of the hall. Her mom was probably watching *Law & Order* like she usually did after Finn went to bed. Maybe if Zadie asked nicely, she could convince her to let her watch MTV for an hour. She turned the corner to find the TV on, but the room empty.

"Mom?" Zadie said. No answer. She made a beeline for the remote and was about to change the channel when she felt a chill on her bare leg. The windows were all closed, but somehow there was a draft. Zadie set down the remote and followed the current of cool air from the living room through the kitchen and into the mudroom, which was connected to the screened-in porch. The doors to the porch and the yard were both wide open, their unoiled hinges squeaking in the wind.

"Mom, why's the back door open?" Zadie said, panic constricting her throat. Had someone broken in? She wheeled around to make sure there wasn't a stranger lurking behind her. Realistically, she knew her mom had probably just left the door open to let in some fresh air and forgot to close it, but if that was the case, then where was she? Zadie stepped onto the porch and looked out at the yard. It was that time of evening right after the sun has gone down, when everything is tinted blue, like looking through a piece of cobalt glass. That's why at first the figure Zadie thought she saw moving at the far end of their yard was nothing more than a trick of the light. It was only after a few seconds of squinting that she recognized her mom's gait.

"Mom!" she called after her. "Where are you going?"

Nora must not have heard her, because she was swallowed by the jagged shadows of the trees. Zadie hesitated. She wanted to follow Nora. She wanted to know what could have possibly driven her out into the night without a word, but that would mean leaving Finn alone in the house. The most sensible thing she could do would be to go back inside, lock the doors, and watch TV until her mom returned. But Zadie was seventeen, and seventeen-year-olds are not always known for making sensible choices.

She shut the door behind her and took off running after Nora. When she reached the edge of the woods, she called for her mom, but her words were swept away by a sudden gust of wind. Then out of the corner of her eye: an apparition. In a clearing at the edge of a ravine, what looked like a statue of her mother had been erected. If it weren't for her hair blowing wildly in the wind, Zadie would have believed Nora had been turned to stone.

Zadie felt a hot surge of fear in her chest as she tentatively made her way toward her. "Mom? What are you doing out here?"

The statue—her mother—did not answer. As Zadie drew closer, she realized just how close Nora was standing to a precipitous drop into the ravine below. Silhouetted against clouds that bloomed violet like bruises, Nora bore a striking resemblance to a heroine on the cover of a Gothic novel. The cliff edge was her widow's walk, and it was unclear whether her sorrow would move her to jump.

Zadie's heart was a drumbeat in her ears. "You're scaring me, Mom," she said unsteadily as she inched closer, afraid that any sudden movement might startle Nora out of whatever trance she was in and cause her to lose her footing. Her mom didn't acknowledge her presence. She continued to stare out at the horizon, the dividing line between flight and flightlessness.

The wind picked up and with it, Nora's arms. She stretched them out to her sides in a T formation, her cardigan billowing beneath them like a sail. Nora had asked Zadie once where she would go if she woke up one day and could fly. "Anywhere in the world," she'd added. Zadie couldn't recall what she'd said exactly, but she remembered her mother's response: "Can I fly there with you?"

"Mom! Stop!" Zadie grabbed Nora's shoulder and twisted her around. Her mother's face, one she knew almost as well as her own, was barely recognizable. "Mom? What are you doing? What's happening?" Zadie realized that she was trembling.

Nora looked directly at her daughter in a way that frightened

Zadie, like she was looking into what she thought was a mirror but was really two-way glass. Without a word, Nora stepped past her in the direction of their house. Zadie tailed her mother all the way home, tears silently running down her cheeks and collecting in the corners of her mouth. When they got close, Zadie hurried ahead and opened the door. Nora wafted into the house along with the cool night air, and once inside, settled herself on the couch in front of the TV, which was in the middle of a *Law & Order* episode. Almost a minute later, Nora finally spoke. "Shoot. I've seen this one already. I think I remember it being pretty good, though." She turned to Zadie, who was standing in the kitchen, watching her. "Hey, hon. Do you want to snuggle with me? We can watch something you want to watch. I promise I won't say anything snarky."

Zadie didn't know what to say. Either her mom had no memory of what had just happened or she was messing with her. All she knew was that she needed to get as far away from her as possible.

"Zadie? You feeling okay?"

"I have homework to do," she finally blurted and hurried down the hall toward her bedroom. She had already finished all her homework in study hall earlier that day. She just wanted to put on her headphones and try not to think about what she had just witnessed. On her way, she stopped in front of Finn's room and peered through the crack in the door at her sleeping sister. She decided not to tell Finn about that night. *She was probably just sleepwalking*, Zadie told herself, although in her heart she wasn't sure if she believed it.

Four

Psychic Karaoke

(Part 1)

Nora looks up
A colorful canopy of wings
Too many to name
Not that she could if she tried
Darting, chittering amongst fan-shaped leaves
She has seeds in her cupped hand
Offers them to the sky
Her daughters watch
Too nervous to hold out their own hands
Something yellow flits down from the trees
And lands in her palm
She sings to it, the bird
A song about itself
And she thinks:
How easy it would be
To open the door to its cage
And let it fly free
But the bird doesn't even look at the door
Her youngest extends a finger
Barely glances off the crown of its head before it takes flight
I scared him, *her daughter says*
No, honey, *she answers*
It was just time for him to go

Finn knew where she was before she even opened her eyes. The familiar squawks and whistles and cries took her back to a time when her mother would hoist her on her shoulders so that she could get a closer look at the cockatoos and parakeets perched in the umbrella trees. What was unfamiliar was the damp feeling on her back.

Finn rolled over and found that she had been lying in a puddle, runoff from the sprinkler system that misted the giant fan palms above. How she had ended up passed out on the floor of the zoological gardens' aviary, she wasn't sure. The last thing she remembered was standing awkwardly in front of her party guests while Kathy regaled everyone with stories of her youth.

Then it all came rushing back to her: the song, the bird, her mom's outstretched hand.

Her mom.

She *had* shown up to her party after all, just not in the present. Nora's memory was at least a decade old, but to Finn, it felt as fresh as just-cut grass. She could still feel the gentle pinch of the bird's toes on her finger, the way it tickled her palm as it pecked at the mound of seeds. It was the first echo of her mother she'd ever had, the first sign since her disappearance that she had ever existed.

Finn caught the eye of a lovebird nestled among the palm fronds. The little creature was still aside from the visible thumping of its heart in its chest, a lot of effort expended by one organ simply for the act of waiting. Finn had been waiting for her mom for five years. Neither the police nor the internet had yielded any clues as to where she had gone or why she had left. Her echo didn't answer those questions, either, but it had given her one important thing: hope. If Finn could access her mom's memories, maybe she could use them to piece together what had happened the day she left. And maybe, if she was lucky, they would lead Finn to her mom.

"Finn!"

She turned to see Zadie approaching, drenched in sweat and squeezing a cramp in her right side. "I ran all the way here," she said, her breathing labored. "Are you okay?" She leaned over and felt her sister's forehead.

"I'm not sick," Finn said with dry amusement.

"I know that." Zadie pulled her hand away quickly and shifted awkwardly. "I tried to stop you—"

"From running out of my own party like a crazy person?"

Zadie nodded. "Hold on. I need to sit for a sec." She collapsed next to her sister on the concrete and hung her head between her legs.

"Are *you* okay?"

"Yep. Never better." She sucked in a deep breath. "So that must have been a pretty intense one, huh?"

Intense was not the word Finn would have used. *Exhilarating, reaffirming,* even *comforting*: these were all words that described the experience she'd just had. But as eager as she was to tell her sister about the echo, the secret stuck like flypaper to her tongue. "Yeah. I don't remember how I got here."

Zadie raised her head, frowning. "You blacked out?"

"I guess so." Finn shrugged.

"Does that happen a lot?"

"No. This is the first."

Zadie looked like she was about to feel Finn's forehead again, then thought better of it. "Just . . . be careful, okay?"

"I will."

Zadie nodded despite looking unconvinced and dropped her head back between her legs.

Just spit it out! Finn wasn't sure why she was so hesitant to tell her sister about the echo. Zadie's feelings about their mom were complicated, but complicated feelings or not, she still deserved the truth. "Hey, listen. I kind of have something big to tell you. Like, maybe you should just stay like that to brace yourself."

Zadie's head snapped up. "Okay . . . Now, you're making me nervous."

But before Finn could respond, Steve came stomping through

the palms toward them, even more sweaty and out of breath than her sister had been. "Finn! There you are! What happened?"

Finn tried to not let her disappointment show on her face. Her news would have to wait. "Uhh, sorry. I wasn't feeling well."

"So you ran . . . here?"

Finn shrugged. Nothing she could say would sufficiently explain her strange behavior, so she didn't even try. Steve, mercifully, didn't press her. "Want to head back to the party? I saved you girls each a piece of cake."

"Sounds good." Finn stood, swiped the dirt off her dress, then held out a hand to Zadie. As she helped her sister to her feet, Finn leaned in and whispered, "Let's talk more tonight. Over Froyo?"

Her sister examined her curiously, then said, "Uhh . . . sure."

"Meet me there at eight."

As they wound their way through the man-made rainforest toward the exit, Finn began to hum. It was the song she recognized from her echo but couldn't place at first. Then lyrics started coming to her one line at a time like brushstrokes:

Hush, darling, hush
It's almost dawn

It was a ballad her mother used to sing to her.

The birds are singing
I must move on

I can't."

"Just one song. Please?"

Zadie and Finn were seated across from each other at a clear acrylic table next to the karaoke stage where a man was clumsily detangling a microphone cord. The room was humid with hazy pink light cast by neon letters that spelled words like *dance* and *star*. The Fro-Yodel was a little on the seedy side for a frozen yogurt place, partly because of its location right next to the railroad tracks. It was in the girls' old neighborhood, twenty minutes north of San Antonio, where they'd lived with their mother. Every Friday night, the three of them used to walk the four blocks to listen to terrible karaoke and take turns pulling the dispenser levers, marveling as frozen yogurt coiled like snakes in their bowls.

After loading up on toppings, Nora would sometimes embarrass them by hopping up onstage and belting out one of Janis Joplin's greatest hits. Her voice would crack like the strip of sunbaked earth that was the girls' driveway, but that just made it sound more rock 'n' roll. Finn remembered men sometimes leaning their elbows on the edge of the stage as she sang. As soon as she was finished, they'd ask to buy her a beer at the bar across the street. Nora refused most of them, but to a select few, she'd write her phone number on the back of a napkin and say, "Rain check." Then she'd return to their table, to her girls, because that's why she was there, to be with them, to hear about their days and laugh at their jokes and play Psychic Karaoke.

The game was simple: Zadie would use her gift to try to predict the next song in the karaoke lineup. If she got three correct in a row, Nora would reward her daughter with another trip to the soft-serve machine or extra toppings.

"I don't play that anymore," Zadie said matter-of-factly, licking yogurt off the back of her spoon.

Finn sighed. "What's the point in having an awesome talent if you never use it? I'd trade mine for yours any day."

"Yeah, well, if I could give it to you, I would."

"Speaking of giving things away, are you gonna finish that?" Finn pointed to Zadie's half-eaten frozen yogurt.

"Nope. Go for it." Zadie pushed the bowl to her sister, who received it with a little happy dance, then asked, "Will you tell me what mine sounds like?"

Psychic Karaoke wasn't the only game the girls used to play at the Fro-Yodel. The other relied on Finn's skills. "Gimme a minute." She spooned Zadie's yogurt into her mouth but did not swallow. Instead, she let it turn to fruity liquid on her tongue and waited.

Finn remembered the first time her mom had taken her to the Fro-Yodel. She was sloppily eating chocolate yogurt with gummy worms when a song got so viciously stuck in her head that she dropped her spoon on the floor. "The yogurt tastes like music!" she gasped. As a kid, Finn was prone to silly outbursts, so her mom probably thought nothing of it, but over the next few months, her proclamations became more and more specific:

> "This one tastes like jazz!"
> "This one tastes like a banjo!"
> "This one tastes like the drum solo from 'In the Air Tonight'!"

Each Friday, Finn would eagerly anticipate what music she'd "taste" later that night. She wasn't sure why the Fro-Yodel triggered so many musical memories. Her best guess was that they were linked to whoever had made it that day. However, it was more fun to pretend that the yogurt itself was singing to her.

"Well?" Zadie had been waiting on Finn for almost a minute.

Finn silently asked for more time by holding up an index finger. A few more seconds passed; then a song began playing in her head. It was in another language—French, maybe—with an accordion and what she thought was a washboard.

Finn finally swallowed the warm yogurt and looked up at Zadie. "What's that type of music they play in New Orleans?"

"Zydeco?"

"Yeah. That's it. Wait—" Steel drums began playing a competing tune. "Did you get a swirl?"

Zadie nodded. "Passion fruit and coconut."

"Oof. Those two songs do not work together." Finn shook her head, trying to knock the cacophony between her ears loose. "You should have gotten plain vanilla like I did. That one sounded like acoustic guitar."

Finn's echo died off at the same time the man onstage started singing "We Didn't Start the Fire" by Billy Joel. Hopefully, by the time the song was finished, Finn would figure out how to tell her sister about her big idea. She'd spent the thirty-minute car ride rehearsing it in her head. First, she'd tell Zadie about her echo. Then, once Zadie had recovered from the shock of it, she would pivot toward her plan. It would be a hard sell. Her sister liked surprises even less than she liked talking about their mother, and Finn's idea involved both.

The performer had only just finished singing the names of Soviet politicians when Zadie beat Finn to the punch. "So what's this thing you needed to tell me?"

Finn swallowed. "I had an echo."

"I know. You told me."

"Yeah, but I didn't tell you whose memory it was."

"Mom?" Zadie wasn't sure if she'd heard her sister correctly. "It was Mom's memory?"

"Yes."

She'd had a knot in her stomach ever since she'd walked into Finn's party that afternoon. Now it cinched so tight she felt breathless. "How . . . Are you sure it was her?"

Finn nodded. "Positive. She was singing the song."

"The song?"

"The one she used to sing to us when we were kids. The one about the bird."

Zadie remembered. She had loved that song. Now she turned off the radio any time it came on.

Finn started talking so fast her words tumbled over each other. "It was incredible! It was like I was in her body. But I didn't just see what she was seeing, I felt everything she was feeling. I could hear her *thoughts*. That's the first time that's ever happened." Finn paused, taking in her sister's expression. "You don't look excited."

"It's just . . . a lot."

"I know. It is for me, too. To be honest, lately I've been feeling like I was forgetting her, you know? It was so long ago, and I was only a kid. But now I feel like we've been given a second chance."

"A second chance at what?"

Finn shifted in her seat. There was more she wasn't telling her. Zadie could feel it.

"I think we should go looking for her."

Zadie didn't answer at first. Maybe she could pretend that she hadn't heard her sister. After all, the karaoke machine was loud and the poorly executed vocal runs of the two middle-aged women onstage were even louder. If she didn't answer, maybe Finn would drop the subject and they could go back to talking about things that didn't make her want to scream: funny dog videos, maybe, or people who weren't their mother.

"Zadie? Did you hear me?"

"Hmm?"

"I think we should go find Mom." It was clear by Finn's determined expression that she wasn't going to let this go.

"But we don't know where she is." *Or if she's even alive.* "If the police couldn't find her, what makes you think we can?"

"Because we have something the police don't." Finn leaned over the table, nearly setting her elbow down in Zadie's yogurt. "I've never had an echo of Mom. Not before she disappeared, not after. Until today."

"So?"

"So that's got to be significant. Don't you think?"

Unable to give Finn the response she was fishing for, Zadie didn't answer.

"It's fine if you don't. That's not what matters here. What matters is that we now know I can pick up on Mom's memories. I just have to do it again. Maybe then we can figure out where she went."

"But don't you find memories where they happened? If we don't know where she went, how would you even know where to look?"

"I know where we could start."

Zadie hadn't been back to their childhood home since the day Finn and she had moved out. Sometimes she thought about its red shutters, the way the pipes clicked when the hot water was running, the screen door that snapped shut like a mousetrap every time you went outside. She tried not to think about the time their mom had made a sprinkler for them in the backyard by poking holes in an old hose, or the time they'd tried to make a cake for Finn's ninth birthday and ended up with something that tasted good but was definitely not cake. She didn't need a gift like Finn's to know that their old house was full of memories. That's why she'd elected to stay as far away from it as possible, even moving an hour away so that she never had to accidentally drive past it.

"Nope. Nuh-uh. I'm not going back there."

"But it's just down the street—"

"No."

"Fine. You don't have to, but hear me out," Finn insisted. "Let's say I find another memory. We might be able to retrace her steps. If we can retrace her steps, then we might find more memories. If we find more memories, we might find *her*. Make sense?"

"Yes, but"—whether or not it made sense was not the issue—"what about Steve and Kathy? I don't think they'll be wild about the idea."

"They think we're going on vacation, anyway. They wouldn't need to know."

And in an instant, Zadie's beach plans were washed away. She could practically see the tide dragging her romance novels out to sea. "So you want to cancel our beach vacation to go looking for

Mom?" she said, measured, trying not to let her disappointment crack open like an egg and run all over the floor.

Finn must not have known how much this trip meant to Zadie, or she wouldn't have said what she said next. "The beach would be fun, but, I mean, this is more important, right?"

Who's more important than the mother who abandoned you? How about the sister who didn't? Five years had passed since Nora's disappearance, and yet her mom had still managed to find a way to intrude on their lives. Zadie didn't just want Nora in her rearview mirror, she wanted to smash the mirror into a thousand tiny shards. She wished that Finn understood how she felt. But instead of telling her, she did what she usually did when she felt hurt: she lied. "Sure, it's important. But what if she doesn't *want* to be found. Have you considered that?"

"No." Finn was adamant. She reached down under the table and reappeared with Nora's anklet in her hand, their tiny initials glittering pink in the light. "I used to think this had just fallen off her ankle by accident, but now I'm thinking maybe she left it behind on purpose. She was trying to tell us something."

"Tell us what?"

"To follow her."

"Wouldn't it have been easier to just leave a note?" Zadie said hotly. The irony of this statement was not lost on her—having declined her own opportunity to leave such a note that morning. The breakup, the pregnancy—these were words Zadie was waiting to say out loud until the air was salty enough to cure them. But with her beach plans dashed, she could feel them start to rot in her mouth.

"You really think she just ran out on us, don't you?" Finn's eyes flashed.

Zadie thought carefully about her answer. "I don't think there's any way of knowing why Mom did what she did, and I think chasing after her based on one echo would be a mistake."

Unlike Zadie, who tried her best to bury her emotions, Finn flew them like a flag. Her indignation was borderline patriotic. "I don't know why I even told you. You don't care where she is."

“That’s not fair.”

“Then why don’t you want to look for her?”

Zadie *had* looked for Nora. The day she went missing she’d driven around town for hours asking everyone she knew whether they’d seen her mother. When she returned home that evening, she couldn’t stop staring at the iridescent oil stain on the driveway where Nora’s car had once been parked. It was another twenty minutes before she could bring herself to go inside, to tell her sister she’d failed.

Finn got tired of waiting for an answer. “I’m doing this. With or without you.” With that, she pushed her chair away from the table, feet screeching across the linoleum, then hurried out the front door.

“Shit,” Zadie muttered. The woman singing onstage made brief eye contact with her. She’d heard their argument. Most of the room probably had.

Zadie slinked past the other tables and pushed open the front door. Warm air rushed at her face, as did the lonesome sound of an approaching train. The horn sounded again and the warning bells began to chime, an oddly cheerful reminder of something so deadly. Zadie watched Finn’s car pass over the tracks just as the barriers began to fall and the mile-long train split the neighborhood in two.

FIVE

A SECOND SLEEPING BAG

Several days went by; long, hot, drawn-curtain days that made Zadie yearn for a sea breeze. Most of her evenings were spent slouching in front of her window air conditioner, waiting for Finn to call. The girls hadn't spoken since their fight, and they were supposed to leave for Galveston the next day. With less than twelve hours to go, Zadie thought it was pretty safe to assume that they would not be going to the beach tomorrow or perhaps any other day.

Maybe it was for the best. Had she really expected one vacation to rebuild a relationship that had been eroding for years? She'd read an article about homes on the Atlantic coast that were slowly succumbing to the ocean as tides ate away at the cliffs they were built on. Owners were being forced to decide whether it was worth the money to move their homes back from the cliff or to just let them tumble into the ocean. At the time, Zadie had thought the decision was a no-brainer: move the house. Now she wasn't so sure. Maybe that house belonged at the bottom of the ocean where it could start a new life as a hotel for fish.

The one thing she was certain of, however, was that Finn's grand plan to reunite them with their mother was a bad one. Even if she set aside her personal feelings, the idea that they could somehow track her down using nothing but a series of memory fragments was ludicrous. If all Finn had wanted to know was what kind of sandwich their mom had eaten on a given day, maybe she'd have some luck, but reconstructing the days after her disappearance would require more than hearing Nora humming a song. It would be a huge investment of their time and energy, and at six weeks pregnant with a full-time job, Zadie had very little of either to spare.

Zadie's suitcase sat expectantly by the front door, faintly smelling of coconut sunscreen. She picked it up with the intention of unpacking it, then stopped. Instead, she pulled one of her romance novels, *The Fisherman's Desire,* from the side pocket. It featured a sea-drenched bearded man wearing an unbuttoned yellow rain slicker that exposed his bare chest. He was standing on the bow of a fishing boat forcefully pulling a rope that hung from overhead, which Zadie found odd, considering the craft he was on was clearly not a sailboat. This was an inaccuracy that she was willing to overlook, considering that there were more pressing matters at hand—namely, chiseled fisherman abs.

She settled back onto her spot on the couch and spent the next four hours devouring the story of a lonely fisherman trying to capture the heart (and body) of an aristocrat. Dustin had never understood how she could read a book cover to cover in one sitting. "Clearly you've never read a romance novel," she had answered.

"Should I be jealous?" he'd joked. Only it wasn't a joke. Dustin was so deeply insecure that he made the same comment every time he saw her reading anything with an attractive man on the cover. At least her wandering eyes—if you could call them that—were fictional. His ogled flesh-and-blood redheads while they were standing in line at coffee shops.

She tapped her smartphone and the screen lit up. It was midnight, an hour past when she usually turned in for the night, but she wasn't tired. She was anxious; anxious that Finn hadn't called her back; anxious that she had possibly messed up the only relationship that meant anything to her. Maybe she just should have agreed to Finn's plan. Yes, she would have been disappointed when their search came up empty, but at least they'd get a few kitschy refrigerator magnets out of it.

Zadie picked up her phone and scrolled through her contacts until she found Finn. It rang. One, two, five rings and no answer. *I shouldn't be calling this late*, she thought. *She's probably asleep.*

But something didn't feel right. It wasn't a premonition, just old-fashioned intuition that was telling her she needed to talk to Finn as soon as possible.

Zadie dialed again, but it went straight to voice mail:

Yo, it's Finn. My mom taught me not to talk to strangers, so only leave a message if I know who you are or you're calling to tell me I won a bunch of money.

She must have turned off her phone when she saw me calling, Zadie thought. In seventeen years, she'd never known Finn to hold a grudge. Zadie could think of only one other reason why she might decline her call.

She shoved her phone in her pocket, grabbed her suitcase, and let the door slam behind her.

The house was just as Zadie remembered it. Even in the dark, she could make out the same red shutters, the same aluminum mailbox, the same withered persimmon tree in the front lawn. And for a moment she was sixteen again, sneaking in after a night of watching friends set off firecrackers behind the quarry. Her mom had waited up for her and had been thoroughly unimpressed when Zadie had told her where she'd been. "Firecrackers? I'd assumed you'd be doing something fun." She was right. It hadn't been that fun, certainly not fun enough to justify the two-week grounding she got as a result.

These were exactly the kinds of memories Zadie had been hoping to avoid.

As she pulled closer, her headlights illuminated a hooded figure standing in the driveway. The person turned around and waved her arms frantically. She seemed to be mouthing, "Turn it off!"

Zadie turned off the engine and Finn marched up to her window and tapped on the glass. "What are you doing?" she hissed as the window rolled down.

"Me? What are *you* doing?"

"I told you I was going to do this with or without you. This is what 'without you' looks like."

"Really? Because it kind of looks like trespassing."

Finn glanced over her shoulder at the house. The windows were dark. "You've gotta get out of here. You're going to blow my cover."

"So were you just going to stand in this stranger's driveway all night, waiting for an echo?"

"If necessary."

"You're lucky no one has called the police."

"They don't get up till six."

"Wait . . . how many times have you done this?"

"Uh. Three."

"You've been out here three nights in a row?!"

"Ssshhh!"

"And how many echoes have you had in that time, huh?"

Finn pursed her lips. "Will you just leave already? I can't concentrate with you here."

"I'm not leaving until you do."

"Fine. But stay here." Finn pushed away from the car and marched back toward the house, glancing over her shoulder to glare at her sister.

"I will," Zadie muttered, watching Finn sit down in the driveway and pointedly turn so she was no longer facing her. After a moment, her sister reclined so that she was lying flat on her back on the concrete.

"This is insane." Zadie looked up at the house and into the window of her old bedroom. She used to run to it anytime she heard a car pull into the driveway, ever hopeful that it was some boy who'd come to woo her. She wondered who lived in that room now, and prayed to whatever God would listen that whoever it was didn't look out the window to see the strange girl splayed out in their driveway.

She looked back at Finn, who as far as she could tell hadn't moved since she'd lain down. *She's probably asleep,* Zadie thought, yawning herself. It was almost two in the morning. Just that knowledge alone made her want to shut her eyes.

Zadie didn't remember the clock turning three, and yet the neon green digits on her dash read 3:17. *I must have dozed off,* she thought, blinking heavily. Her eyes darted from the clock to her sister, who was no longer in the driveway but was standing on the front stoop with one hand on the doorknob.

"You've got to be kidding me." Zadie was wide awake now. As quietly as she could, she opened her car door and padded across the lawn. "Finn!" she hissed and grabbed her sister's arm. "What are you doing?"

Just then the porch lights blinked on. "Shit! Finn, come on. We gotta go." But Finn couldn't hear her, and by the far-off look in her eyes, it was clear she didn't see her, either. Zadie could hear noises coming from inside the house. She didn't have time to wait until Finn came out of the echo on her own, and she didn't have the strength to drag her back to the car, so she did the only thing she could think of in the moment: shove her sister up against the brick wall of the house and flatten herself next to her. Finn let out a small gasp as the impact woke her from her trance, so Zadie clamped her hand over her sister's mouth to silence her.

The front door swung toward their hiding spot and a beam of light stretched over the lawn. Zadie held her breath as she waited for whoever was behind the door to step into the light and discover them lurking in the shadows. Several throat-tightening seconds passed. Then the door closed and the porch light clicked off, plunging the sisters back into darkness.

Zadie hazarded a step in the direction of the car when Finn whispered, "She didn't have a choice."

"What?"

"Mom. She didn't want to leave, but she had to. I just saw it."

Zadie nervously glanced back at the front door. "Can we talk about this later?"

"I watched her walk out the door and get in her car. I watched her drive away. She was sad. Really sad." Even in the dark, Zadie could see tears collecting in her sister's eyes. "I never really believed she left on purpose, but now I'm sure of it."

Zadie didn't think Finn's echo proved anything. Did she believe her mom was sad about abandoning her kids? Yes. Only a complete monster wouldn't be in that situation. But she still left, and Zadie had no interest in revisiting the issue. Not now. Not while they were trespassing on private property.

"You can tell me more about it in the car. Come on." Finn let Zadie lead her away from the house and into the station wagon. "Where'd you park?" Zadie asked, not seeing any other cars parked on the street.

"On Brushwood. I didn't want to draw attention from the neighbors."

Zadie nodded and put the car into drive. As they pulled up behind Kathy's maroon SUV, Finn said, "There's something else. Remember that compass Mom used to hang around her rearview mirror?"

"Yeah."

"In my echo it was pointing west."

"Okay . . ." Zadie had expected more to the story. "Is that it?"

"Well, yeah, but—" Finn paused and shook her head. "Wait. No. You don't get to make me feel bad about this. I finally have a clue. A *real* clue." A second later, Finn was outside and slamming the car door behind her.

"Finn. Wait . . ." Zadie followed her sister to the driver's side of the SUV. It was then that she noticed the bags in the back seat. "So that was your plan? To drive off without telling anyone where you're going?"

"That's *still* the plan," Finn said defiantly, one hand on the steering wheel.

Zadie groaned. She loved her sister, but her obstinance was infuriating. "You're seventeen! Do you even have any money?"

"I have a few thousand saved up, plus graduation checks."

"I can't let you do this alone. It's dangerous."

"Don't worry. I'll be fine. I'll tell Mom you said hi." Finn tried closing the door, but Zadie braced it with her elbow.

"What are you doing?" Finn said, exasperated.

"Just . . . give me a minute." Zadie looked out at the road that was only faintly visible by moonlight, a road to nowhere. She was silent for a few moments—at least from Finn's perspective. In Zadie's mind, a lot was being said.

Then finally, "Throw your shit in the car."

"But—"

"My car," she corrected. "I'm driving."

Barely suppressing a squeal, Finn dove out of her seat and pulled her sister in for a tight hug. "Thank you! Thank you! *Thank you!*"

"Don't thank me yet," Zadie said as Finn pulled away and air rushed back into her lungs. "I have conditions."

"Shoot."

"We'll drop off the SUV. Then you have to text Kathy and tell her we left early for Galveston."

"I already left a note."

"Okay, fine," Zadie said impatiently. "Second: don't wander off. I need to know where you are at all times."

"I have just the thing." Finn reached into the SUV, pulled out her giant sun hat, and placed it on her head. "How's that for conspicuous?"

Zadie ignored the attempt at a joke. "Finally: be prepared for the possibility that we don't find her."

Finn's smile waned a little, as if the thought hadn't actually occurred to her until just now. "I am."

"You might be disappointed."

"I know."

Zadie gave a nod, then opened the back door of the SUV and pulled out an orange nylon bag. She turned to Finn. "Mom's tent? Really?"

Finn grinned. "I brought a second sleeping bag, just in case."

Zadie groaned, walked the tent to the back of her thirdhand Subaru station wagon, and tossed it next to the inflatable watermelon lounger she'd bought for the beach-house pool. She hadn't been camping since she was seventeen, and she hadn't liked it then, either.

Finn gathered the rest of her belongings and carried them to Zadie's car. "Are you *sure* you want to do this?" Zadie asked.

Finn's smile answered for her.

SIX

SIX MONTHS

(UNTIL NORA WILDER'S DISAPPEARANCE)

They had been on the road for eight hours, although the bleakness of the desert highway made it feel like they'd been driving for as many days. The arid landscape looked like a beach at low tide, an expanse of sand dotted with wiry black sea-urchin shrubs and not much else. Nora had barely said anything since they'd left. Zadie, who was sitting in the passenger seat, was unnerved by her mother's silence. Normally, Nora would be singing along with the radio or goading her daughters into playing I Spy or some other inane game conceived for the sole purpose of tricking children into thinking that road trips are actually fun, but today she held her body with a military stillness, elbows locked, hands clamped at ten and two on the steering wheel.

"Where are we going?" Zadie asked for what was probably the tenth time.

Nora's eyes barely flicked in her daughter's direction. "Man, you really don't like surprises, do you?"

Zadie crossed her arms. She *did* like surprises, just not this one. She'd spent the last three hours wishing a premonition would come along and ruin it.

She turned to look at her sister in the back seat. Finn had barely uttered a peep, thanks to a book of crosswords she'd found in the seat-back pocket. If Zadie had had time to pack, she would have brought her iPod or a magazine, something to pass the time other than reading bumper stickers, but Nora had shaken the girls awake at seven A.M., tossed each of them a banana, and practically shoved them out the door with no explanation.

"Seriously, Mom. Do you even know where we're going?"

"Cool it, Zadie! Jeez . . . what has gotten into you lately?"

Six months had passed since Zadie had followed her mom to the edge of the cliff. Ever since that night, she'd been keeping a close eye on Nora, spying on her through the front window as she wheeled the trash can to the edge of the road; offering to drop her off and pick her up from work. She even hung a bell on the back door that she'd listen for at night when she was supposed to be sleeping. But Nora didn't go anywhere, and she appeared to have no memory of the incident that had been haunting Zadie for months. The burden of that night should have belonged to both of them, but it became apparent that Zadie was going to have to carry it alone.

"It's nothing."

"Fine. If we're not going to talk, then I'm putting on music." Nora punched the power button on the stereo and the cassette deck whirred to life. Zadie leaned her seat back, closed her eyes, and pretended she was still in her own bed.

Finn didn't like it when her mom and sister fought, and it had been happening a lot lately. It hadn't always been this way. Something in the past few months had shifted between them, some cosmic disturbance that forced them to say things to each other that they didn't really mean, then go hours without speaking. Whenever she asked her mom about it, she would just sigh and say, "Teenagers." Finn didn't bother pointing out that she, too, was almost a teenager. Sometimes she worried that the moment she turned thirteen, she and her mom would suddenly start hating each other as well.

The fighting had stopped. For now. Zadie's eyes were closed, but

Finn couldn't tell if she was asleep or just trying to avoid another argument. Her mom was playing Simon & Garfunkel, which did little to liven the mood. It continued this way for an hour or more until her mom suddenly announced, "I think it's time for a slushy break! Who wants one?" Whatever had been bothering her mom was apparently old news, because she was smiling now and drumming on the steering wheel.

"I do!" Finn said, relieved at the prospect of getting out of the stale car. "The green kind."

"One Soylent Green coming up."

Nora got off the highway at the next exit and pulled into a gas station labeled GO FOR GAS. The lettering on the sign was so faded it looked as if it had been hastily colored in with marker, and a bird had built a nest in the cradle of the second O.

The door chimed as they walked inside, and the girls made a beeline for the Slushie machine, two plastic chambers filled with roiling icy slurries of Yellow No. 5 and Blue No. 1.

"Aww. No green," Finn said with an exaggerated pout.

"Yeah, there is. Watch." Zadie filled half a cup with yellow slush, followed by blue, then snapped on a lid and shook it vigorously. When she was done, she pulled off the lid and handed the cup to Finn.

"You're a genius." Finn slurped from the edge of her cup, then looked around for their mom and spotted her chatting with the cashier. Three Pepsis, several sticks of jerky, and a bag of marshmallows sat on the counter between them. The cashier must have noticed how pretty Nora looked in her white tank top, her arms lean and freckled from the hours she spent outside at Sunnyside Dairy. She'd worked there for as long as Finn could remember, working her way up from feeder to manager in only a few short years. There was a large bruise on her right thigh from where a cow had kicked her the week before. Finn thought it looked like a sunflower.

"Where do you think Mom's taking us?" Zadie asked.

"Dunno. The zoo?"

"The zoo's only an hour from our house."

Finn furrowed her brow thoughtfully. "You don't think she's taking us to that doll museum again, do you?"

"Ugh. I hope not. That place was creepy." Zadie stole a glance at Nora. "Don't you think it's a little weird, though?"

"What's weird?"

"Dragging us out here to the middle of nowhere. Not telling us where we're going?"

Finn hadn't really given it much thought. Nora often sprung plans on them last minute, so it wasn't a stretch to think that she would wing a trip like this, too. Her sister was probably worried over nothing. "I dunno. I think it's fun."

Zadie exhaled heavily, then held out her hand. "Can I have a sip of that?"

Finn passed her the Slushie. Zadie popped off the cap and straw and took a large gulp, leaving a green mustache on her upper lip that she quickly wiped away. "Thanks," she said, passing the drink back.

"Zadie! Finn! Come here." Nora gestured for them to join her at the register. Finn was first to her mom's side. "Look at this," Nora said when Zadie had finally caught up. She held out a brochure for something called the Constellation Campground. The picture on the front flap showed a family of four posing in front of a sandstone mesa, blithely smiling at their own good fortune for booking—according to the small print—THE ONLY CAMPGROUND WITH SPECTACULAR VIEWS OF THE RED ROCKS.

"How would you guys like to stay here tonight?" Nora asked.

"Really?" Finn gasped. She loved camping. She loved sleeping outside with the crickets and the owls, eating charred marshmallows, splashing through creeks looking for arrowheads. She even loved bugs and would collect the ones she found in a plastic terrarium her mom had gotten her from the dollar store. Finn would always release them after an hour or two, but she liked being able to see them up close: the bristles on their legs, their stained-glass wings, the iridescent orbs of their eyes.

"Yes, really!" Her mom's enthusiasm bordered on frantic. Maybe, Zadie had been right. There was a strangeness to her mother in that moment, an undercurrent of panic beneath her toothy smile.

By the expression on Zadie's face, she'd noticed it, too. "Are you okay, Mom?"

"Of course I'm okay." Nora laughed mirthlessly. "Don't you think this place looks like fun?" She shoved the brochure at her elder daughter as if that would somehow convince her.

"Can't we just go home?"

"No." The word was cold and sharp, as if it had been chipped from ice. Just as quickly, Nora grinned again. "I guess you don't want any marshmallows, then."

There was an uncomfortable pause, after which Zadie said, "But marshmallows are literally the only thing I like about camping."

"Tell you what . . ." Nora straightened her shoulders in an attempt to appear composed. "You can have all the marshmallows you want if you at least try to have fun this weekend. And I mean *really* try. Got it?"

Zadie hesitated. "Okay. I'll try."

"Even if it rains?"

"Sure."

"Even if there are bugs?"

"Uhh . . . yeah, I guess."

"Even if the woods turn out to be haunted?"

"Mom!" Zadie clapped her hands over her ears.

Nora laughed. "I'm kidding!" she said. "The woods aren't haunted."

Zadie let her arms fall to her sides, watching Nora warily.

"The tent is."

"No, no, no, no, no!" Zadie plugged her ears again and ran out of the convenience store.

"Why is she so afraid of ghosts?" The idea of ghosts didn't scare Finn like most children her age, probably because she was so used to sensing things that were no longer there.

"Because people are scared of things they don't understand."

Finn noticed the new freckles on her mother's nose before she noticed that her eyes were wider than usual, like she was watching a scary movie. Her hands were trembling a little, too. When Nora saw Finn looking at them, she shoved them in her pockets. "Come on," she said. "Let's go camping."

Camping. Finn loved camping. Then why did she feel anxious?

Seven

The Early Bird Gets the Pancake

Zadie felt the gas pump shudder against her forehead. She had rested it there just as a headache was beginning to swell behind her eyes and the cool metal had seemed soothing. *What the hell am I doing?* she thought—not in regards to why her face was pressed up against a dirty gas pump, but to the broader question of why she was pumping gas at a rest stop in Middle of Nowhere, Texas, at six in the goddamn morning. Zadie pushed herself off the pump and blinked into the sheet of cherry-colored sky where the sun would soon be. She loved sunrises, but she rarely woke up early enough to see them. *I'll probably be seeing a lot of them on this trip,* a thought that was supposed to inspire her but just ended up making her feel preemptively exhausted.

She turned to see Finn heading toward her with two plastic grocery bags in her hands, a bottle of Snapple sticking out of her left armpit, and a six-pack of mini-doughnuts tucked under her chin. "No coffee?" Zadie asked. She knew she wasn't supposed to have caffeine while she was pregnant, but given the choice between that and falling asleep at the wheel, she opted for the less lethal of the two options.

"Oh, crap," Finn said, dropping the bags at her feet. "I knew I forgot something."

Zadie glanced inside the bags. *And yet you remembered to buy three different flavors of Combos.* "It's fine," she said, trying to hide her irritation as she placed the gas nozzle back on its cradle. "I'll get it. You want one?"

"Nah," Finn said, popping open a peach Snapple. "I don't drink coffee."

"You don't drink coffee? How do you function in the morning?"

Finn shrugged. "I just get out of bed and then, you know, do stuff."

"You mean, you don't wake up and immediately want to fall back asleep?" Zadie said, mystified. She usually spent an hour swatting the snooze button before her day got started, and it took two cups of Colombian before she could safely operate the toaster. She even had one of those mugs that read: DON'T TALK TO ME UNTIL I'VE HAD MY COFFEE.

"Not really. Why would I sleep when I could—"

"*Do* stuff?"

"Exactly." Finn popped a mini-doughnut in her mouth and washed it down with a swig of her Snapple.

It's gotta be the sugar, Zadie thought. *That's where all her energy comes from.* "Well, we're not all as motivated as you," she said mid-yawn. "Speaking of doing stuff, do you have any idea what we're supposed to be doing now?" Gas and coffee weren't the only reasons the sisters had pulled off at Exit 258. There was also the small matter of not knowing where the hell they were going. They had started driving west only because that was the direction Finn saw on their mom's compass. Two hours later, it was starting to look like they'd need a lot more to go on than just a cardinal direction.

"Not yet. Don't worry. It'll come to me."

"Well, while you're waiting for Mom's memory ghost to give you directions, I'm gonna get some coffee." That came out sounding more bitter than Zadie had intended, but she was tired and wasn't particularly interested in engaging in talk about Mom before she had some caffeine in her.

As Zadie disappeared through the automatic sliding doors of the gas station, Finn half sat on the hood of the car and craned her face toward the light like a flower. She couldn't remember the last time she had been awake from sunset to sunrise. It was dizzying, as if she could actually feel the rotation of the earth beneath her feet. She should have been tired, but all she felt was this propulsive energy coursing through her the way she did before a big track meet. It wasn't just the possibility of finding her mom that excited her. It was the journey ahead. It was waking up every morning to a new sky, exploring new places. She had been on vacations before, but never anything she would consider an adventure. *This* was an adventure.

It would likely only be a matter of minutes before Steve and Kathy woke up and found her missing. She winced, imagining Steve knocking on her bedroom door and saying something like "Finn, I made pancakes! Better hurry before Milly decides to jump up onto the table again." When she didn't answer, he would let himself in and find her bed messy as usual, but unoccupied. Thirty more seconds would pass before he found her note, thirty seconds that would feel like an eternity to him, each millisecond unfurling in slow motion like a new leaf. Finn could picture his face in those moments, as confusion quickly metamorphosed into panic.

Suddenly she wasn't so sure that she'd done the right thing. She could have waited until morning, told her foster parents to their faces, not skip out of town in the middle of the night. *Don't worry. I didn't run away!* she'd written in her note. Finn just now realized how flippant those words were, as if she'd anticipated Steve's pain and had crudely placed an exclamation point beside it.

She unlocked her phone and opened the text app. SORRY ABOUT THE NOTE, she typed. I'LL CALL YOU WHEN WE ARRIVE. It was a soft lie. She and Zadie would arrive, just not at the destination she had given Kathy "in case of emergencies." She would call them from her fictional room overlooking the Gulf of Mexico, and they would believe her because she had never given them a reason not to trust her word. *I'll just tell them I have my toes in the sand*, she decided as she gazed out at the burnished landscape. For all she knew, she could be looking at the same sand that—hundreds of miles southeast—was tangled with seaweed and gull feathers. Maybe, the beach was simply one edge of the desert, and she was standing on the other end.

To assuage her guilt, Finn reminded herself why she was there. *Mom is missing, and I can find her.* It was then that the weight of the commitment she'd made truly hit her. Their success—or failure—hinged on her. She would have to harness her ability in a way she never had before, not simply waiting for memories to come to her, but seeking them out. She would have to learn to hunt with a spear, not a trap.

Finn inhaled until her lungs trembled with fullness, closed her eyes, and cast her mind out like a net. She could feel memories all around her, floating like pollen; memories about flat tires and jumped batteries, counting change on a car hood, and collect calls that said "come home" on the other end of the line. They were all stories about people on a journey, just like hers.

Then she sensed one memory that seemed to have a stronger presence than the others. She could feel it, like a vibration in her chest. *Mom, is that you?* Finn's question hung in the air, unanswered. She tethered her mind to the memory, just as she had done all those times at the Fro-Yodel, and tried to reel it in. After several seconds of intense concentration, she could feel the memory start to yield to her. A moment later, it docked.

Finn's ears filled with a dull roar. *It sounds mechanical,* she thought. *Like an engine.* She concentrated harder. The sound sharpened.

No. Not an engine. Water. A waterfall. She heard thousands of gallons of water succumb to gravity; the thunder of erosion. Finn flinched as she imagined her mom being pulled along by the current, then tumbling into the billowing white cloud over the rocks. She shook her head, trying to focus on the only thing she knew was real: the roar of the water.

Then the sound changed once again. It was not a continuous flow of water, she realized. It was a short, loud burst followed by a gentle trickle and a long hiss.

"Ahhh . . . that's the good stuff." Zadie appeared beside her, holding a cardboard coffee cup. "Actually it's not that good, but at least it's caffeinated." She paused, trying to read her sister's expression. "You okay?"

Finn burst out laughing.

"Wow, okay. What did I miss?"

"I finally got one."

"An echo?"

Finn was laughing so hard that she was gasping for air, but she managed to squeak out a *yes*.

Zadie squinted, confused. "Must have been funny."

"For a second, I thought—I thought Mom had *drowned!*"

"That's not funny at all."

"No, it's not." A breath. "Then I realized the sound I was hearing was a—a toilet flushing!"

Zadie starting laughing, too—probably just because her sister was—and soon both of them were doubled over, clutching stitches in their sides. By the time their laughs had turned to sighs, Zadie said, "Well, we're off to a great start."

Finn let out one last chuckle. "Yeah, we're killing it."

"I'm kinda hungry. How about you?"

"I could eat."

Zadie nodded at a diner across the street that looked like an old saloon. A yellow A-frame sign outside the door read:

EARLY BIRD PANCAKE SPECIAL

50¢ EACH

5 A.M. TO 7 A.M.

Did you know that armadillos carry leprosy?" Finn said, petting the scaly shell of the taxidermy animal displayed on the hostess stand of the restaurant.

"Then why are you touching it?" Zadie backed up a step.

"You can't catch a disease from a stuffed armadillo. Just live ones." She scratched it behind the ears, then spoke in a baby voice, "You wouldn't give me leprosy, would you?"

"It looks a little . . . *off*." The armadillo gawked back at Zadie, one eye noticeably higher than the other.

"I think he's cute," Finn countered. "Just look at how happy he is." Whoever had immortalized this particular armadillo had formed its mouth into a grotesque smile. Zadie shook her head in disgust.

A hostess wearing a red-and-white-checked gingham shirt greeted them at the podium. "I see you've met Luanne!" she said, nodding at the armadillo.

"Oh, yes. We're best buds," Finn answered.

She chuckled. "Just the two of you?"

"Yes, ma'am."

"Follow me." The hostess pulled out two menus from a basket hanging under Luanne's tail and gestured for the girls to follow her through a pair of swinging saloon doors into the main dining area. She walked them over to a booth pushed up against a wood-paneled wall decorated with framed portraits of Hollywood cowboys. "Your server will be right with you."

Zadie gazed up at a signed picture of Burt Lancaster. "They committed to their theme. I'll give them—"

A very loud ringing sound interrupted her. "Order up!" cried a voice. Zadie clapped her hands over her ears. "Shit! What was that?"

"The dinner bell." Finn laughed and pointed to a cast-iron triangle swinging from the kitchen pass-through window.

Zadie's face sank. "Do you think they're going to do that every time an order comes out?"

Finn shrugged. "Oh, come on. It's fun!"

"Ugh. Well, if the coffee doesn't wake me up, that will."

The crumpled ten-dollar bill in Zadie's pocket bought each of the girls a short stack and a side of bacon, a glass of orange juice for Finn, and another cup of coffee for Zadie. Their ears were still ringing from the dinner bell when the waitress placed their steaming plates on the table. Finn promptly drowned hers in syrup like she was trying to put out a fire.

"So what has Dustin been up to?" she asked, passing Zadie the syrup dispenser. "I haven't seen him in a while."

Zadie realized that she hadn't thought about Dustin once since they'd started driving. The thought was both simultaneously liberating and depressing. "Oh, uhhh . . . we broke up."

Finn looked up, startled. "What? Seriously?"

She nodded. "A few days ago."

"Are you okay?"

"Yeah. I was the one who called it off." Zadie wondered if she appeared sad. She didn't *feel* particularly sad—not over Dustin, anyway.

"Damn . . ." Finn looked reflective for a moment. "But he was so good at caricatures."

Zadie raised an eyebrow. "Are you suggesting I shouldn't have broken up with him because he's a good cartoonist?"

"I'm just saying. He never drew one of me, and I kinda wanted one," Finn continued, mouth full. "Why'd you break up with him?"

It was a simple question with a Rubik's Cube of an answer. "Because . . ." Zadie turned it over in her head, trying out different combinations of words that essentially meant *I didn't think he'd be a good father* without letting it spill that she was pregnant. The phrase she decided to go with was: "He didn't have his shit together."

"I get that," Finn said. "He never struck me as the responsible type."

"Me neither. It didn't used to bother me as much before—" Zadie paused as she debated whether the mustard-colored booth under the watchful eye of Luanne the Armadillo was the right venue to tell her sister the big news. Thankfully, the waitress swooped in at just that moment to refill Zadie's coffee. "Can I interest you girls in anything else?"

"Just the check, please," Zadie answered, then wiggled her finger in her right ear as if that would somehow cure her of her dinner-bell tinnitus.

"So what've we got planned for today?"

"You tell me," Zadie said, emptying her coffee cup. "You're the reason we're out here."

"There must be a ton of fun things to do in"—Finn read the address at the bottom of the menu—"Filbert, Texas."

Zadie looked skeptical. "Yeah, okay."

"Oh, come on. Live a little." Finn vigorously shimmied her shoulders.

"That's weird. Don't do that." Zadie looked around the diner to see if anyone was watching, but all the other patrons were focused on their breakfasts. If there was one thing that hadn't changed about her sister, it was her willingness to embarrass herself in public.

"You *do* remember how to have fun, don't you?"

"Yeah, I have fun all the time," Zadie said, although the uncertainty in her tone belied her words.

"Okay, if you say so." Finn leaned back, casually draping her arms over the back of the booth.

"I do."

"I believe you," Finn said, humoring her, then examined a hangnail on her left ring finger.

"Fine. You want to know what I do for fun?" Zadie stood up, wincing as the vinyl upholstery nearly ripped the skin off her bare thighs. She spotted a Wurlitzer-style jukebox pushed up against the far wall and headed toward it. Finn swiveled around to watch her, hiding a grin behind the back of the booth. Zadie slid a quarter into the jukebox, punched a button or two, and returned to her seat.

A second later, the opening bars of "Baba O'Riley" started playing. Zadie first looked around to make sure no one was watching. Then as the drums kicked in, she started air drumming along with them. After she'd banged out the first verse, Finn said, "So that's how you have fun? Pretend drumming while making awkward eye contact with people?"

"No. Most of the time it's with my cat. Well, Dustin's cat, I guess. It's actually really cute. Once he didn't break eye contact with me for the entirety of 'Bohemian Rhapsody.'"

"Okay, so just to recap, you like air drumming . . ."

Zadie nodded.

"And staring contests with cats."

"If the mood strikes."

"Anything else?"

Zadie thought for a moment, then reached into her bag and pulled out her copy of *The Fisherman's Desire*. "And this."

"You're still reading that stuff?"

"That *stuff*?" Zadie playfully raised her eyebrows.

"I didn't mean it like that," Finn corrected, but the trouble with backpedaling is that you can't see where you're going. "I just meant—"

"It's okay," Zadie said. "Romance novels aren't for everyone."

Finn sat forward and leaned her elbows on the table. "What do you like about them?"

Zadie hadn't thought much about it, so she took her time answering. "Because I like the idea that two people can have all the odds stacked against them, but they figure out a way to make it work, because their love for each other is more important than all the other bullshit." Then she added, "I'm not stupid. I know that's not how real relationships work, but that doesn't make it any less satisfying."

Finn picked up the book and started flipping through the pages. "Can I borrow this?"

"Sure. I'm done with it, anyway." It felt good to chat like this with her sister. She was reminded of the nights she used to read to Finn when she was young. Finn would nod off to sleep mid-story, and soon it was just Zadie reading *The House at Pooh Corner* to the owls.

"If you like it, I have a whole stack of others," Zadie said.

Finn held up *The Fisherman's Desire* and waggled her eyebrows. "Are they all as hunky as this guy?"

"Hunkier."

The girls paid the bill and left the tip on the table. "Goodbye, Luanne," Finn said, patting the armadillo on the head on their way out. As she stepped out into the parking lot, shielding her eyes from the desert sun, her phone buzzed in her back pocket; eight missed calls and three voice mails, all from Kathy. "Hey, I need to make a call."

Zadie nodded and headed back to the car to give her sister privacy. She didn't need to ask who Finn was calling.

Finn sucked in a breath and tapped on her foster mom's icon on her phone. Kathy answered on the first ring. "Finn?" Her voice was shrill.

"Hey."

"Are you okay?"

"Yeah. I'm fine. Did you get my note?"

"I did. After we called half the neighborhood."

Kathy didn't get angry that often, so Finn knew she had screwed up. "I'm sorry. I should have put it somewhere more obvious."

"What you *should* have done is tell us you were leaving early, not sneak out in the middle of the night. Your dad about had a heart attack." Kathy normally caught herself when she started to refer to Steve as Finn's dad, but she was too upset to notice.

Finn felt herself shrivel inside. "He didn't get my text?"

"He forgot his cell at the office."

"Oh . . . I'm sorry. It was stupid. *I* was stupid."

"Stupid is right." There was a pause. Finn could hear the sound of traffic in the background. Kathy must have been driving. "Was this Zadie's idea?"

"No. It was mine."

More silence. Somewhere in San Antonio, a car honked. "I'm just glad you're safe," Kathy said, the edge in her voice sanded off.

"I really am sorry."

Her foster mom sighed. "It's okay. Have fun. Bring me back a seashell."

A lump formed in Finn's throat. When she opened her mouth, the lump turned into a lie. "I will." She hung up and took a moment to compose herself. She'd betrayed Kathy's and Steve's trust. It made her feel small and ungrateful, because in her heart she still felt like she owed them something for taking her in. Since they'd proposed to adopt her, that feeling had only intensified. After five years of providing for her, loving her, had they not earned the right to call her their daughter? Was it wrong of her to deny them that? Whether it was objectively selfish or not, she *felt* selfish in that moment, and that made it real.

"Kathy?" Zadie said as Finn returned to the car.

"Yeah."

"Was she pissed?"

"Kinda."

"Why does that not surprise me?"

Finn felt heat rush to her cheeks. "She's just worried. I don't blame her." She could hear the defensiveness in her voice.

Zadie must have heard it, too. "Sorry, I didn't mean to . . ."

An awkward silence followed. The sun was higher now, and the air rippled with heat. Finn shaded her eyes with her hand. "So what do we do now?" The question felt more daunting than it had earlier that day. She had exactly seven days to find their mom; actually, now it was more like six and three-quarters.

Zadie looked equally overwhelmed by the decision. "We could keep driving west, I guess, but at some point, we'll end up in the Pacific Ocean."

Finn had hoped an echo would come to her by the time they were done with breakfast, but she'd had no such luck. "I can try again once we start driving," she said, uncertain.

"We don't really have any other options, so I guess we'll just keep heading toward Tucson."

"Well," Finn started, "there's one other thing we can try."

"Oh? What's that?" Zadie narrowed her eyes at her sister.

"You know . . ." Finn put her fingers to her temples and scrunched up her face.

"What's that supposed to be? A migraine?"

"No. A psychic."

"On behalf of all psychics, I have to say that's an offensive stereotype," Zadie said dryly.

"Please?" Finn pleaded. "I'm getting nothing here. You can help."

"I'm going to get in the car now and pretend you didn't just suggest that." Zadie ducked into the driver's seat and started the engine. Finn followed her in through the passenger side.

"Come on. Do the thing!"

"Nope."

"Why? Why won't you use it?"

Because *if I tell you, you'll never speak to me again*, Zadie thought.

She cleared her throat. "I have a box of Mom's old cassettes in the back seat if you want to pick something out to listen to."

"You didn't answer my question."

"If you don't pick one, I'll put on public radio."

"And if you don't answer me, then I'm going to play . . ." Finn leaned into the back seat and thumbed through the box of cassettes until she found one that made her bark with laughter. "This!" Before Zadie could see what it was, Finn stuffed the cassette into the car's ancient tape deck. It made a labored whirring sound, then coughed out the first few bars of "Escape (the Piña Colada Song)."

Zadie grimaced and said, "I forgot that one was in there," then pressed the stop button.

"Uh-uh-uh." Finn shook her head. "Not until I've listened to it, oh . . . twenty more times."

"Listen to it as many times as you want. I don't care."

"Fine. I will," Finn said, then began to sing along at the top of her lungs.

Thirty miles and seven renditions of the song later, Finn was no longer singing along. "I can't take it anymore." She lurched forward and hit stop. Zadie heaved a sigh of relief. "If I had to hear that one more time, I was going to drive us both off a cliff, *Thelma & Louise* style." She ejected the tape and tossed it unceremoniously over her shoulder onto the back seat. "Pick something else."

Finn twisted around in her seat and leaned over the box once again. This time, she perused the tapes more carefully, her eyes lingering on the handwritten spines like SUMMER MIX '94 and RAINY DAY MUSIC. One tape in particular caught her eye. It had no writing on the spine and a blank cover. She held it up for Zadie to see. "What's this blank tape?"

"I don't know. I've never opened it."

Finn unlatched the case and saw, in her mother's handwriting, a label that read: DO NOT RECORD OVER!!! Her curiosity was piqued. "I'm gonna play it. See what it is."

"A wild card. I like it." Zadie smiled. "Put it in."

Finn tried to not look too eager as she fed the tape into the player. She held her breath as she waited for music to start, but what came out of the speakers was not music. It was their mother's voice.

Eight

Six Months

(until Nora Wilder's disappearance)

"My name is Nora Wilder.
I am forty years old.
I live at 828 Marigold Lane in Switchback, Texas.
My daughters' names are Zadie and Finn.
We drove to Arizona this morning, to the Constellation Campground."

Nora looked down at the recorder in her lap, watched the tape spin slowly through its little plastic window. She didn't have the money to record in a booth with the foam on the walls like Dolly or Bowie, so she'd bought the tape deck to record herself singing in the bathroom where the acoustics were best. In recent years, she'd hardly ever used it. In fact, the only reason it was in the car with her was because she'd lent it to a friend the week before.

Nora considered what to say next—what, if anything, future her would need to know. "The feeling you are having right now will pass. It always does."

A knock on the driver's-side window startled her, and she turned to see Finn waving at her through the glass. "Are you recording a song?" her daughter asked as Nora opened the door.

"Uh, no. Not exactly." Nora quickly changed the subject. "Hey, do you want to help me pitch the tent?"

"Okay!"

Nora tucked the recorder under her arm and set it on the picnic table before kneeling down next to the tent she'd already spread out on the sand.

"See that hole?" Nora pointed to a grommet on the tent floor closest to Finn's feet. "Put the end of the pole in there and hold it steady while I attach the sides."

Finn followed Nora's instructions and held the pole upright while her mom clipped the nylon sides to it. As they worked, a shadow from the rocks above crept slowly toward them. They had arrived at the Constellation Campground just in time to see the Martian-red cliffs catch fire in the evening sun.

"I like this place," Finn said as Nora snapped the last of the fabric in place. "I like the way it sounds."

Nora froze and listened to the wind piping through the fluted rocks; a colony of quail chirping in a patch of prickly pear; the rustling of the cottonwood trees. "Cool, huh?"

Finn nodded.

"How about you, Zadie?" Nora called to her other daughter, who was seated at a picnic table reading a book. "What do you think of this place?"

Without lifting her eyes, she replied, "It's all right."

Nora sighed and turned back to her youngest. "I don't think your sister likes camping."

She had forgiven Zadie for her surliness. After all, Nora had dragged her out of bed at seven in the morning on a weekend with no warning. She would have been grumpy, too, if her own mother had done that to her.

And confused. Nora knew her behavior had been erratic. That morning, it had almost felt like a ghost had taken over her body. Thankfully, neither of her daughters seemed particularly distraught, and she wanted to keep it that way.

Nora pulled the stakes out of their nylon bag and handed one to Finn. "Do you want to help hammer in the stakes?"

She nodded.

"Here . . ." Nora kneeled beside the tent and fed one of the stakes through its designated loop and into the grass. "Take this." She handed Finn a rubber mallet. "Now hit it as hard as you can."

A wildness flashed behind Finn's eyes, the kind children get when they're given permission to be destructive. She squatted like a toad in front of the stake and, using both hands, struck a wobbly blow to the head of the stake. "Nice one!" Nora cheered. "I should hire you to fix the squirrel hole in the deck." Finn beamed and pounded on the stake again, pushing it another half-inch into the red earth.

They had finished with three of the stakes and were about to start the fourth when Nora's hands began to tremble. *Not again*, she thought. It had taken all her energy to get through that morning's episode. She was worried she didn't have the strength to do it again. "Finn, honey, just leave that stake there. I'll finish up."

Finn pouted. "But I want to do it."

"I know, but I have a better idea," Nora said, trying to keep the alarm out of her voice. "How about you and your sister go explore the campground. You can take my tape player and record some sounds for me."

Finn considered her mother's offer. "Okay," she chirped, dropping the mallet on the ground and running back to the fire ring. "Zadie! Mom says we gotta go record sounds for her!"

After a little muttering to herself, Zadie closed her book and followed her sister down the trail leading to the camp office. When they were out of sight, Nora crawled into the tent, curled onto her side, and tried not to cry out. Her body felt like it was ripping in two, like the fault line of her sternum was shifting inside her and all she could do was wait and hope whatever it was didn't kill her.

Terror gripped her as she made a tight fist around the stake in her hand. As the pain escalated, she drove the stake downward, piercing a hole in the tent floor. Through clenched teeth, she repeated to herself, "This feeling will pass. It always does."

"*Sssssh!*" Finn hissed at Zadie, pressing her finger to her lips. "Quit moving around." She held the recorder inches from a striped lizard clinging motionless to a boulder.

"It's a lizard. It doesn't make noise," Zadie grunted.

Finn answered her with a quick glare, then returned her attention to the tiny reptile. A moment later, the lizard skittered down the side of the rock and disappeared into the brush. "You scared it away!"

"Are you sure it wasn't the big black machine you were sticking in its face?"

Finn stood up, her knees stained with red dust. "Fine. You try." She shoved the recorder at Zadie.

"I'd rather just go back to camp." They had been walking around the campground for only twenty minutes and Zadie was already bored.

"But we haven't been that way yet." Finn pointed to a paved road lined with gnarled conifers and a brown sign posted next to it that read: AUTHORIZED PERSONNEL ONLY.

"Wait, we're not supposed to go down . . ." But before Zadie had even finished her sentence, Finn was already running toward the road. Zadie groaned and followed her sister, dragging her feet as she went.

"Don't forget to record!" Finn called over her shoulder. Zadie rolled her eyes theatrically and looked down at the recorder. It was still rolling. She lifted the microphone to her mouth and said in her best narrator voice, "On today's episode of *The Lizard Whisperer*, Finn takes her show name literally and believes that lizards are actually whispering to her."

Finn scowled. "What does *literally* mean?"

"Will she learn to commune with her reptile friends, or will she make a fool of herself on national TV? Tune in to find out!"

"Don't be an asshole."

Zadie gaped at her sister. "Wha'd you just say? You know I'm recording, right?"

"So?" Finn shrugged, trying to play it cool. "Asshole," she said again, giggling to herself this time.

Zadie grinned and put an arm around her sister's shoulders. "Mom's gonna be so proud of you when she hears this."

The road they were on opened up into a sandy clearing where a couple of dozen RVs were parked in a horseshoe formation. By now the sun was almost completely behind the red rocks. Only the crowns of the buttes to the east glowed their postcard orange. The rest of the valley was bathed in a smoky shade of violet.

The camp was mostly deserted save for one person: a woman, sitting alone in a lawn chair, facing the rocks. As if she sensed them watching her, the woman turned around in her seat and held up a hand to wave at them. The girls waved back silently. Then the woman turned back around toward the sunset.

"Do you think she lives here?" Finn asked.

"Probably."

"Where's her family?"

"I don't know."

The girls stood for a few more minutes, watching the sky change color before their eyes. Zadie was about to suggest they head back when the woman turned around in her seat once again and pointed to the hills.

"What is she pointing at?" Zadie squinted but saw only mountain-shaped shadows.

Finn gasped. "Over there!" Zadie followed her sister's index finger to a four-legged creature climbing over the rocks. "It's a coyote. Hit record. Hurry up!"

Zadie pushed the red button and the recorder began to softly whir. Then, as if on cue, the coyote lifted its chin toward the sky and a series of yips and howls echoed throughout the valley. Zadie shivered. It was the first time she remembered hearing something beautiful that also made her feel like crying.

Moments later, the coyote bowed to its audience and slipped

behind the rocks. "Whoa," Zadie whispered. "That was awesome." She looked for the lady who had pointed the coyote out to them, but all she saw was an empty chair.

When Zadie and Finn arrived back at their campsite, they had expected to find their mom tending a roaring fire and, in deference to their noisy bellies, cooking something over said fire. However, what they found was just the opposite. The camp was dark and Nora was nowhere to be found.

"Mom?" Finn called. There was no answer.

Zadie felt her heart plummet into her stomach as Finn unzipped the tent and stuck her head inside. "She's not in here," she said, then backed out on her hands and knees and added, "There's duct tape on the floor."

Zadie looked inside the tent. Sure enough, there was an *X* of duct tape in the middle of the tent floor. "Mom must have fixed a hole."

"Where do you think she went?" There was an uneasiness in her little sister's voice that Zadie wasn't used to hearing.

"She's gotta be around here somewhere." Thankfully, the car was still where their mom had parked it hours earlier, so she couldn't have gone far. Zadie had to decide if they should go looking for her and risk getting lost in the desert at night or stay put and hope she came back. She wasn't particularly wild about either option, but the thought of stumbling through a moonless desert, unable to see any scorpions and snakes that might be hiding in the dark, made her blood run cold. "She'll be back soon. Don't worry."

"I want to play her the coyote," Finn said, clutching the recorder to her chest like a security blanket.

"Do you want to listen to it now?" It was the only thing Zadie could think to do that might distract her.

"Okay." The girls sat down on the log bench next to the firepit.

But before they could rewind the tape, a voice behind them said, "Get anything good?"

"Mom!" Finn spun around to face Nora. She was wearing a headlamp and her arms were heavy with firewood. "Where were you?"

Nora dumped the logs out of her arms and into the firepit. "Can't eat hot dogs without a fire."

Zadie's shoulders relaxed as the scorpions in her mind retreated back into their holes. *False alarm,* she thought, although something in her gut still wasn't sitting right.

"You guys hungry?" Nora asked as she knelt down next to the pit and started snapping dried-out pine branches to use as kindling.

"I am!" Finn practically shouted. "I bet the coyote is hungry, too."

"What coyote?"

When the fire was lit and the campsite flickered with amber light, the Wilder women roasted hot dogs over the open flame and listened to the end of Finn's recording. Finn held her breath as the lone coyote cried. He sounded farther away than she remembered, smaller. She rewinded the tape back thirty seconds and played it again, then five more times. *Maybe he'll hear it,* she thought, scanning the manzanita bushes for pairs of glowing eyes. But the coyote did not visit their camp that night. The only proof he existed at all was on that tape.

Nine

Follow the Music

What did she mean? 'This feeling will pass'?" The tape had gone silent many seconds ago, but Finn was still holding out hope that her mother's voice would bring it back to life.

"I don't know," Zadie answered. She also appeared to be waiting for something.

"There aren't any other tapes like this, are there?"

"Not that I know of."

Finn waited several more seconds before finally pressing stop. "Do you remember that campground? What was it called?"

"Constellation."

That trip must have been important to her, Finn thought. Why else would her mom not want anyone recording over the tape? It wasn't an echo, but it was a memory, one her mom wanted to preserve.

She pulled out her phone and typed "Constellation Campground" into the search bar. The first result was a campground in central Arizona, not far from Sedona. "I think I found it," she said, clicking on the map.

Zadie took her eyes off the road briefly to look at Finn's phone screen. "Yeah, that's the one. Wait . . . you're not suggesting . . ."

"Do you have a better idea?"

Her sister sighed. "This means we're going to have to camp, doesn't it?"

It should have taken the girls only a little under seven hours to get to the Constellation Campground. With bathroom breaks and a stop to look at the World's Biggest Mousetrap, it took them over eight. "Imagine how big a mouse would have to be for that to work," Finn wondered out loud (roughly the size of a cow, they decided).

It was almost seven P.M. by the time they rolled up to the camp office, a tiny log cabin whose front porch danced with an array of wind chimes, dream catchers, and whirligigs. The hand-painted OFFICE sign above the door was written in connect-the-dots style lettering that resembled constellations.

The girls walked up the stairs to the porch. Finn pulled open the door and a tiny wind chime hanging on the inside of the handle tinkled as they walked inside. A bony middle-aged woman hiding her graying hair behind a vibrant silk scarf smiled at them from the check-in desk. "Hi, girls. What can I do for you?"

"We'd like to reserve a site for tonight," Zadie replied.

"Excellent!" The woman slapped the desk with her palm and stood up from her stool. "If you wouldn't mind signing the guest book. I'll also need a credit card and your signs."

"Signs?"

"Your zodiac signs."

Zadie raised her eyebrows at her sister, who shrugged in response. "I'm a Leo," Finn said, then picked up the pen tethered to the guest book and wrote her name on the next free line.

"A fire sign! You must be out looking for adventure."

"Always," Finn answered with a confident smirk.

Zadie handed the woman her credit card, who waved it at her like a wand. "And what about you?" she asked. "What's your sign?"

"I'm not sure."

"What's your birthday?"

"September tenth."

"Then you're a Virgo. That's an earth sign."

"What does that mean?"

"In many ways, you're the opposite of fire. You like to feel grounded, stable. You don't like taking big risks."

"Yep. That's Zadie, all right." Finn clapped her sister on the back. Zadie shot her a playful glare.

The woman handed back her card along with a map of the camp. "The Leo and Virgo sites are already booked, so you'll park at site 23, Perseus. Please don't leave any food out and throw away your trash in the proper bin. We've had some bear sightings recently. Oh! I almost forgot . . ." She opened a rusty recipe tin sitting on the counter, pulled out two slips of paper, and handed one to each of the girls. "Here are your horoscopes."

Finn read hers aloud. "You will face tough challenges ahead, but you have the determination to face them." It wasn't a legitimate premonition like Zadie's were, but it was a nice little pep talk all the same. "Thanks."

"Don't thank me. Thank the stars," the woman answered earnestly, her eyes slowly drifting skyward.

Finn glanced over at Zadie, who was biting her lip to prevent herself from laughing. Finn was about to laugh, too, when she cleared her throat. "Have a nice day."

The girls left the office and walked back out onto the porch. Finn whispered, "That lady was a trip."

Zadie nodded. "I don't understand how anyone believes in that stuff."

"Says the psychic. What's your horoscope say?" Finn asked, peering down at the paper in her sister's hand. Zadie passed it to her. It read:

Don't try to make predictions about the future. Live in the present.

"The stars have spoken," Zadie said with a smirk, then trotted down the porch steps.

"Don't think this lets you off the hook," Finn called after her. She still didn't fully understand why Zadie had denounced her premonitions after their mom's disappearance. It was like a switch had been flipped. One day they were playing Psychic Karaoke, and the next, Zadie had sworn off her psychic gift altogether. The best explanation Finn could come up with was that her premonitions reminded her of their mom, and Zadie had made it painfully clear that she did not like being reminded.

While Finn mulled this over, the wind chimes played a discordant melody. There was something about them, something about this place that gave her a good feeling. She felt it in the music, as if she'd heard it before, as if her mother had heard it before. She could feel the line between present and past getting blurry, like crossing her eyes, and she felt what she thought was an echo coming on. *Could it be . . .*

Then it was gone.

"Live in the present," Zadie's horoscope had read. *How do you live in the present if your present is someone else's past?* That was a question for another day. Today she had more pressing questions she needed answers to.

A short drive later, the sisters arrived at their campsite, a spacious patch of rusty earth shaded by grizzled junipers and cottonwoods whose heart-shaped leaves fluttered like confetti in the breeze. In the center was a stone fire ring circled by benches made from logs that had been sawn in half lengthwise and flipped on their curved backs like turtles. On top of the pit sat a grate, presumably for cooking, although Zadie hadn't the first idea how to use it. There was also a rickety picnic table that, from the looks of what remained of the peeling paint, had once been red.

And then there was the view: extravagant sandstone formations layered like pastry and carved by time into rococo columns, spires, and buttes. The rolling clouds above cast dramatic shadows that crept across the landscape like molasses, plunging the valley into darkness one minute and drenching it in golden light the next. It was both exactly how Zadie remembered it and nothing like it all at the same time.

Finn offered to pitch the tent while Zadie got cleaned up. "Are you sure you don't need help?" Zadie offered, although she wasn't sure how much help she could possibly be when it came to camping-related tasks.

"Nah. I'm good. Remember I was a Girl Scout back in the day."

"Back in the day? Wasn't that, like, three years ago?"

Finn waved her off. "Go take your shower. I'll set up the tent, then build a fire so we can eat."

Zadie slung a towel over her shoulder, slipped on her flip-flops, and started down the dirt path toward the women's locker room. Inside, there were two shower stalls with hospital room–style curtains pulled across them. One had a sign taped to it that read: OUT OF ORDER. Zadie pulled back the curtain of the presumably in-order shower to find a bagel-sized spider splayed out on the tile. After flinging several choice expletives at the intruder, Zadie removed one of her flip-flops and hurled that, too. By some stroke of luck, the shoe hit the spider dead-on and it crumpled to the floor. *This is why I hate camping*, she thought miserably as she picked up her sandal and slipped it back on her foot.

With some effort, Zadie turned the spigot and walked face-first into the hot water. Rust-colored dirt trickled down her ankles, forming a gruesome sanguine puddle at her feet. *Between that and the spider, I could be in an Alfred Hitchcock movie*, she thought, then yawned. The gentle patter of the hot water on her skull was making her tired. It had been almost thirty-six hours since she'd last slept. Her body swayed with exhaustion, and she leaned on the wall to steady herself. All she wanted to do was collapse onto a warm bed with a down comforter. The thought of sleeping on the hard ground that night made her wince.

Once again, Zadie was nearly winded by the reality of what she had agreed to. *Two weeks—maybe more—of sleeping on the ground.* Her body ached in anticipation. She wondered briefly if the Ladybug would be okay with the sleeping arrangement, then reminded herself that the Ladybug had a comfy uterus to sleep in. It didn't need a down comforter.

After she'd wrung her hair out and toweled off, Zadie pulled on a fresh pair of gym shorts and a T-shirt for the walk back. The sun had set by the time she left the locker room, and the red rocks were nothing but imposing shadows against a navy sky. As she was about to turn right onto the path that led back to the campsite, she stopped. Music fluttered into her left ear and she turned toward the sound. The notes were delicate and bright like filaments in a lightbulb, but they were not particularly melodic. The song—if you could even call it that—had a stream-of-consciousness quality to it. It would stop and start. There was no obvious meter, no refrain, just arbitrary notes bunched together like wildflowers a child had picked.

The sound seemed to be coming from what looked like an old maintenance road that disappeared into a stand of Arizona white oaks. The corral-style gate was open, but the sign hanging from it read AUTHORIZED PERSONNEL ONLY. Zadie knew she probably wasn't allowed back there, but the music was so strange and entrancing that her curiosity got the better of her. She followed the road into the trees and down a short hill. What she found at the bottom was not a maintenance building. It was an RV park. Two dozen RVs were parked in a horseshoe formation around the perimeter of a large desert lot, but in the center was a shantytown of sorts; saltbox-style shelters with steep asymmetrical roofs that appeared to have been constructed from whatever the residents had lying around, from salvaged wood to corrugated sheet metal, old tires to cinder blocks. No one seemed to live in these structures. It was a gathering place filled with mismatched patio furniture, a fire ring, and long banquet-style tables. String lights swooped from roof to roof, but not the white globes Zadie was used to seeing over restaurant patios. These were black lights, and they cast an eerie purple glow over the camp. It took a minute or so for Zadie's eyes to adjust, but once they did, she saw a dozen or so people milling around, not at all bothered, it seemed, by the darkness.

The music was still playing. Zadie squinted, trying to find the source, then spotted a woman sitting on a lawn chair using a red headlamp to illuminate the keyboard in her lap. Her fingers glided slowly across the keys, stretching out the notes as if tapping them for sap. Every sixty seconds or so, she'd stop, look up at the sky, then continue playing, occasionally taking breaks to write something down in a notepad sitting on the arm of her chair.

Zadie took a few steps forward to get a closer look at this strange person in this strange place. The woman looked up, this time not at the stars, but directly at her. *How can she see me?* she wondered before looking down at her own glow-in-the-dark shirt. Above her, hanging from an old signpost, was a black light.

Zadie backed up out of range of the ultraviolet light, but it was futile. The woman had already seen her. She watched Zadie curiously for a few moments as if she were a wild animal, then raised her hand and gestured her over. Something curdled in Zadie's stomach that at first felt like shame, but as the feeling intensified, she realized it was the beginning of a premonition. She scrambled into the shadows, clamped her eyes shut, and tried to think of a song, any song that would keep her mind in the present and not allow it to be sucked out with the tide that was lapping at her feet.

The sky is full of birds.

She looked up, but all she saw were stars.

The sky is full of birds.

Then the keyboard music began again. While the woman's eyes were on her fingers, Zadie slipped back into the night.

When Zadie returned to camp, she saw a tent, but no Finn. "Dude, this place just keeps getting weirder—" she started, then parted the tent flap and found her sister passed out on top of her sleeping bag, *The Fisherman's Desire* fanned open on her chest. Zadie gingerly lifted the book, set it on the tent floor, then grabbed the wool blanket that was bunched up at Finn's feet and pulled it over her. Her sister grunted softly and nuzzled into the blanket.

Exhaustion tugged at Zadie's eyelids. Ignoring the hollowness in her belly, she crawled into her own bag and sank into a cavernous sleep.

Finn could have slept in. She hadn't set an alarm, trusting her body to wake when it felt ready. As it turned out, *ready* meant six A.M.

Finn crawled out of the tent carefully so as not to wake her sister, then stretched her limbs like a cat, digging her toes into the sand. It was a gorgeous day. The burnished cliffs glowed in the early morning sun, and the air was cool and smelled like smoke from neighboring campsites. It was a contradictory landscape. On the one hand, it was arid and severe, the color of heat. On the other, it was veined with verdant gullies that sang with insects and bloomed like moss at the feet of the hills. Finn let the vastness of it all sink in. Having lived her entire life in the largely flat state of Texas, she felt overwhelmed that there were things in the world that existed at such heights. She trembled with excitement at the prospect that she could see *more*: more mountains, more world. It made her feel like her vision was widening, becoming a panorama. Eventually she just stopped turning her head. She could see everything.

This is the place, Finn thought, surer than ever that her mom had passed through here five years earlier. If she had to, she would overturn every rock, climb every butte until she found where her memories were hiding.

Finn walked to the outskirts of their campsite and climbed onto a boulder that had been sheared flat on top. It was warm and gritty against her thighs. She pressed her palms into the warm stone and felt a scar. Someone named Alison had carved her name into the rock. A few other names were etched into the surface, too—Michelle, Tim, Alberto—but no Nora. When Finn was young, her mom had carved their initials, NZF, into everything: rocks, trees, restaurant booths, bathroom stalls. "How else will people know we exist?" she'd said. Finn didn't care how many people knew she existed. The only people that mattered already knew.

Finn closed her eyes and another world opened. The memories here were older than any she'd felt before. They yielded like clay between her fingers; drummed like hoofbeats and smelled like smoke. They belonged to people who lived before she was born, before anyone she'd ever known was born. It seemed that the desert had preserved them somehow, kiln-fired them and put them behind glass just for her.

As fascinating as these memories were, none of them belonged to her mother. She drew a deep breath and tried again. Snakebites and sunburns. Hunger. Thirst. The desert had been unforgiving to many. Before this was a place for tourists, it was merely another stop on a long journey west. An old mutt slept in the shade of a wagon. Somewhere a gun fired.

Then a chime. Not a memory, but her phone. She fished it out of her pajama shorts pocket and found a text from Steve:

HOPE YOU'RE HAVING FUN!

Finn was instantly awash with guilt. She hated lying to Steve even more than she did Kathy. He was the more trusting of the two, the one more likely to hand over his car keys and believe Finn when she said she would be "home by ten." His trust was precious to her, something she wore like a locket around her neck. The thought of his realizing that she had broken that trust—well, she tried not to think about it.

She swallowed her reservations, snapped a picture of her bare feet against the sand below—being careful to frame out the prickly pear to her right—and texted it to her foster dad with the caption: MY FEET ARE!

He texted back: PUT SOME SHOES ON, followed by a winking face emoji.

Finn smiled and replied, WHAT ARE SHOES? She realized then that she was actually a little homesick. She missed Kathy and Steve and Milly, even if the dog did steal her socks out of the laundry hamper and bury them in the yard. She missed them the way anyone would miss their family on a long trip.

She thought back to the month before when the three of them had sat in a TGI Fridays, sharing a basket of buffalo wings. "You're already part of our family," Kathy said, her eyes darting nervously to her husband. "But we want to make it official." With bright orange sauce smeared all over her mouth and fingers, Finn stared back at her foster parents, speechless. She could see them squirm as they waited for her to respond. *This must be what it feels like to be publicly proposed to,* she thought. Eventually she stammered something like "Wow, you guys. That . . . that's awesome."

Kathy and Steve smiled at each other. "You don't have to give us an answer now," Steve continued, shifting restlessly in his seat. "Just . . . something to think about."

And Finn was still thinking about it, even as she followed in her mother's footsteps. She knew she couldn't make a decision one way or another until she looked her mom in the eye. It was the only way she would know for sure where she truly belonged.

And then there was Zadie. *She would be hurt the most by all of this,* Finn thought. She looked over her shoulder at the tent where her sister was sleeping. There was no reason her sister needed to know. Not yet.

Finn switched her phone to silent and slid it back into her pocket.

She didn't need any more distractions. Instead, she decided to explore the rest of the campground. After all, her mom could have stayed at any one of these campsites. If she was lucky, she'd get back before Zadie even woke up.

The camp was long and winding and appeared to follow the curves of a gurgling creek Finn glimpsed through a tangle of juniper trees. Almost immediately, she came upon a picnic area, a tiny mini golf course, and a cactus garden. They were empty aside from a picnicking couple who were tossing chunks of watermelon rind to their large dog.

If Mom was here right now, where would she go? Finn wondered. She walked over to the cactus garden and sat on the wooden bench in its center. The garden was full of memories, mostly happy ones—proposals, first kisses, enjoying a really good sandwich—but none of them stood out to her. None of them were Nora's.

She left the garden and continued down the rows of campsites. Each of them had a decorative wooden sign posted out front with the name of a constellation. As the woman at the front desk had explained, the one they were staying at was Perseus. Their neighbors' was Sagittarius. She passed a Taurus, Draco, and Scorpio.

Aries . . . Her mom was an Aries. If she had checked in here, the lady at the front desk probably would have assigned her that site if it was available.

Finn was jogging now, reading signs as she passed: Cancer, Cygnus, Lyra, Pisces . . .

Aries.

She stopped in front of a sign with a painted ram on it. It was her lucky day. The campsite was vacant.

Finn made her way over to the fire ring. Several charred logs sat inside, along with a few glass bottles. She picked the bottles out of the ash, walked them over to the recycling bin, then surveyed her surroundings. The site was identical to the one she and Zadie were in, except that it was by the creek and thus more shaded. There was a picnic table, too. She sat down on its bench, then listened to the creek bubble and tried to imagine her mom doing the same. But the only memories that visited Finn belonged to other moms, other families. Hers was silent.

Then as she absentmindedly ran her fingers across the surface of the table, she felt a deep scar. Finn let out a short gasp as she looked down and saw the initials NZF carved into the wood. A moment later, her mind began to slide, lose its purchase on the present and drift into another time. The heat from the sand dissipated. The sky plunged into darkness and stars descended upon her like rain. A heart that was not hers raced.

Music.

She heard music.

She was lost, but the music made her feel found.

Where am I? *she said aloud.*

Who am I?

The sky was a dusting of faint stars. Sailors used them to navigate across oceans.

The music would be her compass.

If she told it her name, maybe it could tell her something, anything about her life.

My name is Nora, *she said.*

No one answered.

A gate. The music was on the other side.

She *was on the other side.*

She would follow the music.

Ten

The Stars Are Brighter in the Desert

Zadie woke to the color orange and the smell of coffee. The tent walls were aglow with morning light, and Finn's sleeping bag lay crumpled and empty. She wiggled her toes and discovered that the inside of her sleeping bag was coated in a fine layer of sand. *This must be what it's like to live in the desert,* she thought. *You wake up feeling like an excavated mummy.*

Zadie sat up slowly, groaning. As she had predicted the night before, every part of her body ached: her shoulders, her neck, her back, even her hips. *One week,* she thought grimly, fluffing her pillow. She did a quick calculation in her head of how much it would cost if they stayed in motels every night: at least four hundred dollars, probably closer to five. She hadn't budgeted for lodging—a friend in Galveston had generously offered her family's beach condo for the first iteration of their trip. Five hundred extra dollars would almost clean out her savings. She supposed she could ask Finn for money, but as usual, her pride got in the way. *I'd rather sleep on the ground.*

A sudden wave of nausea rocked Zadie. Worried she was about to be sick, she scrambled out of the tent and found Finn seated in front of a crackling fire holding *The Fisherman's Desire* in one hand and a thermos in the other. "Good morning!" Finn chirped.

Zadie swallowed. It appeared she wasn't going to be sick after all. "Morning."

"How'd you sleep?"

"Like a rock. Sorry, I mean like I was sleeping *on* rocks. Which I was."

Finn smiled, amused by her sister's surliness. "I made you coffee." She poured coffee from the thermos into a speckled enamel mug and extended it to Zadie. Zadie threaded her fingers around the cup and inhaled the fragrant steam. She had promised herself she wouldn't drink any more coffee while she was pregnant, but that didn't mean she couldn't smell it. "Thanks."

"I tried some before you got up."

"And?"

"I hated it."

"To each his own." Zadie inhaled deeply while pretending to sip her coffee. Wisps of steam swirled over her cheekbones. "You were really out last night."

"Yeah, sorry." Finn held up the book. "I took a break to acquaint myself with the enigmatic Captain Neptune, and I must have passed out. I had a really weird dream about fish, though."

"I hate to break it to you, but the book isn't really about fishing."

"Yes, I gathered that from the first sentence." Finn flipped the book to the first page and read aloud, "'Captain Neptune was not a god, yet he commanded the sea.'"

"That's not the only thing he commands," Zadie said, wiggling her eyebrows.

Finn snorted and closed the novel around a receipt she was using as a bookmark. "I'm glad you're up," she said, smiling coyly. "I have something to share."

"Okay . . . What is it?"

"It's better if I just show you."

Uh-oh. "Can you at least give me a hint?"

Her sister shook her head as the kettle over the fire began to whistle. She pulled it from the heat and poured some of the boiling water into a bowl filled with instant oats. "Eat up," she said, handing the oatmeal to her sister. Zadie stared down at the gloopy substance the color of uncooked dough and weighed her hunger against her sudden aversion to all things mealy. She usually liked oatmeal, but apparently, the Ladybug was not a fan.

Zadie dutifully took a bite. Her sister smiled and said, "Today's gonna be a good day." Then she took a large gulp from the coffee thermos in her hand. Her face scrunched up in disgust. "Nope. Still bad."

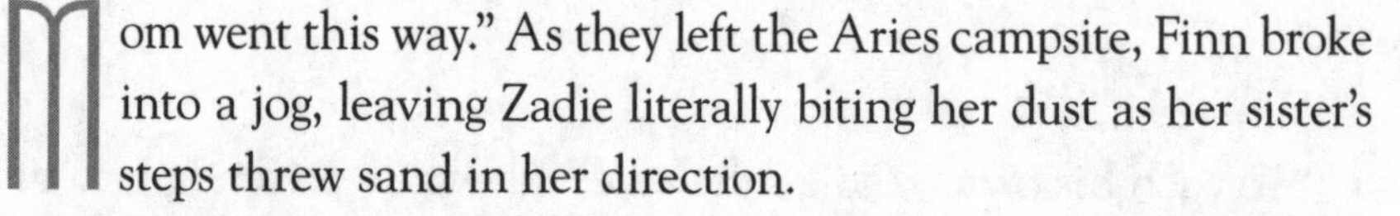

"Mom went this way." As they left the Aries campsite, Finn broke into a jog, leaving Zadie literally biting her dust as her sister's steps threw sand in her direction.

Zadie's platform sneakers weren't designed for speed, but she attempted to run anyway. "Whoa. Slow down!"

Finn waited for her sister to catch up. "Sorry. I got excited. Anyway . . . so, she headed this way . . ." She continued at a walk over a decorative footbridge flanked by mesquite trees. "She heard music, so she followed it."

"Music?" Zadie thought back to the piano tune she'd followed herself the night before. Had her mother heard the same?

"Yeah." Finn bounced a little with each step. She clearly wished they were moving faster, but she kept to Zadie's pace. "Something was wrong. She seemed . . . lost."

It appeared that Finn might have witnessed secondhand what Zadie had experienced firsthand years ago. It made her sad to see the concern in her sister's eyes. She had tried to shield her from it, but Finn was almost an adult now. Maybe it was better that she knew. "Yeah, I remember Mom being kind of out of it sometimes."

"Out of it? How?"

As Zadie remembered her mother teetering on the cliff's edge like a tightrope walker about to step onto the wire, she had a sudden change of heart. She didn't want to be the one to tell her sister. If Finn found out on her own, fine. She would deal with it then, but if she confessed now, Finn would know she'd kept this from her for the past six years.

"Oh, umm . . . she would just kind of stare off into nowhere, that kind of thing."

"Like she forgot where she was?"

"Yeah, maybe."

Finn's sun hat cast webbed shadows on her face, making her expression all the more inscrutable. "I wish you could feel it, too," she said. "I'm not just remembering something that happened to her. It's like I'm living it right there in that moment. I've never felt anything like it before."

"Is it scary? To be someone else?"

"Not scary, just . . . weird. In a good way." Finn turned to her sister and smiled. "We're going to find her, Z. Mom's lost, and we're going to find her."

Lost . . . Zadie thought that was a charitable characterization of their mother's absence. Even if that was true, even if she had momentarily forgotten where she was as she had that night on the cliff, why didn't she return the moment she came to? Why didn't she ask for help? Something didn't add up.

"I hope you're right," Zadie said finally.

For several minutes they walked in silence past campsites populated by squealing kids and adults too tired to chase them. A short-haired dog lying in the shade lifted its head to watch them pass and thumped its tail once in greeting.

"We're almost there." Finn grabbed her sister's hand. "Come on. I want to introduce you to my friends."

How long had Zadie slept for? Finn had always made friends easily, but this was a record, even for her.

"You'll like them. They're just like us."

"Like us how?"

Finn let the question dangle as she led them around a corner and toward the service road Zadie had explored the night before. Zadie stopped.

Her sister looked at her curiously. "Something wrong?"

"I don't think we're supposed to go down there." What if she ran into the keyboardist who caught her spying on her? Zadie cringed at the thought.

Finn waved her off. "Don't worry. It's cool. They told me to stop by anytime."

Zadie followed her the rest of the way without protest. *It was dark*, she reasoned. The woman probably wouldn't even recognize her.

When they arrived at the RV camp, there was already a group of people gathered by a picnic table as if they had been expecting them. "Finn!" one of the women cheered. "You came back!"

"Of course! I wasn't about to miss the barbecue."

The Ladybug fluttered. Barbecue sounded much better than oatmeal.

"Everyone, this is my sister, Zadie."

Zadie waved awkwardly. They returned her greeting with smiles and friendly nods.

"I was just telling her about you guys. Cynthia over here"—she pointed to an elderly woman with a braid—"can tell you what you're going to dream tonight."

Now Zadie understood what Finn had meant by *they're just like us*. Before she could comment, Finn continued. "Tonya"—she turned to a middle-aged Black woman with wire-framed glasses—"can sense the exact temperature without looking at a thermometer, and Earworm can get a song stuck in your head without even opening his mouth."

A man sporting a bandanna and a bushy red beard said, "You can call me Brian." Brian's eyes lingered on Zadie a second longer than she was comfortable with. She looked away.

"Finn, I think we should—"

Finn turned to look over her shoulder. "Hey, Chuck! Do that thing to my sister." A gaunt man with the facial hair of a mountain goat looked up from fiddling with an overturned mountain bike.

"Sure."

Zadie started to object, but the man cut her off. "Coffee."

"Excuse me?"

He carefully applied oil to the chain of his bike, his tone distracted. "You want coffee. It's all you've wanted for days."

Zadie looked at her sister, puzzled.

"Chuck can tell people what they're hungry for," Finn explained. "He knew I was craving mac and cheese this morning."

"For *breakfast?*"

Her sister shrugged.

The man spun the front wheel of his bike. It clicked as it turned. "I can brew a pot if you'd like some." The offer was clearly intended for Zadie, but he didn't so much as glance in her direction.

"No, thank you. I'm fine," she answered, then turned back to her sister. "Can we talk?"

Finn nodded. "I'll be right back, guys." She followed Zadie to a bench out of earshot of the residents. "What's up?"

"*What's up?*" Zadie repeated, incredulous. Her head was spinning. She couldn't decide whether to believe everything she'd just heard. She'd gone her whole life assuming that her sister and she were some kind of exception to the laws of time and space. Only now was she starting to consider how conceited that belief actually was, like the presumption that Earth is the only planet with life in the universe. She and Finn weren't special, or at least maybe they weren't the only special ones.

"You're mad."

"I'm not mad, it's just . . . you don't seem fazed by any of this."

Finn grinned. "Cool, huh?"

"Are you sure they're not some kind of cult?"

"What makes you think they're a cult?"

"I saw this place last night on my way back from the showers. You know they only use black lights at night?"

"So?"

"So they probably use them to see the blood of all the travelers they've sacrificed." Zadie was only half joking.

Finn let out a sudden bleat of laughter. Their mom used to say she sounded like a sheep on nitrous oxide. "Are you sure you don't have heatstroke?"

Now that her sister mentioned it, she was feeling a little woozy. "I don't know. What does heatstroke feel like?"

Finn took her sister's arm. "Come on, let's sit down. I'll get you something to drink." Zadie started to let her sister lead her, then stopped abruptly. "No, wait. I'm not finished."

"It's not a cult, Zadie. They have a volleyball net."

"Not that. Do they know about *us*?" Zadie knew she sounded dramatic, but she didn't care.

"I mean, I showed up here in the middle of an echo, so they saw me all—you know." Finn unfocused her eyes and stared into space.

"Right."

"Don't worry. I didn't tell them about you."

They were quiet for a moment. A fleeting breeze sent sand slithering past their toes. Then Finn said, "I thought we were the only ones, you know?"

"I know."

"And now"—Finn looked back at her new friends—"to know we're not alone . . ."

Even Zadie had to admit it was kind of cool to find out that she and Finn might not be the only weirdos in the world. It was like they were mutants who had just discovered the X-Men. "I still don't want them knowing about me."

"Don't worry. Your secret's safe with me. Come on," Finn said, taking her sister's hand. "I think Samir is firing up the grill."

Zadie gave in and let Finn lead her to a picnic table under a canvas tarp where a few of the residents were chatting and eating. "I'll grab us some drinks," Finn said and hurried off, leaving Zadie alone.

In the daylight, the camp square looked a lot more cheerful than it had the night before. In lieu of the black lights were multicolored strands of Christmas lights trimming the makeshift shelters that had been painted in vibrant shades of turquoise and burnt orange. Zadie had been correct in assuming no one lived in them. One was currently being used as a taco stand, another appeared to be some sort of arts and crafts studio complete with a potter's wheel, and another was a desert greenhouse whose windows were made from recycled glass bottles. It appeared nothing went to waste in this little community. Not even broken pots and dishes, the shards of which had become part of a circuitous mosaic walking path that seemed less concerned with getting from one end to the other than it did about meandering from one neighbor to the next. When you finally made it to the end, however, you arrived at a bonfire area next to an abandoned boxcar that had been converted into a performance stage. There was even a playground nearby constructed entirely out of tires, where a small group of children were playing the lava floor game.

A mother bent down to tie her child's shoe. A young man taught a slightly younger woman to play guitar. Neighbors waved to one another from hammocks and petted each other's dogs and read quietly in the shade of a desert willow. Finn was right. This was no cult. It was a neighborhood like any other—friendlier than most, even. It just so happened that its residents were all . . . *gifted? special?* Zadie hated those terms, but she couldn't think of a better one. It made her feel self-conscious, being surrounded by people who accepted who they were when she was so reticent to do so herself.

Someone sat down next to Zadie. It was Tonya, the human thermometer. She smiled warmly. "Is this your first time meeting other sixes?"

"Sixes?"

"People with sixth senses."

A little on the nose, she thought. "Uhh . . . yeah."

"Are you also . . . ?"

"Me?" Zadie's voice cracked slightly. "No. I'm boring." She scanned the faces of the people milling around the square. "How'd you end up here?"

Tonya smiled brightly. "I came here on vacation and never left, but I'm unusual. Most of the others have a different story."

"And what's that?"

"They were driving by on their way somewhere else and this place just sort of sucked them in. Like a black hole." The woman laughed. She had a gap between her front two teeth, a tiny courtyard.

"So, is everyone here a . . . six?"

Tonya shook her head. "No. Some folks are like you. Everyone is welcome here."

Zadie thought she saw Tonya glance over at Earworm, who looked both ways before picking food off a paper plate that had been abandoned on a neighboring picnic table.

"So you can really tell exactly what temperature it is?"

"Yes, ma'am."

"What is it right now?"

"Eighty-four degrees."

"I dunno. Feels like eighty-five to me."

Tonya laughed again. "Whatever you say."

Finn watched Zadie from the buffet table, which had been set with a bright array of condiments, paper plates, and several large orange beverage coolers. There was something different about her sister, a small spark. It was as if she—despite her best efforts to mask it—was enjoying herself.

Finn made her way back over to the table and placed a cup half full of pink lemonade in front of Zadie. "Yours used to have iced tea in it, but I spilled it, so I gave you half of my lemonade."

Zadie grinned. "Thanks."

Then something caught Finn's eye: a small cluster of residents gathered around a pile of painted rocks. It stood about five feet tall and was shaped like a piece of coral—vaguely conical with several asymmetrical spires. "What's that thing over there?"

"The Cairn?" Tonya answered. "It's like a guest book of everyone who's ever been here. We add a rock to it every time someone new comes to camp."

"Does that mean we get one?" Finn asked eagerly.

Tonya nodded. "See that woman in pink?"

Finn turned and spotted an elderly Hispanic woman in a salmon-colored tunic. She was speaking intently with a young woman who looked like she could be her granddaughter. "Yeah."

"That's Estrella. She's the one who paints the rocks. She's probably discussing yours."

"Do I need to model for it?"

Tonya laughed and shook her head. "She doesn't paint *you*. She paints where you're going. Sometimes that place is right here. Other times, she knows there's more to your journey. She's never wrong."

Finn watched Estrella vanish into a single-wide trailer carrying a smooth orange rock in one hand. Hours later, she would presumably emerge carrying a piece of art depicting a single frame of Finn's future. Her heart lunged at the thought of her fate being swirled around on a palette, turning from blue to purple to lavender back to blue again, a kaleidoscope of possibilities. She looked at her sister, who, as usual, did not appear convinced. "Whatever she paints, we can't stay," Zadie said matter-of-factly.

"If that's the case, then Estrella will know," Tonya said evenly. "I came here four years ago, and when it was my turn, she handed me a rock with those mountains painted on it." She pointed to the red buttes that towered above them. "I knew I was meant to stay."

"Isn't that just a self-fulfilling prophecy?" Zadie countered.

"Maybe." Tonya didn't seem bothered by the implication. "Everyone has free will. You can choose not to follow her advice, but I've also never known anyone who said she got it wrong."

Finn watched her sister struggle for something to say. Did Zadie recognize the hypocrisy of her objection? Here she was, a psychic herself, suggesting that prophecies weren't real. Maybe she'd spent so much time in denial of her ability that the irony was lost on her. After a pause, her sister gave a tepid nod and said, "When's the food supposed to be ready?"

The rest of the Wilders' afternoon was spent at the RV camp. Finn asked every person she met whether they had seen their mother, but their responses were nearly identical: new travelers came through Constellation every day. It was possible that they had met Nora, but it was just as likely that they hadn't. Despite their lack of progress, however, Finn remained in high spirits. "*Some*one has to remember her," she kept saying. Zadie wasn't as certain but held her tongue.

As the sun went down, the temperature dropped from precisely 84 degrees Fahrenheit to 76 and falling. When the last drops of daylight had drained from the sky, they heard a low chime echo throughout the canyon. Then all at once the lights went out and the camp was plunged into darkness.

Zadie's voice cut through the hush. "What's happening?"

"I don't know," Finn answered.

After a few seconds, the black lights blinked on and the camp was transformed into an ultraviolet wonderland. The saltbox shacks and mosaic path glowed with bold geometric patterns that hadn't been visible in daylight. The succulents that dotted the grounds now looked like tiny prickly aliens that lived in holes in the ground. Zadie leaned in to look at the flower of a nearby cactus. It gave off an undersea glow and glittered with the spray of pollen. A pocket-size neon lizard skillfully scaled its spiny flesh, pausing beside the flower as though even a reptile could appreciate its loveliness.

But it wasn't just the flora that caught her eye. She soon realized that everyone in the square was looking up. When she followed their gaze, she finally understood what the black lights were for. Above her were an impossible number of stars glinting like faceted jewels against the ancient vastness of space—more stars than she'd seen even in the most rural corners of her home state. It was both peaceful in its stillness and terrifying in its enormity. "They're so bright," she heard Finn whisper.

They *were* bright. And beautiful. As Zadie searched the sky for Ursa Major (the only constellation she knew), she heard one lonely piano note sing out in the desert air. At first she thought she was hearing things, but that note was followed shortly by another, then another. The song was faint but familiar. As her sister and the rest of the camp were busy admiring the stars, Zadie snuck off in the direction of the music.

She found the stranger sitting on the stairs of the boxcar stage, keyboard balanced on her lap. As with the previous night, the woman didn't seem to be playing for anyone but herself. She kept her long, gray-streaked hair tucked behind her ears as she leaned over the keys, rocking slightly as if she were pressing on an invisible pedal. She was neither old nor young. She was the age of someone who had lived enough life to know what she liked and gave little thought to who was watching. Unsure of whether to approach the stranger, Zadie hung back, half-hidden behind a trellis of bougainvillea.

Without looking up, the woman said, "Hi again."

This was the second time she had caught Zadie watching her. *She must think I'm a creep,* Zadie thought, flushing with embarrassment. "Hi," she answered, stepping out from behind the trellis.

"Zadie, right?"

"Yeah. How'd you know?"

"My wife, Nic, runs the front office during the day. I'm Ursula. I own the place." She finally stopped playing and studied Zadie with guarded curiosity. "I hear your sister is a hit with the neighbors."

"She has that effect on people. I'm more of an introvert."

"Me too." The woman smiled thoughtfully.

Zadie nodded at the keyboard. "I like your music."

Ursula looked surprised. "Really? You don't think it's sad?"

"Well, yeah . . . but that's kind of the point, right?" The stranger nodded. It appeared that they shared an appreciation for a good dirge. "Did you write it?"

"Yes and no." Zadie waited for Ursula to elaborate, but she didn't. Instead she looked up at the sky. "Have you looked at the stars yet?"

Zadie nodded—forgetting the woman wasn't looking at her—then said, "They're so much brighter out here."

"That's because there's no light pollution. I lived in Sacramento most of my life, so I never really saw the stars until I came down here. At least not like this, anyway." Zadie wasn't sure what to make of the stranger. She didn't appear sad, exactly, just distant, as though her mind were floating at the end of a tether.

The contemplative silence was broken by hurried footsteps. Zadie turned to see her sister walking up from behind. Under the black lights, she was all teeth and whites of eyes, a Day-Glo Cheshire cat. "Zadie, I heard that same music— Oh, hi," she said, noticing Ursula's presence. "Was that you playing?"

Ursula nodded.

"I'm Finn."

"Ursula. Your sister and I were just looking at the stars," she answered. "Actually, I was thinking about taking my telescope out tonight if you two are interested in joining me."

Zadie caught Finn's eye. It was clear by the look on her little sister's face that the answer to Ursula's question was yes.

They took Ursula's Jeep up to a little-known bluff that acted as a fulcrum for a rotating dome of stars. Zadie and Finn sat on camping chairs while Ursula unlatched the telescope case. "We're lucky. It's a clear night. Perfect for stargazing." She unfolded the tripod legs of the telescope stand and positioned them in the dirt. As she bent down to retrieve the telescope itself, Finn asked, "So how long have you owned the campground?"

"About thirteen years. I used to be a security guard at a mall in Roseville. Night shift. Then like most malls, it closed. It was a blessing in disguise, really. I never got to see the stars in that big white box." She looked wistfully above her head. "A few months later, Nic and I bought the campground."

Once Ursula had mounted the telescope to the base, she pressed her eye to the eyepiece and adjusted the aim of the lens. "There it is." She stepped back from the telescope and turned to the girls. "Who's first?"

Finn hurried toward the telescope and eagerly pressed her eye to the eyepiece. "Be careful not to bump it," Ursula instructed. "And if you can't see it at first, squint a little."

"Whoaaa. Is it that bluish light?"

"Yep. That's Denebola, Tail of the Lion, the third-brightest star in the Leo constellation."

"That's so cool."

Ursula turned to Zadie. "Your turn." Finn stepped aside and let Zadie look into the eyepiece. Sure enough, a small blue light winked back at her. "I see it."

"Denebola is a young star," Ursula began, walking to the back of the open Jeep. "Less than four hundred million years old. It's blue in color because of its surface temperature. The bluer the light, the hotter the star." She sat on the back bumper and pulled her keyboard onto her lap. "I've found the hottest stars sound the prettiest."

Then she started to play. Like whale song, the music had no discernible melody. It was a ship lost at sea, but it wasn't trying to find the shore. It didn't raise the sails or lower the oars, but instead gave itself over to the tide, dipping and swaying in the starlight. The music was the reflection of the moon on the water.

But it wasn't just the music that was strange. It was Ursula herself. It was as if she wasn't really in her body. She was lost at sea, too, but she didn't seem scared. She looked peaceful. Content, maybe.

Finn felt it, too. The music made her body feel like it was levitating, and for a moment, she was an asteroid, alone and weightless. Then she remembered her mother's memory: lost, afraid, following the notes like a beacon in the fog. Ursula must have met her. Now all Finn could hope was that she remembered.

No one moved until the song was over. After the last note was finished echoing off the vermilion cliffs, Ursula said, "That's what Denebola sounds like tonight."

Barely louder than a whisper, Finn said, "You can hear stars?"

"Every star has a song," she answered plainly, sliding the keyboard behind her. "I'm the only person I've met who can hear them. The first one I heard when I was a kid was Polaris. It was years before I could hear more distant stars, and years after that before I figured out how to tune them in and out. Other kids used to think I was weird because I wore these." Ursula reached back into the Jeep and pulled out a pair of noise-canceling headphones. "I wear them during the day. It's the only way I can sleep. The sun is so loud. It's like radio static being blasted into my ears."

"That's why you work the night shift."

Ursula nodded. "It's not so bad, really. I mean, I get to see this every night." She gestured to the starry sky.

Finn beamed. "Yeah, not bad at all."

"Why are you telling us this?" Zadie asked.

Ursula, to her credit, simply smiled and said, "Because Nic and I have worked hard to make this a place where people feel like they can be themselves, no matter how the rest of the world sees them. I gave up hiding a long time ago." She shot a pointed look at Zadie, who promptly averted her eyes.

Finn, on the other hand, took her invitation to heart. "Actually, we could use your help."

A searching look crossed Ursula's face. "Oh?"

"We're looking for someone. Nora Wilder. I think you might have met her."

"I don't recognize the name, but we have thousands of guests every year. Why?"

"She's our mom." Finn glanced over at her sister. By her expression, it was clear that Zadie would have preferred they keep that particular detail to themselves.

"Your mom . . ." Ursula's words hung in the air for a moment like mist.

Finn pressed on. "Do you keep records of all the people who've stayed here?"

"Yes, but they're all paper. The ones we haven't thrown away are all packed away in boxes."

Finn's heart sank. "Oh."

Ursula paused, as if contemplating which of her own policies she would be willing to break to help them. "When do you think she stayed here?"

"Five years ago."

"Tell you what . . . I've been meaning to go through those boxes anyway. I can take a look through them later tonight."

"Really? Thank you!" Finn practically dove at Ursula and pulled her into an awkward side hug.

"Uh . . . it's no problem." Unsure of what to do with her arms, Ursula patted Finn lightly on the back. When Finn finally released her, she cleared her throat and said, "At this time of year, I wake up around eight, when the sun's going down. Why don't you come over tomorrow around nine?"

"Nine is great."

They spent the next hour searching for stars through the telescope. The Pleiades, Sirius, Betelgeuse, and Castor were just a few of the stars they saw that night. Ursula could hear them all and played their songs softly as the girls took turns peering into other worlds.

It was almost eleven-thirty by the time Zadie and Finn arrived back at camp, so they wasted no time in crawling into their respective sleeping bags. But the second Finn's head hit her pillow, her mind took off at a gallop. She had barely any time to process each thought as it raced by, thoughts about neon cacti and singing stars and magical strangers. For some—what now seemed absurd—reason, it had never occurred to her that anyone outside her family had abilities like hers. She'd always just accepted it as a family quirk and nothing more.

But now an entirely new world was making itself known to her. It had been there all along, of course. She had just needed someone to shine a little ultraviolet light on it, and now it glowed.

She turned onto her back and stared up at the stars through the plastic skylight. "Hey, Zadie?"

Her sister had her back turned to Finn. She was breathing deeply.

"Zadie?"

She stirred. "Hmm?"

"Can I ask you a question?"

"You just did," she mumbled wryly.

"Can I ask you another question?"

Zadie groaned and rolled over to face her sister. "Yeah. What is it?"

"How many other people in the world do you think are like us?"

"I don't know. A hundred?"

"I bet there are thousands."

"Sure. Sounds good. Now go to sleep."

"What about Mom?"

A pause. "What about her?"

"Do you think she was a six, too?"

"Oh, we're calling it that now?"

"Well?"

Zadie didn't answer. The tarp of the tent flapped in the breeze.

"Zadie?"

"Mom didn't talk about that stuff."

"You mean you never thought about it?"

"No."

Finn searched the darkness for her sister's eyes. "I think she was, and whatever it was made her leave."

"Sounds good. I'm tired. I'm going to sleep now." Zadie rolled away from Finn and yanked her sleeping bag over her head.

She just needs a little more time, Finn thought. They'd been looking for their mom for only two days. Had she really expected her sister to have a change of heart that quickly? It was going to take a lot more than a few echoes to undo five years of bitterness, she realized. *But she's here. That's something.*

Finn peered back up through the skylight. If she could figure out what their mom's sixth sense was, maybe she could figure out where she went. Slowly her mind began to settle. She searched for Leo in the night sky but couldn't figure out which grouping of stars it was. A dream visited her a few moments later in the shape of a silver lion.

Zadie, on the other hand, was wide awake. Something was keeping her up, something that had kept her up many nights over the past five years. Finn was right to think something was wrong with their mom. It was even possible that Nora had a sixth sense she'd been hiding from them; in fact Zadie was almost sure she did. But was it the sole reason she'd walked out on her daughters? Zadie doubted it. When Nora had stepped out that door, she'd looked calm, collected. She'd deliberately slipped off that anklet like it was gum on her shoe, like she didn't want to be reminded of who F and Z were.

Zadie knew all this because she'd seen her mom do it.

And she'd done nothing to stop her.

Eleven

Six Months

(until Nora Wilder's disappearance)

"Tell me a story."

Nora gently brushed her thumb over the apple of her younger daughter's cheek, wiping away a smudge of campfire soot. An electric lantern cast an orange light on their faces, projecting their shadows onto the tent wall. Nora had dimmed it as low as it would go so Zadie could sleep. Her older child was almost an adult, but with her eyes closed and her mouth in a sleepy pout, she still looked like the little girl who couldn't fall asleep unless Nora rubbed her feet and hummed "Sweet Baby James."

"I thought you said you were too old for bedtime stories." Nora said in a whisper that sounded like beach grass on a windy day.

"A scary one."

"Are you sure? Right before bedtime?"

Finn nodded, then quickly added, "But no monsters."

"Okay. No monsters. And you're not afraid of ghosts. What else do you find scary?"

"I dunno . . . bears?"

Nora smiled, amused. "Bears, huh? I like it. A more plausible threat than monsters. Heightens the tension."

"Nice bears, though."

"Well, that's not a very scary story, is it?"

"I guess not." Finn rolled onto her stomach and began absentmindedly zipping and unzipping her sleeping bag. "I like camping with you."

Nora brushed a stray hair off her daughter's forehead. "I like camping with you, too."

"Did you go camping with your mom?"

Nora stiffened. "No, honey. My, uh, mom and I didn't do things like this together."

"Was she special like me and Zadie?"

"No one's as special as you girls."

"Are you special?"

Nora had fielded this question a hundred times before, but today she was tired, tired of fighting the unnamed thing that threatened to tear her apart. She had kept it at bay for now, but she knew it was only a matter of time before it emerged again: her demon, the thing that made her *special.*

Before she knew what was happening, tears were streaming down her face.

Moments later, Finn had her arms around her mother and was patting her back the same way Nora would when her daughter was upset. "It's okay," she said. "It's okay."

Nora clung fiercely to her child, afraid that if she let go, Finn would vanish.

Twelve

Every Star Has a Song

Do you think Ursula found anything?" Finn asked her sister for what had to be the tenth time that day. It was all she could think about while she ate her breakfast banana and oatmeal; all she could think about during her morning hike and the hour she spent helping Chuck change a tire on his Oldsmobile. Now, as they walked up the aluminum steps to Ursula and Nic's double-wide, she realized she was nervous to hear the answer.

"Well, getting stressed about it definitely isn't going to help." Zadie had been more sympathetic the first nine times her sister had posed this question. "Let's just go in and see what she says." Then she knocked.

A voice from inside called, "It's open!" and they let themselves in. The trailer was cozy in the most non-patronizing sense of the word. Terra-cotta-colored walls peeked out from behind colorful artwork. The floors were a patchwork of Turkish rugs, and a beaded curtain separated the living area from a hallway on the other side. Trailing jade and philodendron spilled over the sides of baskets that hung from the ceiling, along with bundles of dried herbs and copper pots and pans.

"Leo and Virgo!" Nic rushed at the girls, her arms in a wide V like an inverted cowcatcher. Before either of them knew what was happening, they were being hugged. Ursula stood at a more respectful distance, as though she were waiting in line at an ATM. "Their names are Zadie and Finn," she corrected her wife, then addressed the girls. "If you couldn't tell, Nic's really into astrology." Then in a loud whisper, "I think it's all bullshit."

"You only think it's bullshit because you're a Taurus. It's in your nature," Nic said with a wink.

Ursula rolled her eyes dramatically. "Since Nic takes the day shift, I only have to put up with this a few hours a day."

"That must be weird being on different schedules like that," Zadie commented.

Ursula shrugged. "It's not so bad. It just means I get to eat a lot of pizza for breakfast." She moved toward the kitchenette and opened the refrigerator door. "Do you girls want anything to drink? We've got Diet Coke and— Nic, what *is* this?" she said, holding up an unmarked jar of pale pink liquid with globules floating in it.

"It's prickly pear kombucha."

"Where did it come from?"

"I made it."

Mercifully, Ursula returned the strange jar to the fridge, pulled out two cans of Coke, and handed one to each of the girls. Zadie cracked hers open with a satisfying hiss while Finn fiddled nervously with hers. She was about to inquire about the ledgers when Nic spoke. "So do you ladies camp often?"

"I do," Finn answered, trying not to let her impatience show.

"Yeah, my sister is the camper. I'm just along for the ride," Zadie added.

"Oh, really?" Nic was courteous enough to feign surprise that the young woman in the platform sneakers and skintight jeans was not a seasoned camper. "You know, when Ursula and I bought this place, she had never camped a day in her life."

Ursula glared at her wife playfully. "Yeah, well, at least I didn't almost blow us both up."

"What happened?" Zadie asked.

"It was the night we met," Nic began. "We were at a party. I saw her over by the firepit, stacking logs."

"She told me I was doing it wrong."

"I was flirting."

"Then she poured lighter fluid all over it," Ursula said, shaking her head, then turned to her wife. "How much did you have to pay in damages again?"

"I don't remember. Whatever a garden shed costs."

"It was a lot."

"You still went out with me, though. That's worth a million sheds."

Ursula arched an eyebrow while attempting to hide a smile. "Anyway . . . you guys didn't come over to hear about us. How about we talk in my office?"

She stepped through the beaded curtain, and Zadie and Finn followed her into a hallway. At the end of the hallway was a door, and behind the door was what could best be described as an observatory. Most people would have referred to it as a sunroom, but unlike a sunroom, all the windows were on the ceiling. It didn't really have any walls, either, as every vertical surface was covered up by rickety wooden bookshelves lined with old astronomy textbooks, musical instruments in various states of disrepair, and hundreds of clear plastic tubes filled with rolled-up paper. The only bare patch of wall was occupied by a yellowing roll-down star chart that looked like it had been lifted from a high school in the 1970s. An even older wooden drafting table sat in the center of the room, cluttered with sheet music.

Ursula attempted to straighten up the clutter on her table. "Make yourselves comfortable." Zadie and Finn looked around for somewhere to sit, but the only other chair was being occupied by a wooden crate filled with piano keys.

"This place is awesome," Finn said, looking up at the night sky through the windowpanes.

"Thanks. Obviously, it wasn't original to the trailer. Nic built it for me three summers ago. Before that, I was storing all my music stuff in the front office."

"Is Nic a six, too?"

Ursula shook her head. "I think that's why she got so into astrology. She wants to understand that world, and why I can do what I do, so she can help me in some way. I joke about it, but I wouldn't take that away from her."

Finn knew the feeling. She would do anything—including studying astrology—if it brought her closer to understanding her mom. "So what do you do in here?"

"A lot of things, but mostly, it's where I come to document star songs."

Finn drifted over to one of the bookshelves stacked with plastic tubes and read the label of one of them out loud. "Eta Piscium. 1 H, 31 M, 29 . . . What do all these numbers mean?"

"They're astronomical coordinates. You can open it. It's just paper."

Finn popped the top off the tube and slid out a roll of sheet music. She ran her fingers carefully along the handwritten notes. "This is a star?"

"Yes. I record as many of them as I can, so their songs don't get lost." There was a melancholy note in Ursula's voice. "Obviously, there are too many stars to be able to do it for all of them, but if I can immortalize even a hundred, I'll feel like I've done something worthwhile with my life."

"That's beautiful." Finn gently rolled up the sheet music and placed it back in the tube. She turned back to Ursula and saw hesitation, like she had something to say but didn't know how to begin. Finn spoke for her. "Our mom's name wasn't in the ledgers, was she?"

Ursula shook her head. "No Nora Wilder. It's still possible she stayed here. Our records are a little spotty. I'm sorry. I really wanted to help."

Finn could tell she was being sincere, so she smiled graciously despite the sinking feeling in her stomach. "It's okay. Thanks for trying."

"I hope you find her. I really do." Then Ursula paused, thinking.

"I know it's not much of a consolation, but would you like to hear what they sound like tonight?" Ursula looked up through the glass ceiling at the stars.

"Sure." Finn smiled meekly. She would have preferred to be alone at that moment, but didn't want to insult their host, especially when she had taken the time to dig through old records for them.

While Ursula was setting up her keyboard on its stand, Finn tilted her head back to observe the stars glistening through the glass panes. Then all at once they blinked out of existence.

When the stars reappeared, they were different somehow.
She saw Orion, the hunter. Canis Major. In fact, she could name all the constellations in the sky that night.
Ursula could. This was her memory, not Finn's.
Then. A note.
The only word she could think of to describe it was shimmering.
It sounded like a sequined dress looks under stage lights; a tincture made of starlight dropped straight into the soft shells of her ears.
Another note joined the first, followed by another, then another.
Soon the whole sky was shimmering.
Then her eyes adjusted from the infinite blackness of space to the lamplight of Ursula's observatory. Neither Ursula nor Zadie were there.
I must still be in the echo, *Finn/Ursula thought.*
Ursula's memory wrestled a pencil into her hand. She began furiously scratching out notes on a piece of sheet music.
The door to the observatory opened.
Nic. Her wife's mouth was moving, but all she heard was a loud ringing sound.
A flash of recognition on Nic's face. She switched to sign language.

Finn/Ursula found herself signing back: I'LL BE DONE SOON. I JUST HAVE TO FINISH UP THIS PIECE.

OKAY. I LOVE YOU, Nic answered, then closed the door.

As the lock clicked shut, Finn was jolted back to the present. Both Ursula and Zadie were staring at her. "What did you see?" Zadie asked.

The ringing in her ears was gone, but it still took Finn a few seconds to find her voice. When she did, it was unsteady. Her eyes, she realized, were wet. "The stars. I heard their music. It was . . . I've never heard anything that beautiful."

Ursula studied her for a moment. "You saw something else, didn't you?"

Finn nodded solemnly.

"What is it?" Zadie asked.

Finn cast her eyes on the ground. It was not her story to tell.

"I'm going deaf," Ursula said bluntly, then looked up at the stars as if they gave her the courage to continue. "I found out six months ago. Turns out, even my headphones aren't strong enough to block the damage the sun is doing to my ears. I can hear okay most of the time, but there are moments when everything just goes silent. That's why I'm rushing to get all this music written down, because soon I won't be able to hear it anymore."

Finn finally raised her eyes to Ursula. "I'm sorry." She was both sorry that Ursula was losing her hearing and sorry that she had found out the way she did.

Ursula waved her off. "Don't be. I don't regret a thing. It's the price I paid for being able to hear the most beautiful sound in the universe . . . Do you guys want to see the sign for star?" She pointed both her index fingers toward the sky and swiped them against each other like she was trying to start a fire. "That's Nic's favorite. She says it looks like I'm trying to start a new dance craze and failing miserably."

Finn laughed as she blinked away a tear. "It does kinda look like that."

"Enough of the sad talk," Ursula said, shuffling the sheet music on her desk into a pile. "It's Friday."

"What happens on Friday?"

The bonfire roared. Huge tongues of flame thrashed against the night sky, spitting embers into the stars. Ursula wandered off to talk to a gathering of her neighbors while Zadie and Finn settled themselves onto one of the serape-style blankets that encircled the fire. They were quiet for a while, observing the other residents as they danced and laughed and tossed bottles into the fire to see if they would melt. They seemed happy, the kind of happy that comes with feeling truly at home in a place. Zadie envied them. She had yet to find somewhere like that for herself.

"This place is so weird," Finn said wistfully. Zadie looked over at her sister, a blue aura of moonlight outlining the coils of her hair. From anyone else, this would have been an insult, but not her. She had an affinity for all things strange. After all, it was an exclusive club of which she considered herself a member. People like Finn didn't live in the suburbs. They lived in places like this, on the fringes of society surrounded by Technicolor cacti.

Finn began absentmindedly picking at the tassels on the end of the blanket. "I feel like I failed her."

"You didn't fail anyone. You got us this far." Zadie should have been relieved. The trail had ostensibly gone cold, and maybe now she could salvage what was left of their trip by driving to the closest beach, or if there was none nearby, the closest swimming pool. But if she was being honest with herself, there was a small part of her that had hoped her mother's signature had been in one of those ledgers. Maybe it would have absolved her of some of the guilt she'd been feeling for the last five years.

It was a premonition that had guided Zadie to the window just in time to see her mom leave, a premonition that could have prevented every gut-wrenching second that followed. But the words themselves were vague and forgettable, so forgettable that, to this day, Zadie couldn't recall what they were. It hardly mattered. She had given up that life. What was the point of knowing a future she had no power to change?

But the more she tried to rationalize—*there was nothing I could have done*—the guiltier she felt. It was that guilt that sat with her now in the firelight, that jammed its limbs into her ribs like her baby would do in a matter of weeks. Her anger was guilt in a Halloween mask. It made her feel in control.

But she wasn't in control. Her premonitions made sure to remind her of that.

Then, as if taunting her: *The sky is full of birds.* The phrase lunged at Zadie. Instinctively, she put up a wall, but the premonition beat itself against it like a bird flying into a window.

The sky is full of birds. She held her breath, trying to starve it of oxygen, then looked up at the stars and started counting: *One, two, three—*

The sky is full of birds.

Four, five, six . . .

As she counted to seven, the stars didn't look like stars anymore. They were a flock of birds flitting through space on wings made of luminescent dust, a murmuration of starlight.

"It's taking a long time, don't you think?"

Finn.

Zadie blinked the rest of the starbirds from her eyes. "What's taking a long time?" she said, disoriented. Her sister often did this. Start a conversation that had already begun in her head. Or perhaps she had been speaking this whole time and Zadie had been too preoccupied to notice.

"Our rocks. You don't think it would take Estrella that long to paint."

Zadie had forgotten about the rocks. She rubbed her brow. The premonition may have subsided, but a headache had taken its place. "She probably forgot. I wouldn't get hung up over it. It's just a rock."

"No, it's not." It was as if a switch inside Finn had just been flipped. "It could be a clue," she said and jumped to her feet.

Zadie followed her. Someone would have to apologize for the elder harassment that was about to take place. "Whoa, slow down. What clue?"

"If the paintings are supposed to show our futures, maybe they can tell us where to go next."

"So, you want to see *our* futures so you can see into *Mom's* past?"

"Exactly."

Zadie's brain hurt. This was why she didn't watch time travel movies.

As they approached the front door of Estrella's trailer, they saw a sign hanging from the knocker that read:

PALM READINGS: MONDAYS AND WEDNESDAYS

TAROT: TUESDAYS AND THURSDAYS

PAINTINGS AVAILABLE UPON REQUEST

Zadie rolled her eyes. There was nothing that got under her skin more than phony prognostication. "If you want your palm read, I can write *bullshit* on it with a Sharpie."

Finn glared at her sister and hissed, "*Sssh!* She'll hear you." Then, deadpan, "Good one."

"Thank you."

Finn knocked on the door. She could hear someone shuffling around inside. "Someone's home," she whispered.

A few seconds later, the door opened, but it wasn't Estrella who answered. It was the young woman Finn had noticed her talking to the previous day. A long black braid was draped over her right shoulder like a stole. "Can I help you?"

"Yeah, is Estrella here?"

"I'm sorry. She's not seeing any visitors today." Her tone was brusque.

"I was told that Estrella might be painting rocks for us. I was just, um, checking in to see if she had finished."

The woman turned to look behind her, then continued quietly. "Sorry. My grandmother said she couldn't paint yours."

Finn glanced over the woman's shoulder. Estrella was sitting in an armchair, watching TV. She seemed unaware of their presence. "Why?"

"It just happens sometimes." She sounded irritated. "I'm sorry. Have a good night." The woman moved to close the door.

"Wait! Could I come in and speak to her? Just for a minute?"

"Finn, we should go." Zadie tried to pull her sister away from the door, but Finn held firm.

"I don't think that would be a good idea." Then from behind her, a voice called, "Mija, do we have visitors?"

"Yes, Abuela. But they're just leaving."

"Let them in! I want to say hello."

The granddaughter reluctantly stepped aside to let Finn and Zadie pass. Estrella was a petite woman with a round face and salt-and-pepper hair. She had a smattering of sunspots on the apples of her cheeks and eyes whose corners were folded into joyful little fans. The lobes of her ears were stretched out from both age and the heavy silver earrings that dangled from them. She waved the girls over. "Come here. What are your names?"

"I'm Finn, and this is my sister, Zadie," Finn answered. "Sorry to bother you—"

"You're not bothering me!" The woman laughed. "Luna, maybe."

Her granddaughter Luna smiled hollowly.

"To what do I owe the pleasure of your company this evening?"

Finn sat across from Estrella on a claw-foot ottoman upholstered in raspberry velvet. "Tonya mentioned you might be painting rocks for us."

"Ah, yes . . ." she said, trailing off.

"I know you weren't able to paint them, but I hoped I could maybe talk to you instead."

"What do you want to know?"

"Well, it's a long story, but our mom went missing five years ago. We're trying to find her, but we're kind of stuck. I thought maybe you would know where we should look next." Estrella's eyes darted from Finn to Luna, a peculiar expression on her face that Finn couldn't read. Luna quickly turned away and began straightening a pile of magazines. Estrella shook her head and sighed. "I'm sorry, girls. I can only paint if a vision is delivered to me. I'm just a conduit."

"So you saw nothing for us?"

"I did not."

"Okay. Thanks anyway," Finn said, deflated, and stood to leave.

Zadie had been watching Luna since they arrived. There was something about her that felt familiar, something she couldn't quite put her finger on.

Until now. "It's *you*."

Luna snapped around to face her. "What?"

"You're the psychic one." Zadie surprised even herself with her certainty. For lack of a better term, it was as if they had some kind of psychic connection. She'd heard of twins reuniting after years apart being able to read each other's thoughts. She didn't know what Luna was thinking, but she was pretty sure they had more in common than met the eye.

"How would you know?" Luna bristled.

"Because . . ." Then reluctantly she mumbled, "I'm a psychic, too."

The woman gaped back at her. "You *are*?" She seemed just as stunned as Zadie to be meeting another one of her kind.

"Well, I used to be," she said, walking it back. "I don't use my ability anymore. At least, not on purpose."

"Luna's been wanting to stop for years." Estrella was looking at her granddaughter. "But the palm readings and tarot are how we make a living. Believe it or not, there aren't a lot of job opportunities out here in the desert," she said dryly. "Luna tells me what she sees and I paint. I agreed to be the face of the operation so she could stay anonymous."

"And I'd like to keep it that way," Luna interjected, her eyes burrowing into Zadie's.

Zadie returned the hard look. "Me too." It was like looking into a mirror. *Are all psychics this grouchy?* she wondered.

Luna's suspicion began to give way, the hard line of her mouth slackening. She turned to Finn. "I'm sorry. I tried to read your fortunes, but I couldn't. Every time I tried to look into the future, I kept getting thrown into the past. It was like my wires were getting crossed with someone else's memories."

Finn sucked in a quick breath. "Whose memories?"

"It was a long time ago. I don't remember her name. Actually, now that I'm thinking about it, I don't think she ever told me her name. It was like she'd forgotten it or something."

"Did you guys paint a rock for her?"

"I think so." Luna looked at her grandmother for confirmation. The old woman nodded.

"Can we see it?" Finn asked.

Luna led Finn and Zadie out of the trailer toward the Cairn. Estrella must have used glow-in-the-dark paint, because the colors that had already seemed brilliant in the sunlight had turned neon under the black lights. Rather than a pile of painted rocks, it looked like some kind of totem from an alien planet.

Luna knelt near the base of the Cairn. Her fingers lightly skimmed the rocks as though she were blessing them. "Here it is."

Finn and Zadie bent down to see the rock she was pointing to. It wasn't colorful like the others. In fact, the only color was the cornflower blue Estrella had used for the sky. Underneath was what appeared to be a gray, barren mountain range.

"It's a mountain," Finn said.

"No. Look closer." Luna pointed to several curls of white paint above one of the peaks.

Clouds? No. Smoke.

Finn turned to her sister. "Mom was looking for a volcano."

The Wilders rose with the blushing dawn. Finn wanted to hit the road early despite having barely slept the night before. When she had slept, she'd dreamt of magma leaping from the mouths of steaming calderas; viscous fire writhing and bubbling under its black crust. When she was jolted awake, it wasn't from fear, it was from excitement. She'd always wanted to see a volcano, even if it was dormant; even if the only lava she saw had long since cooled and turned to rock.

The only problem was figuring out *which* volcano was the right one. On the pamphlet display in the front office, she found a *Volcanic Parks Map of North America.* A little dot identified the location of each volcano: black for extinct, gray for dormant, orange for active, and red for supervolcanoes. Finn had learned about supervolcanoes in geology class. Three of the twenty known on Earth are located in the United States, and according to her teacher, Mr. Mayweather, any one of them would be powerful enough to possibly trigger another ice age. (Mr. Mayweather had a reputation for trying to terrify his students. His lecture on brain-eating amoebas was the reason Finn didn't swim in lakes anymore.)

Sitting in the open hatch of Zadie's station wagon, Finn stared down at the map in her lap. There were dozens of dots on the U.S. portion alone. There was no way they could visit all of them. They would have to narrow it down somehow.

Finn reached into her bag and pulled out the egg-size rock Estrella had painted for their mother. Luna had pried it from the Cairn and given it to her in hopes that it would help with their search. Finn couldn't prove it was her mother's—although she had floated the idea of dusting it for prints—but she knew it in her gut. Nora's memory lived somewhere inside Finn. She had felt it. Luna had seen it.

Finn felt the heft of the rock in her palm. It was smooth as a river stone and cool as the water that had shaped it. She felt silly for having thought it might be warm to the touch, as if the volcano itself were somewhere inside, its smoke venting through the tiny pores in the rock's surface.

Smoke. She looked back at the map. Only the orange and red dots were active volcanoes. "Do dormant volcanoes steam? Or only active ones?" she asked aloud.

"I dunno." Zadie grunted as she heaved her suitcase into the hatch. The car bounced under its weight. "Could you scoot over?"

Finn moved a foot to her left so Zadie could shove her suitcase the rest of the way inside. "I mean, that makes sense, right? It would vent steam only if there was actual volcanic activity going on down there."

"I guess. Why? Are you planning on pushing me in?"

Finn grinned. "Oh, did I not tell you about the human sacrifice portion of the trip? My bad."

"Here." Zadie shoved the tent bag at her sister. "You can finish loading. I need to save my strength for Mount Doom."

As Finn tossed the tent into the car, she felt her phone buzzing in her pocket. It was Kathy. She owed her a call (she'd been too busy yesterday and had asked for a rain check), but now was not a good time. *I'll call her back later,* Finn thought, and shoved the phone back into her pocket.

As Finn loaded the rest of their camping gear into the car, Zadie lay on the picnic table, staring up at the fast-moving clouds and trying to will away the seasick feeling that she'd had ever since she'd smelled Finn's oatmeal breakfast. It wasn't all the pregnancy's fault, however. She was also dreading another day of aimless driving. Even though Luna had been psychic, it didn't mean that her premonitions held the weight Finn thought they did. Just because Nora had glimpsed a volcano once didn't mean she was still there, despite what Tonya had told them. So far the next leg of their journey was looking just as speculative as the first.

Zadie heard footsteps. When she sat up, she saw Nic's spindly limbs bounding down the path that led to their campsite. *If she held her arms above her head, she'd look like a saguaro*, Zadie thought, amused.

"Good morning, ladies!" she sang as she approached.

"Morning," Zadie replied, climbing down from the table. "Here to see us off?"

"Yep. I couldn't let you guys leave without saying goodbye . . . and giving you these." She handed Finn and Zadie a plastic tube each, the kind they had seen in Ursula's study. "Ursula wanted you to have them. She wanted to give them to you in person, but you know . . ." Nic waved dismissively at the sun.

Zadie looked over her sister's shoulder as Finn opened her tube and pulled out several pieces of sheet music. In Ursula's handwriting, it was titled *Denebola in F minor*.

"The Tail of the Lion!" Finn gasped. "I can really keep this?"

Nic nodded. Her eyes were bright. "It's your star now."

Zadie opened hers and read the title aloud: "*Porrima in A major*."

"From your star sign, Virgo," Nic explained. "Ursula wanted me to tell you it's a binary star, two stars that orbit around each other. She said the first few bars sound just like a lullaby."

Zadie's hand instinctively drifted toward her stomach. The Ladybug lifted the two halves of its shell to reveal a pair of gauzy wings. It had outgrown its ladybug body, Zadie realized. Or maybe, it had never been a ladybug at all. Maybe it had always been a star.

Zadie placed the music carefully back in its tube and cleared her throat. "Thank you," she said sincerely.

After they had said their goodbyes, the girls climbed into the station wagon and snapped their seat belts. Zadie slid on her sunglasses and glanced at herself in the mirror before flipping up the sunshade. "Ready?" she said.

"Ready." Finn wrapped her fingers around the rock in her hand, closed her eyes, and waited. As they pulled out of the campground and onto the highway, it hit her:

How long had she been walking?
Finn/Nora wasn't sure.
The buzzards knew. They had been watching her.
Her mouth was dry, tacky.
Eyes hurt from squinting in the unrelenting sunlight.
Suddenly her chest burned. Like a cigarette had been snuffed out on her heart.
I don't have much time, *Finn/Nora thought.*
Her mind was a weak radio signal.
One moment she was there and the next . . .
. . . static.
A pickup slowed beside her.
Out of gas? *a man said.*
He pointed to something in her hand. It was red, plastic, with a long nozzle.
What's your name?
What's my name?
She couldn't remember.
Another bolt of pain. A gasp.
Ma'am? Are you okay?
It's getting worse, *she thought.*
She didn't have much time.

Thirteen

Psychic Karaoke

(Part 2)

The one hundred and fifty miles between the Constellation Campground and the Arizona-Utah border were as varied as they were long. As the girls wound their way north, the red cliffs were replaced with snowy peaks trimmed with fragrant pine forests. Farther north still and closer to sea level were vast badlands, striated hills in hues of orange and lavender that reminded Finn of the sand art she made as a kid. Beyond the hills, copper desert stretched for miles in every direction, high winds whipping sand like snow across the highway. Too low on gas to wait out the dust storm, Zadie had to wear a bandanna over her nose and mouth to fill up her tank. After they crossed into Utah, they began seeing green again—farms and trees and grassy lawns—only to be plunged into harsh desert an hour later.

Just looking at the miles of sand through the window made Finn's mouth feel parched. She could still feel the sun beating down on her—*Nora's* neck; sweat collecting on her forehead, her chest, between her legs; her inner thighs raw and goose-pimpled. *It's getting worse. I don't have much time.*

Time. Finn turned to her sister in the driver's seat. "You know how when people claim they were abducted by aliens, they say it felt like they lost time?"

Zadie squinted. "Uhhh . . . where are you going with this?"

"You know . . . like they wake up in a field and don't know how they got there?"

"Yes, I've seen movies, Finn. If you tell me you think Mom was abducted by aliens—"

"No! I mean . . . I don't *think* so."

"Ha!"

"What I'm trying to say is that whatever was going on with Mom, whether it was a sixth sense or something else . . . she was losing time. There were gaps."

"Okay, Mulder," Zadie said dryly.

"Who's Mulder?"

"Doesn't matter."

"What kind of sense would make you lose your car and forget your own name?" Finn wondered out loud.

"A shitty one."

She ignored the unhelpful comment and thought back to the blank tape she'd found in her mother's collection. In it, Nora had stated her name, her age, her address. What if the reason she'd kept the tape was not sentimental? What if she'd needed it to remind herself of details of her own life? Because she was starting to forget. *I don't have much time.*

Finn didn't have much time, either. This was their fourth day on the road, and she was only supposed to be gone for seven. That meant she had just three days—two if you included the drive home—to find their mom. She would likely have to ask Kathy and Steve if she could extend their trip, a request that her foster mom wouldn't be thrilled about, but Finn also knew she couldn't face her foster parents without an answer to their question. She couldn't face them before she'd answered it for herself.

But despite her eagerness to keep driving, Finn felt guilty. Ever since she'd seen the tired look on her sister's face as she crawled out of their tent that morning, Finn had been feeling bad about canceling their vacation. Zadie looked like she could use a night in a comfortable bed and a belt-compromising quantity of room service. They could spare one evening.

"I have an idea," Finn said.

"Yeah?"

"What if instead of sleeping at a campsite tonight, we got a hotel? My treat."

Zadie looked surprised. "Seriously?"

"I think we've earned it."

It didn't have room service, but it had a pool! And a hot tub (not a particularly clean one, but Zadie was beyond caring). Most important, their room at the Indigo Motel had real double beds with real mattresses and fluffy down comforters that sighed when they sank into them.

"No sand, no rocks, no bugs," Zadie mumbled blissfully, the soft mattress drawing out the ache in her back like a poultice.

"No stars." Her sister frowned as she gazed up at the water stain on the popcorn ceiling. "No birds, no fresh air."

The fan next to Zadie kicked on and a gentle breeze swept across her face. "Aaaaaiiiir-conditioning."

"Yeah, that feels pretty good." At least they agreed on something.

The moment Finn's toes pierced the water's surface, the pool burst open like a ripe fruit. She sank like pulp to the bottom, feeling cool but not cold, and gazed up at the shimmering fractals the late afternoon sun made on the water.

She surfaced and swam to the side of the pool closest to Zadie, who was lying on a deck chair reading. Finn squinted to read the cover. "*Two to a Saddle.* What's that one about?"

Zadie presumably lifted her gaze to her, but it was hard to tell behind the large sunglasses she was wearing. "It's about a misunderstood cowboy named Dash. I'm not that far in, but it looks like he's got the hots for his employer's wife."

Finn rested her arms on the pool deck. "Uh-oh."

"Yeah. Uh-oh."

"My book's under my towel. Can you pass it to me?" Finn pointed to the balled-up hotel towel sitting on the deck chair next to her sister's.

Zadie looked at her like she'd lost her mind. "You want to read *in* the pool?"

"No. I want to read *over* the pool."

"But your body is in the pool."

"My lower body is in the pool. My hands"—Finn wiggled her fingers—"are not."

"Ugh. Fine. But if you drop it, you're buying me a new copy." Zadie stood up from her chair and walked *The Fisherman's Desire* over to Finn.

"Gracias," she said and started thumbing through the pages with her pruney fingers. Zadie cringed.

A few minutes later, Finn gasped in horror. Zadie jerked up to sitting. "You dropped it, didn't you?"

"Worse!" Finn replied. "Eleanor just found another woman's stocking in Neptune's lobster trap!"

Zadie heaved an exasperated sigh.

"How could Captain Neptune do that to her?" Finn continued, incensed. "After she promised to give up her riches to be with him?"

"Just keep reading."

"It doesn't make sense. They were so in love!"

"Just keep reading."

"Wait . . ." Finn's gears began to turn. "It wasn't another woman, was it? It was planted there by Admiral Winsome!"

Eleanor, the noblewoman who had stolen Captain Neptune's heart, had been promised to Admiral Winsome by her father. As was customary at the time the story was set, Eleanor had had no say in the match. When Winsome discovered she was having a love affair with Captain Neptune, a lowly fisherman, he had used every trick in the book of villainy to keep them apart.

"Maybe. Maybe not," Zadie teased.

"Argh!" Finn tossed the book back onto her deck chair. "Guys suck."

One of Zadie's eyebrows peeked out from over her sunglasses. "You sound like you're speaking from personal experience. Did you also find a stocking in your boyfriend's lobster trap?"

"Ha. No. That would require having a boyfriend to begin with." Finn found herself thinking about Jonathan and his green—or sometimes brown—eyes. "The guy I'm into . . . it's not gonna happen."

"Why not?"

"I'm pretty sure he thinks I'm weird."

"Does he know about your—?"

"God, no. He thinks I'm weird for totally normal reasons. But I have his old locker, so let's just say I know him better than he knows me."

"Yikes."

"Right?" Finn groaned. "Every time I'm around him I have to make sure I don't say something too personal, like 'Hey, how's your dog's diabetes?'"

"That sucks."

"Yup. Kathy says he's just intimidated by me. That's why he hasn't asked me out."

"Mom told me the same thing once. Mike Hayworth. I had to remind her that *I* was the one who asked *him* out, and he still said no."

"I wonder what Mom would say about Jonathan."

"Probably that you're too good for him. And then she'd stick a picture of his face up on the dartboard."

Finn laughed. "You're right. That's totally what she'd do." Just then it struck her that this was probably the first time Zadie had voluntarily brought up the subject of their mother since they'd left Texas. Not only that, but she seemed almost *happy* to be talking about her. Not wanting to jinx it, Finn left her sister to her thoughts.

"I'm going to do laps," she announced, then pushed off the side of the pool.

Half an hour later, Finn climbed onto the pool deck and observed the long rectangular shadow splayed across the concrete. "I'm hungry. Are you hungry?" Zadie nodded as Finn leaned her head over the pool and squeezed the rest of the water out of her dark curls.

There were only a few restaurants near their motel, most of them fast-food chains. Hungrier than they were picky, they decided on a place called Dry County Bar and Grill. It was in a squat brick building with a flashing neon sign in its window that read: GOOD FOOD, BETTER SERVICE.

Inside, a waitress carrying two giant foaming pitchers of beer told them to seat themselves. Pulling up, Zadie had wondered if the name Dry County was ironic or not. Based on the size of the pitchers, it clearly was. The room was dim, illuminated only by the neon signs above the bar and strings of lights threaded through drop panels in the ceiling. One whole wall was covered in old license plates, a reminder that this was a place for travelers, just another stop on a long journey.

Finn plopped herself down at the closest table and picked up a menu. "I hope they have chicken fingers. And honey mustard."

Zadie smiled to herself. When Finn was little, they always used to split an order, although Zadie usually opted for ketchup over mustard. "I might get the same," she said. "And a salad, so I can say I ate something healthy today." So far that day, all she'd eaten was a string cheese that she'd bought at a gas station. She had been too nauseated that morning to eat anything and was in serious caffeine withdrawal. The Star formerly known as Ladybug must have appreciated the gesture, because it hadn't made her throw up even once that day.

The girls ordered their chicken fingers and a basket of fries to share. As they waited for their food, Zadie watched a small crew of people prepping the stage at the far end of the bar. "There must be a band playing tonight," she said.

Finn looked over her shoulder at the stage. "That's not a band," she said, glee glazing her voice. She turned back around, eyes twinkling. "That's a karaoke machine."

"Nope."

"It's fate."

"Absolutely not."

Zadie scrunched her left eye closed, a spinning disco ball reflecting in her right, bright white sparks that gave off the illusion of genius. The bearded man onstage chuckled into the microphone nervously as his friends whistled at him from the back of the room. Zadie held her stare for a few more seconds, then turned to her sister and said, "Michael Jackson. 'Beat It.'"

Finn raised one eyebrow. "You sure?"

Zadie was *not* sure. Her premonition had been fuzzy. All she'd been able to glean from it was that the first letter of the song started with a *B*. That was like guessing one letter correctly on *Wheel of Fortune* and going straight for the win. "Uh . . . yes?"

The song that began to play did start with a *B*, but it was not performed by Michael Jackson. It was by America's most famous flightless Eagle, Don Henley.

"Did I say 'Beat It'? I meant 'Boys of Summer.'"

"So close," Finn said sarcastically.

"I guess I'm a little rusty." How had Finn convinced her to play Psychic Karaoke? She had cajoled her, of course. Her sister had given some speech about missing the time they spent together as kids, and that this game reminded her of those days, and would she please, *please* play just this once?

"One song," Zadie had conceded after Finn's begging had started to turn heads, but now that she'd gotten the first guess wrong, she felt a need to redeem herself. When the next performer was announced, Zadie focused all her mental energy on the stage.

"Got anything yet?" Finn asked.

"Shh! I'm trying to concentrate." Zadie let out a slow breath and the weightless feeling in her stomach returned; with it, a name. Zadie blurted it out as if it would vanish if she didn't get it off her tongue. "Aretha Franklin."

"Song?"

Zadie hesitated. She had only a name. Before she could even make a guess, the opening bars to Franklin's "Think" started playing over the karaoke speakers. "Shit," she muttered.

"If you wanna stop playing, I get it," Finn teased.

Zadie gave her sister a withering stare. "I'll get it next time. Watch me."

"Oh, I'm watching." Without breaking eye contact, Finn clumsily grabbed a fry from the basket, dipped it in ketchup, and shoved it in her mouth. "Tell you what. How about we make it interesting?" she said, chewing.

"Go on."

"If you get it right, I'll give you the rest of the fries in this basket. If not, I eat them all."

"Deal."

A few minutes later, as "Think" drew to a close, Zadie threw the shutters of her mind wide open. A premonition was there waiting for her. Without hesitation, she said, "'Friends in Low Places.' Garth Brooks."

"You sound pretty confident."

"I am." Although her voice wavered.

An older gentleman wearing a leather vest and cowboy boots climbed onto the stage. He pulled the microphone from its stand and began tapping his toes to the rhythm of the cymbals playing through the speakers.

Was this how the song started? Zadie couldn't remember. Then the man began to sing, "Blame it all on my roots . . ."

"Boom!" Finn was in the middle of reaching for another fry when Zadie snatched the basket away from her. "I'll take my winnings. Thank you."

Finn didn't look mad about the fries. Instead she grinned in a toothy, self-satisfied way. Zadie eyed her suspiciously. "What?"

She shrugged. "Nothing."

"Seriously. Why are you smiling?"

"I just missed this side of you."

"The *fun* side?"

"No. Not more fun. Just . . . relaxed."

Finn was right. Zadie was feeling better than she had in years. Maybe this road trip wasn't such a terrible idea, after all. "Let's play again, only with higher stakes this time."

"I'm listening."

"Whoever loses has to go up there and sing."

This brought a devilish grin to Finn's face. "Winner gets to pick the song."

Zadie hesitated momentarily. "Fine."

The cowboy belted out his last "I'll be okay" and the instrumental faded out. A woman with teased blond hair stepped onto the stage to take his place and he handed her the mic with a small nod. Zadie zeroed in on the woman and waited for a premonition to come knocking. But nothing happened.

Zadie blinked hard and tried again. Every muscle in her body clenched from concentration, even her bones felt the strain, but it was not enough. Whatever magic had been working through her minutes ago was now out to lunch.

"Well?"

"Well, nothing. You win," she said, defeated.

Finn slid her a glass of water. "Here. You'll need this." Zadie took a huge gulp and tried not to think about all the ways she could potentially humiliate herself.

Four songs later, it was Zadie's turn to perform. Thankfully, only a handful of people were looking in her direction. Most of the patrons were understandably more interested in the bottles in their hands than the woman standing uncomfortably onstage clearing her throat for the third time.

"*Woooo!*" called a voice from the back of the room—Finn's, obviously. For some reason, this show of support succeeded only in making Zadie more nervous, and she inadvertently heaved a shuddering breath into the microphone. *How did Mom used to do this every week?* she thought helplessly.

The instrumental track began to play. Zadie thought back to Nora and her singing along to "Piece of My Heart" by Janis Joplin as they drove home from a swim lesson at the YMCA. The memory was so strong, she could almost smell the chlorine.

"'Didn't I make you feel . . .'" Zadie began timidly.

She had belted it out at the top of her lungs, wet tendrils of hair dripping on the leather seat. Nora rolled down the windows, and Zadie sang into the street like her life was a musical. She hadn't sung like that in years. She wasn't as talented as her mom, but she was better than this, better than the shrinking violet who was being drowned out by her own instrumental track. So she closed her eyes—

—and sang. "'*Take it!*'"

A few more heads turned in her direction. She spotted Finn dancing along in her seat. Zadie could feel her body start to move with the music, too.

Zadie was pretty sure she was enjoying herself. She felt free. It didn't matter that barely anyone was paying attention to her. In fact, it was better that way. In that moment, she was singing out an open window, hair flying behind her, with no audience but the passing cars.

As the second chorus started to build, she looked back at their table, expecting to see Finn singing along, but she wasn't there. Thinking she might have looked at the wrong table, she scanned the bar, holding up her hand to block out the glare of the stage lights, but saw no sign of her sister.

In an instant, the high Zadie had been riding was gone and panic had set in. If Finn wasn't in the bar, where was she? The bathroom was behind the stage. She would have noticed if she'd gotten up to use it. Zadie stopped singing while the instrumental continued to play. "Finn? You there?" she said into the mic. More heads turned in her direction, but none of them were Finn's. She hastily shoved the mic back into its stand and ran off the stage.

Zadie burst through the front door into the parking lot. The moonlit outlines of cars were all that Zadie could see as her eyes adjusted to the darkness. She scanned her surroundings but saw no people, no Finn. Beyond the parking lot were more cars moving at blurring speeds. Zadie hurried to the edge of the highway. "Finn!" she called out. A truck shot past, its wheels spitting dirt at her: a warning. She thought she might find her sister wandering along the shoulder sticking out her thumb, lost in the memory of some aimless hitchhiker, but all she saw was a tumbleweed caught in a piece of construction fencing. As she watched it struggle to break free, her mind went to a darker place. She shifted her gaze from the side of the road to the road itself.

She didn't see any sign of Finn between the bright orbs of white and red, although, without streetlights to see by, there was no way to know for sure. Zadie shouted her sister's name again, but the drivers of the speeding cars couldn't hear her. No one did.

Pulse hammering, she turned back toward the bar. That's when she saw her; still in one piece, astride a parked motorcycle. "Finn!" Zadie cried as she sprinted over to her. "What the hell are you doing?"

But as Zadie drew close, she realized her sister couldn't hear her. With every involuntary twitch of her body stilled, Finn looked as though she had been turned to stone. On her face was a wrenched expression, encapsulated in marble and polished until her eyes glistened so much they appeared wet. Zadie recognized the expression. She'd seen it on their mother.

She grabbed her sister by the shoulder and shook her hard. "Hey! Wake up!"

Finn snapped out of her hypnosis as if someone had just thrown water on her. She looked at Zadie, confused, then down at the bike.

"Whoa!" Finn vaulted off the motorcycle and backed away. "Holy shit," she muttered, threading her fingers behind her head.

Just when Zadie thought the nightmare was over, Finn threw one of her cryptic curveballs. "It was real," she gasped. Finn may have not wandered onto the highway, but hearing her talking like she'd just stumbled out of Narnia didn't exactly put Zadie's mind at ease. "*What* was real?"

"The motorcycle."

"I don't understand."

Finn wasn't sure where to begin. This particular memory of her mother's was different from the others. It had a sense of urgency to it. Her heart was still racing from the moment she—or rather, Nora—had stolen that motorcycle.

The echo had begun in the very parking lot they were standing in. The bass from the music playing inside the bar thrummed like a beehive. Finn/Nora had a set of keys in her hand that didn't belong to her, keys she'd sweet-talked a deliriously drunk man into giving her so he wouldn't try to drive home. She may have been stealing his bike, but she might have also saved his life. At least that's what she told herself when she climbed on and revved up the engine.

Desperate times . . . She knew there was a second half to the saying, but she couldn't remember what it was. Her mind was spotty. One second she was there and the next—well, she wasn't sure where she went in between. The only thing that grounded her was an unflinching instinct telling her to *go, go, go.* Go where? Finn/Nora couldn't remember what had happened to her car. This bike was the only thing that could get her back on the highway, and she *needed* to be back on the highway before it was too late. *It's getting worse.*

When she was finished recounting the echo, Finn looked up at her sister. "Then I heard you calling my name." She could still feel the phantom tremor of the bike's engine coursing through her muscles. She looked back at the motorcycle. In the side-view mirror, Nora peered back at her. Finn blinked and her mom's face was replaced with her own reflection. "I—*Mom* was scared. Like she was running from something."

"What would she be running from?" Nora wasn't perfect, but as far as Zadie knew, she hadn't been involved in anything particularly nefarious.

"I don't know, but whatever it was, she had to get out of there quick."

Zadie sighed heavily. "You scared the crap out of me, Finn. Sneaking out, jumping on a stranger's motorcycle . . . You could have gotten hurt. Maybe you should try to cool it on the echoes for a while."

Finn shook her head defiantly. "No way. It's the best chance we have of finding—"

Just then two bikers exited the bar. Zadie and Finn halted their conversation and moved aside to let them pass. Finn held her breath, hoping that the one whose bike she'd sat on didn't notice the smudges she'd left on the handlebars.

Once the bikers had peeled out onto the highway, Finn continued, "I'll be more careful, okay? I promise."

"No more running away?"

Finn almost corrected her but decided against it. She hadn't been aware that she'd left the bar. But if she admitted to Zadie how little control she'd had in that moment, her sister would probably try to pull the plug on the whole operation. "No more running away." It was a promise Finn knew in her heart she was likely to break.

Fourteen

One Month

(until Nora Wilder's disappearance)

If anyone tries to hassle you, you just tell them you're with Nora Wilder. And if they still hassle you"—Nora snapped her right knee toward her chest like a drum major—"kick 'em in the balls."

"Mom, I'll be fine," Zadie insisted, although her gaze drifted nervously across the room of strange men with their full beards and half-full pint glasses. This was the first time Zadie had been to see her mom perform at Hound Dog's open mic night. Finn was at a sleepover, and rather than make Zadie sit at home alone, Nora had offered to take her along. She was friends with the doorman, so he had let Zadie through on Nora's word that she was twenty-one, even though that particular milestone was still three years away—three years that felt like a hundred in the dim bar that smelled like cigarettes and simmered with intoxicated laughter.

"I know you'll be fine," Nora said. "You always are." There was a tinge of melancholy in her voice.

Zadie flashed the stamp on the back of her hand. "If I'm supposed to be twenty-one, does that mean I get to drink?"

"Nice try," Nora said, playfully pinching her daughter's nose between her thumb and forefinger. She flagged down the bartender and pointed to Zadie. "She'll have a Coke." The bartender nodded and Nora placed two dollar bills on the counter.

"I'm on next," she said, waving toward the stage, where a wiry young man with an incongruous mustache was playing guitar. "Stay here. I'll come find you after."

"Good luck," Zadie said.

Nora winked at her daughter and disappeared into the crowd.

A few minutes later, the emcee took the stage. "Most of you know our next act. She's the down-home rocker who lives up to her last name." Several whistles pierced Zadie's ears. She knew her mom was popular, but at Hound Dog's she was practically a celebrity. "Performing 'Edge of Seventeen,' please, give a big round of applause for Nora Wilder!"

As prompted, the crowd erupted in cheers and applause. The emcee returned the mic to its stand and walked off stage left. Zadie looked stage right at the glittering emerald curtain that her mom would ostensibly emerge from in her four-inch leather boots and Van Halen T-shirt that she had artfully torn and safety-pinned back together.

Ten seconds went by and the curtain still hadn't stirred. The cheers were slowly replaced with people murmuring, *Where is she?* Zadie wondered the same thing. She slid halfway off her stool, planting one foot on the floor, debating whether to go back behind the curtain herself and look for her. She spotted the emcee. Someone was whispering in his ear. He nodded and climbed back onto the stage. "Looks like Nora has stepped out for a sec." The crowd groaned in disappointment. "While we wait for her, let's welcome our next act . . ."

Zadie stopped listening as a seed of worry sprouted inside her. Had her mom's friends ever witnessed her disappearing act? Had they covered for her before? Based on the emcee's reaction, she guessed not. *It's probably nothing*, Zadie told herself. And again, *It's probably nothing.* She repeated the phrase in her head throughout the entire next act, the words marching to the rhythm of "Black Velvet" by Alannah Myles.

When the song was over, another performer who was not her mother took the stage. Then another. Twenty minutes went by. Zadie nervously stirred the ice in her empty glass with a straw, looking for her mom in the throng of neon-irradiated faces. She opened her phone to the ten unanswered texts she'd sent Nora and considered sending another. Instead, she shoved the phone into her pocket, climbed off the stool, and weaved through the crowd to the edge of the stage, where the emcee was standing, smoking a cigarette.

"Hi," Zadie started nervously. The emcee looked down at her without smiling. "Umm, I was wondering . . . Do you know where Nora went?"

"She bailed," he said gruffly. "One of our guys saw her sneak out the back."

"Oh."

"Do you know her?"

Zadie nodded.

"Good. Tell her if she wants a spot next week, she has some ass-kissing to do." Something across the room stole the emcee's attention. "Excuse me," he said and walked off.

Zadie stood there, dumbfounded. Had her mom really just left her teenage daughter alone in a bar with no money? The worry she felt moments ago was quickly engulfed in anger. The late-night wandering, the urgent trip to the desert, the way she evaded every one of Zadie's questions—all the memories from the past year that Zadie had tried to suppress burst forth like a geyser. She had never thought of Nora as a bad mother, but now—as she stood helpless in a room full of inebriated strangers, armed with only two knees and the world's most insufficient self-defense course—she had a change of heart.

By the time Zadie crossed the train tracks and saw the glowing orange tiles of their house's windows, it was almost midnight. She had walked most of the way home along the shoulder of a country road, muttering prayers to herself every time she felt the wash of headlights on her back. With every fraught step, she felt her anger grow, so that when she finally reached the front door, she was ready for a fight.

Before she could even touch the knob, the door lurched open, and Nora was standing there with a severe expression. "Zadie! Where the hell were you?"

Zadie gawked at her in disbelief. "What do you mean, 'Where was I?' You're the one who left me there!" She shouldered past her mother into the house.

Nora tailed her into the hallway. "Good one," she scoffed. "If you're going to lie to me, maybe don't use me as your alibi."

Zadie whipped around to face her mom, body trembling with rage. "What about this, huh?" She held up the back of her fist.

Nora clearly recognized the insignia of the stamp and hesitated. "How'd you get that?"

Zadie didn't dignify her question with a response. "I can't believe you just bailed. I had to walk all the way home. Did you not get my texts?"

A look of horror came over her mother's face. She touched her right hand to her bottom lip like it was bleeding. "I think . . . I lost my phone."

"Maybe you left it at the bar with your daughter."

Nora folded her arms in front of her and shook her head, either in disagreement or disbelief. Zadie couldn't tell. "No. No, I would have remembered."

"You think I'm lying?"

"I didn't say that." Nora dragged the nails of her right hand across her left arm.

"Then what? What do *you* think happened, Mom?"

"I don't know, Zadie." She moved toward her daughter, arms outstretched. "But I'm so—"

"Don't," Zadie said, backing out of her mother's reach. "Don't apologize. I just want to know why. Why'd you leave me there?" This was her mother's chance. If she came clean, Zadie would have forgiven her. She would have helped her overcome whatever it was that had turned her mom into a stranger. But when Nora didn't answer, Zadie said, "You know what . . . don't bother. I don't wanna know." Then she marched down the hall to her room and slammed the door behind her.

Fifteen

A Well-Traveled Hat

It was one of those dreams you know isn't real.

Finn clawed her way out from underneath the covers of a bed. A quick inspection of her hands revealed a complexion several shades lighter than her own; black nail polish; a jute friendship bracelet that she recognized as once belonging to her sister. The Joan Jett poster tacked to the inside of the door confirmed Finn's suspicion: in this dream, she was Zadie.

Cooool, she thought. Finn had never had an echo of her sister. Zadie's memory was like one of those secret doors with a sliding window in which a pair of suspicious eyes asks you for the password. Finn had promised never to use the password, so her mind must have invented a memory of Zadie's for her to explore. Dream Finn had no qualms about this. Dream Finn was a lot less considerate.

An unsteady feeling caused Finn/Zadie to sit up. She didn't feel dizzy exactly, just off-center. Her stomach lurched like she was falling. Then she stood on wobbly feet and swung open the bedroom door.

In front of her: an empty hallway, mustard-yellow carpet, photos on the walls, a clock somewhere was counting seconds like pennies: *click, click, click*. At the end of the hallway was a staircase, and beside the staircase was a window shaped like a piece of honeycomb. The light that filtered through it was the color we think honey is (gold), not what it really is (brown).

Finn/Zadie was now walking down that hallway, her feet pillowed by the ugly carpet that their mother couldn't afford to replace. The yellow brick road, that's what Nora had called it, and so they had held hands and skipped. *We're off to see the wizard!* Her sister and mother used to sing together. Finn had forgotten that.

But that was the past. Finn/Zadie was more interested in the future. She reached the golden staircase and began her descent.

Suddenly her childhood home vanished and Finn was back in her bed at the Indigo Motel. She flopped onto her side to face the bed next to hers. All she could see of her sister was a tuft of hair sticking out from underneath the duvet like one of Goldilocks's bears. It was only a dream, not a real memory, but Finn felt guilty nonetheless.

Her phone buzzed on her nightstand. It was a text from Kathy in all caps: CALL ME. *Oops,* Finn thought. She'd meant to call the night before, but she'd been distracted. *Inhabiting your missing mother's body will do that to you.* As quietly as she could, Finn slipped from beneath the covers and out the front door, gently pulling it closed behind her.

Finn padded barefoot down the concrete walkway until she reached the entrance to the pool. The water glittered with help from the fledgling sun, the deck empty save for an abandoned towel draped over one of the chair backs. Finn sat on the edge of the pool by the walk-in stairs and plunged her feet into the shallows.

She dialed Kathy, but after several rings it went to voice mail—her foster mom had a bad habit of leaving her phone on silent. "Heeeyyy, it's me," Finn began. "Sorry, I didn't call last night. Zadie and I went karaokeing and it was loud so . . ." She searched for something else she could tell Kathy without giving away her location. "I'm at the pool right now. I swam over a mile yesterday. Zadie just spent the whole time reading. That's kind of her thing.

"Anyway . . . uh, we were thinking about extending the trip by a few more days, so I wanted to see if that would be cool with you. Just give me a call back and let me know. Say hi to Steve and Milly for me. Love you. Bye!"

Finn hung up the phone and looked down at her feet. Beneath the water, her toes danced like tiny fish nibbling on the concrete. For a brief, disorienting moment, she couldn't remember who the toes belonged to.

"Finn," she said finally. That was her name. The toes belonged to her.

She swiped at the water, scattering her feet into a hundred identical ripples.

Zadie didn't hear Finn come in, but she did hear the gentle patter of the shower running. At first she thought it was rain; then she remembered where she was. It wouldn't be long before they left the desert. Another day's car ride and they would be in volcano country, the Pacific Northwest. It rained there, Zadie had heard. A lot.

She shut her eyes, hoping to get at least another half hour of rest before she had to drive again, but the Star formerly known as Ladybug had other plans. A wave of queasiness rocked Zadie. Without a bathroom to escape to, she had only one option. She leaped from her bed and sprinted out the front door, clamping her hand over her mouth. The trash bin of a housekeeping cart was the lucky recipient of her morning sickness. The bin took it admirably, Zadie less so. As she wiped her mouth with the back of her hand, she spotted a man in an orange polo and cargo shorts walking out of the room next to hers with a caddy of miniature soaps and shampoos. He had a thick brown beard and was wearing an olive bucket hat with decorative patches sewn onto it. Only one person Zadie knew wore a hat like that. "Joel?" she gasped.

The man turned toward the sound of his name. Stunned, he lost his grip on the caddy. It crashed to the ground, sending an avalanche of lavender hand soaps tumbling in every direction. Joel clumsily got on his hands and knees and began picking them up.

"Shit. Sorry!" Zadie rushed over to him. "Let me help."

"It's cool. I got it," Joel said with forced nonchalance, but Zadie bent down to help him anyway, scooping up a handful of soaps and placing them back in the caddy.

Joel stole a glance at Zadie and ventured a smile. "It's really you, huh?"

"More or less," she replied. "You look the same." It wasn't really a compliment, but it wasn't intended as an insult, either. Joel also seemed unsure of which one it was, but thanked her anyway. "How long has it been?"

Zadie wasn't surprised he didn't remember when they had broken up. In the fourteen months they'd dated, Joel had forgotten almost every plan he'd ever made, including his own birthday. "How could you forget your *own* birthday party?" Zadie had shouted while stabbing a balloon with a needle. It had exploded into fleshy shreds with a loud bang, causing Joel to flinch. What had he done to incur Zadie's wrath? He had wandered into her apartment only minutes after she'd sent the last of their friends home with a slice of uneaten cake. Confused, Joel had asked earnestly, "Wait. It's my birthday?" That had made Zadie even angrier, and she popped another ten balloons like she was auditioning for the part of the cannon in the *1812 Overture*.

That was the beginning of the end. They broke up eight weeks later, citing irreconcilable differences.

And now here they were, three years older and marveling at how little either of them had changed. "Three years," Zadie answered. "It's been three years."

Joel nodded awkwardly. "Wow. That's older than Jackson."

"Who's Jackson?"

"My nephew. He's two. I guess you never met him, huh?"

"You literally just said he was born after we broke up."

"Right."

Just as the conversation was about to irretrievably slip into a black hole, Finn appeared behind Zadie. "Cute reunion."

"Finn! Holy shit!" Joel jumped to his feet to greet her. "Man . . .

last time I saw you, you were only this tall." Joel held his hand out, palm side down. Then, realizing that it was basically level with Finn's scalp, he added clumsily, "You looked a lot taller from down there."

Finn pinched her lips around a laugh. "I bet."

"Cool hat," Joel said, pointing to the oversize sun hat perched on Finn's head.

"Thanks! I like yours, too. Is it the same one?"

"Yep. Got a bunch of new patches, though." He pulled off the hat, revealing a sweaty, matted head of hair, and pointed to a patch that looked like an alligator. "I got this one in Florida from an airboat captain."

Finn leaned in to get a better look. "Cool. How many states you got left?"

"Six. Hawaii, Alaska, Minnesota, Delaware, and one of the Dakotas . . . North, I think."

"Nice. Hey, remember that dance we used to do?"

Zadie cringed. She remembered.

Joel waved Finn off dismissively, turning his back to her. "Nah. My dancing days are behind m—" Then he spun back around suddenly and began doing a dance that resembled the Running Man being performed by the cast of *West Side Story*, replete with finger snaps. Finn joined him, laughing, and Zadie hid her face in her hands until the humiliating public display was over.

"We still got it!" Joel held up his right hand and the two high-fived. "So what are you guys doing here, anyway?"

"We're trying to find our mom," Finn said.

Joel's gaze snapped back to his ex. "Wait. Seriously?"

He had met Zadie only a year after Nora had disappeared, when she was broke and still sleeping on friends' couches. They'd met on one such couch the morning after a mutual acquaintance's party. Each of them thought they were the only person crashing there until they woke up with the soles of their feet pressed together. Zadie instinctually screamed and kicked him in the shin. Joel also screamed, but from pain, not surprise. After a solid minute of confused yelling from opposite ends of the couch—

What are you doing here?

What are you *doing here?*

—they were laughing at the burgeoning bruise on Joel's shin. An hour later, Zadie found herself spilling the story of her mom's disappearance to this guy she barely knew. If she had met him at any other point in her life, they would have been good friends and nothing more, but Zadie was lonely, and he made her happy. At least for a while, anyway.

"Yeah. That's why we're here," Zadie said sheepishly, remembering all the times she'd cried in Joel's arms saying things like: *I hate her. I hope she never comes back.*

Joel ran his fingers through his sweaty hair. "Whoa. That's crazy. Do you know where she is?"

"Not yet," Finn answered, then added, "but we're getting closer."

Joel appeared to have more questions, but a shout from behind him broke his train of thought. A man in a stiff collared shirt beckoned him over to the pool deck. "Shit. That's my manager. I'll be right back."

When Joel was out of earshot, Finn asked, "Did you know he was here?"

"No idea."

The two men were now standing face-to-face on the pool deck. From the way the manager was jabbing his finger in Joel's face, it appeared he was not pleased.

"What do you think he did?"

Zadie shrugged. "Knowing Joel, I'll bet it was probably something stupid."

The heated exchange continued for another minute until Joel had apparently had enough. He shoved the soap caddy into his boss's chest with such force that the man lost his balance and staggered backward over the edge of the pool. Zadie winced at the sound his body made as it slapped against the water.

Moments later, a wild-eyed Joel hurried past the Wilders. "Can I come in?" he said, not waiting for an answer before entering their room.

Zadie and Finn followed Joel inside, but they couldn't see him anywhere. Zadie sighed, exasperated. "You don't have to hide, Joel. He didn't see you come in here."

Joel hesitantly rose from behind one of the double beds. "What's he doing now?"

Finn peeked through the curtains. "He's climbing out of the pool. No, wait . . . he slipped . . . now he's climbing out again."

"Does he look mad?"

"Well, he doesn't look *happy*."

Joel buried his face in his hands and let out a pitiful groan. "I really fucked up this time."

"What was he yelling at you about?" Finn probed.

"It wasn't a big deal. The room wasn't even being used. I was just keeping my stuff there until I found a place."

"You've been living at the motel?" Zadie tried to sound surprised, but a motel was far from the strangest place Joel had called home. When they first met, he was living in a friend's RV that had previously been used exclusively for a canning business. During those first few weeks, he'd show up to every one of their dates smelling like sauerkraut.

Joel looked neither ashamed nor remorseful. "Like I said, they weren't even using the room. It was supposed to be fumigated for bedbugs last fall, but the owner hadn't gotten around to it yet." He was about to lower himself onto the end of Zadie's bed when Zadie shook her head forcefully.

Joel hovered in a half squat for a moment, then straightened back up to standing. "Right. Sorry . . . Anyway, I guess I'm fired now. It sucks because I only have, like, a hundred bucks in my bank account." He looked plaintively out the window. "I don't even have a car."

Finn looked over at her sister. *He has nowhere to go,* she mouthed.

Zadie shook her head. *He's not coming with us.*

Why not?

Because he's . . . Joel.

Finn gave Zadie a chastising look and nodded in his direction. *Look at him.*

Sniffing back tears, Joel bumped against the lamp on the desk and attempted to straighten the crooked shade to no avail.

Did Zadie have a burning desire to spend hours, possibly days, in a car with her ex-boyfriend? Not really. But sometimes, rather than start an argument, she found it easier to just hitch her cart to Finn's horse and hope it didn't run them into a bog.

Zadie sighed. "Joel?"

"Yeah?" he replied feebly. The whites of his eyes were pink like they'd been washed with a red sock.

Cart. Horse. Bog. "Do you want to come with us?"

"Really?" He brightened. "But . . . I thought you hated me."

"I never hated you, Joel."

"I annoy you, then."

"You annoy the shit out of me, but most people do."

By the way he smiled then, you'd think she'd just professed her undying love. "Thank you, thank you!" he said, brimming with new tears, happy ones. He circled behind Zadie and hugged her shoulders with his forearms as if he was strapping her in for a roller-coaster ride. Zadie stiffened, as she did in ninety-nine out of a hundred hugs, and waited for it to end. She could see her sister grinning out of the corner of her eye, like she was Dorothy watching the Tin Man finally get a heart. *I guess that would make Joel the Scarecrow,* Zadie thought, and couldn't help but smile herself.

I can't believe you still have the Wedgie Wagon," Joel, laughing, commented from the back seat of Zadie's car.

Zadie raised an eyebrow at him in the rearview mirror. They'd just pulled out of the parking lot, and it was obvious to Finn that her sister already regretted her decision to let him tag along. "Don't call it that."

"Why not? It's funny."

"No, it's not."

"Is it because the seats make your underwear ride up?" Finn asked.

"Yes! See? Finn gets it."

Zadie looked at her sister pointedly. "Whose side are you on?"

"I'm on the side of funny nicknames." She twisted around in her seat. "So, Joel. What have you been up to these days?"

"Oh, you know me . . . various pursuits. I have many irons in the fire, as they say." Joel wasn't aware of the origin of that particular expression, but he used it liberally. That was because he always had some project he was working on, some "big idea" that was going to make him rich. Finn thought some of his ideas weren't actually terrible—the Cookie Toaster, for example—but no matter how good the idea was, Joel lacked the follow-through to make any of them a reality.

"Like what?"

"I'm writing a screenplay."

"Oh. Cooool."

Zadie made eye contact with Finn and shook her head as if to say, *Don't ask him what it's about.*

But Finn pressed on. "What's it about?"

"Get this," he said, animated. "It's like *Freaky Friday*, but with dogs."

"So, like, a dog and its owner switch bodies?"

"No. Two dogs switch bodies."

Zadie and Finn shared a baffled look. "Do the dogs talk?" Finn asked.

Joel laughed as if the question were inherently absurd. "No. They're dogs."

Unable to contain herself anymore, Zadie cut in. "How are you supposed to know they've switched bodies if they don't talk?"

"What do you mean?"

"If they both look like dogs and act like dogs, how do you know which one's which?"

Finn watched Joel grapple with the hole Zadie had poked in his plot. "They act different." he said defensively. "When you see the movie, you'll get it."

"Okay. Sorry," Zadie said, amusement curling the edges of her voice like ribbon.

Now it was Finn's turn to give Zadie a withering stare. *What?* Zadie mouthed in response.

"What's this for?" Joel had spread the *Volcanic Parks Map of North America* open on his lap.

"Here, I'll show you." Finn unbuckled her seat belt and clumsily climbed into the back seat, accidentally kicking Zadie in the arm as she went. When she had settled, she pulled the painted rock Luna had given her out of her pants pocket and handed it to Joel. "*This* is where we're going."

Joel looked down at the trinket with a baffled expression. "I don't follow."

"I have it on good authority that the volcano in this painting is where our mom went when she disappeared."

"Which one do you think it is?"

"Well, we think it's an active volcano, so that eliminates all of these." Finn gestured to the gray dots on the map. "And see how the volcano in the painting is steaming? I looked it up and that can be a sign that an eruption is imminent. If it was steaming when our mom saw it, that means we're most likely looking for a volcano that erupted recently."

Joel's eyes widened. "There was that eruption on the news a few years ago. Where was it again?"

Finn pointed to an orange dot on the northwest quadrant of Washington State. "Mount Ire."

"Yeah! Mount Ire. Man, that shit was scary."

"Well, get ready," Finn said as she folded up the map, "'cause that's where we're going next."

They wouldn't make it to Mount Ire by nightfall. It was summer. The days were long, but not long enough. They would have to make camp somewhere in the old-growth forests of northern Oregon, a land where trees dramatically outnumbered people. While Zadie appreciated the oxygen they provided, she did not appreciate the cover they gave to a host of creatures that might want to eat her. Snakes and scorpions seemed like windup toys compared to the cougars and bears that roamed the wilderness of the Pacific Northwest. Even the vegetarians—elk, bighorn sheep, moose—had menacing horns protruding from their skulls. What were those horns for if not to gore her to death? Zadie knew she was spiraling down, but just because she knew it was happening didn't mean she could stop it.

It took her several seconds to realize her marshmallow had ignited into a ball of flame. Finn leaned in and with a quick puff of air extinguished it, leaving behind a blistered black lump of sugar on the end of Zadie's stick. Zadie barely glanced at the marshmallow before her gaze was dragged back to the dark wood beyond the ring of firelight.

"You're freaking out, aren't you?" Finn said.

"No," she said, defensive. "Why would I?" Zadie couldn't see the moon. Where was it? When she looked up, all she could see were dark spires of ponderosa pine looming over her. *They must have the moon*—an irrational thought that made perfect sense in the moment.

"Are you gonna eat that?" Joel said, pointing to the cremated marshmallow on the end of her stick. Zadie shook her head and handed it to him. "I like 'em crispy," he said and ripped the charred remains from the stick with his teeth.

Finn draped an arm around her sister's shoulder. "It's okay to be scared. I mean . . . these woods *are* haunted."

Zadie elbowed her sister in the ribs. "Ow!" Finn recoiled, clutching her side, and laughed. "Sorry, I forgot you were scared of ghosts."

"I'm not," she lied. At twenty-three, Zadie still hadn't gotten over her irrational fear of the paranormal. *I have Mom to thank for that*, she thought bitterly, remembering the time Nora had recorded spooky noises on her cassette player and left it playing under her bed.

"The woods are definitely haunted," Joel said, sucking marshmallow out from behind his teeth. "I saw a ghost out here once."

"Joel, cut it out."

"I'm serious! His name was Tom and we shared a pineapple. It was dope."

"That wasn't a ghost. You just ate pineapple in the woods with some stranger."

"Classic, Zadie," Joel muttered under his breath.

"What was that?"

"I didn't say anything."

"Oh, it wasn't you? I guess it must have been Tom, the pineapple ghost."

Joel let out an acerbic laugh. "Zadie, I know you think the world revolves around that big brain of yours, but it revolves around the sun. I learned *that* in science class."

"Well, you must not've paid attention or you'd have known what poison ivy looks like."

"Oh, we're bringing this up again?"

"I had to apply that cream three times a day."

"It was on my *back*. I couldn't reach it."

"Yes, you could! I saw you reaching back there constantly to scratch it."

"You were my girlfriend. That's what girlfriends do."

"No, that's what nurses do."

Finn let out a sharp whistle through her teeth. "Whoa! Cool it, you two. You guys broke up already, remember?"

Zadie and Joel averted their eyes. They didn't need reminding.

"Mom's counting on us. We can't be fighting with each other. Now say you're sorry."

“‘*Mmm*, sorry,” Joel mumbled.

Zadie gave her sister a begrudging look, then said halfheartedly, “Sorry.”

Finn smiled and handed each of them a marshmallow. “See? Isn’t it nice when we all get along?”

If there were any bears or cougars or ghosts in the woods that night, they steered clear of the Wilders’ camp. The women retired to their tent, and Joel retreated to the station wagon, where they had made him a makeshift bed out of Zadie’s watermelon pool lounger and an old blanket. From their sleeping bags, Zadie and Finn watched him crawl inside the back hatch and turn in circles, trying to find a comfortable sleeping position.

“It’s like a dog making its bed,” Finn observed as Joel pawed at the rumpled blanket.

“Oh my god.” Zadie snorted. “You’re totally right.” As if on cue, Joel flopped belly-first onto the pool lounger, nuzzled his nose under his arm, and let out a low grunt. Once he had settled, Zadie continued, “How are we supposed to do this with him here?”

“What do you mean?”

“Your echoes. What if Joel sees you . . . you know?” Zadie gave Finn a dead-eyed stare.

Finn waved her sister off. “*Pssht.* I’m not worried.”

“You know him. He doesn’t exactly keep a low profile.”

“It’ll be fine. Just tell him I’m meditating.”

“He’ll never buy that.”

A loud squeak came from the station wagon. By some miracle of psychics or possibly an act of stupidity (likely the latter), the watermelon had flipped itself on top of Joel. Finn turned back to Zadie, one eyebrow arched.

“Okay. I’ll say you’re meditating.” Zadie sighed.

Finn couldn’t help but grin as she watched Joel crawl out from under the watermelon and attempt to remake the bed while muttering to himself. "He's a hoot," she said. "I'm still bummed you guys broke up."

"That makes one of us."

"Oh, come on. You must have missed him a little."

Zadie hesitated. "Yeah, kinda. He can be . . . a lot, but he was the only person who was really there for me after Mom left."

Finn studied her sister's face. Zadie was usually hard to read, a letter written in invisible ink, but Finn could tell Zadie had meant what she'd said. Joel had been there for her during a time when no one else was.

No one—including her.

Finn cringed, remembering all the times she had been too busy with school or sports or dinner with her foster family to answer Zadie's calls; all the times she'd had to cancel their plans to go out for frozen yogurt. *Oh, and then there was that one time I canceled the beach vacation she'd been planning for months to drag her out to the desert, where she could get stuck in a car with her ex-boyfriend.* Had her sister been hurting all those years, and she'd just now noticed? Finn had been only a kid when their mom left, but that now felt like a feeble excuse.

"I was thinking . . ." she began. "Rice is only two hours from Austin. You can come visit me in the dorms, or I could drive down on weekends to see you."

Zadie turned her face away, but Finn could tell from the crack in her sister's voice that her offer had meant something to her. "I'd like that," she said.

Black nail polish. Joan Jett poster. Finn must have been asleep because she was back in Zadie's childhood room.

Yellow carpet. She was in the hallway now. Honeyed light spilled down the stairs.

Finn/Zadie kept one hand on the banister. She counted her steps: *one, two, three . . .*

Fourteen. A bird somewhere was singing. Her mom would leave the windows open on days when the weather wasn't too hot.

Fresh air. Fresh air is good for you.

But it was windy that day. Fresh air had knocked over a pencil cactus and spilled its dirt onto the windowsill. The words *close the window* filled her head as if it were her own thought, but it wasn't. A premonition was telling her to close the window.

Another gust rattled the window screen, and the clay pot rolled to the edge of the sill, then over it. Finn/Zadie outstretched her arms instinctively, swiping air. When the pot smashed, she felt the impact in her bones.

Finn woke with a start, but not wrapped up in her sleeping bag. She felt pine needles underneath her, glimpsed the moon through a web of branches. *I must have sleepwalked.* How far was she from camp? It couldn't be that far. She could still smell the lingering scent of their campfire. Hopefully, she could find her way back before Zadie noticed she was missing. If Zadie knew that on top of her echoes, Finn was now sleepwalking, she would probably drive them back to Texas first thing in the morning, and she couldn't let that happen.

It occurred to Finn that their mom's gift—if that's what it was—was a lot like sleepwalking. Where did she go in those in-between moments? Did she go backward as Finn did or forward like Zadie? Or did she lose time because she was somewhere in her own head, somewhere no one could follow?

It's getting worse. The phrase sent a chill through Finn's bones. She had found herself thinking about it more often since the echo at the bar, not just out of a desire to know what her mom meant by it, but because she'd started to feel something like it herself. She would never admit it to Zadie, but the moment she'd touched that bike, she'd felt like a different person. In the echo, she was no longer Finn, the casual observer. She wasn't just feeling her mother's memories. She was living them.

Zadie's heart had nearly stopped when she woke up to find Finn gone and the tent flap open. Her heart nearly stopped a second time when she saw a dark shape emerging from the woods.

"*Gah!*" Finn shielded her eyes with her hands as Zadie aimed her flashlight at her sister's face. "Are you trying to blind me or something?"

"Sorry. I thought you were a bear," Zadie said, lowering her flashlight. She looked agitated. "Where were you? I was freaking out."

"Bathroom."

"Oh," Zadie said, relaxing a little. "I thought you'd run away again. I was about to go in there looking for you."

"Nope. Just had to, you know—"

Zadie raised her hand, preventing her from elaborating further. "Got it."

Finn waved a hand in the direction of the tent, and said, stilted, "Well, I should probably . . ."

"Yeah. Sorry." Zadie stepped aside to let her pass, but something was gnawing at her. She looked down at the flashlight in her hands. Why hadn't Finn taken it with her? Surely the forest was too dark to see where she was going without it. To test her theory, Zadie clicked off the flashlight and stumbled her way back to the tent in the dark.

SIXTEEN

JOEL VS. THE VOLCANO

If they were going to climb a volcano, they would need supplies. Most important, Zadie would need to trade in her platform sneakers for real hiking boots—an expense she wasn't thrilled about, but it beat blisters. A quaint general store with a carved wooden bear lurking by the front door had exactly what they needed: boots and socks; water bottles; sunscreen; bear spray; enough jerky to distract a bear if spray failed; and a topographic map of Mount Ire National Monument. While the girls were shopping for essentials, Joel was browsing a display of men's T-shirts. He had been wearing the same sweaty hotel polo for a day and a half, and Zadie had noticed him sniffing it minutes earlier.

"How amazing do I look?" Joel said, completely unironically as he spun around to show off his new outfit. The shirt he had selected depicted a brightly colored tableau of a pack of wolves howling at an oversize moon, the kind of art you'd see spray-painted on the side of a rusty Chevy Astro.

"It's . . ." Zadie began, flipping through her mental index for a word that was complimentary, but not so disingenuous it was glaringly obvious.

Finn completed the thought for her. "It's very *you*."

Joel brightened. "I know, right? I almost bought a shirt with one wolf on it, then I saw this one had *five*!"

"You can never have too many wolves," Finn said without cracking a smile.

"Totally." Presumably satisfied that he had made the right decision, Joel pulled the shirt back over his head and went to the register to check out. The sisters followed behind, covertly picking up a few more items Joel would need but had neglected to purchase for himself (a toothbrush, spare socks, deodorant) and adding them to their haul.

Less than an hour later, they arrived at Mount Ire National Monument. The route Finn had plotted for them would take them within yodeling distance of the volcano—the trails leading up the mountain itself were far too advanced for even a moderately seasoned hiker, let alone Zadie, who, even with proper footwear, was unsteady on her feet.

The hike was surprisingly pleasant. Unlike the Constellation Campground, the Obsidian Trail had long stretches of shade from the towering pines. *And the best part of all,* Zadie thought. *No sand.* (Although a particularly sharp pine needle still managed to find its way into her right sock.) Indeed, she was enjoying herself, despite the relentless ramblings of one Joel Magliano.

She'd forgotten how much he could talk. Zadie used to refer to Joel as her "pet parrot" because he would talk even if no one was listening. Sometimes she would leave the room during one of his soliloquies, only to walk back in several minutes later to find him still yammering on, waving a spatula around like he was conducting an orchestra. It was no wonder that he and Finn got along so well. The two of them hadn't stopped chatting since they'd left the trailhead. Zadie had heard Joel's opinions on everything from the two-party electoral system to cinnamon gum.

As Finn walked, she turned Joel's green bucket hat over in her hands. She pointed to a patch depicting a cowboy riding a bucking bronco. "Where's this one from?"

"Wyoming. I was a rodeo clown for a summer."

"For real?"

"My stage name was Droopy Drawers. I used to pop out of a barrel with my pants around my ankles and try to pull them up before the bull got me."

"That's insane. Did you ever get hurt?"

Joel rotated his shoulders so that Finn could see a three-inch long scar just above his right scapula. "Ten stitches."

"Cooool."

"You shoulda seen the bull," Joel cracked. Then his tone turned earnest. "Just kidding. Bulls are incredibly strong."

"What about the hot dog?" Finn said, pointing to another patch.

"Oh, that's a good one!" Joel beamed like he wasn't used to having someone interested in his stories. "It was from a hot dog eating contest at the Ohio State Fair. I unseated the ten-year reigning champion, and he didn't take it well."

"What did he do?"

"Nothing. At first." Joel paused for dramatic effect, then continued. "I was driving home when I smelled something funny. I pulled over to the side of the road and checked under the hood, and you know what I found?"

"What?"

"Hot dogs."

"No . . ."

"There must've been a hundred of them in there! Then some dude—who probably thought I had broken down—pulled over to help me. When he saw me hysterically laughing at my hot dog engine, he ran back to his own car and left me there."

Finn palmed her forehead. "That's nuts! I can't believe that happened."

Neither could Zadie, but in a more literal sense. Joel was prone to exaggeration—also on the list of reasons she broke up with him. If he said he found a hundred hot dogs under his hood, it probably meant he found one hot dog that he forgot he had dropped himself while changing his windshield wiper fluid. Zadie had seen this exact thing happen with a bean burrito.

Finn, on the other hand, apparently appreciated a yarn well spun no matter how specious it was. "Which one's your favorite?" she asked, handing the hat back to Joel.

"Easy," he said, turning it until he found a patch of a small flame.

"Where'd you get it?"

"From a friend," he said, his eyes darting over to Zadie.

Joel squinted in the sunlight. "Where is it?"

"What do you mean? It's right in front of you," Zadie said, incredulous. They were staring straight at it, a snowcapped peak against a brazenly blue sky that rose from a vast desert of hardened magma that looked like it had been sculpted by mud daubers.

Joel didn't appear convinced. "That's a mountain."

"It's a volcano."

"Where's the lava, then?"

"There isn't any. It's not erupting right now."

"Yeah, okay," Joel said, his voice sticky with sarcasm. "A volcano without lava. Good one."

Finn could tell her sister wanted to respond, but Zadie bit her tongue.

She slung her pack off her back and rummaged through it until her fingers brushed smooth stone. She pulled out the painted rock and held it up to the volcano in front of her. As Finn's eyes flicked between the two, her face fell. The peak in the painting was symmetrical. The one standing in front of them was leaning noticeably to the right. "They look different."

Zadie peered over her sister's shoulder. "Could Luna have seen it from a different angle?"

"The only accessible trails are on the east side of the mountain,"

Finn replied. "If this really was an image from Mom's future, the only way she could have seen it from another vantage point would have been by helicopter or something."

"That seems unlikely."

"I agree."

Not ready to give up hope just yet, Finn passed her pack to her sister. "I think I'm going to go *meditate*."

It took a moment for what Finn was saying to fully register with her sister. "Oh. *Right*," Zadie answered finally. They looked out at the pockmarked landscape, at the crumbling black holes where lava had once pooled and bubbled and spat. Some holes you could see the bottom of; others were so deep, you couldn't. "Do you want me to come with you?"

"No, I'll be fine."

"But what if you *meditate* yourself . . . down there?" she said anxiously, pointing to a particularly perilous-looking drop-off where the volcanic rock had turned to scree.

Oblivious to the wordplay taking place, Joel laughed. "That makes no sense. How would she meditate herself off a cliff?"

"Wait here." Finn left her sister and continued down the trail alone until she arrived at an outcrop that looked like a giant sundial. She sat on the smoothest slab she could find, folded her fingers around the painted rock in her hand, and closed her eyes. If her mother had been here, she would know soon.

She inhaled—the air smelled acrid—and as she exhaled, she cast out her mind-net and waited for a memory to come along, poised like a spider on the edge of a web. *Any minute now,* she coaxed herself.

Several minutes passed and the web didn't so much as tremble. The mountainside felt empty, a story waiting to be written rather than read. *Maybe the last eruption burned away all the memories*, she thought. Defeated, Finn trudged back to the others. "How was your meditation?" Zadie asked.

"Uneventful."

Zadie nodded slowly. Was it just Finn's imagination or did she look disappointed, too?

"I mean, isn't that kind of the point?" Joel asked. "With meditation?"

Finn shrugged.

"You know what else is relaxing and way more fun?" Joel waggled his eyebrows and reached into the pockets of his shorts. "Shit!" He patted down his legs and pulled both pockets inside out. A gum wrapper and several pennies fell to the ground. "I must have left my stash at the motel."

"It's the thought that counts," Zadie said, patting him on the arm as she passed. "Let's go."

"But what about your mom?" he asked as he bent over to pick up the change he'd dropped. "You said you thought she might be here."

"She's not," Finn said, then turned and started back down the trail from which they'd come. *If not here, then where?* She still had the painted rock in her hand. It was probably useless now. They couldn't visit every volcano in the country in hopes that their mom had once been there. That could take months. There was no way Steve and Kathy would let her be gone for that long. Finn considered tossing the rock into the volcanic wasteland to be consumed by the next lava flow, but she didn't. She dropped it into the pocket of her hiking pants and zipped it closed. It was still a piece of her mom's story, one she couldn't let go of just yet.

If Mount Ire was a memory desert, then the American Robin Diner was a rainforest. The moment they stepped through the door, Finn could hardly think as her brain cleaned up decades-old coffee spills, thumbed through sticky menus, and picked up crayons that had been tossed on the floor by bored toddlers. Gravy that was too runny, eggs that had been overcooked, ketchup that needed to be bludgeoned before it could be dispensed onto a basket of fries: all these things had been experienced within the walls of this greasy spoon.

Finn, Zadie, and Joel were seated in a booth in the former smoking section of the restaurant. Finn deduced this from a particularly aggressive echo that smelled like a cigarette had been put out inside her nostril. She kept all of this to herself, of course, until Joel left the table to use the restroom and she finally let herself sneeze.

"Smoking section?" Zadie said, not looking up from her menu.

"Yup."

"Do you want to move tables?"

"Nah. It's going away already." She smiled distractedly.

"Are you okay?"

"Yeah. Why wouldn't I be?"

"Today was a bust. I figured you'd be disappointed."

"I am disappointed."

"Yeah."

"But I'm not giving up."

"Okay."

The sisters watched each other, unblinking, for a few moments.

"Do you know what you're getting?" Finn said finally.

"Chicken-fried steak. You?"

"I'm gonna see what's good here."

Zadie flashed her a warning look. "Joel's gonna be back any second."

"I'm having a crappy day. The last thing I want is a bad lunch, too."

"Ugh. Fine. But be quick."

Finn relaxed her body and followed a memory that smelled like maple syrup.

Zadie was now alone at the table. She held her breath, hoping no one would notice her sister's glassy expression.

Unfortunately for her, Joel did. "What's wrong with Finn?"

Zadie jumped and looked over her shoulder to find him standing behind her. "Uh. Nothing. She's fine," she stammered. "Just meditating, again. It's weird-looking, I know. She gets really into it."

Joel wasn't buying it. "I don't think meditation means what you think it means." He sat down next to Zadie and waved a hand in front of Finn's face, but she didn't so much as blink. Joel's face turned suddenly serious. It was an expression Zadie had seen on him on only two, maybe three occasions in all the time she'd known him. "I think she's having a seizure."

"It's not a seizure."

"Yes, it is. My cousin used to have these all the time. He didn't shake or anything. He just looked like a zombie."

"It's not that."

"How do you know?" Joel's voice climbed in agitation. "We should call an ambulance." He started to stand to flag down the waitress, but Zadie yanked him back by the arm.

"No!" she snapped, attracting the stares of the couple at the table next to theirs. She continued in a whisper, "We can't call an ambulance because she's not sick."

"Then what *is* she?"

Zadie caught the eye of their waitress, who was making a beeline for their booth. She turned back to Joel. "Give me your hat."

Joel instinctively dodged her reach. "Why?"

"Just give it to me."

Moments before the waitress arrived, Zadie had pulled Joel's hat snugly over Finn's head, adjusting the brim so it hid her sister's haunted-doll stare.

"How we all doing?" the waitress asked with a pleasant smile.

"Great," Zadie answered stiffly, while Joel simply stared at the waitress, wide-eyed. Unnerved by Joel's gaze, she refilled their waters quickly and bustled on to the next table.

A moment later, Finn stirred. She tilted her head, then, realizing she couldn't see, clawed at the hat over her eyes. She yanked it off, making chunks of her hair stand on end. "Did I miss something?"

Joel and Zadie both raced to answer Finn first:

"Nope." "You were having a seizure."

An amused smile spread across Finn's lips as she turned to Zadie. "Let's just tell him."

Zadie sighed heavily. "Okay, fine."

"Tell me what? What's going on?" Joel hated being left out of conversations. It was why he instigated so many of them.

Finn looked him in the eye and, without any flourish, said, "I can read people's memories."

"You can *what*?" Joel practically shouted. Zadie and Finn shushed him, fielding more dirty looks from nearby tables. "You can read minds?" He sounded mildly nervous at the prospect.

"No, I don't know what people are thinking," Finn continued patiently. "I can just feel the memories that people leave behind."

Joel looked relieved. "But . . . how?"

Finn shrugged. "Runs in the family."

"Wait." He turned to Zadie. "Do *you* have it, too?"

"Uh, sort of. I'm a"—she lowered her voice—"psychic."

Joel's expression was momentarily blank. Then a low chuckle escaped his lips. "You guys are screwing with me."

"No, we're not," Finn insisted.

He clapped his hand on the table. "Man . . . you guys really had me going there for a second. Psychic!" he hooted. "Good one."

Zadie had spent her whole life hiding who she really was, but for some reason, Joel's laughter got under her skin. In that moment, she wanted to prove him wrong more than she wanted to keep her secret. "I *am* a psychic!"

"*Sure* you are." Joel gave an exaggerated wink, then stood up in his seat, plate in hand. "I'm gonna hit the buffet. When I get back, you can tell me who's going to win the Super Bowl."

"How could he not believe us?" Zadie said, incensed, as she watched Joel make his way down the aisle of booths, dodging platter-wielding waitresses. “He believes in Bigfoot, for Christ’s sake.”

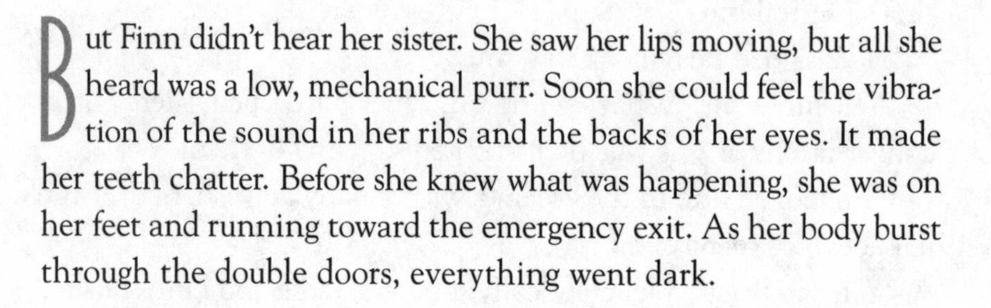

But Finn didn’t hear her sister. She saw her lips moving, but all she heard was a low, mechanical purr. Soon she could feel the vibration of the sound in her ribs and the backs of her eyes. It made her teeth chatter. Before she knew what was happening, she was on her feet and running toward the emergency exit. As her body burst through the double doors, everything went dark.

The air was moving. Or maybe she *was.*
A light, deep in the blackness, was moving, too.
It started small, then grew and grew, divided like cells until not one but two lights were rushing toward her.
Headlights. WHERE WAS HER HEADLIGHT?
Finn/Nora tried to break, but her muscles were frozen, numb.
Stop! *a small voice inside her cried.*
But this wasn’t time travel. Whatever was about to happen had already been decided.
A considerate moon suggested a road ahead, but Finn/Nora couldn’t feel the wheels underneath her.
The air moved faster, dragged her hair behind her like a comet’s tail.
She didn’t have much time.
Someone was expecting her.
Then:
A white-hot pain, the kind that steals the scream from your lungs, uses it as bellows.
It felt like she was being ripped in two. A cracking sound—her ribs?—shifted inside her chest.
Muscles, ligaments shuddered, straining to hold everything together, to hold her *together.*

The pain was too much. She had to turn around.

A bright light.

The bike was gone. She was weightless, airborne, shrapnel.

A new brilliant pain, in her shoulder this time. Her hip.

Her eyes slammed shut . . .

. . . then creaked open.

Letters, numbers snapped into focus. A license plate.

A blurry figure stood over her.

Finn/Nora's mouth was moving. "You're here," it said.

When she came to, it took her a moment to realize who she was. Her name was Nora. No, that was her mom's name. Her name was . . . Finn. Finn Wilder.

A car honked. She was standing in the middle of a road. As Finn ran to the safety of the diner parking lot, a wave of vertigo rocked her, and for a moment she was back in her mother's body. Her elbows collided with the pavement, rocketing pain up her arms. Finn rolled onto her back and pictured the blurry figure hovering over her. *You're here,* Nora had said. Had her mom known the person who ran her off the road?

Finn pulled herself off the asphalt, examined her skinned knees, and limped back toward the restaurant. She was almost at the front door when she ran into Zadie. Had she seen her in the road? It seemed she hadn't, as the frown on her face seemed born more out of irritation than concern. "Dammit, Finn. You've gotta stop running out on me like that. The waitress thought we were dining and dashing. I had to give Joel my credit card so he could pay for the buffet."

"Sorry . . ."

Her expression softened. "You okay?"

"I'm fine." But what about her mom? Finn wondered if she had fared as well. "It's Mom. She was in an accident."

Zadie's face dropped. "Wait . . . what happened?"

"I'm not sure. I just saw bits and pieces. There was a car. The headlight on Mom's bike wasn't working, so I don't think they saw her."

"Was she hurt?"

"I don't know, maybe . . . She was conscious, at least." Finn felt less assured saying the words out loud. Her mom had been conscious, yes, but for how long? She could have passed out only to wake up days later in a hospital bed with tubes coming out of her arms and nose. But it wasn't just the accident that was making her uneasy; it was the dull ache in her sternum, the aftershock of the bone-quaking pain that had driven her mother in front of oncoming traffic. It felt like someone had strapped a bomb to her chest, and all that was left to do was count down the minutes until it went off.

"Remember how I said I thought her gift was making her lose time?" Finn began. Her mouth was dry. She swallowed, but her tongue felt like sandpaper. "Well, that wasn't the only thing happening to her. She was in pain. It was horrible. It felt like I was being ripped in half."

"Her gift was causing her pain?"

"That's just it. I don't think it was. I think she was fighting against it. She had to be somewhere. Whatever it was, it couldn't wait."

Zadie looked out at the road riddled with poorly patched potholes. "Is that where it happened? The accident?"

Finn imagined her mother in slow motion, soaring through the air as her bike skittered into the grassy ditch. "I think so, yeah."

"Do you remember anything else?"

"I saw a license plate. I think it was the car's."

"Do you remember what it said?"

"I think so. Give me a pen."

Zadie pulled a pen and a crumpled napkin out of her purse and handed them to Finn. When she had finished writing, she handed them back to her sister and said, "Washington plates." Had they been detectives, this would have been a clue, but as neither of them had any law enforcement experience or connections, it was just a meaningless assortment of letters and numbers.

"What's that?" Joel appeared beside them, chewing on a biscuit.

"License plate," Zadie answered.

"Whose?"

"We don't know."

Joel didn't ask how they got it or why. "Do you *want* to know?"

Finn perked up. "Why? Do you know someone?"

"One of my buddies works for the DMV. I bet he'd help you out."

"Really?"

Zadie looked nervous. "I don't know . . ."

"He owes me a favor," Joel continued. "It would probably only take him a few seconds to look it up."

"Sure, but we'd probably be breaking a shit-ton of laws."

"Then we break the law," said Finn matter-of-factly.

Zadie was taken aback by her sister's nonchalance. "We could go to prison!"

"We have to find her, Zadie," Finn said, urgency creeping into her voice. "She could be hurt, or—" She let the end of her thought hang, fearing that finishing it would make it true. Her ribs still ached. She wondered fleetingly if she had fractured a bone when she'd fallen but even as she considered if she should see a doctor, she knew nothing would show up on the X-ray. Some aches were deeper than bone.

Zadie finally capitulated. "All right. Joel, call your friend."

Ten minutes later, they had a name and an address:

VAN HOUTEN, MYRON

3763 GRANITE RD

MILLPORT, WASHINGTON

Seventeen

Two Weeks

(Until Nora Wilder's disappearance)

Five days had passed since open mic night at Hound Dog's. Zadie had made pains to avoid her mother when she could, going straight to the library after school and staying there until the voice on the PA system informed her of its closing. When she got home, she'd sneak leftovers from the kitchen—ignoring the place setting that had been left for her on the table—and take them to her room. Nora didn't knock on her door or ask to talk. She gave Zadie her space, even if that meant catching nothing but glimpses of her daughter as she moved from one closed door to another like a ghost.

On the sixth day, Zadie didn't go to the library after school. When it was time for dinner, she emerged from her room and took a seat at the table next to her sister. Nora talked a little, Finn talked a lot, and Zadie listened. When the plates were clean and Finn had scampered off to her room to play with her Legos, Zadie tried to slip away before her mom had a chance to initiate a conversation between the two of them.

"Hey, Zadie. Hold up a minute." Zadie reluctantly turned to face her mom. "I wanted to run something by you."

"Yeah?"

"I was thinking . . ." There was a glint in her eye like a ring catching the light. "Since Finn has that Girl Scout trip next weekend, maybe you and me could do something together."

"Like what?"

"What about the beach?"

"The beach?"

"Yeah. We could get a motel for a night. Lay out on the sand, then fall asleep and get sunburns. Whaddya say?"

It sounded fun enough, but Zadie was uncertain. If her mom could ditch her at a bar, what was to say she wouldn't run off and leave her alone on a beach somewhere? If she did, Zadie wouldn't be able to just walk home. "I dunno . . ."

"Please. I screwed up. Bad. Let me make it up to you."

Her contrition looked genuine even if the gesture was a little over the top. Zadie considered the offer, made it dance for her, do backflips. "Can I pick the music on the drive down?"

"Yes."

"And do you promise not to talk the whole time?"

"I can try."

Eventually, Zadie gave a conciliatory nod, and Nora clapped her hands together. "Great! This Saturday. Pack your swimsuit."

Zadie returned to her room and pulled her suitcase out from under the bed. She blew the dust bunnies off it and began to pack, grabbing two swimsuits, just in case.

They dropped their bags off at the Sailor's Knot Motel, a one-story white stucco building with "views" of the Gulf that required a fair amount of squinting. Once they had claimed their sides of the bed and slathered themselves in sunscreen, Nora and Zadie walked the two blocks to the beach past brightly colored souvenir shops and men selling Popsicles out of refrigerated carts.

The beach itself was crowded, so they chose a spot on the far end next to a rocky groin and spread out their towels on the sand. Sensing her mother wanted to chat, Zadie buried her nose in the book she'd brought with her. Nora took the hint, but her compliance lasted only thirty seconds before she asked, "How is that?"

"Good," Zadie grunted.

"What's it about?" Nora was lying on her side now, with her head in her hand, peering at her daughter through oversize sunglasses.

"It's about a man returning home from war."

"Which war?"

"Two, I think."

"Is it a love story?"

"Yeah."

"Think I'd like it?"

"I dunno." Zadie could tell her mom was trying, but the small talk was making her uncomfortable. "It's kind of depressing."

"Most love stories are."

Zadie nodded, unsure of whether her mom was still talking about books. Nora hadn't had many successful relationships in her life. Neither Zadie's nor Finn's dad had made the list. The only boyfriend whose name Zadie even remembered was a man named Doug, whom her mom had asked out while he was in the process of towing her car. "He was so sweet about it," Nora had said. "He kept apologizing." They'd lasted almost six months, Doug and her mother. She never actually told Zadie why they'd split up.

Nora reached into her bag and pulled out her taxicab-yellow Walkman. "Mom, you know they have iPods, now? You can fit thousands of songs on them."

"But I *like* my Walkman," Nora said. "I got it when I took you to see REO Speedwagon."

"You took me to see REO Speedwagon? How old was I?"

"Six, I think. You didn't care for it."

"I'm shocked."

"We left after three songs and got French fries."

"And a Walkman."

"And a Walkman." Nora smiled and held out an earbud to her daughter. "Wanna share?"

"Is it REO Speedwagon?"

"No."

"Then okay."

The tape reached its end with a pop and Zadie opened her eyes. *I must have dozed off,* she thought as she blinked the floaters from her eyes and turned to face her mother. But Nora was no longer lying beside her.

Zadie sprang up and searched for her mom in the crowd like the world's most traumatizing game of Where's Waldo? It turned out Nora wasn't the only forty-something brunette on the beach that day. Her heart pounded as she scanned the sea of faces. It wasn't until Zadie turned to look behind her that she saw her mother crouched in the sand dunes, inspecting something near her feet. Zadie hurried over and was about to ask Nora what she was doing when her mother raised a hand to silence her. Then she placed her index finger on her lips and waved her daughter over with the other.

Zadie stepped carefully through the beach grass to her mother's side. "Look," Nora whispered and pointed to a small nest made of grasses, pebbles, and bits of seashell. In the middle of the nest were three peeping, pink-faced chicks.

"What are they?" Zadie whispered back.

"Snowy plovers. They must be waiting for Mom to get back with food." Nora's eyes glistened with childlike curiosity as the tiny creatures craned their wobbly necks to the sky. "These little guys are on the endangered species list. They build their nests in the sand, so they often get trampled on by people. You have to be careful when you're clam digging, too. You might not see them until it's too late."

"That sucks," Zadie said. She had the urge to scoop up the hatchlings, feel the warmth of their featherless bodies in her hands. "How do you know all of this?"

Nora looked like she had surprised even herself. "I don't know . . . must have been something I saw on TV." She stood and brushed the sand off her hands. "Let's go for a dip, dry off in the sun for a bit. Then later, I think we should do something crazy."

Zadie didn't particularly like the sound of that. "Like what?"

"Just name something you've always wanted to do and we'll do it."

"Anything?"

"Anything."

She thought for a moment. "I've always wanted to dye my hair."

Nora smiled. "I think we can arrange that."

"Why do you want to be a blonde, anyway?" Nora lingered in the bathroom doorway, looking at a box of goldenrod hair dye as Zadie bent over the motel sink, hair sticky with bleach.

"Because I hate my hair." Like most teenage girls, by *her hair,* she meant *herself,* but hair is easier to change.

"If you really hate your hair, then why dye it a lighter version of itself? What if you did something completely different?"

Zadie's attention was piqued. She looked up at her mom. "Like what?"

"Stay there. I'll be right back."

Twenty minutes later, Nora returned with two boxes of hair dye. Zadie read the label. "Mermaid Blue?"

"I got one for each of us."

Zadie stared at the picture of the woman on the box. Her hair was the color of toilet bowl cleaner. She was in love. "Let's do it."

Nora and Zadie ordered a pizza and took turns painting dye onto each other's roots. While they waited for their hair to transform from that of mere mortals to that of mythic sea creatures, they watched *Splash* on the motel TV and laid the seashells they'd collected that day out on the bedspread. For three inimitable hours, Zadie forgot all about their fight the week before. She felt like a kid again, watching birds outside her window as her mom hummed softly and swayed, and swayed, and swayed until Zadie was too big to fit in her arms anymore. Now that they were the same height, they could sway together. They could dance if Zadie let them.

EIGHTEEN

HOUSE OF MEMORIES

It smelled like rain, like exhumed earthworms and peckish robins; high, fast rivers and overflowing storm drains that turned into their own little creeks in the gutters of roads. It smelled like growth, not bullish leaps of progress, but infinitesimal shifts in color and shape, seedling to flower in many thousands of blinks of an eye. Rain meant change and change was coming. Finn could feel it.

They were winding down a two-lane highway that had been blasted out of a mountainside a hundred years ago by railcars hauling explosives. Not hundreds, but millions of years' worth of sediment towered on either side of them like castle walls, and ahead, the base of an evergreen mountain, the top of which was hidden behind a dense fog that looked like a plume of uncarded wool.

Joel had offered to give Zadie a break from driving and was now behind the wheel. "Almost there," he said as he glanced over at the GPS on his phone. Finn was quiet. She didn't need a GPS to know they were getting close. She could feel it in her gut the same way she could sense a memory. *I've been here before*, she thought, even though she hadn't.

Joel took the next exit onto a narrow unmarked side road that shimmied its way through a jungle of red cedar, hemlock, and giant prehistoric ferns. The house, according to whatever satellite was still able to send them coordinates, was tucked at the end of the road, three miles deep into the forest and about fifteen from the nearest town. "I can't believe we still have a signal," Finn remarked. Then, as fate once tempted is wont to do, the signal dropped.

Minutes later, patches of sky began to pierce the thick canopy and the road widened. Around another bend, part of the forest gave way to a meadow laced with yellow wildflowers. A blue spruce rose from its center, guarded by three small scarecrows. As the car drew closer, Finn realized the scarecrows weren't scarecrows at all, but rather, young girls. All three stood perfectly still as though they had been caught in a game of freeze tag. "Joel, stop the car."

Joel did as he was told without asking why. Zadie, on the other hand, seemed very interested in the *why*. "Why are we stopping?" she asked, sitting up in her seat. Finn pointed out the window to the three motionless girls. "What are they doing?"

"I dunno."

Finn turned to Zadie. "We should see if they need help."

Joel leaned over to peer through the passenger-side window, then instantly recoiled. "Are you crazy? Have you never seen *Children of the Corn?*"

"Are you telling me you're scared of a few little girls, Joel?" Finn teased.

"No," he said defensively. "But someone needs to stay with the car."

"Suit yourself."

Finn and Zadie trudged through the grass slowly, not wanting to startle the girls. When they were about ten feet away, Finn stopped and gestured for her sister to do the same. "Hi!" she called out.

The girls were silent and eerily still. Finn couldn't see their faces, but she imagined they weren't blinking, either. She tried again. "We were driving by and saw you out here. Do you need help?"

"I don't think they can hear you," Zadie whispered, eyeing the girls nervously.

Finn began approaching again, this time making a wide arc so she could face them. By their chestnut hair and the gentle curves of their noses, she guessed they were probably sisters. The youngest was seven, maybe eight, and the oldest looked like she had just finished her first year of high school. Finn had been wrong about one thing: the girls *were* blinking, but their expressions were contentedly blank, like domesticated rabbits.

Finn turned back to Zadie with an inquisitive grin. "Is that what I look like? During my echoes?"

"Yeah. Kinda."

"It's freaky."

"I told you."

The girl closest to her, the youngest, resembled Huckleberry Finn in her dirty overalls that she'd rolled up to her knees. It was only once she saw the girl's sneakers lying beside her that Finn realized why she'd rolled her pant legs up.

"Look." She pointed to the girl's feet—or rather, what she could see of the girl's feet. "Huck" was standing barefoot in a shallow hole, only deep enough to cover her toes and part of her heel. A quick glance at the other girls revealed they were doing the same.

"What are they doing? Mud pedicures?"

"Beats me," Finn said. "Should we try to wake them up?"

"That seems like a bad idea."

"We should probably do *something*."

"Ugh. Okay. But be careful. I've gotten hit more than once trying to do the same to you."

"Sorry."

"It's okay. You get used to it."

Finn extended one hand to Huck while holding her other arm in front of her face for protection. Just as she was about to tap the little girl on the shoulder, she came to, locked eyes with Finn, and let out a shriek. Finn staggered backward, letting out a scream of her own. The outburst woke the two older girls, and in a matter of moments, they had placed their bodies between Finn and their sibling.

"What are you doing to our sister?!" the oldest yelled. She had a defined brow that gave her the intensity of a much older woman and a ponytail so long she could swat flies with it.

Finn backed up a few more steps, holding her hands up in submission. "Whoa. We're not doing anything. We thought you guys needed help."

"Well, we don't!" the middle child snapped. She had softer features than her older sister, but her appearance clearly had no bearing on her temper.

Zadie stepped in front of Finn. "You're right. Clearly you guys can take care of yourselves. We just thought you were lost or something. That's all."

The oldest girl searched Zadie's face, her dark brows knitted together in a skeptical line. "Why are you here?"

"We're on our way to visit someone."

"There are no houses on this road," the oldest said firmly.

"Are you sure? We're looking for Myron Van Houten. Do you know—?"

"No," she answered, too quickly.

"Okay. Well . . . I guess we'll leave you alone, then."

They began retreating to the car when the littlest called after them, "Why do you want to see our dad?" Her older sisters shushed her. Huck, recognizing her slip of the tongue, slapped her hand over her mouth.

The Wilders turned back around and Finn answered, "Because we're looking for our mom, and we think he might know where she is."

The oldest blinked. "Give us a second." The girls huddled around one another and began whispering among themselves. Moments later, they broke and the oldest girl said, "Drive until the road deadends. Look for the fish."

Finn wasn't sure what she meant, but thanked her anyway. "I'm Finn, by the way. This is my sister, Zadie."

"You don't look like sisters," the youngest said frankly.

The middle girl swatted her on the arm. "What? They don't."

"We're half sisters," Finn clarified. They were used to this kind of unsolicited remark, but it usually came from people who were old enough that they should have known better.

The oldest girl traded in her suspicious stare for a guarded smile. "I'm Rowan." She pointed to the middle and youngest sister in turn. "And this is Hazel and Juniper."

"Hi," Juniper peeped.

"Who's he?" Hazel pointed past Zadie and Finn to Joel, who was now outside the car and looking in their direction.

"That's our friend Joel," Finn answered. "Do you wanna play a trick on him?"

Juniper nodded enthusiastically.

"Okay. Here's what we're gonna do. We're all going to turn and look at him at exactly the same time. Ready?"

"Ready!"

"And don't smile," Finn instructed. "Three. Two. One."

When all five girls turned to look at Joel, he visibly flinched. "Very funny!" he shouted back, then ducked into the car to hide his embarrassment.

The Van Houtens' house was the only one on the entire three-mile stretch of road, and even then, it was difficult to see through the tightly packed stand of alder trees. As Rowan had alluded, a fish-shaped mailbox was the first thing to greet them as they pulled over beside the dirt drive.

"Remember," Zadie whispered to her sister as they climbed out of the car, "we don't know for sure this Myron guy was the one who ran Mom off the road."

"I know," Finn replied.

"Just . . . play it cool, okay? I don't want to freak him out."

"Did you see his kids?"

"You know what I mean," Zadie said brusquely. "Let's try to keep the conversation as grounded in reality as possible." Then, after a beat, "*His* reality, not ours."

It was more of a cabin than a house—cedar-shingled with clumps of moss growing on its roof, a crooked stone chimney, and a large stack of firewood on the front porch. It was the kind of home that Finn thought would make a great setting for a slasher movie or—when bundled in freshly fallen snow—a heartwarming family drama about a prodigal son returning home for Christmas.

The moment Finn's foot hit the porch steps, it was as if she had been struck by a wave. She staggered backward and steadied herself. Zadie put a hand on her shoulder. "Whoa. You okay?"

"Yep. I'm fine," she assured her sister, although her voice wavered slightly. She steeled herself and stepped back onto the porch. Once again, she was rocked by the same invisible force: thousands of memories moving as one sorrowful swarm—hard-faced doctors, thrumming machines, pastel gowns, and waiting rooms—but also, a man carrying a sick woman down a flight of stairs, laughter as her head is accidentally bumped against a doorframe, a firecracker of joy made more acute by despair. A love story in three acts: beginning, middle, end.

Somehow she made it all the way to the front door, but couldn't bring herself to knock, scared that the moment she saw Myron's face, she would be moved to tears. "You knock," she said, stepping aside so her sister could do the honors.

Zadie looked at her questioningly, then rapped four times on the solid hardwood door. A few seconds later, from inside, came a muffled voice. "Did you girls forget your keys again?" The door was thrown open, and there stood a slightly disheveled man in his late forties. He had a five o'clock shadow and small, downturned eyes that gave him a somewhat solemn appearance. He didn't look like the kind of guy who would run someone off the road—intentionally or otherwise—and judging by the surprised look on his face, he clearly wasn't accustomed to visitors, either. "Oh, sorry. I thought you were my kids."

"No worries," Zadie said politely. "Are you Myron?"

"I am," he answered tentatively. "How can I help you?"

"I'm Zadie. This is my sister, Finn."

Finn caught Myron's eye. In her head, she heard a man crying. The sound was clearer than any echo she'd had before, as though the memory were only weeks or days old. It was the closest Finn had ever gotten to mind reading and it made her uncomfortable. She held his gaze for only a second before she looked away.

When Finn didn't say a word, Zadie continued with introductions. "And this is our friend, Joel."

Joel waved. "I like your mailbox."

"Oh, thanks." Myron smiled. "Do you fish?"

"It depends."

"On . . . ?"

"Whether eels are fish or not."

Before Joel could elaborate, Zadie cut him off. "Sorry to bother you. This is going to sound strange, but we're looking for someone we think you might know."

"Well, it's not a long list, so that should be easy." He stepped aside, holding the door open for them. "Come on in."

Zadie and Joel followed him inside, but Finn hung back. She could almost see the memories inside the house, long gossamer threads drifting through space like jellyfish tendrils. To enter, she would have to use all her willpower to resist them or risk going catatonic in this stranger's home. She took a deep breath, imagined a protective glass bubble around her mind, and stepped over the threshold.

The inside of Myron's home looked less like a Christmas movie set and more like what it actually was: a home. It had low plaster ceilings, wood-paneled walls, sofas draped in rumpled plaid slipcovers, and an oval cotton rug that had begun to unravel on one end.

A potbelly stove squatted in the corner of the living room, with several damp items of girls' clothing draped over its stovepipe. On the wall above hung a mounted largemouth bass—a real one, not the singing kind—along with family photos, some of which also prominently featured large fish.

"Sorry about the mess," Myron said, making a show of picking up food wrappers that had been left on the dining table. "I try to keep it clean, but with three girls, it's hard."

Finn's eyes landed on a plastic toy horse. She'd had one exactly like it as a kid with a button on its belly that made galloping noises.

"We saw them playing on our way here," Zadie said.

Myron stiffened. "Oh, yeah? What were they up to?" His tone was guarded.

"Uh, tag," Zadie lied. "They were playing tag."

This answer seemed to put Myron at ease. He gestured for them to sit. "I was never into tag myself. Didn't help that I was the slowest kid on the block." He chuckled. "I suppose no one really likes doing things they're bad at."

"Finn wouldn't know what that's like," Zadie said, sitting across from her sister. "She's good at everything."

"That's not true." Finn squeezed out a smile. "I'm only good at *most* things."

Myron laughed. "You sound like Juniper, my youngest. She hasn't figured out she isn't good at everything yet, and I'm not going to be the one to break it to her."

"Must be a youngest sibling thing."

"Must be . . . So tell me about this supposed friend of mine."

Finn was tired. The echoes were coming hard and fast, and it took all her energy just to fend them off. She looked at Zadie, a silent request to pass the conversational torch. Her sister acquiesced. "Her name's Nora Wilder."

"Nora Wilder . . ." Myron said, narrowing his inquisitive blue eyes like he was peering through a keyhole. "Can't say it rings any bells."

Zadie pulled up a photo of her mother on her phone and turned the screen to face Myron. "Oh . . ." A wistful expression crossed his face. "She told us her name was Wren."

Finn and Zadie both sat up in their chairs and exchanged a look. "How do you know her?" Zadie asked.

Myron hesitated, seemingly reluctant to tell the rest of the story. "One night my family and I were driving home from a movie, and we saw this motorcycle make a U-turn in front of oncoming traffic. She didn't get hit, but she lost control of the bike and skidded off the road. I pulled over to help her. Luckily she wasn't really hurt, just stunned."

Finn should have felt relieved—her mother had come out of what could have been a deadly accident with only a few scratches—but the bruised feeling in her ribs reminded her that there was more to the story.

"When was this?" Zadie continued.

"Gosh, uhhh, it was years ago. Two thousand seventeen, I think."

Finn finally jumped in. "And you'd never met her before?"

"No. Never."

So, Nora hadn't known her rescuer after all. *She must have been confused*, Finn thought. If her echoes were any indication, her mom had been confused a lot.

Myron continued, "She refused to go to the hospital, but my wife, Amy, was worried about her, so we let her come home with us."

Zadie looked around, as if her mother was still in the house, watching them from the shadows. "She stayed here? For how long?"

"Just a couple of weeks. She was in no shape to travel. I mean, she wasn't injured really, but her memory was spotty and she had no ID. She seemed lost. Amy offered to let her stay in the apartment above our barn. I didn't think it was a great idea—she was a stranger, you know—but Amy insisted. She had a big heart." Myron smiled to himself and paused for a moment to gather his thoughts, or perhaps to push certain thoughts aside.

"Is your wife here?"

"No," he said, wavering. "Amy passed last year." As Zadie struggled to find a response, he added, "I've got my girls. I'm lucky."

Finn, of course, already knew all of this. She was looking directly at the buffet table they'd set up in the living room for Amy's wake. It had a cheese platter, a perfectly mundane item that appeared profoundly sad sitting next to an arrangement of white lilies. Slowly the room began to fill with black shapes. One of them was Myron, in a black suit and lavender tie. *Lavender was Amy's favorite color.* Finn wasn't sure how she knew that, but she didn't want to know anything else. Without thinking, she held her breath, trying to starve the memory of oxygen, and the cheese, lilies, and lavender tie retreated like ghosts into the wood paneling.

"Can I ask how you knew her?" Myron was speaking again. "We didn't know much about her life. I don't think she remembered enough to tell anyone about it."

Zadie paused, leaving an opening for Finn to speak. When her sister didn't take it, she answered, "She's our mom."

"Your mom?" Myron looked from Zadie to Finn, who deftly avoided his gaze by pretending to look out the window. "Hell, I'm sorry."

In true Zadie fashion, she let his sympathy slide off her. "We're hoping you can help us. We're trying to figure out where she went."

"Yeah, of course," he said. "I'm happy to answer any questions you have."

Before they could take him up on his offer, the front door swung open and Rowan, Hazel, and Juniper bustled inside, screen door slapping behind them.

"Hazel! Cut it out!" Juniper whined as her older sister held her by the Y of her overalls. Hazel let go, and Juniper stumbled forward, nearly falling on her face.

"Hazel, stop strap-dropping your sister." Myron attempted to sound authoritative, but it didn't quite land.

"What? She thinks it's funny," Hazel shot back.

"No, I don't!" Juniper had pulled off one of her boots and looked like she was in the process of deciding how to best hit her sister with it.

"Hey!" Myron said, pointing to the muddy footprint his youngest had made on the floor. "Bathroom. Now." The girls sighed collectively and trudged into the hallway. Myron turned back to his guests. "Their feet are usually dirtier than their shoes."

Finn swallowed the urge to ask him about his daughters' trances. "I'm the same. I love being barefoot," she said.

"Then you get it." He laughed weakly. He was tired. It was etched all over his face, his voice. "Anyway, like I said, I'm happy to tell you everything I know, but if I don't feed these girls soon we're going to have a riot on our hands. Would you guys want to stick around for dinner? We can talk more after."

Zadie answered, "Sounds good."

"Yeah, thanks," Finn said quietly, even though the thought of spending a minute longer in that house made her stomach ache.

The card stuck to Joel's forehead read: POTATO.

"It's a food!" Rowan shouted.

"Uhhh . . . bread!"

She shook her head.

"Bacon! Lettuce, tomato, mayo—"

"Are BLTs the only thing you eat?" Zadie teased.

"Ssshh! I'm trying to concentrate."

The last time Zadie had played this game, she was at a slumber party in the third grade. Watching Joel reminded her of why she often turned down game night invitations from friends. The Van Houten girls, on the other hand, were having a blast watching a grown man struggle to guess kindergarten-level vocabulary words. So much so that they abandoned their teams and decided to all gang up on Joel instead.

It was Hazel's turn. "You fry them."

"Pickles, onion rings, cheese, umm . . ."

"Sometimes they look like a face!" the youngest shouted. The only person worse at this game than Joel, it seemed, was Juniper.

"How is he supposed to guess it from that?" Hazel scoffed.

"Because that's what they look like," she said as if she were stating the obvious. Juniper seemed to live on her own little island. She reminded Zadie of Finn when she was younger: a little odd, with an imagination that outperformed sense.

"Wait. I got it. Potato!" Joel flipped the card over and saw he was right. "The face thing was what did it for me," he said, winking at Juniper. It was clear to Zadie he wasn't humoring the girl. His brain also worked in a roundabout fashion.

Rowan pulled another card and stuck it to Joel's forehead. The word was *valentine*. "Okay," she started. "It's like a card, and you give it to someone you like."

"Like a girlfriend?" Much to Zadie's chagrin, Joel's eyes landed on her. Keen-eyed Juniper caught the exchange. "Why'd you look at her like that?" she asked bluntly.

Flustered, he began, "Umm—"

"Joel, don't—"

"We used to date."

"*Ooo-oooh!*" the girls sang in unison.

Zadie blushed. Now it *really* felt like a slumber party.

"How long for?" Hazel asked.

"About a year."

"Who broke up with who?"

"She broke up with me," Joel said, making an exaggerated sad face.

"Awwwww," they all cooed in sympathy.

Well, I know whose side they're on, Zadie thought. "He's lying. It was mutual."

"That's not how I remember it," Joel said. "I remember you stomping on my heart like one of those grape-stomping ladies."

"Vintners," Hazel corrected.

"What?"

"Vintners. That's what they're called."

"How do you know that?"

Hazel shrugged. "I dunno."

"Do you think you'll ever get back together?" On Juniper's island, no question was too personal.

Zadie and Joel locked eyes for one awkward second before Myron walked into the room, drying his hands on a dish towel. "All right, girls. It's ten. Time for bed."

"Nooooooo," Juniper protested.

"Yeeeeesss." Myron lifted his littlest by her underarms and placed her on her feet. "Go brush your teeth. With a *toothbrush* this time."

"But monkeys clean their teeth with feathers."

"I don't care how monkeys do it." Myron gently shooed his youngest daughter away. "Now put your pajamas on."

The youngest kids reluctantly obeyed, dragging their feet all the way up the stairs. Rowan was already ahead of them, because somewhere upstairs, water was running. When the stomping ceased and the bedroom doors clicked shut, Myron turned back to his guests and ushered them out onto the screened-in porch.

Much like the rest of the house, the porch was function over form. The screen itself had a few holes that had been temporarily—or perhaps permanently—mended with duct tape. The floor was covered in artificial turf and smelled faintly of mildew. An oil lantern hung from a bent nail in the ceiling. Zadie and Finn squeezed onto a wicker love seat while Joel stretched out on a chaise longue, kicking off his shoes as he did so.

"Anyone over twenty-one want a beer?" Myron walked in carrying a six-pack.

"I'll take one," Joel said.

He handed him a beer, then extended one to Zadie. She shook her head. "No, thank you."

Myron sighed as he lowered himself into a rocking chair. "I love it out here," he said, cracking open his bottle and peering out at the waning sunlight outlining the steeples of distant pines. Beyond that, a snow-kissed mountain glowed like a beacon. He rocked silently for a few moments, the floor creaking under his weight. Finn didn't need to read his memories to guess that this is what he did every night after the kids went to bed. This was his quiet time.

"See that ledge way over there?" he said finally, pointing to a rocky cliff jutting out from the swath of green. "When it storms and the creek floods, it turns into a waterfall."

Joel's bottle hissed as he twisted the cap off. "Nice. Can you walk out there?"

"I wouldn't recommend it. It's shallow but slippery. One wrong step, and you'll fall and bust your tail. Amy and I would go fly-fishing in the creek on Sundays. I fell once. Doctor said I'd broken my coccyx. We were both too embarrassed to ask what that was, so we googled it when we got home." He laughed, but just barely. "Truth is, she was the real fisherman. I just keep all this fish stuff around 'cause she'd kill me if she knew I'd taken it down."

"I'm the same," Zadie said. "I still drag our mom's old cassette collection around with me."

"Oh, yeah . . ." he started thoughtfully. "She was a good singer, wasn't she? I remember her walking around the house singing to herself."

"Yeah, she performed onstage sometimes."

"That's right. She mentioned that."

"So she did remember some things?"

"Some. Amy would know better. The two of them were always talking. I— Well, I mostly keep to myself, as you can see."

Their mom must have sat on this porch, Finn thought. She searched for a memory of hers, some sign that she'd been there, but felt nothing. "She didn't remember us, did she?" she asked.

Myron hesitated and looked down at the beer in his hand. "She didn't say she had kids."

Finn hadn't expected him to say yes, but the truth still stung.

In an effort to change the subject, Zadie asked, "Did she ever black out?"

Myron thought for a moment, then slowly shook his head. "No, I can't say I remember her blacking out. Although . . . Amy said she would do this thing sometimes. They'd be standing around talking, then Amy would turn away, and when she turned back around, Wren—sorry, *Nora*—was gone. A lot of times, she'd find her outside just staring up at the sky."

"Did she ask her what she was doing?"

"Uhh . . . I think she said she was looking at the birds? I'm not sure. We were worried. We tried again to get her to go to the doctor, but she wasn't having it. Then one day she just left. Never came back." His expression was apologetic. "If I'd known she had kids . . ."

"It's not your fault," Finn said. "She couldn't control it."

He looked at her curiously. "Control what?"

Finn glanced over at her sister, who gave an almost imperceptible shake of her head. She ignored her warning and continued, "Our mom was *different*."

"Different how?" he said, eyes narrowing from either curiosity or suspicion, she couldn't tell.

"She wasn't like other people. Like your girls—" Realizing the mistake she'd made, she stopped short.

Myron's guard was up. "What *about* my girls?"

Finn faltered, so Zadie went on defense. "She just means that our mom was kind of eccentric. That's all."

He studied the Wilders for a moment, then said, "You never told me how you found me."

Although her echoes had retreated for the time being, Finn could still feel them lurking in the back of her mind. If she told Myron about the echo she'd had of the accident, she ran the risk of his thinking she was crazy and asking them to leave. But based on the suspicious tone of his voice, she wagered that some version of the truth was still preferable to whatever story Myron was currently cooking up in his head.

He continued, "I'm not trying to be rude. You guys seem nice, but you just show up out of the blue. You know my name, where I live. I just need to know what's going on."

Seeing no other option, Finn answered, "You might not believe it."

"Try me."

Finn told him everything: about her echoes and the accident, about how she had not only seen it, but felt it as if she had been the one who'd crashed that bike. Not wanting to get Joel in trouble, she conveniently left out the part about the DMV, explaining, instead, that the only compelling piece of information she'd gleaned from the crash was Myron's name and license plate.

Finn ran out of breath and locked eyes with Myron. His were blue and drowning in memories. "That's a wild story."

"I know it's hard to believe, but it's the truth," Finn said.

Joel cut in. "Wait! You were serious about all that stuff?" Zadie swatted him, and he took the hint and shut his mouth.

"You know, my wife was kind of like you," Myron told Finn.

She sucked in a short breath. "Why do you say that?"

He hesitated, as if there was more than one answer to her question and he was trying to decide which one to tell. "She had some pretty . . . *out-there* beliefs, too."

Finn tried not to look offended.

"She was a very open person. I, on the other hand, can be a little too cautious, especially when it comes to my daughters."

"I understand. Really. We're just here to find our mom. I didn't mean to bring your family into it."

Myron nodded, ostensibly accepting her apology. Finn wasn't sure if he believed her story or if he was just being evasive, but it didn't matter. He appeared to be on their side. For now.

The sun had dipped below the mountain and the crickets were

singing. "Look, I don't normally do this, but it's late and the roads are a little sketchy in the dark. If you guys need a place to crash tonight, the barn apartment has a couch and a double bed."

"That would be great," Finn answered. Her mom had stayed in that apartment, and she wanted to know what memories she'd left behind.

"All right." Myron threw back the rest of his beer, then stood. "You guys wait here. I'll wrangle up some clean towels."

Joel was the first to speak after Myron left the porch. "I thought you guys were joking," he said, still in shock. He turned to Finn. "So you're really . . . ?"

She nodded.

Then Zadie. "And you're . . . ?"

She nodded also.

"I think I need a minute." Joel stood up slowly and wandered into the yard. The girls watched him sit down and flop onto his back like he was about to make snow angels in the grass.

"He does this when he feels overwhelmed," Zadie said. "He'll be fine in an hour."

A warm step pyramid of freshly dried towels in his arms, Myron led the girls to their quarters. "Neither of you are allergic to hay, are you?" he asked as they crossed the barn's threshold. Sure enough, there was a large stack of hay against one wall, but this was clearly not an ordinary barn. It appeared the rest of the space was being used as a workshop. Several half-finished woodworking projects were in the middle of being either clamped, sanded, or routed. A heavy-duty steel rack on the far end of the shop organized the raw lumber into neat rows of oak, walnut, maple, and pine, planks that would someday become tables and the chairs gathered around those tables.

"This is my workshop." There was pride in Myron's voice as he swept his palm across the top of a dresser he was in the middle of finishing. "This girl could use another coat," he said, examining the slightly patchy stain.

"It's beautiful," Zadie said, admiring the delicate hand-routed molding. "Is this what you do for a living?"

"Part of it." Myron surveyed the shop like a stranger would. "The girls hate it, though." Before he could explain why, he said, "Apartment's upstairs."

The sisters followed Myron up a flight of rickety wooden stairs to the second floor. To their surprise, they arrived to find the apartment already occupied. "Scooter! What are you doing up here?" The goat peered up at Myron with its elongated pupils. A partially chewed pillow lay at its feet, stuffing clinging to its beard.

"Come on. Time to go." He led the goat by the collar to the top of the stairs. Scooter let out a bleat of consternation and squeezed past Finn and Zadie, bell jingling as he trotted down the stairs. Myron bent down to pick up the disemboweled pillow. "Sorry about that. Left the door open."

"It's cool. I like goats," Finn said.

"Anyway," he continued, setting the towels down on the arm of the couch, "make yourselves at home. There's soap and shampoo in the bathroom if you need it. We're on a well here, so the water smells kinda funny, but there's nothing wrong with it. I promise."

The girls thanked Myron, and he made his way back down the stairs. A few moments later, they could hear him chastising Scooter again for another transgression.

Zadie lay down on the sofa while Finn took in the apartment. It still looked like a barn in many respects, with chunky wooden beams poking out of the plaster at odd angles. The ceiling was pitched on one end with dormered windows that appeared to be painted shut. The living area was small—there was only one sofa pushed up against the peninsula of the adjoining kitchenette—and across from the sofa was an old TV that looked like it had last been used when Johnny Carson was still on the air. There was some art on the walls—paintings of fish, mostly—and a couple of Thomas Kinkades.

"It's like she was never here," Finn said quietly.

"What were you expecting? That was five years ago."

"I don't know . . . Honestly, it's hard to even hear yourself think with all the memories in that house." She picked a small stone statuette of an owl off a bookcase. "They're all so sad."

"Must be hard," Zadie said, staring at the ceiling. "Having to take care of kids all by yourself."

"Mom did it."

"For a while, anyway."

Finn was too tired to argue. Battling echoes for hours had taken a lot out of her. She moved toward the bedroom. "I'm gonna go lie down for a bit."

Zadie studied her. "Do you feel okay?"

"Yeah. Just tired." Finn faked a smile and shut the door behind her.

Zadie rested her head back down on the pillow. Her body was tired, but her mind was alert. *Mom laid on this couch*, she thought. Or at least some version of their mother had lain there. Based on the way Myron had described her, there hadn't been much left of the Nora she'd known. If she had truly forgotten who she was and that she had a family, could she really be held responsible for leaving them behind?

The thought took Zadie by surprise, but she didn't try to push it away. She sat with it for a few moments, let it soften between her fingers until she felt a buoyancy in her heart (best known by its street name *optimism*). Even then, she wasn't ready to forgive Nora, not yet. It was one thing to know your mom left you; it was another thing to have watched it happen, to have seen each deliberate-looking step in real time. That wasn't something a person got over easily, but Zadie decided then that she was willing to try.

She climbed off the couch and began poking around, opening drawers and cabinets, pulling back curtains, and peering under furniture. She wasn't sure what she was looking for. As she had been quick to point out to Finn, Nora hadn't been there in five years. Whatever trail she'd left had probably gone cold a long time ago.

She opened the refrigerator. The only thing inside was a box of baking soda and a mostly empty bottle of ketchup. She closed the fridge door and moved to the sink. Over the sink was a square window that had a compact version of the same view they had seen from the screened-in porch. It was almost dark, but Zadie could still see the rocky ledge that was sometimes a waterfall. This was not what caught her attention, however.

Suspended on the other side of the glass, within arm's reach, was a bird feeder. She looked down. Like the others, this window had been painted shut at one point, too, but it appeared someone had taken a razor blade and chipped away at the paint to get it to open. Zadie pulled up. With some effort, the window gave way and slid open.

Fresh mountain air filtered inside and Zadie inhaled deeply. Moments later, a robin swooped down and landed on one of the feeder's perches. It pecked daintily at the tiny avalanche of seeds at its feet.

The sky is full of birds.

"No, not now," Zadie said aloud, scaring the robin into flight. Suddenly she felt like she was falling. She grabbed the edge of the sink to steady herself.

The sky is full of birds.

"I know!" she growled to no one. "You told me already."

Zadie let herself sink onto her hands and knees, comforted by the feeling of solid ground beneath her. Her head was spinning.

The sky is full of birds.

The sky is full of birds.

The sky is full of birds.

The words were like a drumbeat inside her skull. She pressed her hands to her ears as if that would somehow stanch the flow of thoughts into her brain.

THE SKY IS FULL OF BIRDS.

"Please, just leave me alone!" she pleaded.

"Zadie?"

She snapped her head up and saw Joel standing at the top of the stairs.

The sky is full of—the premonition receded.

"Was that one of your . . ." Joel pulled a Finn move and put his fingers to his temples.

"Premonitions. Yeah." Zadie used the countertop to pull herself to standing.

Joel blinked, processing. "It doesn't look very fun."

"It's not." It felt good to say it out loud. "It sucks, actually."

He nodded as if she were simply telling him about a bad day she'd had at work. "What was that one about?"

"To be honest, I have no idea. A lot of them are like that. I just try my best to ignore them."

She half expected him to ask why but, to his credit, he didn't. "I get it," he said, his tone understanding. "I wouldn't want to know the future, either."

"You wouldn't?"

"Nah. Too much pressure. I mean . . . what if you had a premonition about the end of the world or something? That's a lot of responsibility."

"That's what *I* said! Try telling that to Finn, though. She loves being the hero."

"Heroes are overrated."

"Totally."

They smiled then, reminded of the friendship they'd once had.

"Wanna watch TV?" Joel asked.

"Sure."

Joel and Zadie made their way to the couch and took their seats on opposite ends, leaving a sizable gap between them. An awkward silence followed as each of them waited for the other to turn the TV on.

"Do you have the remote?" Zadie asked finally.

"I thought you had it."

"Nope."

"It must be around here somewhere." Joel twisted around in his seat, looking for the controller. Not spotting it on either the coffee table or TV stand, he stood up and overturned the couch cushion he was sitting on, then the cushion next to it, then turned to Zadie expectantly.

"Oh. We're doing this now. Okay," she said, standing up.

He flipped her cushion over and, sure enough, hiding underneath it was a remote control. Joel whooped as if he'd been panning for gold and just found his first nugget. "Got it!"

"Yeah. You sure did," Zadie said dryly, surveying the deconstructed sofa. *I lived with this person once,* she thought in mild disbelief.

Joel reassembled the cushions in the most haphazard way possible and plopped down on his end, remote in hand. "What do you wanna watch?" he said, pressing the power button.

"Whatever you want to watch."

Joel gave her side-eye. "So we're gonna play *this* game again, huh?"

"What?"

"You pretend not to care what I put on, but then when I put on something you don't like, you suddenly have an opinion."

"That's not true," Zadie said, indignant.

"Fine." Joel skimmed through the channels until he landed on one airing professional wrestling. "Still don't care?" he said, eyeing his ex.

Zadie put on the most congenial smile she could muster. "Nope. I love wrestling."

"Oh, yeah? Who's your favorite wrestler?"

"Umm. The . . . Zam . . . boni . . . Man."

"The Zamboni Man?"

"Yup."

"Never heard of him."

"That's 'cause only real wrestling fanatics know about him."

"What's his signature move?"

"He mows the other guy down with his Zamboni, obviously."

"Obviously."

They looked at each other then, bemused. They used to laugh a lot, Zadie remembered fondly. Maybe that was why they stayed together as long as they did. Then Joel's expression softened, his gaze settling into hers. It was the kind of gaze that felt like being touched. Zadie squirmed and turned her attention back to the TV. She could feel Joel's eyes linger on her for a moment longer; then he, too, turned back to the screen.

"How about a movie?" he said, flipping the channel.

"A movie sounds good."

Nineteen

If Trees Could Talk

Finn hadn't meant to fall asleep, but the room was dim and the bed was soft and she was tired, so tired it felt like moving underwater. Sealed off from the memories of the main house, her mind had been given a much-needed reprieve, and so it did the first thing it could think of, and that was to not have to think. She hadn't even had time to crawl under the covers before she was climbing out of them again in a dream:

Close the window.

The bird in the tree had stopped singing. Shards of clay scattered across the tile floor. A helpless cactus lay on its side, root ball exposed. Finn/Zadie combed her fingers through the spidery roots, scooped the sandy soil up with her hands, poured it into an empty coffee can.

Close the window.

Finn/Zadie picked up a piece of clay pot sharp enough to draw blood. She pressed it against her palm—a test—then set it aside.

The bird started singing again. Finn/Zadie could see its tiny apple head, its pinstriped wings. She had never seen a bird like it before.

Close the window.

She didn't want to close it. She wanted to listen.

Close the window.

Finn/Zadie moved toward the window, the bird. She leaned in

until she could feel fresh air against her cheek. Then something out of the corner of her eye moved.

Finn awoke to not one, but a chorus of songbirds outside her window. The bed she was lying on was pushed up against the wall, so she barely had to lift her head to see the ruddy limbs of cedar trees. Light twinkled through their scaly needles as they swayed gently like a queen's wave. Finn waved back. After seven hours of undisturbed sleep, she finally felt like herself again, and was invigorated by the prospect of a day spent retracing her mom's footsteps.

She quickly changed her clothes and pushed open the bedroom door. In the living room, Zadie and Joel were both fast sleep on opposite ends of the couch. The TV was still on at a low volume, airing a generic drama from some three-letter cable network. Not wanting to wake them, she crept across the living room, then slipped out the front door and down the stairs.

Finn stepped out into the dewy dawn. The yard, the house, the mountain: all were still. She liked the feeling of being the first person awake. It was a comforting kind of solitude, like listening to a song with your headphones on. It was also the time of day when, generally speaking, her echoes were least active, when her memories were hers and only hers.

In contrast, the flock of starlings overhead were hungry for attention, flitting from branch to branch, sharing worms and gossip (both juicy). Finn watched them and wondered what had happened to her pigeon, Chris Five. She hoped he was okay on his own and hadn't ended up in some street magician's hat with a deck of playing cards and a chain of multicolored scarves.

Finn turned in the direction of the main house and spotted Rowan slipping out the back door carrying a small trowel. Finn waved, but Rowan must have not seen her, because she darted across the yard and into the forest without so much as a glance in Finn's direction.

Why is she sneaking out this early in the morning? Finn wondered and decided to follow.

When she reached the bank of trees through which she'd seen Rowan disappear, she noticed a narrow trail leading up the hillside. It wasn't an official trail but likely one that had been carved out over many years by many pairs of boots. Even the bulbous tree roots that protruded from the earth had been worn smooth in places like river rocks. Without hesitation, Finn began to climb.

She moved as quietly as possible, not wanting to frighten Rowan before she'd had a chance to announce herself. The only noise she made was the occasional swish of her calves against the fern fronds. The vegetation was strangled, jungle-like, but that only made the blazed trail more obvious, like the first set of tracks in newly fallen snow. Finn ducked under a half-fallen spruce that looked like it had been the victim of a lightning strike, charred and peeled down the middle like a banana. Several of the surrounding trees had burns as well from the ensuing fire, although the damage was minimal.

The trail hooked sharply to the left. Then Finn spotted Rowan crouching in a small clearing at the base of an enormous maple whose branches were dripping in tree moss. She paused, unsure of how to approach, then realized what Rowan was doing. She was digging. The girl drove the trowel she was holding into the dirt, then deposited a small clod of soil on the ground next to her. There were dozens of holes like this one surrounding the tree, not more than a few inches deep and a foot across. It was like she'd stepped into a gopher colony.

Finn hazarded a step forward. "Hey."

Rowan nearly jumped out of her skin as she spun around to face her. She gasped, eyes flashing. "What are you doing here?"

"I saw you sneak out of the house. What are *you* doing?"

"I'm not doing anything," Rowan said, defensive.

"Sorry. I wasn't trying to be nosy."

"Weren't you?"

Finn considered this. "Yeah, I guess I was."

Rowan's hard façade crumbled. "Promise you won't tell anyone. Especially not my dad."

"Tell him what?"

"Just don't tell him you saw me out here."

Finn knew she should walk away and leave Rowan to what was probably just an eccentric hobby, but her curiosity, as usual, got the better of her. "What are all these holes for?"

Rowan frowned. "I'm looking for something."

"Buried treasure?" Finn softened the joke with a smile, but the girl didn't smile back.

"I can't tell you what it is."

"Are you sure? Maybe I can help." Finn took a step forward.

"Watch your—!" Rowan shouted just as Finn's foot slipped inside one of the holes.

She was standing on the earth.

Then she was part of it.

Her toes spreading down and out like roots.

Her legs, back, chest were solid, steady.

Her arms quivered and shook and held back the rain.

Her head . . . well, she no longer needed one.

Her thoughts, senses, feelings now lived in all of her, from root to leaf.

Am I a tree? *her subconscious asked her conscious.*

No, *her conscious answered.* That's impossible.

But was it? She angled her leaves toward the sunlight, took a long pull of groundwater.

If I'm not a tree, then what am I?

Finn opened her eyes to find Rowan lightly shaking her. "Finn?"

"Yep. I'm here," she said, woozy, and sat cross-legged on the ground. She was relieved to see that she still had legs and toes and that her skin was smooth, not made of scratchy bark.

"What *was* that?" Rowan backed away, warily.

She'd already confessed her ability to Myron. What did it matter if his daughter knew, too? "It was an echo." *Was it?* It felt like one, but trees didn't have memories, as far as she knew.

"What's an echo?"

"It's like a sixth sense. I can feel memories that aren't mine."

Rowan had the look of someone trying to do math in their head. "Whose memories?"

"Anyone's. People leave memories behind, or at least parts of them. I can usually ignore them, but not always."

"Was it *my* memory?"

"I don't think so."

"Then whose was it?"

"I don't know. It was weird. For a second, I felt like I was . . . a tree."

The girl's eyes popped. "A tree?"

"Yeah. I know that sounds crazy, but—"

Rowan cut her off. "No! It doesn't. Not to me, anyway." She joined Finn in the grass, folding her legs underneath her and nervously twirling her hair in her fingers. She was only three, maybe four years younger than Finn, but she had a childlike quality about her. "My mom"—Rowan quickly glanced around to make sure no one was listening—"could talk to trees."

Finn couldn't hide her shock. "Seriously?" Once again, she was overwhelmed by what seemed like magic to her. Her own ability suddenly felt mundane in comparison. Why did some people get to listen to star music and talk to trees while she was stuck reliving strangers' pollen allergies and middle school dances? "That's amazing."

Now it was Rowan's turn to look surprised. "I wasn't expecting you to believe me."

"Well, I wasn't expecting you to believe me, either." Finn looked down at the soil trapped underneath the girl's toenails. "What about you and your sisters? Can you guys talk to trees, too?"

Rowan stopped winding her hair around her finger and tugged. A nervous habit. Finn had a few of those herself. "Yes."

"Is that what all the holes are for?"

"Yes."

"How does it work?"

"I just stick my toes in the ground. Like this," she said, burrowing her toes into the loose earth. "And they send me messages."

"Oh, yeah! I remember learning in school that trees communicate with each other through their roots using bacteria or something. Is it like that?"

"My science teacher taught us that, too," she said, a coy smile on her lips. "They have feelings, you know. They can be sad or happy or scared, just like us."

Finn could see traces of all three emotions in Rowan's face. "So they tell you what they're feeling?"

"It's not like I hear them talking or anything. I just sort of *know*."

Finn guessed that Rowan, like her, had only a basic understanding of how her ability worked or where it came from. In the end, what did it matter if they'd been genetically programmed or cursed by a witch with twelve toes? It didn't change anything. They would still be different. They would still elicit curious looks from strangers and find creative new ways to explain themselves, which is a creative way of saying they would have to lie.

"Can you show me?"

Rowan hesitated more out of habit than actual reticence. "Sure." Then, "It works better if I stand." She stood and slipped her feet into the hole in front of her. Moments later, her eyes glazed over and she was still, her breathing so shallow that Finn could barely see her chest rise.

She stayed like this for several minutes. Finn waited for something to happen, some sign that it was working, but Rowan didn't turn green or sprout leaves like some fairy-tale creature. She did what all trees do: stand and wait.

Finally life flickered back into Rowan's eyes. "Well?" Finn asked. "How's it feeling today?"

"Tired. It's been fighting off an aphid infestation for weeks. And now that it's summer, the spruces have been hogging all the afternoon light." She smiled. "This tree is . . . What's the word?"

"Ornery?"

"Yeah! Ornery." Rowan laughed. "They all are, kinda."

"That's wild . . ." Finn shook her head in astonishment. "Can we do another?"

"Sure."

The next tree Rowan "talked" to was a silver fir. It was less ornery than the maple, but still had some strong opinions about the family of voles burrowing between its roots. The aspen next to it didn't mention the voles, but had similar feelings about the woodpecker that was making Swiss cheese out of its trunk. The Pacific yew, on the other hand, had no particular grievances to air. It was just kicking back, basking in the sunlight and sipping on groundwater like its roots were curly straws and the earth was a coconut.

For Finn, the forest came alive in a way it hadn't before. Every twitch, sway, and shimmy felt like a form of sign language. The *hissssssss* that she'd come to think of simply as wind was now a slip-into-a-hot-bath sigh at the end of a long day. It was magical, and Finn needed a little magic. The previous day's barrage of heartbreaking memories had left her feeling drained, but the forest had restored her, the forest and her new friend.

"Does your dad know you can do this?" Finn asked as Rowan brushed the dirt off her feet.

"Of course," Rowan said, as if it should have been obvious. "Doesn't yours?"

Finn shook her head. "My foster dad just thinks I'm spacey, which is kind of true." A pause. "But if your dad knows, then why are you sneaking out here alone?"

"Because he doesn't like it."

"He doesn't like you talking to trees?"

"No. He's fine with that. It's just . . . Forget it. It's stupid."

"I won't think it's stupid. A minute ago, I thought I was turning into a tree. I'm the last person you should feel stupid around."

Rowan had a wary look in her eye. She reminded Finn of her sister, distrustful, easily spooked. "Okay," she said finally, biting her lip. "But you have to promise not to tell my dad I was out here."

"I promise," Finn said, hoping she wouldn't have to break it.

Rowan averted her eyes. "He doesn't like us looking for her."

"Who?"

"Mom."

"Your mom? But—" Finn let the question hang.

Rowan continued, "I have this feeling like she's not really gone. Like part of her might have gotten left behind or something. In one of the trees."

Finn looked back at the giant maple. With the exception of its size, it looked like any other tree. Her heart ached for Rowan. She knew how it felt to miss someone so much that you saw signs of them everywhere, in everything. "And you think she's in this one?"

"I thought so, but now I'm not sure. As you can see, I've tried a lot."

Finn counted at least thirty holes surrounding the trunk, thirty failures.

"Dad says it isn't healthy. That I 'can't properly grieve' if I think Mom is still out there somewhere. I'm not crazy. It's not like I think she's a ghost or something. I just think . . ." Rowan stared down at her calloused feet. "She spent hours every day with these trees. They were part of her." She blushed. "Like I said, it's just a feeling. I'm probably wrong."

"People said stuff like that to me about my mom, too. That she was gone. Never coming back."

"What did you do about it?"

"Honestly? I didn't believe them."

Rowan smiled solemnly. They sat in silence for a few moments, the morning sun warming their bare feet.

"I liked your mom," Rowan said finally. "She was nice. And funny."

"Yeah, she was."

"I should get home before my dad wakes up."

"Yeah, I should get back, too. Zadie freaks out when she doesn't know where I am."

"I'm probably going to head back out here this afternoon if you wanna come."

"I'd like that."

When Zadie woke, she thought that she had traveled back in time. She peered down the length of the couch and saw Joel dozing at the other end, just as she had the morning they'd met. She could even feel the traces of a hangover and the gummy sensation of day-old makeup on her face, of which only the latter was possible. Their feet were intertwined like a dance frozen midstep. Zadie delicately slipped hers free and swung her legs over the side of the couch.

She snuck another glance at Joel and realized, with some consternation, that he'd gotten better-looking with age. He'd talked about growing a beard when he was younger, but always quit a couple of weeks in out of insecurity about its lack of fullness. She thought the beard he had now suited him. In fact, she would have told him so were she not concerned he would read too much into it.

I'm flattering myself, she thought. Joel wasn't interested in her romantically anymore. They were friends . . . kind of. And she could use a friend, especially during the times she was worried about Finn or—

The baby.

The Star formerly known as Ladybug sent out a small flare.

I will, she replied. *I'm just waiting for the right moment.*

She would wait to tell her sister about the pregnancy until they got home, she decided. Finn already had enough on her mind as it is.

It was almost nine. Finn was usually up before her, but the door to the bedroom was still closed. Zadie padded across the hardwood floor and carefully opened the door so it wouldn't squeak. "Finn?" she whispered as she entered. But not only was the bed empty, it was still fully made up as if Finn hadn't slept there at all.

"Oh no," she muttered, then ran back into the living room. "Joel! Joel, wake up!"

Joel lifted his head, groggily. "Huh? What's up?"

"Finn's gone," she said breathlessly, while cramming her feet into her sneakers.

More alert now, Joel sat up, his hair squished to one side. "She's what?"

"She's not in there and the bed's made."

"Maybe she made it?"

"Finn *never* makes the bed." She grabbed Joel's shoes and tossed them to him. "Will you help me look for her?"

"Yeah," he said, rolling off the couch. "Yeah, of course."

Within seconds, they were out the door and jogging down the stairs to Myron's workshop. Finn was not in the barn, so they continued outside. The morning was brisk for summer and scented with pine. The mist that had hovered over the treetops the day before had dissipated and had been replaced with a lemon slice of sun. Zadie shaded her eyes with her hand and looked around. "You check the house," she instructed Joel. "I'll look out here."

"No problem," Joel said and ran toward the Van Houtens' porch.

Zadie began circling the barn. *I shouldn't have left her alone,* she thought. She hadn't meant to. The couch was just so comfortable and Joel—

No. This isn't Joel's fault, she rebuked herself. Finn was her responsibility. If anything happened to her, she was to blame.

Once she had circumnavigated the barn, she checked the goat pen and the detached garage. With no Finn in sight, all that was left was the forest. Zadie froze, staring into the deep green shadows shaped like trees. This wasn't the woods behind their old house, nor was it the sparse landscape of the desert, where you could see fifty miles in every direction. This was real wilderness, forest so dense that millions of people believed that it could hide an eight-foot-tall primate for generations. If she went in there alone, she'd likely never find her way out.

Where was Joel? She'd assumed he would come back outside and fill her in once he'd finished searching the house. He'd probably gotten distracted and forgotten why he was there. *I guess I'll have to do it myself,* she thought.

When she opened the front door, not only did she find Joel, but Finn as well, seated around the dining table with Myron's daughters, happily stuffing fresh-baked banana-nut muffins into their mouths. Not bothering to swallow first, Joel exclaimed, "I found her!" and pointed to Finn.

Her sister looked up and smiled. "Hey, Zadie. Did you need something?"

Zadie did her best to hide her irritation. "Nope. I'm good," she said, clipped, and took a seat at the table.

"How about a muffin?" Joel held one out to her, oblivious to Zadie's indignation. She wordlessly accepted the muffin and began picking at its paper wrapping.

Myron whipped out of the kitchen carrying a pan of scrambled eggs. "Ah, you're up." He sat the pan on a trivet along with a spoon so people could help themselves. "I've got bacon going, too, and OJ in the fridge."

"Dad always burns the bacon," Juniper said matter-of-factly while plucking nuts from her muffin and dropping them onto her plate.

"I don't *burn* it," he contested. "I make it crispy."

"Burnt."

"Fine. You don't have to eat it. And what's this?" he said, nodding at her plate. "You don't like nuts now?"

Juniper shook her head.

"Is there anything else I should know about? A tattoo perhaps?"

"Nope."

"Okay," he said with a mixture of amusement and exasperation, then turned to his guests. "How about you guys? You want some of my burnt bacon?"

All three nodded, Joel most emphatically.

"All right, then. Be right back," he said, hustling back into the kitchen.

Zadie turned to her sister. She also seemed in better spirits than she'd been the day before. "How are you feeling?" she whispered.

"Great. Why?"

"You were kind of out of it yesterday."

"I feel fine," she said, shrugging and helping herself to a spoonful of eggs.

Either Zadie had imagined her sister's distress the previous day, or Finn was gaslighting her. "Okay, if you say so," she said, uneasy.

Finn appeared oblivious to her disquietude. "So we were thinking . . ." She looked around the room as though a consensus had been come to without Zadie's knowledge. "We should probably stay here for another day or two. You know, in case something *jogs my memory*," she said with an unnecessarily winking tone.

Zadie didn't detect any recognition in Juniper or Hazel's faces, but Rowan notably averted her eyes. She turned to her sister. "Can I talk to you outside for a sec?"

Finn grabbed another muffin and followed Zadie out onto the front porch. "What's up?"

"You tell me."

"I don't know what you're talking about."

"Yesterday you could barely speak, and now you're practically ready to move in. What happened?"

"Nothing," Finn insisted.

Zadie shot her a skeptical look. "You had an echo, didn't you?"

"No . . . Okay, yes," she whispered. "But I promised her I wouldn't tell anyone."

"Promised who?"

"Rowan."

"What did you promise Rowan?"

Finn bit her lip, but if she was trying to stop herself from smiling, it didn't work. "She's like us, Zadie. They all are."

Zadie stole a glance through the window at the family seated around the dining room table. Myron had just sat down to find a large bite out of the toast he'd made for himself. He held up the piece of bread with the half-moon-shaped hole and suspiciously raised one eyebrow. All three girls broke into fits of laughter, and in an act of playful retribution, Myron grabbed Hazel's muffin off her plate and took a bite of his own.

"Even Myron?"

"I don't think so. But their mom was. Zadie, she—" Finn hesitated. "They can talk to trees."

Zadie stared at her sister blankly for a moment. "Is it weird that I actually believe you right now?"

Finn looked taken aback. "Honestly? Yeah, kinda."

"I knew there was something weird about them."

"That's what they were doing when we showed up. They stick their feet in the ground and the trees are like, 'Hey, see any caterpillars today?' 'Nah, I saw a beetle, though.'"

Amused, Zadie half smiled. "Is that what you think trees talk about?"

"Sometimes. At least, that's what Rowan said. Oh, and there's one more thing . . ." Finn's smile faded. "Rowan thinks her mom is *in* one of them."

"What? A tree?"

Finn nodded.

"Huh." The cracks in Zadie's suspension of disbelief were beginning to show. "Do you believe her?"

"I don't know. Maybe . . ."

Zadie looked through the window again at Myron and his kids. "Myron's really cool with us staying here another night?"

"That's what he said."

Zadie accepted her answer with a nod, and Finn turned to go back inside.

"Finn?"

She withdrew her hand from the door handle and turned to face her sister.

"You'd tell me if something was up, wouldn't you?"

"What do you mean?"

"Like, if all of this was too much? The echoes and everything. It's just that yesterday, you—"

"I'm fine. I swear." Finn stepped inside, leaving Zadie alone on the porch.

The second Finn entered the house, she felt a twinge in her chest, a thumbprint of the pain she'd felt the night of her mom's accident. Rather than rejoin the Van Houtens, she slipped into the hallway that led to the downstairs bathroom. The sound of their laughter trickled away and her ears began to ring as if a bomb had just gone off. She shoved open the bathroom door and quickly locked it behind her just as an echo began to dig its claws in. The twinge in her chest had intensified to a bright spark of pain. She closed her eyes and pressed her back against the wall, fists clenched so tightly they were nothing but veins and bone.

After several excruciating seconds, the pain subsided, leaving behind a faint burn like acid in her throat. When she opened her eyes, a face blinked back at her.

It must have been her reflection. It had to be.

But why didn't she recognize the person frowning in the mirror?

She lifted a hand to her chin.

There was a bandage there and a plum-colored bruise on her jaw.

She'd been in an accident, that much she remembered.

But everything that came before it was a fog.

A knock at the door.

Ma'am? Are you okay? *a voice said.*

Amy. That was the woman's name.

But what about hers? She must have one, too.

Ma'am?

Yes. I'm fine, thanks.

We'd like to help you. Will you tell me your name?

A pause.

My name's Wren. *She'd always liked that name.*

It's nice to meet you, Wren.

Wren was crying now.

Her real name was not the only thing she'd forgotten.

Then it came to her like coming up for air:

Her girls! She had daughters!

Wren threw the door open.

What is it? *Amy asked.*

I have—

I *had*—

I . . .

Amy took her hand. It's okay, Wren.

It's okay.

When Finn came to, she realized that she'd been crying. She recognized the reflection in the mirror—the bowed mouth, tight curls, and round, tawny cheeks—but even though she looked like herself again, she didn't *feel* like herself. The echo may have passed, but she could still feel its presence, like a shadow hitching a ride on the soles of her feet.

"My name is Finn," she said to the face in the mirror, but the name felt like paste on her tongue. She swallowed, and she and her shadow made their way back down the hall.

After all the eggs, muffins, and burnt bacon had been eaten and the plates were stacked in neat rows in the dishwasher, Rowan and Finn announced they were going on a hike.

Juniper leaped out of her chair and ran after them, nearly tripping over her too-long overalls. "Can I come?"

"Not until you do your chores." Myron watched his youngest's face sink.

"But Rowan has chores, too!"

"She did hers already. So did Hazel."

"But it's Saturday," she pouted.

"What does it matter if it's a Saturday? You're on summer break. Every day is a Saturday to you. Now go brush the goats."

"Ughhh. Life's so unfair." Juniper moved toward the door like she was stomping mud off her boots.

"You're telling me," said Myron, deadpan, as the screen door slapped behind her. Zadie and Joel were the only two left in the room. He smiled at them wearily. "So got any plans for the day?"

"Not really," Zadie said. What she really wanted to do was keep an eye on Finn, but it appeared she'd made a friend, and Zadie didn't want to intrude. After her overreaction this morning, she needed a few hours to herself to unwind, maybe take the hammock for a spin and crack open a book.

Just then a loud, nasal sound filled the room. Zadie thought for a moment that a goose had found its way inside, but then she turned toward the sound and saw Hazel sitting in front of a flimsy music stand, a long black instrument in her hands. Myron shouted over the noise, "Hazel, could you practice your oboe in your room?"

Hazel pulled the reed out of her mouth, making a slurping sound as she did so. "But the acoustics in here are way better!" she protested.

There was no acoustic configuration, Zadie decided, that would improve the sound coming out of that oboe. *Can I just skip the part of being a parent where my kid is learning an instrument?* she thought. That, or she would have to invest in some noise-canceling headphones.

"Okay, okay." Myron caved. "Carry on."

Hazel impatiently resumed her solo. Halfway through a shaky first measure of Pachelbel's Canon in D, the instrument started to make a gurgling sound. "Oops, forgot to dump it." Hazel unscrewed the bell of the oboe, releasing a dribble of spit onto the rug.

Myron winced apologetically to Zadie and Joel. "Do you guys want to go fishing?"

Zadie had never been fishing before, and she didn't have a burning desire to learn, either. Joel, on the other hand, already had the hat, which perfectly complemented the waders Myron let him borrow. Zadie was wearing a pair that had once belonged to Myron's wife. They were slightly more flattering than Joel's, but not by much.

"That's a good look on you," Joel teased as Zadie joined him on the Van Houtens' front porch.

"Yeah, my mom was always telling me I looked good in rubber, but I didn't believe her."

Joel put his hand to his chin in a thinking pose. "I mean, it's *good*. There's something missing, though . . ." He felt around inside his pockets, fished out a pair of aviators, and placed them on Zadie's face. As an added flourish, he flipped up the tinted clip-on lenses. "There."

"I feel like a retired baseball coach."

Even with the door closed, the melody of "Clair de Lune" as performed by a terminally ill goose drifted out of the house.

Joel shifted his weight awkwardly. "So you want to explain to me why you were so freaked out about Finn this morning?"

The question caught Zadie off guard. "Oh. Yeah, sorry about that," she stumbled. "I know I overreacted."

"What did you think was going to happen to her?"

Zadie wanted to tell him how scared she'd been the first time

Finn had gone catatonic; how her sister would run off without warning; the panic that would set in as she called her name and got no response. She wanted to tell him about the distant look she sometimes saw in her sister's eyes, like there was a mist floating in them; that she'd seen her mother's eyes look that way, too. She wanted to tell him everything, and she almost did before Myron bustled out the front door carrying three fishing poles and a large tackle box. "You guys ready?"

The creek was knee-high and so clear Zadie could actually see rocks rippling on the bottom. A fish passed by her leg, lazily swishing its tail back and forth like it was fanning itself on a muggy afternoon, which it was. The temperature had climbed steadily since that morning, as had the humidity. As she swatted a fly buzzing past her ear, she felt like she was back in Texas. All that was missing were the cattle.

"Put your thumb on top like this, and keep your rod in line with your forearm," Myron instructed. Zadie copied his form, trying her best to keep her forearm straight.

"Good," he said approvingly. "Now, on the back cast, you want to think about drawing a straight path with the rod, not an arc. You want to pull back smooth, stop and pause, then just before the line straightens out behind you, you cast. Watch me." Myron whipped his line behind his body, the bright yellow fly sailing across the blue sky. Then he snapped the line back, reversing the fly's trajectory and landing it gracefully in the water downstream. "Now you try," he said, circling to the other side of her so she would have room to cast.

"Uhh, okay." Zadie ran through the steps in her head, but despite her best attempt, the fly landed only a few feet in front of her. "Well, I suck at this."

Myron smiled. "You cast a second too late. Reel it in and try again."

It took Zadie several more tries before she made an acceptable cast, but it was still nowhere near as good as Joel's. His first cast elicited a long whistle from Myron. "You're a natural."

"Thanks!" Joel grinned proudly, catching Zadie's eye as he did so. Zadie looked away but could still feel his eyes on her.

Myron stepped to the side, cast his line out, and the three of them stood there quietly, listening to the gentle gurgling of the creek and waiting patiently for a tug on the other end of their lines. Zadie finally started to understand the appeal of fishing. It was an excuse to do absolutely nothing besides stare out at a body of water, which was, if she really thought about it, exactly what she did at the beach. "Do your kids like to fish?"

"Not even a little." Myron chuckled. "I was hoping at least one of them would be into it, but Rowan feels bad for the fish, Hazel thinks they're slimy and refuses to touch them, and the one time I took Juniper out, she spent the whole day looking for turtles. I guess none of them got the fishing gene."

"Our mom used to make us go camping."

"I take it you weren't so keen on it?"

"I would come down with a lot of mysterious last-minute illnesses."

"Ah, yes. Hazel once told me she thought she had scurvy the night before a recital."

"Oh, I had that once before a spelling bee."

"Must have been going around." Myron chuckled again. "Was it just you girls and your mom?"

"Yeah. Our dads were never really part of the picture. Mom didn't really trust a lot of other people."

"I get that." Myron's smile slipped a little. "It can be hard, though. Doing it on your own."

Zadie realized with a tinge of shame that she hadn't given it much thought. Until the year before her disappearance, her mom had always seemed so unflappable, so independent. But it couldn't have been easy, taking care of two girls with only the money she earned at the dairy farm. And still she somehow found the energy to make them dinner, brush the knots out of their hair, and bend over their math homework with them until one or both of them fell asleep at the kitchen table. *That Nora would never have left her children,* Zadie thought. *Maybe that Nora was still out there somewhere.*

"Yeah. It was hard for her." Zadie turned her attention back to her line, half hoping they didn't catch anything and they could just continue to stand there, watching the water.

Ever since she was little, Finn had loved to climb trees. The maple was excellent for climbing. Its branches were broad and sturdy and hung low enough that you could pull yourself onto them without needing a boost. The moss provided a bit of cushion, too, so once Finn had found a perch, she lounged on the bough like a leopard, letting her limbs dangle, and pressed her ear against the bark. She wasn't sure what she expected to hear. A pulse, maybe? Whispers? If trees could feel, did it hurt when she dug her heels into its trunk? She suddenly felt guilty for climbing it without first asking permission.

On the ground below, Rowan heaved a frustrated sigh as she stepped out of a fresh hole. "I give up," she said, throwing her spade down at her side. "I was sure it was this one."

Finn sat up and swung her leg over to face her. "Have you tried any other trees?"

"Yeah. A bunch. But we used to play here all the time as kids. If she was going to be in any of them, I assumed it would be this one." She sat down hard on the ground and groaned. "Maybe my dad's right. This is a waste of time."

"What's a waste of time?" Juniper and Hazel appeared behind her.

Rowan frowned. "You guys followed us?"

"You should be thanking me," Hazel said, hands on her hips. "I got Dad out of the house. Now he can't catch you out here."

"Where'd he go?"

"He's fly-fishing with Zadie and Joel."

Fishing? Finn couldn't picture her sister participating in any activity that involved sticking her fingers in an animal's mouth.

"Whatcha doin'?" Juniper asked, looking from Rowan up to Finn, then back to Rowan again. She looked like a forest sprite in her ragged shorts and unwashed hair.

"Don't worry. She knows," Rowan assured her little sister.

Juniper grinned playfully at Finn. "Cool, huh?"

"Very cool," Finn agreed.

Hazel bent down and picked up Rowan's discarded spade. "I think it's time we tried a different tree."

"What tree?" her sister answered bitterly. "I tried all the ones I could think of."

"What about that one?" Juniper asked, pointing to a nearby cedar. "Or that one?" Another cedar.

"Juni, we can't just check every tree in the forest. Do you know how long that would take?"

Juniper started chewing on the end of a cornflower stem, which only amplified her puckish appearance. "The whole summer, probably."

"Well then, *you* can spend the summer digging holes, 'cause I'm out."

Juniper shrugged, plucked the spade from Hazel's hands, and started digging at the base of one of the cedars.

Finn called down to Rowan: "Do you mean that? Are you really giving up?"

"No, she's not," Hazel answered for her. "She says that every day."

"I mean it this time."

While Hazel and Rowan bickered, Finn pulled the painted rock out of her pants pocket, felt its heft in her palm. "I've wanted to give up, too."

Rowan gazed up at her. "You have?"

"Yeah." She reached down from the branches and held the rock out to Rowan. "This rock was supposed to help me find her. I was sure I'd figured it out, but we showed up and nothing happened."

Rowan examined the stone in her cupped hand. "You went to the coast?"

"It's not the coast. It's a volcano."

Rowan turned the rock a hundred and eighty degrees. "Ohhhh. Right. I see it now," she said, then passed it back up to Finn.

Finn rotated the rock until it was upside down. Sure enough, it looked like a bird's-eye view of a craggy coastline. Finn studied the wisp of white paint that had once looked like smoke and now looked like the frothy curl of a wave. Then, before she had time to properly brace herself, she heard a telltale ringing in her ears . . .

It was her favorite spot. A knobby old pine.
Its bark scratched her bare thighs.
Like saying grace, her fingers threaded together, resting on top of a pumpkin-round belly.
In the branches of a giant maple, two young girls were climbing. Her girls.
"Too high!" Her voice seemed to echo.
The oldest stopped and said something to the youngest. The youngest clung sloth-like to a branch, hair hanging like Spanish moss.
The sky was so bright and clear it seemed to chime.
Sun. Water. Air. Love.
Everything Amy needed to live.
A tap on her arm like a butterfly landing. A woman, face green with bruises, sat beside her.
She said the words beautiful *and* family. *She was talking about hers.*
The woman called herself Wren. Amy didn't think it was her real name.
I could sit here forever, *Amy said.* Watching them.
Her girls. Her audacious, smart, wild girls.

When Finn opened her eyes, she was facedown. She *had* been in the tree, and now she was on the ground.

"Finn!" Someone was shouting. Finn rolled onto her back and looked up to see Rowan, Hazel, and Juniper hovering over her. Juniper gave her a light slap on the cheek, a move she'd probably learned from cartoons. "Are you okay?"

"I'm fine," Finn groaned, sitting upright. "Just another echo."

Rowan helped her to her feet. "What was this one about?"

Finn looked to her left. Thirty feet away, in the middle of the clearing, stood a crooked old pine. Its trunk was squat and gnarled and stooped to one side; its limbs bowed chivalrously low to the ground, bristly clumps of needles clinging to their tips. It wasn't a pretty tree, but it looked to Finn like the perfect tree to sit on and watch your children play. "Try that one," she said, nodding in the pine's direction.

Rowan followed Finn's gaze to the twisted pine. "Really? It looks half-dead."

"Just try it."

Juniper offered the spade to her older sister, who took it with a shrug. She stopped a few feet from the crooked tree and began to dig while the others watched. When the hole was deep enough, she gave a cursory glance over her shoulder, then stepped into the soil and slid into a trance.

Seconds passed. Then minutes. After five or so, Juniper started to squirm. "She's been in there a long time." While they debated whether to wake her, Rowan abruptly stumbled backward, nearly losing her balance. When she turned around, she appeared to be in shock. "What happened?" Juniper blurted.

Rowan gazed out at the pock-holed clearing, her words faltering. "She—she said I made a mess of the grass." Her sisters gaped back at her, speechless, then Juniper let out a part gasp, part sob, ran to the trunk of the pine tree, and pulled it into a bear hug. Hazel was slower to react, but even she started to tear up. "You're serious?" she asked.

A smile broke over Rowan's face like a wave. "I'm serious."

"What . . . How . . ."

"You know how we're the ones who have to reach out?"

"Yeah."

"She reached out *first*. I didn't even have to ask questions. She did most of the talking, as usual." The girls broke into a complicated amalgam of laughter and tears and grabbed one another's hands. Finn couldn't help but feel a prickle of envy as she watched them. They had found their mom. She was still looking.

Finn backed away to give them some space. She watched them from the maple as they dug two more holes. By the time all three of them had slipped their feet into the soil, Finn was gone.

When Myron's truck pulled up to the house, Zadie spotted Finn sitting on the porch steps, squinting in the sun. "Hey," she said as she dropped down from the cab, "how was the hike?" Zadie, of course, knew there'd never been any hike, but she wasn't going to ask *so what did the trees have to say?* with Myron in earshot.

"Good" was all Finn said in return. She had that distant look in her eyes again, the one she'd had when they'd arrived the day before.

Myron had climbed into the truck bed with the fishing gear and was handing a tackle box down to Joel. "Will you take that inside for me?"

"Sure thing," Joel answered.

Myron turned to Finn. "The girls in the house?"

Finn shook her head. "No, they wanted to keep hiking."

"Hazel and Juniper, too?" He sighed, then grumbled, "I guess I'll brush the goats myself."

By the time they'd finished unloading the truck, Zadie heard excited whispers coming from the woods. When the Van Houten girls stepped out of the trees to find their dad glowering at them, their chatter swiftly abated.

"Juniper, I wasn't joking when I said you have chores to do."

"I know, but—"

"Why can't you just do what I ask you to do, instead of turning it into an argument every time?"

"But, Dad! We talked to Mo—" Rowan shot her sister a warning look, and Juniper bit her lip. Zadie thought she saw the girl trembling—from fear? Excitement? It was hard to tell.

Myron's face was hard. "Hazel, take Juniper inside. I need to talk to Rowan."

Hazel and Juniper scurried away, ostensibly grateful not to have to face what was likely about to be an unpleasant conversation. Finn quietly excused herself as well and made her way toward the barn. Zadie was about to do the same when she remembered her phone was still in the truck.

Myron trained his eyes on his daughter. "Were you talking to that tree again?"

"*That tree?*" she snapped. "She has a name."

"Just answer me."

Rowan's eyes glistened. "It's *her,* Dad! She wasn't in the maple, she was in the pine, the one she used to sit on. I talked to her. We all did."

As quietly as she could, Zadie stepped up into the cab of the truck, but her phone wasn't on the seat where she'd left it.

Myron closed his eyes and threaded his fingers behind his neck. "Dr. Mallick—"

"Dr. Mallick doesn't know anything."

"She said you need to grieve, honey."

"Why would I need to grieve? She's *right there*!" Rowan pointed accusingly up the hillside. "It was her, Dad! How else would she know that Mom's favorite ice cream was cookie dough?"

"Rowan—"

"Or that she used her fingers to wet envelopes because she was scared of getting a paper cut on her tongue?"

"Rowan, please—"

Zadie's phone must have slid under the seat. She felt around on the floor for it, trying unsuccessfully not to eavesdrop.

"She said to tell you that she misses you and that she wants to see you—"

"That's enough!" Myron's cry was simultaneously formidable and heartbreaking. *I shouldn't be hearing this.* Zadie stilled herself, hoping to fool Myron into thinking she'd already left.

She barely heard his next words, but somehow they felt louder than anything else he'd said. "It's not your mom, Rowan. It's a tree."

Hurried footsteps. A door slammed.

The truck rocked slightly as Myron sat down on the tailgate. After a few seconds of uncomfortable silence, he said, "I'm guessing you heard all of that?"

Zadie tentatively angled her head toward the open back window. "Yeah."

"If anyone ever found out about them—"

"I won't say anything. I promise."

More silence.

"I really fucked up."

"She'll be okay."

"Will she?" Myron answered, glancing over his shoulder.

Zadie hesitated, remembering the last fight her mom and she ever had. Had *she* turned out okay? Not exactly. But her mom had left. Myron was still here. "You're a good dad," she said. "You're sticking it out. Not everyone would."

"Thanks." He sounded unconvinced.

The truck was still running, Zadie realized. She killed the engine and listened to the gentle clicks it made as it cooled.

After a moment, Myron said, "Amy called it *tree talk*."

Zadie turned around to face him and tried to sound surprised. "Your wife could talk to trees?"

"My wife could do anything, including talk to trees," he said with a wistful smile that said *better to have loved and lost.* He picked up a loose fly from the bed of the truck and twirled it between his fingers.

"Sometimes I wish Amy were here instead of me. She was better at this kind of stuff. If the kids walked up to her and said, 'Dad's in a tree,' she wouldn't hesitate. She'd do something crazy like grab an old sheet and a projector and play movies outside so we could all watch them together." Myron chuckled sadly, imagining the scene. "Me? I can't even say hi."

Zadie paused, then answered, "That sounds like a good place to start."

Finn stared out the window of the little barn apartment, unable to recall her own name. In every echo she'd ever had, her name had always been her North Star. She knew who she was and who she wasn't. She knew which memories were hers and which belonged to someone else. That distinction is what kept her sane.

But as she looked down at what she knew intellectually to be her own hand, she had the unsettling thought that the hand, the arm, and everything it attached to did not belong to her, that this body was just a vessel, one she was currently using to reach out the window, pull the bird feeder from its hook, and upend a bag of seeds.

Her name? Her name was irrelevant now, it seemed.

She turned to see a woman standing at the top of the stairs to the apartment, watching her.

"Hey."

"Hey."

It was Zadie, her sister. That would make her Finn.

Finn. Finn. Finn. She would need to think of some way to remember it. Write it in permanent marker on her arm perhaps, or somewhere more discreet so Zadie didn't suspect she was losing herself. *If losing myself is what it takes to find Mom, then that's what I'll do,* she thought, although the prospect made her uneasy.

She screwed the top of the feeder back on and returned it to its hook outside the window. "How was fishing?"

Zadie lingered in the doorway. "It wasn't that bad, actually."

"Who are you and what have you done with my sister?" *Zadie's the one who really should be asking that question*, Finn thought as she struggled to remember her own birthday.

"I know, right?" Zadie moved into the living area and sat on the arm of the couch. "So what do you think happened?"

It took a moment for Finn to realize she was talking about the Van Houten girls. "I believe them."

Zadie looked thoughtful for a moment. "I can't believe I'm saying this, but I do, too."

Finn looked out the window to see a sparrow perched on the feeder, completely unperturbed by her presence.

"Have you heard anything from Mom yet?" Zadie asked.

Finn remembered the feeling of her mother's hand on her shoulder. *Like a butterfly landing*. "I had one of Amy Van Houten. Mom was in it."

"What was she doing?"

"She was just sitting with her on a tree. Amy's tree. They were friends, sort of."

"Yeah, Myron mentioned that."

"If they were friends, maybe Mom told her where she was going."

Zadie looked wary. "I mean . . . maybe, but I don't think Myron's gonna let those girls go back out there any time soon."

"You're probably right . . ."

"He might let us stay a little longer if you need more time."

Finn nodded noncommittally. More time was exactly what she needed, but she'd already asked her foster parents to extend her trip once. What were they going to say when she broke the news that she wasn't coming home the following day like she'd promised?

"There's also this . . ." Finn fished the painted rock from her pants' pocket and tossed it to Zadie, who looked back at her quizzically. "Turn it upside down."

Her sister did as she was told. "What am I supposed to be seeing?"

"What does it look like to you?"

"An upside-down volcano."

"Rowan thinks it looks like a coastline."

"Oh. Yeah, I can see that." She handed the rock back to Finn. "Are you telling me you want to drive to the coast?"

"I don't know. I just thought it was interesting, that's all."

Zadie studied her for such an uncomfortably long time that Finn thought she was trying to start a staring contest. "You seem . . . different," her sister said finally.

Finn. My name is Finn. "In what way?"

Zadie held her gaze a second longer, then stood up from the couch. "Sorry. That was a stupid thing to say." She smiled apologetically. "I'm gonna go to the house. See if Myron needs help with dinner. Wanna come with?"

"Actually, I might take a shower."

"Okay." Zadie stood and walked to the top of the stairs. "I'll come find you later." She pulled the door behind her with a soft click.

Finn turned her attention back to the wilderness out the window. Wind swept through the valley and, for a moment, she thought she could hear the thousands of evergreens whispering to each other, sharing the secrets of the forest. More than anything, she wanted to know what those secrets were, and whether any of them had to do with Nora Wilder.

It wasn't Myron who Zadie found in the kitchen this time but Joel, wearing his favorite wolf shirt and a pair of oven mitts. He glanced over at her as he reached into the microwave. "Oh, hey, Zadie!" he said, pulling out a large steaming green jar.

The smell made Zadie's stomach turn. "Are those *pickles?*"

"Yeah," he said, setting the jar on the counter and fanning it with his right mitt. "Want one?"

Zadie gagged slightly. "No. I'm good."

Joel shrugged and retrieved one of the warm, limp pickles from the jar and took a bite. It didn't so much crunch as squelch. "Wanna watch TV or something?"

Zadie could feel bile rising in her throat. She tried breathing through her mouth. "Actually, I might go down to my car and listen to music for a bit."

"Can I come with you?"

"Sure. But you have to leave the pickles."

Joel didn't object, but when Zadie turned toward the door, he grabbed one for the road.

Blue hair looks rad on you." Joel was holding a photograph inches from his nose. It was of a teenage Zadie and her mom jumping on a motel bed, their matching lapis-blue hair branching out around their heads like coral.

"Yeah. Not sure I could pull it off now." Zadie was sitting cross-legged next to him in the back of the station wagon, thumbing through the box of Nora's cassettes.

"I think you could."

Zadie gave him side-eye, then plucked a cassette from the box and held it up for Joel to see.

He nodded approvingly. "Good with me."

Zadie climbed over the console, popped the tape into the player, then settled next to him.

Joel flapped the photo as if he were waiting for it to develop. "I think me and your mom would have gotten along."

"Why do you say that?" Zadie laughed.

"We've both got cool hair. Good taste in music. Magnetic personalities."

"Inflated egos."

"That, too."

A piano began to play over the speakers. A few bars later, a voice joined it.

Hush, darling, hush
It's almost dawn
The birds are singing
I must move on

"I love this song," Zadie said. "Mom used to sing it to me all the time when I was young."

"A little depressing for a kid, isn't it?"

"I don't think it's depressing."

"Isn't it about a woman leaving her husband?"

"Well, yeah, but not because she doesn't love him. It just isn't working out and they both know it."

"That's depressing."

"No, it's sweet. Listen . . ."

I want more for you
And for that I'll take less of you
I've taken enough from you
Already

Joel appeared unconvinced. "I thought songs like this would make you sad, considering—" He stopped himself.

"Considering my mom left?"

"Yeah."

She shrugged.

Joel handed the photograph back to Zadie. "Can I be real with you for a sec?"

Zadie tossed him a questioning look. "Sure."

"Why do you want to find her? I mean, all I remember is you talking about how much you hated her for leaving."

Zadie hesitated. The change of heart had snuck up on her, too. They'd been at the Van Houtens' for only a little over twenty-four hours, but in that time she'd received a crash course in being a single parent. Every hour contained dozens of decisions, big and small, that determined how healthy and happy and loved your children felt. Nora had committed the worst sin of all: she'd made Zadie feel unloved. But what if the decisions Nora had made the day she left—walk out door, get in car, drive away—had not been her own? Then she was no more to blame than Zadie, who made the decision not to stop her. "Because," she began, "I'm starting to think it wasn't her fault."

Joel, skeptical, continued, "I just remember how much you used to cry over her. It made me so angry. I wanted to find her myself so I could tell her—I don't know what I would've said . . . that you deserved better or something."

Zadie lifted her eyes to meet Joel's, testing his sincerity. He didn't flinch. Gratitude welled inside her. She remembered nights spent crying in his arms, how he would hum soothing songs and stroke her hair until she fell asleep. "Thank you," she said, threading her fingers through his. Joel squeezed her hand back. Then his fingers drifted up her wrist, her forearm, her shoulder. When his fingers reached her neck, she knew he was about to kiss her.

Twenty

Three Days

(until Nora Wilder's disappearance)

"It's not fair! I want blue hair, too." Zadie had thought Finn might be jealous that Nora and she had gone to the beach without her, but that didn't even come up. After almost two weeks of her little sister sulking and attempting to make her own dye by breaking open ballpoint pens, their mom finally gave in and painted a blue streak into Finn's curls. "I can't wait to show it off at the festival," she said as she ran the blue tendril through her fingers.

Nora and Finn attended the Hog-Wild Chili Fest every year without fail. Despite its name, it was so much more than just chili. There were bands, barbecue, carnival games, and contests that involved men putting hot peppers on their tongues and trying not to cry in front of a bunch of strangers. It was an activity that Zadie—averse to both crowds and spicy food—had no desire to participate in, so it had become Nora and Finn's own little mother-daughter tradition.

"Are you sure you don't wanna come this year?" Nora asked Zadie, who was watching TV upside down, her legs slung over the back of the couch.

"Nope."

"Zadie hates fun," Finn said.

"No, I just hate chili."

"Well, if you change your mind," Nora continued, guiding her younger child toward the front door, "we'll be in the chili tent, eating our body weight in beans."

"Gross."

"Love you." Nora took a moment to blow her daughter a kiss before leaving the house.

Ever since their trip to the beach, Zadie and Nora had been in a good place. It helped that Nora had been acting more like her old self. Her eyes were clear and they made Zadie feel seen. It felt like they'd turned a corner: that maybe whatever it was that had made her mom act so strange was finally over.

That is, until two hours later when she got a call from her sister.

"I need you to come pick me up." Finn sounded annoyed.

"Why? Where's Mom?"

"I don't know. She's not answering her phone."

Zadie kept her voice even. "Where are you now?"

"I'm at the security tent. They tried paging her, but she probably didn't hear it. It's pretty loud."

"Okay. Stay there. I'll be there in fifteen minutes."

Through the bustling crowd, Zadie spotted her sister sitting on a bench outside the security tent, absentmindedly swinging a bag of kettle corn between her legs. "Finn!" Finn looked up as she approached. "Are you okay?"

"Yeah. I guess."

"Still no sign of Mom?"

"No. She's probably looking for me, too." There was an anxiousness in Finn's voice that broke Zadie's heart. *How could Mom do this?* Forgetting to give your teenager a ride home was one thing; leaving your twelve-year-old alone at a busy festival was another.

"Yeah, you're probably right," she answered, trying her best to disguise her anger. "Come on. I'll walk you home. Then I'll come back and see if I can find her."

"Why don't we just look for her now?"

"Because . . ." *I don't want you to see Mom that way.* "I think I left the door unlocked. I want to lock it before Mom gets home."

How hard could it be to find someone with blue hair? As it turned out, very hard. Zadie searched every booth, every tent, every bathroom line, but Nora was nowhere to be found. There were fleeting moments when she would worry that something had happened to her. But then she would remember the anxious look on Finn's face and the anger would come rushing back. After she had spent an hour wandering the festival grounds, the anger was all that was left.

The one place she had yet to check was the event stage, where a corn-fed rock band was in the midst of a harmonica solo. A sea of mostly middle-aged spectators was grooving along on a grassy slope, sipping from their beers as they danced. This wasn't exactly Nora's scene, but Zadie scanned the crowd for her anyway.

Finally she spotted her standing off to the side of the stage next to a tall man with a tattoo sleeve. Something he said must have been funny, because she was touching his arm and laughing. The sight of her mother yucking it up with some stranger while she'd been combing the whole park for her made Zadie's blood boil.

She charged toward her. "Mom!"

The man with the tattoos was the first to notice Zadie, followed by Nora, who gave her a curious look. "Hey, hon. What are you doing here?"

"I've been looking for you," Zadie shot back.

The man with the tattoos quietly slipped back into the crowd. Nora glanced after him briefly, then returned her attention to her daughter. "Is something wrong?"

"Yeah. You're over here flirting instead of taking care of your kid."

"I'm confused . . ." Nora narrowed her eyes. "What, exactly, are you accusing me of here?"

"Where's Finn right now?"

"Finn?" she answered like it was a trick question. "I . . . I don't know."

"You don't remember leaving Finn alone?"

"What? No!"

"If you don't remember ditching your daughter, what *do* you remember?"

Nora looked around. Several other festivalgoers were staring at them now. "Can we wait to do this at home?"

"No," Zadie said, defiant. "I've been waiting for months for you to tell me what the fuck is going on. We're going to talk about this now."

Her mother anxiously ran her fingers through her mermaid hair. Zadie suddenly found herself resenting the fact that Nora's hair matched hers. "I don't know what you want me to say."

"Okay. I'll talk, then." Zadie squared her jaw. "I don't want you around Finn anymore. She's not safe with you."

"Zadie—"

"You're a bad mom."

The hardness in Zadie's voice cut right through Nora. She could see it in her mother's eyes.

"You don't mean that," she said, shell-shocked.

"Then tell me! Tell me why I should trust you."

With two words, Nora emptied all the breath in her lungs. "I can't!"

Zadie fell into a stunned silence, as if her mother's voice was still echoing off the walls of a cave. Then the sobs started. Nora clasped her hands to her mouth as her body rocked and dirty tears stained her cheeks. Zadie stood there awkwardly, unsure of what to do. She'd never seen her mother cry like this. It was unsettling, Zadie thought, to see a grown woman, her mother, nearly choking on her own tears.

Once Nora's sobs were under control, Zadie mumbled, "Are you okay?"

Her mother nodded, pushing hot tears off her cheeks with the heel of her hand. "I'm fine."

Zadie was too drained to comment on her hypocrisy. Her mom was not fine. She waited, giving Nora one last opportunity to tell her the truth. When she didn't take it, Zadie turned her back on her mother and walked away.

TWENTY-ONE

SEARCH PARTY

The sun ostensibly rose the next morning, but the clouds kept it hidden. Finn used the dimness to her advantage, slipping out of bed while Zadie was still asleep. It was six A.M. She had an hour—two if she was lucky—to do what she needed to do.

She pulled on a pair of hiking boots, slipped past a snoring Joel, and made it all the way down the squeaky staircase without his waking (his snores were so loud, she could hear them from the floor below). As she cut across the yard, the main house appeared on her left, and with it, a rip current of memories. She hurried past, head down. *Parallel to the shore.* That's what her surf instructor had told her two summers ago.

She turned onto the trail and was almost at the top of the hill when her phone dinged in her pocket. It was Kathy.

WHAT TIME WILL YOU BE HOME TODAY?

Shit. Not only was Finn apparently forgetting her own name, but she'd forgotten what day it was. Kathy was not going to be pleased when she told her they were at least two days' drive from home. It was not a conversation she was prepared to have right then, however, so she switched her phone to silent and left it and her boots under the maple tree.

Barefooted, Finn approached the crooked pine. "Hi, Mrs. Van Houten." She probably could have called her Amy, but she figured good manners couldn't hurt. "It's just me today. I hope that's okay."

A sudden breeze made Amy's tree's needles shake like rattlesnake tails. Finn shivered. She raised her voice so it would carry over the wind. "It must have been nice to talk to your kids again." As expected, the conversation so far was one-sided. She knew she wouldn't be able to communicate directly without Rowan there, but she still had one card she could play.

"I'm not sure if you can hear me, but if you can, I have some questions I'd like to ask you."

If Amy understood, she didn't show it. Finn placed her toes in the dirt like she'd seen Rowan do. She looked back up into Amy's twisted branches. "My name is Finn. You knew my mom. She told you her name was Wren, but it wasn't. It was Nora Wilder, and I'm trying to figure out where she went."

The wind died down and Amy's branches stilled. Finn felt an earthworm wriggle against her big toe.

"I know she probably didn't tell you where she was going, but if you know anything that might help me . . ."

Finn waited. Minutes passed. The soles of her feet began to feel clammy. The wind picked up again and hurried pewter clouds across the sky. She pulled the painted rock from her pocket, squeezed it until its cool surface began to feel warm in her fist.

It's not working, she thought, starting to feel self-conscious. She pulled her feet out of the dirt and sat on one of the pine's stooped branches, leaning her back against the trunk. "This is a lot harder than I thought it would be," she said, disheartened. Finn looked down at the rock in her hand and stared at the blobs of blue paint. Whether they were meant to represent sky or water, it didn't matter. Like her sister had said: *It's just a rock*.

So she threw it. Where it landed, she didn't care.

Maybe Zadie was right. Mom doesn't want to be found.

The wind stirred what remained of Amy's tree's branches. Finn closed her eyes. When she opened them again, she had a different name.

Amy watched her girls play.

The woman who called herself Wren stood under the maple tree, held out her hand.

She had mother's arms, strong but gentle. In them, Rowan floated like a dandelion seed to the ground.

The woman wrote something on her daughter's palm, then appeared next to her, smile like sun-softened butter.

You have a way with kids.

My girls like to climb, too.

Your girls?

Confusion like oil, fogging her eyes.

A flock of geese flew overhead. Wren watched them, rapt, unblinking.

I have to go.

And then she was gone.

Rowan ran over, held out her palm. Four letters were written on it:

N-E-S-T

There were other letters, too, but the ink was smudged, illegible.

Did she say anything to you, Rowan?

She said to come find her.

Is that all she said?

Rowan blinked. She called me Zadie.

Thunder rolled across Zadie's pillow. Her eyes fluttered open just as the first spots of rain dotted the windowpane. She turned to see Finn's side of the bed rumpled but empty. *She must be at breakfast.* Zadie was hungry, too, but she was in no hurry to run into Joel after last night. *He kissed me,* she thought, hardly believing herself. It was a fine kiss, the kind of kiss that would have most people buzzing the next day, but Zadie's stomach ached with guilt.

Once again she had gotten caught up in his kindness, mistaken it for something more. He was there for her then and he was here for her now, but that didn't mean they were getting back together. They couldn't. She would be a mom soon, and he would still be the guy who bounces from job to job, town to town, crashing in motel rooms without permission. But despite his faults, Joel still deserved better than to be her emotional crutch.

I'll let him down easy, she thought, knowing full well that there was no such thing.

Zadie waited until she heard Joel clomping down the stairs to the workshop before she left the bedroom. By the time she left the barn, she'd convinced herself that Joel might not even harbor any romantic feelings toward her. He'd imbibed that night (at least two fingers of whiskey and some of Myron's home-brewed beer). His wits were suspect on a normal day, let alone after a drink or two. Her theory, however, fell apart the moment she walked into the Van Houtens' kitchen and saw the way Joel looked at her.

"Zadie, heeeyyy," he said, awkwardly half standing at the dining table to greet her.

"Hey." Zadie's response was more succinct but no less uncomfortable.

Mercifully, the clumsy exchange went unnoticed by their host family. Myron looked up from his newspaper. "Morning. Pull up a seat. Finn on her way down?"

"You haven't seen her?"

"No. Why? She's not up there?"

"She got up before me." Zadie turned to the girls, who had been uncharacteristically silent since she'd walked in. "Have any of you seen her?" All three shook their heads.

Joel stood again. "You want me to help you look for her?"

"No, that's okay," she said, not wanting to repeat the embarrassing display of the previous morning. "I'm sure it's nothing. She probably just went for a walk."

"Bad morning for it," said Myron, glancing out the window. Outside, it was still only drizzling, but the wind had picked up. A storm was on its way.

Zadie took a seat at the dining table and helped herself to a bowl of Cheerios, but after only a few bites, she was no longer hungry. A clod of worry had formed in her throat. She couldn't swallow even if she wanted to. "Excuse me," she murmured and pushed away from the table.

Zadie checked the bathrooms, the whole second floor, and the sunroom. She walked back up to the barn apartment, but it was still empty, as were the woodshop and the surrounding yard. Zadie looked out at the gray clouds gathering over the mountain and felt a tingle down her neck. Then she heard the door to the house open. It was Joel. "Hey," he said, a nervous smile twitching across his lips. "I was wondering where you went. You worried about Finn?"

"Yeah. I checked the house and the barn. Couldn't find her. Something feels off." *Off* was a mild way of putting Finn's more alarming episodes, but she didn't feel like getting into it with Joel right then. She just wanted to find her sister.

"Do you have any idea where she might have gone?"

Zadie did, but getting there would require the Van Houtens' help. She went to the window and caught Myron's eye, waving him over. "What's up?" he said as he stepped out onto the porch.

"The tree the girls were climbing yesterday . . . where is it?"

Myron tensed and closed the door behind him. "Not far. About a third of a mile up the hill. Why?"

"I think that might be where Finn went. I hate to ask, but with the storm—"

Myron waved her off. "I'll grab us some rain gear."

The trail was slick. Even in hiking boots, Zadie could feel her feet slipping on the mossy rocks. Glassy pearls of water collected on her jacket sleeve, something between rain and mist that both fell and floated like the air behind a waterfall. Despite the conditions, it took Myron, Joel, and Zadie only ten minutes to reach the pine tree Finn had described. But Finn was nowhere in sight.

Zadie turned to Myron with a look of contrition. "Sorry. I thought for sure she'd be here."

"That's okay," he answered, distracted by the dozens of holes that encircled a giant maple tree. Zadie noticed them, too. They were similar to the holes she'd seen the girls standing in when they'd first arrived. Then Zadie spotted a pair of boots sitting at the foot of the same tree. "Shit." She ran over to them. "These are hers." Inside one of the boots, Zadie found her sister's phone.

"Why would she leave her boots behind?" Joel asked. Zadie had seen Finn running around on grass and sand and pavement in her bare feet, but even she would never trek through the deep woods without proper foot protection. It had to be an echo.

Myron pushed back the hood of his jacket and crouched down to look at one of the holes. The rain had started to turn them into puddles. He flicked the muddy water, and as he did, his fingers brushed up against something hard.

"Do you recognize this?" Myron held up something for Zadie to see. It was the painted rock her sister had been carrying everywhere.

"Yeah," she said, taking it from him. "She must have dropped it."

Something else caught Myron's eye. He stood and walked to the edge of the clearing. "I see a couple of prints here. Looks like she wandered into the woods. Why do you think she'd do that?"

The question was directed at Zadie. If she told Myron that she was almost certain that an echo was the cause of Finn's disappearance, that would mean admitting to both him and Joel that her sister had run off before. Thankfully, it was Joel who responded first. "Do you think it has to do with her . . . thing?"

"Her echoes? I guess it's possible." Zadie could feel her heart pounding through her jacket. Rain droplets began collecting in the folds, creating rivulets down her sleeves that looked like lightning bolts. "We have to find her."

Myron stood up abruptly. "My satellite GPS is in my car. Let's head back to the house and grab it along with anything else we might need. I doubt she got far, but we should be prepared in case."

Zadie felt both fear and relief simultaneously. Fear that her sister was possibly lost, and relief that someone else was taking charge of the situation. Joel placed a reassuring hand on her back. "We'll find her, okay?" Myron looked less certain but nodded in agreement.

When they arrived back at the house, Rowan was waiting for them on the front porch. She jumped off the swing as soon as she saw them approaching. "You didn't find her?"

Myron shook his head and opened the door to his truck. "She wandered off the trail. We're going to search the woods."

"I'm coming," she said without hesitation.

He didn't hesitate, either. "No, you're not."

"Please? This is my fault. I'm the reason she went up there in the first place."

He leaned into the cab of the truck and opened the glove compartment. "You need to stay here and watch your sisters."

"They don't need me to—"

Myron turned and said directly, "I'm not asking."

Rowan gave her dad a hard stare, then marched back into the house, slamming the door behind her.

Myron rejoined Zadie and Joel, GPS in hand. "Let's get moving. She can't have wandered far. We just have to put ourselves in her shoes."

Zadie hoped he was right, but her instincts were telling her otherwise. If an echo was responsible for her disappearance, then the thing they were looking for wasn't really Finn. It was a memory.

Twenty-Two

Not the Same Zadie

Finn was running. Nora *was running.*

She had no car. No bike. Just legs. She ran like her ancestors did before the invention of the wheel.

Amy was calling for her. She thought Nora was running away, but she wasn't. She was running toward.

Nora would have stopped and said goodbye, but stopping was impossible. All she needed was a running start—like the early flying machines—then her wings would do the rest. Any moment now, they would unfurl.

Any moment now.

Amy's voice was getting smaller and the water was getting louder.

Any moment now.

Rocks stamped themselves into the flesh of her bare feet. There must have been blood.

Any moment . . .

If she couldn't fly, she would have to swim. Some birds could do both.

Cool water, ankle-deep. Then knees. Waist.

Puffins could dive to depths of two hundred feet. Nora just had to make it to the other side of the creek.

The other side of the creek. Then the ocean. She had to make it to the ocean before . . .

Nora's thoughts were dropped stitches. Her feet, bloody. Amy's voice had been swallowed up by the forest and now she was alone.

Zadie, Joel, and Myron hiked back up the hill to Amy's tree and followed Finn's prints into the woods. A few minutes of walking led them to what would, on a normal day, be a spectacular view of the valley—vast evergreen forests shrouded in drizzle and fog—but under the current circumstances, it was more daunting than it was beautiful. Without any more footprints to follow, Zadie froze. "So, where do we go now?"

Myron wiped raindrops off his GPS. "Well, usually, when people get lost in the wilderness, they take the path of least resistance."

"You don't know Finn."

"I mean that they let the terrain lead them. Rivers, ridges, anything flat that gives the appearance of a way forward. If I had to guess, I'd say she most likely went that way." Myron pointed to what appeared to be a path that had been combed over with wild grasses. "It's not a man-made trail. Probably deer."

Zadie imagined her sister charging down the foot-wide path, kicking up rocks that skittered down the hillside, miniature previews of what could happen to her if she lost her footing. Supposing she did. Would self-preservation kick in, or would her body fall while her mind was somewhere—someone—else? She pushed the thought away. *It's going to be fine,* she told herself. Finn was lost, not dead. They were going to find her, and then they were going to find their mom. That was the plan.

Joel fell in step beside Zadie as they followed the deer trail past misty knolls covered in wagging wildflowers and tender-leaved saplings, before being swallowed by a grove of mature pine trees pressed into the ground like unlit birthday candles. Their stubby branches radiated out like spokes on a wheel, sky-high trunks moaning like old doors being opened. A carpet of bronzed needles, molted bark, and moon-shaped pinecones baffled the search party's footfalls. *They like quiet,* Zadie thought, allowing herself to indulge in the possibility that the trees were in fact listening.

Eventually Myron slowed to a stop. "Trail's gone," he said, surveying the forest floor.

He was right. The deer path was now a fork in the road with at least five branches that split off in different directions. Zadie looked from one identical path to the next. "What do we do now?"

"Well, we could try going downhill. If she was trying to find her way back to the house, she'd probably assume that was the right direction."

But what if she wasn't *trying to find the house?* If Finn had had an echo like Zadie suspected, she could have taken any one of these routes. Whatever world she was navigating in her head didn't have north, south, east, and west. It didn't have uphill or downhill. It only had forward. If Zadie was going to find her sister, she had to think like her echoes. She had to think like Nora.

Myron looked down at the illuminated shapes on his GPS screen. "If we keep heading straight, we'll hit the creek we were fishing at yesterday."

Zadie couldn't see the creek—it was somewhere deep in the veil of drizzle and ferric green shadows—but if she listened closely, she could hear its faint hiss. Devoid of a better idea, she said, "Let's try there."

"Why don't we split up?" Joel suggested. "We'll cover more ground."

Myron shook his head emphatically. "Because then I'd have three missing people instead of one."

Joel's eyes widened slightly and he said nothing more. Myron peered back down at his GPS and pivoted until his directional arrow was facing the thin blue line on the screen. "This way."

Because of the rain, the creek was much higher than it had been the day before. Then, it had come up to Zadie's knees, but now it appeared to be chest deep. It was much faster, too. Water churned over rock-shaped moss, throwing foamy spittle into the air. Whole tree branches were being whisked downstream, only to then get lodged in a dam that had been started by beavers but would likely be finished by mother nature.

"Creek's high." Myron may have been stating the obvious, but the subtext of what he was saying made Zadie's pulse climb. The creek was high; therefore it was dangerous.

As if being pulled by the current themselves, they began walking downstream. The rain picked up, pockmarking the water's surface. Exposed tree roots dangled from cut banks that had receded like swollen gums. Joel dropped to his knees and leaned over one such ledge. "Joel? What are you doing?" Zadie was about to pull him back by his pack when he sat up and pointed to something on the bank below. "Look! Down there!"

Zadie peered over the edge, and there in the backwater-soaked mud was an imprint. Not of a shoe, but of a human foot with five distinct toes.

"The rain hasn't washed it away yet," Myron observed as droplets fell from the brim of his hood. "It must have been made pretty recently."

"So we're going the right way, then?" Zadie silently admonished herself for the hope that crept into her voice.

"It's a good sign, at least." Myron didn't offer any more reassurance, and Zadie didn't ask for it.

But why was there only one set of footprints? Had Finn fallen in the water? Had she been carried away by the swift current only to end up as just another log in the dam downstream? Zadie left the two men behind and hurried along the bank, squinting through the curtain of rain at every human-size log, root, and rock. Then something ahead of her caused her to stop abruptly.

Someone appeared to have climbed up the creek bank. There were skid marks in the mud and clods of torn grass that had probably been used as handholds. If Finn *had* fallen in the creek, at least she'd made it out alive.

Thunder echoed through the valley like it was the inside of a drum. "Storm's here," Myron said as he caught up with her. Zadie's eyes flitted to the gathering clouds above. Behind one of them was a ghost sun wrapped in gauze. "We better get moving," he said, taking the lead once more.

Zadie could hear the downpour coming before she felt it. She pulled her hood up just in time to deflect the worst of the cloudburst, but the percussion on the fabric was deafening. Myron was moving his lips. She had to pull the hood back from her ears to hear him. "I said we should find shelter. Wait this out," he shouted over the rain.

"You want to stop? What about Finn?" Zadie shouted back, tasting rainwater on her lips.

"She probably stopped, too. See that tree?" Myron pointed toward a Douglas fir with great boughs that sagged under the weight of their own needles. The earth beneath the tree appeared mostly dry. "You guys take cover. I'll be right back."

"Where are you going?"

"I want to check that rocky overhang. Make sure Finn didn't hide out there."

Zadie was about to protest again when she imagined a tiny flicker in her abdomen. She couldn't risk getting hypothermia with the little Star inside her.

She and Joel settled themselves on the bed of needles and leaned their backs against the trunk of the fir. Joel's beard was dewy and wet strands of hair clung to his forehead. "Aren't you not supposed to sit under a tree in a thunderstorm?" he said.

"There's nowhere that *isn't* under a tree."

"I guess so." Joel gave Zadie a sidelong glance. "What are you thinking about?"

"I'm thinking that I'm cold, and if *I'm* cold, Finn's probably freezing right now."

"Maybe she brought a jacket."

"Maybe."

They watched a curtain of water cascade off the outermost boughs, creating their own little Cone of Silence.

"You know you can trust me, right?" Joel said, finally. Zadie didn't say yes, afraid of what would come next.

"If something's going on with Finn, I want to help."

"She's lost, and you *are* helping." She could feel Joel's scrupulous gaze on her like a magnifying glass.

"Then why for the last two days has she looked like she's just seen a ghost?"

The word "ghost" made Zadie shiver. She supposed Finn was haunted in a way, hearing and seeing things that weren't really there. Since they'd arrived at the Van Houtens', it had seemed like her sister was dragging all of those memories behind her like a sled. "I think she's overwhelmed," Zadie said. "That house has a lot of memories in it."

Joel nodded, indulging her half-truth. "Must be tough having all those thoughts in your head at once."

"Yeah . . ." There was more she could have said, more she wanted to say about her sister, her mom, herself; but Zadie had spent most of her life biting the heads off her fears before they had a chance to speak. She thought of it as self-sufficiency when it was really silent suffering. She had cried in front of Joel many times, but once her tears were dry, she would pretend as if nothing had happened. She was like a stray cat who cries at the back door for food, then once it has had its fill, slinks off as if it never asked for it in the first place. Joel had left his door wide open, and even now she couldn't bring herself to walk inside. "I hope the rain lets up soon."

"Me too" was all Joel said in response, his door clicking shut.

Myron appeared a moment later, flush-faced and breathing heavily. "Did you find anything?" Zadie asked him, grateful to have someone to break the awkward silence.

"Sorry. No luck." He pushed his hood back and sat knees-to-chest to catch his breath. "I'm gonna be straight with you . . . we've been out here for over two hours now. This might be too big a job for the three of us. We might want to start thinking about getting the sheriff involved."

"The sheriff?"

"She could send out a search-and-rescue team. I volunteer for them sometimes. If anyone's going to find Finn, they will."

Just then Zadie felt a vibration in her jacket pocket. It was Finn's phone. She pulled it out and tapped the screen to life. On it was a text from Kathy:

WHY AREN'T YOU ANSWERING YOUR PHONE?

WHERE ARE YOU?!

Zadie's mouth felt dry. If they called the sheriff's department, they would have to tell Steve and Kathy about Finn's disappearance. If the Andersons found out, their trip was over; their search for their mother was over. And as resistant as Zadie was at the beginning of their journey, she was invested now. So was Finn. If her sister had to go home early because Zadie contacted her foster parents, she would probably never forgive her. She finally had her sister back, and she wasn't going to give her up that easily.

Zadie returned the phone to her pocket. "There's one thing we haven't tried yet."

Myron studied her, then said warily, "And what's that?"

"I just need a minute alone."

Joel and Myron looked at each other. Zadie didn't wait for them to answer. "Please?" She thought it best not to share that the only recent success she'd had at deliberately using her psychic ability had been during a round of Psychic Karaoke.

"Sure." Myron climbed to his feet and gestured for Joel to follow.

"We'll be right outside if you need us," Joel said tentatively, before ducking back out into the rain.

Zadie waited until Joel and Myron were out of sight, then crossed her legs in front of her. If Finn could draw out her gift, so could she. After all, she'd mastered the art of pushing it away; she just had to do the opposite.

She had to relax.

Zadie drew in a deep breath and focused on the hammering of the rain on the forest canopy. She had never tried meditating before, but her impression was that it was about emptying your mind of all thought—a task, she soon realized, that was easier said than done. As soon as she closed her eyes, her worries started buzzing around her like gnats.

What if Finn's hurt?
What happens if I don't find her?
Am I doing this right?
Who am I kidding? I can't do this.
We should call the sheriff.

Flustered, Zadie's eyes popped open. "Fuck." She took another drag of damp air, felt her stomach rise and fall. "Come on. You can do this," she whispered on the exhale. She closed her eyes again and tried to think of something relaxing. *The beach . . .*

Warm sand. Sea breeze. Sun glinting off the water.
A good book and a good chair.
Waves tumbling and breaking.
Her mother beside her, pointing to a storm on the horizon.
Nora wading into the ocean as the waves turn gray.
A wave swallowing her whole.

Zadie shook her head in frustration. If the beach couldn't mollify her, then what could? Maybe she was doing it wrong. She needed something to focus on that had no expectations of her, that didn't try to force her to be happy but allowed her to find peace in whatever she was feeling.

Zadie placed her hands on her abdomen and began to hum.

She didn't think about what she was humming at first. She couldn't even hear herself over the rain. She could just feel the vibrations in her throat. Once she realized what the melody was, lyrics began to mold themselves around the notes, dove-soft syllables that melted like wafers on her tongue.

"Hush, darling, hush
It's almost dawn
The birds are singing
I must move on"

Zadie's pulse began to slow in time with the song.

"You'll say I didn't say goodbye
But we've been over this a thousand times
Wings were not meant for flying
In place"

Her mind was a screen door. Music flowed in like air while her thoughts paced outside.

"I want more for you
And for that I'll take less of you
I've taken enough from you
Already"

Her stomach sank while her head seemed to float.

"Hush, darling, hush
It's almost dawn
The birds are—"
Falling.

It was brief, but a premonition all the same. She started the chorus over.

"Hush, darling, hush
It's almost—"
Creek.
"Hush, darling, hush—"
The creek is falling.

The creek is falling? The strange message meant nothing to Zadie. Her premonitions were always a little cryptic, but this one didn't even make sense. The water level was rising, not receding. If the rain continued the way it was, it wouldn't be long before the creek flooded.

When the creek floods . . . She half remembered Myron saying something about this that first night on his back porch. They were looking out over the valley—

Zadie jumped to her feet and ran out into the rain. "Myron!" The men whipped around as Zadie stumbled to a stop in front of them, hair already drenched, blinking the raindrops out of her eyes.

"That bluff you can see from your house. You said it turns into a waterfall?"

"When the creek floods, yeah," Myron answered.

"Do you think it might flood today?"

Myron looked over at the rushing water. "I'd say it's likely."

"How far is the bluff from here?"

"Mile. Mile and a half. Why?"

"I think Finn's there. Or she *will* be. If we hurry, we can catch her."

Myron's skepticism caused him to hesitate momentarily before finally assenting. "Okay. Follow me."

The creek continued to rise as the rain continued to fall. They reached a bend in the creek, and the water was so high that the lowest boughs of the cedars were fighting against the current and the ferns clinging to the mossy bank were gasping for air. "We're almost there," Myron said, peering down at his GPS.

As they rounded the bend, it was clear the creek had indeed flooded. The forest floor was now a rippling pool of gray water that extended from the creek bed to the base of the granite cliffs to the south. "It looks like the swamps I used to kayak on when I lived in Georgia," Joel said, coming to a stop. "Without the gators."

Zadie dipped a boot into the floodwater, and all but the top lace disappeared. Myron looked out over the floodplain and pointed west. "Bluff's that way," he shouted over the rain. "We have to cross it."

Without another word, the three of them waded into the water. Zadie looked down and almost didn't recognize the murky, quivering reflection staring back at her. This woman with the wet hair and determined gaze was not the same Zadie as the one who'd left Texas with a beach bag full of romance novels.

That Zadie wouldn't have trudged through a rainstorm in the middle of the wilderness.

That Zadie wouldn't have broken the promise she'd made to herself to never use her ability.

That Zadie never wanted to see her mother again.

This Zadie, she realized, did.

She ignored the water splashing inside of her boots, ignored the stitch in her side and the burn in her muscles. Her sister needed her. Her mom needed her. And so she forged ahead through the drowning wood.

Myron slowed as they came to what appeared to be the western edge of the white pine forest. "We're here," he said. Zadie's heart vaulted into her throat. She was about to rush ahead when Myron held her back. "The rock is slick." His tone was sobering, parental. "Be careful."

Zadie nodded and stepped out of the forest onto a rocky outcropping. If Myron hadn't told her otherwise, she would have assumed she was wading through another branch of the creek. The water wasn't stagnant here, but flowed steadily across the smooth sheets of shale down a nearly imperceptible hill to the lip of a cliff. Where the water went after that, Zadie couldn't see, but what she could see through the rain was the thin frame of her sister silhouetted by an expanse of ashen sky. She was wearing a bright yellow raincoat, hood down. Her normally buoyant black curls hung in sad wet clumps like kelp washed up on the sand after a storm. She didn't move, but the wind moved her, the same gentle swaying motion that tricks birds into thinking scarecrows are alive.

Instinctively, Zadie took a hurried step forward and felt the ground slip underneath her. Her heart leaped, and she took a moment to steady herself before calling out, "Finn!"

Finn didn't give any sign of having heard her, just like her mom hadn't heard her when she'd found her teetering on the edge of another precarious drop-off six years earlier. That cliff, however, had been still and dry. This cliff had a current.

Zadie looked over her shoulder and locked eyes with Joel, who was following a few steps behind. He looked frightened. "Do you want me to grab her?"

"No," Zadie replied, trying to keep her voice steady. She caught Myron's eye, too. "I don't want to spook her. Let me try and talk to her before we try anything else."

Joel was about to respond, but Myron beat him to it. "We'll be right behind you."

Zadie turned back around and began inching forward. If she startled her sister on the slick rocks, Finn might vanish over the edge of the cliff with the floodwater. From their back porch, the Van Houten girls might see her fall, a drop of yellow amidst the shower of blues and grays. If they blinked, they would miss her.

Panic had Zadie by the throat. She could feel it tighten the closer she got to the edge of the bluff. Zadie tried talking to Finn again, hoping that maybe she hadn't heard her the first time she'd spoken. "Finn, it's Zadie. Are you okay?" she said. She tried to sound calm, but her voice wavered.

No answer. The rain was falling sideways now. Mist rose from the exposed shale that had spent the previous day baking in the sun. To Zadie, it both looked and felt like a bad dream.

"Look. I don't know if you can hear me, but I'm just going to start talking." Zadie swallowed. "Wherever you think you are, you're not. Whatever you do, do *not* take another step. I want you to turn around very slowly. Turn toward the sound of my voice."

Finn did not turn. She did not move.

Zadie took another cautious step forward. "You're having an echo, Finn. Do you remember what that means? It means you're not yourself. It means whatever you think is happening happened a long time ago . . . to someone else."

Six feet of water still stood between her and her sister, only it wasn't really her sister. Finn was trapped in a memory, and Zadie had a pretty good guess as to whom it belonged to. It was her she needed to reach.

"Mom?"

Finn stirred. She was listening.

"Mom, I know it's you. Look, I know things didn't end great between us." She crept closer. "Some of that is on me."

Finn's head turned slightly.

Zadie continued, "I was angry. But I'm not anymore. I want us to work this out, but I need you to come to me."

Slowly Finn began to turn, like a music box ballerina on her last pirouette. When she finally faced her sister, Zadie's breath caught in her throat. The light behind Finn's eyes reminded her of their mother. The similarity was striking enough that it was a few moments before Zadie could find her voice again. "Something was wrong, wasn't it?"

Finn gave no indication of having heard her, but the eyes glinted in confirmation. Zadie hazarded another step in her direction.

"You needed help. I wanted you to talk to me, but you wouldn't. I think you were trying not to scare us. You were trying to protect us from something you couldn't explain." Zadie realized she was crying. Finn's eyes were wet, too, but whether it was from tears or rain, she couldn't tell.

A few more steps. She was within arm's reach now.

"I let you down," Zadie said, her voice cracking. "I'm so sorry."

Something in Finn's face changed then. Nora's light made its way from just her eyes to her brow and lips. She was now looking at Zadie the way their mother would when she thought her daughters weren't looking. It was a look that said: *You don't know how wonderful you are, but I do.*

Zadie had missed that look. It took everything she had in that moment to not start sobbing. She took a moment to compose herself, then continued, "But now I need you to help me. I need Finn back so I can get her to safety. Can you do that for me?"

Finn's gaze drifted down to Zadie's outstretched hand as rainwater pooled in her palm. Then, as if in slow motion, Finn extended hers, too. Zadie threaded her fingers through hers and guided her sister—her mom—gently away from the waterfall's edge.

Once they were a safe distance from the cliff, Joel hurried forward just in time to catch Finn as her legs gave out. He lifted her in his arms and carried her to a mossy hillock on the edge of the floodplain. As soon as he laid her down, it became obvious to everyone why she had collapsed. The soles of her bare feet were bloody. Several of her toes were bruised and swollen, and one was missing a nail. Zadie gasped loudly enough for Joel to hear. He turned to Myron and asked, "Do you have a first-aid kit?" but Myron was already ahead of him. He pulled a red plastic box out of his pack and handed it to Joel.

"It's okay, Joel. I can do it," Zadie said, her squeamishness apparent.

"I got it. I trained as an EMT."

"You *did?*"

"I mean, I just completed the training. I ended up bailing on it for a job at a haunted house."

Zadie was simultaneously impressed by his expertise and unsurprised by his lack of commitment to it. "What are you doing now?" Her hands were shaking.

"Cleaning the wounds so they don't get infected. Will you hand me the alcohol?" Zadie passed him a bottle with a small red plus sign on it, and he rinsed the soles of Finn's feet with it. She groaned but didn't say a word. When the wounds were clean and free of debris, he applied antibacterial ointment and wrapped her feet in gauze. "We'll need to carry her." Then, to Myron, "How far's the hike back?"

"Three miles, give or take. Do you want me to take the first shift?"

"No, you navigate. I'll carry." Joel turned back to Finn. "I'm going to lift you, okay?"

Finn's gaze rolled slowly skyward, as if her reply were trapped in the clouds.

"Has she ever done this before?" It took a moment for Zadie to register that Joel had asked her a question. She was too busy searching her sister's face for signs of their mother. But it appeared she was gone. "No. She usually snaps out of it by now."

Joel didn't need to hear any more. He scooped Finn up in his arms like a rag doll, her mummified feet dangling at his side.

We did it. We found her, Zadie thought. But as they hiked back down the mountain, she couldn't shake the feeling that Finn was still somewhere out there wandering the forest, leaving muddy footprints in her wake. It took an hour and a half to reach the Van Houtens' home, and in all that time, Finn's eyes—Nora's eyes—never left the sky.

Twenty-Three

Waves of Smoke

Finn came to in a dark room. The first thing she felt was a throbbing sensation in her feet. Unable to wiggle her toes, she sat up in bed and looked down at the bandages that bound them together. She had no memory of hurting her feet. In fact, she had no memory at all of the past twelve hours. The last thing she remembered was sitting on Amy's tree and looking into the mossy branches of the maple.

She'd spent every moment between then and now lost in her mother's memories. Even now, as she looked down at the body that was ostensibly her own, something didn't feel right. She felt like she was Nora assuming her daughter's body, that *this* was the echo, not the other way around. All of a sudden, the room felt stifling. She needed fresh air.

Zadie lay next to her on the bed, softly snoring. Finn moved slowly, so as not to wake her, and tenderly placed her weight on her feet. She sucked in a quick breath as all the nerves in her feet fired at once. When the worst of the pain had passed, she limped out of the bedroom and down the stairs to the workshop.

There was a light on downstairs. As soon as Finn saw Myron bent over his workbench, she froze for fear that one more step would lead her into another of his heartbreaking memories. He looked up, glasses precariously clinging to the end of his nose. "Hey, there. How are you feeling?"

"Okay," she said. "My feet hurt."

"I bet." Myron pushed his glasses further up his nose. An awkward pause followed as if he was waiting for her to ask him a question he didn't want to answer.

Finn pointed to the piece of wood on his workbench. "What are you working on?"

"Oh, this?" Myron glanced down at the wood like it was the first time he was seeing it. "Just taking some measurements for a bookshelf I'm building."

"To sell?"

"Hopefully."

Finn nodded. She wasn't really interested in the bookshelf. She was more interested in the man building it. "My mom built a chair once."

"Oh, yeah?"

"It was really wobbly."

"Chairs are hard to build."

"I used to sit in it so she wouldn't feel bad."

"That was nice of you."

Finn shrugged and took the last few tentative steps down the staircase. Thankfully, no echoes were waiting for her at the bottom. "It was the least I could do. She was always complimenting every ugly piece of pottery I made in art class."

Myron chuckled. "I have three homemade ashtrays, and I don't even smoke. If only my wife had let me homeschool them . . ."

"Why did you want to homeschool?" It was a prying question, but Finn was genuinely curious.

Myron avoided eye contact by resuming measuring the lumber in front of him. "I didn't want them getting made fun of because of their . . . you know. Especially Juniper. She doesn't know how to turn it off sometimes."

Finn understood. She remembered her mom worrying the same thing about her when the echoes had started. "Are they picked on?"

"Sometimes," he said, marking the wood with his pencil. "But for normal kid reasons. Honestly, I think they're better adjusted than I was at that age." He paused. "I still worry about them, though."

Based on what Zadie had told her about Myron and Rowan's fight, he was still not ready to take his daughters at their word. There was no reason, then, that he should trust a stranger, but Finn decided to try anyway. "I was the one who found your wife."

Myron's ruler slipped and the pencil veered off course, scoring the wood at a strange angle. He paused for a moment, eyes downcast, then said tersely, "My wife is dead."

"I know." Finn pictured him in his black suit and lavender tie. "But maybe . . . she's not totally *gone*, either."

Myron kept his head bowed. His glasses had begun to slip back down his nose. Sensing that she'd crossed a line, Finn excused herself and began hobbling gingerly back up the stairs.

"Hold on."

She turned back around. Myron set down his pencil and locked eyes with her. "You really saw her?" His voice was quiet, uncertain.

"Yes."

"What was she doing?"

"She was watching the kids play."

Myron nodded thoughtfully, then resumed his work as if they'd never spoken.

Zadie expected Finn to be gone when she awoke, but there she was, peacefully lying next to her, bandaged feet poking out of the bottom of the comforter. The amount of relief she felt at seeing her there was as palpable as if her sister had returned from the dead. She was safe now. But for how long? Could Zadie really keep track of her every move? *I'll handcuff us together if I have to*, she thought.

Of course the other option would be to turn back, to come clean to Steve and Kathy so they could lock Finn in her room until she broke free of whatever force had taken hold of her. It would have been the responsible thing to do. But every time she contemplated this, she pictured the look on her sister's face—her mom's face—as they stood facing each other in the rain. She wanted, *needed* to see that face again. And she could only do it with Finn's help.

"Hey," Zadie said when Finn's eyes eventually fluttered open.

"Hey." She looked dazed, unfocused. She pointed to her feet. "Do I want to know how this happened?"

"I'll tell you later."

Finn nodded in agreement, then slumped back onto her pillow. "Later sounds good."

"You scared the shit out of Joel."

"I did?"

"Not me, though."

"Just Joel."

"Yeah."

Finn attempted to smile but grimaced as it stretched the skin on her chapped lips. "I know you want to talk about this later—"

"Right."

"—but I have something to tell you."

Zadie gifted her the silence to continue.

"I think Rowan was right. The painting wasn't a volcano. It was the ocean."

"How do you know?"

Finn's tone was uncharacteristically flat, unmoved. "Because in my echo, I needed to get there for some reason. Nothing else mattered. I just kept running."

"You mean *Mom* needed to get there."

"Yeah. That's what I meant." Finn tried smiling again. "Looks like you're going to get your beach vacation, after all."

It was true. Zadie would get to see the ocean. But the thought of lounging on a beach chair—after everything they'd been through—felt hollow. "I don't want a vacation," she said decidedly. "I want to find Mom."

Finn searched her sister's face, but if she was looking for falsehoods, she wasn't going to find any. Zadie had meant what she'd said.

"Crap." Finn sat up suddenly. "I left my boots and phone up there."

Zadie pulled Finn's phone and the painted rock out of the drawer in her nightstand and handed them to Finn. "I didn't have room for the boots. I'll head up there now and fetch them for you."

"You sure?"

"Absolutely." Then, in a spontaneous and uncharacteristic show of affection, Zadie gave her sister a quick hug. "I'm glad you're okay." But before Finn could hug her back, she was on her feet and out the door.

Ding. Finn swallowed. She knew who the text was from before she even looked at her phone.

Twenty-three texts. Fifteen missed calls. Eight voice mails. The text that Kathy had just sent read:

IF YOU DON'T CALL ME BACK IN FIVE MINUTES, I'M CALLING THE POLICE.

One ring. "Finn?"

"Yeah. I'm so sorry, I—"

"Where are you?"

She hesitated. *No more lies.* "Washington State."

"What the hell are you doing in Washington?"

No more lies. "Zadie and I went to find our mom."

Kathy was silent for so long, Finn thought the line had gone dead. "You still there?"

"I'm still here."

Her foster mom had a habit of playing with her wedding ring when she felt hurt. That's what Finn pictured her doing while she waited for Kathy to speak.

"Was this Zadie's idea?"

"No. It was mine. I didn't say anything 'cause I didn't want to hurt you."

"And look how that turned out."

Finn closed her eyes as if her shame were something she had to see to feel.

She heard Steve's voice, faint, in the background. "Yes, it's her," Kathy said. "Do you want to talk to her?"

He must have declined, because Kathy continued. "You know what really makes me sad?" There was a sort of resignation in her voice. "That you felt like you had to hide this from us."

"I know. I—"

"I'm not finished." A pause. "Look, I know I'm not your mom, but I've always considered you my daughter. Even if your mom showed up on my doorstep today, I'd still consider you my daughter, adoption or no adoption. If you feel like this is something you have to do, I get it, but when it's over just . . . come home. Please."

The greatest gift Finn could have given Kathy in that moment was to tell her she was giving up her search, that she'd jump on the next flight to San Antonio and be there by the evening. But she couldn't, so she did the next best thing. "See you soon . . . Mom."

Zadie managed to get herself all the way up the hill without getting winded. The Star formerly known as Ladybug would have applauded if it had had hands, but those wouldn't come for another few weeks, so Zadie had to settle for taking pride in her own accomplishment without any external validation.

She saw Finn's boots sitting under the maple and started to move toward them when a figure in the clearing made her stop abruptly. His back was turned, but it was clear by the stoop of his shoulders that the man was Myron. He was standing before the gnarled pine, speaking in hushed tones. Zadie couldn't make out what he was saying, but she had a guess as to why he had come up here alone.

She watched him for a moment. His body language was awkward, circumspect, but when he placed his calloused palm tenderly against the trunk, Zadie felt a surge of emotion on his behalf. Maybe his wife was somewhere behind the crust of bark, busy crafting the tree's next ring, or maybe she wasn't. It hardly mattered. The love was real. It lived outside both of them in the whispering leaves and bubbling creek. It lived in mountaintops and pollen and on the wings of birds. It lived in their children.

Before Myron could notice her, Zadie quietly retrieved Finn's boots and slipped back into the forest.

Finn sat on the front porch stoop watching Joel help Zadie load the station wagon. The out-of-body feeling she'd experienced that morning still lingered, but at least the echoes had subsided. She felt like she was finally seeing the Van Houtens' house for what it was, not some den of loss and misery, but a home—a home where the saddest thing that happened inside its walls was vastly outnumbered by the thousands of beautiful things.

The Van Houten girls had spent the last hour on the porch swing telling their favorite stories about their mom. From the picture they painted, it was no wonder Amy and Nora had sparked a friendship. To borrow her mom's expression, they both "marched to the beat of their own xylophone."

"Thank you," Rowan said, taking a seat next to Finn on the stoop.

Finn waved her off. "It's no big deal."

"Seriously. If it weren't for you, we never would have found her. I'd still be digging holes all over the forest."

"I'm just happy my echoes could be useful for once."

"I can't wait to talk to her again." Rowan smiled briefly before her eyes drifted downward. "That is, if my dad lets me."

At that moment, Finn spotted Myron sneaking out of the woods. "I bet he will," she said.

"Headed out?" Myron strolled up to the station wagon just as Zadie slammed the back door closed.

"Yeah," her sister answered. "We should get on the road if we want to get to the coast by dark."

"The coast?" Joel said, confused. "I thought you were heading home?"

"Not yet. We still need to find Mom."

"But Finn—"

"I'm fine." Finn stood and approached the others with as normal a gait as she could muster without wincing. "We're so close. We have to finish this."

Joel shook his head slightly. He clearly had reservations about the plan, but he held his tongue.

"Well, it's been a pleasure having you here," Myron continued. He seemed lighter somehow, a shade or two shy of happy. "Now who am I supposed to fish with?"

Zadie shrugged. "You could try convincing the girls again."

"Nope!" all three of them said in unison.

"Well, there you have it!" Myron laughed easily. "When you find your mom, tell her I say hi."

They finished saying their goodbyes, and Zadie and Joel climbed into the car. Before Finn could join them, Rowan pulled Finn into a tight hug and whispered, "I hope you find her."

"Me too," she answered.

The six-hour drive to the Washington coast was too quiet for Zadie. Finn sat in back, her injured feet propped up on the seat next to her, drifting in and out of sleep. The previous day had been hard on her, so Zadie was content to let her rest. Joel rode shotgun but spent most of the drive gazing out his window at the islands dotting Puget Sound and the jagged forests of the Olympic Peninsula. "Whoever sees Bigfoot first, wins," Zadie tried joking after an achingly long silence between them. "You're on," he said halfheartedly, then never mentioned it again.

He'd been acting distant all morning: avoiding eye contact, mumbling one-word answers to her questions. Zadie could only assume it had something to do with that moment between them in the station wagon. Joel must have picked up on her lack of interest in pursuing the relationship further. If that was the case, then why tag along? Why not ask her to drop him at the nearest bus station?

Zadie hoped the ocean would lift their spirits, and as she caught a glimpse of her sleeping sister in the rearview mirror, she hoped that everything they had been through, everything *Finn* had been through, would be worth it.

Zadie had called ahead and booked an oceanside motel room for them to stay the night in, but as she was about to pull into the parking lot of the single-story building with the neon narwhal on the side, her gaze drifted down to the beach at the end of the road. At least two cars were parked on the sand, with tents erected next to them. One belonged to a man and his dog playing a game of Frisbee on the misty edge of the waves.

For some reason she couldn't quite put her finger on, she didn't turn into the motel parking lot. She continued straight, toward the ocean. *I'll get sand in my sleeping bag again*, Zadie thought, remembering the way it crunched between her teeth when she woke in the morning. But it didn't matter. Something about it just felt right.

The station wagon rolled onto the beach and Joel glanced behind them, confused. "I thought we were going to a motel?"

"You can take the room if you want. I'm camping."

The black sand beach was littered with driftwood, some logs as big as whole trees. Zadie set up their tent next to one such trunk that was angled toward the sinking sun while Joel dug a hole for a fire. Finn sat on a picnic blanket, staring out at the monolithic sea stacks that rose from the waves. Many were boulder-like and crested with conifers, while one was shaped like an arch. Finn wondered if when the tide was low enough, you would be able to walk through it like a doorway into a fantasy world. The longer she stared, the more she felt drawn to them, and the more drawn she felt, the more her mind slipped. Soon she could look at nothing but the flock of gulls orbiting around the pinnacle of the nearest sea stack. Zadie was the first to notice the far-off look in her eyes and followed her gaze up to the looming rocks. "Creepy-looking, aren't they?"

Finn knew someone was speaking to her, but she didn't recognize the voice. She didn't even recognize her own voice when it left her mouth. "Yeah, creepy." Her mind was still circling the rocks.

"Hole's done," Joel said, clapping the sand from his hands. "I'll collect some wood."

"Do you want help?" Zadie asked.

He wouldn't look at her. "Nah, I'm good," he said and wandered off down the beach.

Zadie stared after him for a moment, then sat down next to Finn on the blanket. "He's mad at me."

"Why?" Finn's own voice sounded tinny, like she was hearing herself through a bad phone connection.

"Because I think he wants to get back together, and I don't."

Finn shifted her weight, but otherwise gave no indication that Zadie had spoken.

"We kissed."

This got Finn's attention. "What?"

"Yeah . . . I really screwed things up."

Finn followed Zadie's gaze to Joel, who was now a hundred yards down the shore digging through a pile of driftwood. High above him, the halo of gulls called out to each other and the sea.

Joel stayed in the motel room that night while the girls slept in the tent. Zadie blocked the door with her body so that if Finn had another echo and tried to leave, she would have to crawl over Zadie to do so. Thankfully her sister slept soundly, and so did she.

The next morning Zadie woke to the sound of her name being whispered by a silhouette on the nylon door. She leaned forward and unzipped it, being careful not to disturb her sleeping sister. Joel poked his head inside. "Can I talk to you?"

"Yeah. Sure . . ." Zadie crawled out of her sleeping bag and followed him down to the waves. He held his bucket hat in one hand and a plastic grocery bag in the other. "I considered leaving without telling you," he began, staring out at the ocean, unsmiling. "Then I realized that would be an asshole move."

Zadie was momentarily dumbstruck. "Wait . . . where's this coming from? Does this have to do with the other night? Joel, I'm really sorry, but—"

"You don't think we should date again. I know." His voice was calm, measured, as if he had practiced this conversation already in his head. "I knew that's how you felt the second I kissed you."

Zadie blushed with shame. "Why didn't you leave then? Why now?"

"Because that's not why I'm leaving," he said, defensive. Then, regaining his composure, "At least it's not the only reason."

Zadie's first instinct was to beg him to stay, but then she realized that would be selfish. Joel had loved her once—and maybe still did—but what she had given him in return wasn't love at all. It was grief in love's clothing. She had worn the disguise well, well enough that she herself hadn't realized she'd used Joel to fill a void, one that her mother had left, and it didn't matter how Joel contorted himself, how many limbs he disjointed, he would never quite fit.

And now he was trying to let her go, and she owed it to him to not make it harder than it had to be. "I get it. I really do. I still care about you. You know that, right?"

"Stop it. You're giving me déjà vu."

"Déjà vu?"

"You said the exact same thing when we broke up."

Zadie fought the urge to explain to him what déjà vu really meant. "I still mean it."

"Do you want to know the real reason I'm leaving?" Based on the hard look on his face, Zadie wasn't sure she did. "It's because I think you're making a huge mistake."

"What are you talking about?"

"Finn." Joel's mouth was a tightrope. "She could have died in those woods. Now you're dragging her out here?"

"I didn't *drag* her anywhere. This is what she wants."

"Do you think she's really in a position to be deciding anything? Have you seen her lately? She's a zombie, Zadie."

"She's just tired."

"Those echoes are messing with her head."

"She promised me she has it under control."

"Oh, yeah," Joel scoffed. "She can barely walk or speak, but everything is cool, I guess."

Zadie's temper was a pilot light and Joel had just struck a match. "Who are you to tell me what's best for my own sister?"

"What about Finn's foster parents?"

"What about them?"

"Shouldn't they have a say in what's going on here?"

"They have nothing to do with this."

"What are you talking about? They're her family, Zadie!"

"*I'm* her family! I'm not going to let you or anyone else take her from me."

"Is that what you think I'm trying to do?" Joel said in disbelief.

"It's what everyone's trying to do! Five years we've been kept apart because of people like you who thought they knew better. Mom leaving ruined everything. Everything was broken. Now I finally have a chance to fix it, and you think I should just go home?"

Joel looked stunned and hurt. "Are you listening to yourself right now? I know you think the world is plotting against you, Zadie, but it isn't. You got dealt a shitty hand, but you're not the only victim here. Finn lost her mom, too."

"You think I don't know that?" she snapped. "I'm doing this for her. I drove across the country for *her*."

"Finn needs help."

"She has me!" Zadie was trembling with anger. She barely noticed the frigid wave that broke around her ankles. "I'm the one who found her in those woods. I can keep her safe."

The heat behind Joel's eyes tempered. "I hope you're right," he said sadly, then turned abruptly and walked back to camp. Zadie watched him stop beside the tent and briefly bend down next to Finn's pack before disappearing behind the wooden fence that separated the road from the beach. Zadie returned to camp herself and noticed something small safety-pinned to the strap of Finn's pack: an embroidered patch of a bright yellow bird. *He must have taken it off his hat,* Zadie thought as the fire in her gut diminished and was replaced with regret.

"Joel, wait! I'm sorry!"

But by the time she reached the fence, he was already gone.

That morning, it felt like a starter pistol had gone off in Finn's brain. For the first time in days, she felt like something resembling her old self. The heartbreak that had been her near-constant companion during their stay at the Van Houtens' had dissipated. Now she was free to feel as sad or as happy as she wanted.

The tent flap was open and waved in the salty sea air. Finn peered out at the wedge of gray sky and water. This wasn't the kind of beach you spread your towel out on and worked on your tan. It was the kind of beach on which you found yourself shipwrecked. *Maybe that's all driftwood is,* Finn thought. *Broken masts worn smooth.*

Zadie stepped into view, a blanket wrapped around her shoulders. For several minutes, Finn watched her watch the ocean. She'd heard raised voices earlier that morning. She'd only caught bits and pieces of Zadie and Joel's conversation, but she'd picked up enough to know it hadn't gone well.

Finn crawled out of the tent and hobbled over to Zadie on her bandaged feet. "Where's Joel?"

Zadie turned to her, withdrawn. "He had to go."

"Oh . . . He didn't say goodbye," she answered, disappointed.

"He left you something, though. Check your bag."

Finn smiled when she saw the tiny yellow bird. "I'm going to call him Chris."

"Are you sure you want to do that? You've had pretty bad luck with Chrises."

"Yeah, but this one can't fly away," she said as she pinned the bird to her hoodie.

Zadie squinted at her. "What's that on your hand?"

Finn flipped her hand over and pulled up her sleeve. In black permanent marker, the word *nest* was scrawled repeatedly from palm to elbow. She let out a sharp breath. "I must have done it in my sleep."

"Do you know what it means?"

"I think it's from the echo I had when I was lost in the woods. Mom wrote it on Rowan's hand."

"Why Rowan?"

It was only then that Finn remembered what Rowan had said to Amy: "*She called me Zadie.*" She turned to her sister. "Because Mom thought she was you."

"Me?" Zadie pulled her blanket tighter around her shoulders. "She was trying to give me a message?"

"I think so. There were other letters, words maybe, but they were smudged. *Nest* was all I could make out." *Nest.* The word meant nothing to Finn. What could her mother have possibly been trying to tell them?

"What happened next?"

"I don't know. I just kept running." Suddenly an echo crashed into Finn's field of vision. It was so brief that she hardly knew it was happening, but the image lingered.

She wades into the ocean, the fog
Hair wet
Arms at her sides
Black waves crash around her
But she doesn't waver
She needs the sea to come and take her

Zadie must have seen it in her face. "What's wrong?"

"I think it was Mom . . . She was in the water." She looked out at the whitecapped tide barreling down the black sand. "The waves looked like they were made of smoke."

Zadie followed her gaze. "Are you feeling up for a walk?"

Finn nodded. How she was "feeling" was irrelevant, and both of them knew it.

As Zadie and Finn made their way slowly down the volcanic beach, the air cooled and more fog rolled in. The sea stacks now seemed to float on the mist like a cloud city. Waves would burst from the fog, then retreat back to it, hissing like injured sea creatures. It was the kind of dreamlike place that should have been full of memories, but either they had all been carried away by the fog or Finn just couldn't sense them.

"Getting anything?" Zadie asked.

"No. It's like this place has no memory, like we're the first people ever to come here." She knew this couldn't be true, of course, but the quiet and stillness were unnerving and a bad explanation was better than none at all. A place without memory was a place without life. Had they unwittingly stumbled into some kind of underworld? Finn pulled the reins on her imagination. They weren't dead. They were on a beach—a dark, lonely, unsettlingly quiet beach.

A small colony of sandpipers appeared on the sand in front of them, then scuttled out of the way. As Finn watched them run, her attention was brought suddenly back to the stinging in her feet. "So you were the one that found me? In the woods?"

The question was so out of the blue, it seemed to catch Zadie off guard. She looked at Finn questioningly.

"I heard you and Joel fighting," Finn clarified.

"Oh. How much did you hear?"

"Not a lot. Is that why he left?"

"He was scared you were going to get hurt." Zadie tucked her hands into her jacket pockets, then continued. "He thought we should quit."

"What did you say?"

"I told him you had it under control."

Finn swallowed. Not even she believed that anymore.

"I had a premonition," Zadie added. "That's how I found you."

"Seriously?"

She nodded. "I can't believe it worked."

"I can."

The girls shared a knowing smile like it was a telephone made from two cans and a piece of string.

Then through a break in the mist, Finn spotted a figure. "Look . . ." It was a long-limbed woman with wavy hair that reached the middle of her back. She was wading into the waves as if she were going for a dip, but she didn't move like she had any intention of swimming. She barely disturbed the water, arms limp at her sides as the ocean slowly pulled her into itself.

"Mom!" Finn took off in a hobbling sprint down the sand.

She had heard of time slowing down in moments of crisis, but as she raced toward her mother, time did not slow so much as it reversed. Finn was eighteen, then a few steps later, she was seventeen. By the time her toes touched the freezing water, she was thirteen and crying into the pillow of a strange bed. And when she had waded through the last of the sea and fog, when she was in arm's reach of the person she'd spent five years hoping to find, she was twelve years old again, picking up her mom's discarded anklet, squeezing it in her fist until it made painful impressions of their initials in her palm; calling out for her mom in every room of the house until the windows steamed with her breath and the despair she'd expelled from her lungs was inhaled again, starting the cycle all over. And so it was in an unexpected flash of anger—not joy or longing—that she forcefully grabbed her mother's shoulder.

But the startled woman who wheeled around to face her was not Nora, and by the bewildered look on her face, she clearly didn't recognize Finn, either.

Finn's heart bottomed out. "I'm—I'm sorry. I thought—" she stammered, but before she could finish her sentence, she was already wading back to shore.

"Hey! Hold on!" the woman called after her, but Zadie was already helping Finn out of the water and onto the sand. They were both drenched from the waist down. The wind blowing against Finn's legs made her skin prickle.

"You guys are gonna freeze like that," the woman said, catching up to them. "Come with me. I have towels and hot tea in my car."

Embarrassed, Finn declined. "It's okay. Thanks, though." As she tried to slink away, dripping and shivering, Zadie hung back. "She's right, Finn. It's a long walk back." She turned back to the woman. "I'll take some tea."

The woman smiled and adjusted the zipper of her wet suit. She looked to be in her late thirties, muscular with violet shadows under her eyes and a slight dimple in her chin. "Earl Grey, okay?"

"Earl Grey is great," Zadie answered.

Finn reluctantly followed Zadie and the woman to her car, which was parked at the end of a short boardwalk. She opened the back of her hatchback and pulled out three towels. "I'm Yasmine, by the way," she said as she passed one to each of them.

"Thanks. I'm Zadie."

"Finn." Finn wrapped the towel around her shoulders and stared sheepishly at the ground. "Sorry, again. I thought you were someone else."

Yasmine waved her off and pulled out a thermos. "Don't worry about it. The sea has a way of making people see things." Yasmine extended a cup of tea in Finn's direction. Finn accepted it but did not drink. "Although you've got me curious . . . Who did you think I was?"

Finn felt a sudden urge to scream. She had been so certain this was her mother, so certain and yet, so flagrantly wrong. Had she simply seen what she wanted to see? And if that was the case, could she trust any of her instincts? "Our mom."

Yasmine handed Zadie a steaming cup, too. "Was she supposed to be meeting you here?"

"Something like that."

The woman sat on her car's bumper, blew on her cup, and gazed out at the waves. "I've been swimming here every day for ten years. Not many people are willing to come out on a day like this."

"You swim every day?" Zadie asked.

"Twice a day. I can't help it." There was a coyness in her voice, as if she was hoping one of the girls would ask her to elaborate. When they didn't, she continued, "What does your mom look like? Maybe I've seen her."

"You didn't," Finn said flatly. "She's not here."

Finn could sense her sister wanted her to stop there, but she kept talking. She no longer cared who knew about her echoes. "I see things from the past. My mom stood on a beach just like this." She turned back to the ocean. "But that was probably a long time ago."

Yasmine exhaled suddenly, disturbing the gentle S of steam from her tea, but otherwise she seemed unruffled by Finn's story. "I used to be a horrible swimmer, you know," she said after a long pause. "Nearly drowned five, six times. Once I had to be dragged out by an elderly member of the Polar Bear Club." She laughed, clearly more amused by her own near-death experience than her audience. "People used to ask me why I kept going in the water if I couldn't swim. I told them, 'Because the ocean calls to me.' I made it sound like a joke, but they wouldn't have believed it, anyway."

She took another sip of tea, then continued. "Every low tide. That's when it happens. The ocean just sort of pulls me to it. I figured, either I could sit around waiting for the day I finally drowned, or I could learn to swim."

Finn finally looked Yasmine in the eye. Here was another kindred spirit, another person at the mercy of something beyond her control, but out of everyone they had met on their journey, this woman seemed the most at ease with herself.

"You're not afraid?" Zadie asked.

"Sometimes. When it's stormy. On those days, I wear a life jacket. But even on stormy days, I'm still a hundred times safer than I was back when I was in denial about my . . . whatever you want to call it." She patted her toned biceps and grinned. "I'm also in better shape."

Finn stole a glance at her sister. "What happens if you don't go out at low tide?"

Yasmine's smile faltered a little. "It's awful. It feels like I'm being ripped in two, like half of my body is moving with the tide and the other half is swimming against it. I'd rather take my chances with the ocean."

Finn thought back to the night on the motorcycle, to the popping in her chest that felt like her ribs were expanding. She turned to her sister. "That's like what Mom felt. The night of the accident."

"Do you think that's what it was? She was being pulled by the tides?"

"If that's true, then why hide it from us? Why wouldn't she just move us closer to the coast?"

"I don't know. It doesn't make sense."

Yasmine turned her cup upside down and watched her last remaining drop of tea dissolve in the sand at her feet. "Maybe she didn't know." Both girls turned to look at her. "I was almost thirty before I finally figured out what was happening to me."

Zadie turned to Finn. "It's possible."

Finn finally took a sip of her tea and felt the warmth not just in her throat but everywhere, from her toes to her temples. The fog had mostly cleared, and she could now see miles down the coast. Somewhere on that horizon was Oregon, then California, and beyond that, Mexico. Eight thousand miles: that's how long she would have to walk on blistered feet in the hopes that her mother would happen by the same beach at the same time she was passing. The improbability of it felt like a slap in the face. She felt stupid and naïve. "We should get back."

"Yeah, we should," Zadie agreed. "I could use a hot shower."

Yasmine stood. "I'll give you guys a ride."

True to her word, Yasmine dropped the girls off at the motel down the street from their camp. "Let me know if you need anything else," she said. "You know where to find me."

"Actually, there is something . . ." Zadie leaned on the passenger-side window. "Does the word *nest* mean anything to you?"

"Nest?" Yasmine tapped her index finger thoughtfully against the steering wheel. "Nest, nest . . . There's a little beach town about ten miles south of here called *Ear*nest. Cute place. Great waffles . . . Sorry, that's all that comes to mind."

Zadie nodded. "No worries. Thanks for the ride. And the tea."

"Anytime. Good luck." Yasmine waved and drove off. When Zadie turned around, Finn was no longer there. All she saw were her wet footprints leading to their motel room.

Pepperoni and sausage with extra cheese . . . yeah, and a side of garlic bread . . . uh-huh . . ." While Zadie ordered pizza, Finn lay on the starchy motel comforter, watching the local weather forecast on mute. Animated rain clouds hovered over most of the Washington coast. The weatherman pointed to them with a look of resignation.

"Yeah, that's it. Thanks." Zadie hung up the phone. "Food will be here in thirty minutes."

Finn kept her eyes on the spiky blue cold front sweeping across the screen. "Cool," she said, distant.

"Wanna watch a movie?"

"Sure."

"What do you feel like? Comedy? Drama? Action?"

"You pick."

"Hey . . ." Zadie sat down on the bed and leaned her shoulder against her sister's. "I know you're disappointed. I am, too, but it's not over yet. Okay? We'll drive down to Earnest tomorrow. Ask around. See if anyone knows her."

"Okay."

"We're going to find her," Zadie insisted.

Finn nodded because it was the only way she knew how to put an end to the conversation.

"Shit," Zadie muttered to herself. "I forgot to order drinks. You want anything from the vending machine? Coke? Snapple?"

"Just a water."

"Okay. I'll be right back." Zadie grabbed her wallet from the nightstand and slipped out the door. Cool, clammy air wafted against Finn's cheek through the open window. She turned toward it, watching Zadie cross the dark parking lot to the glowing blue vending machine outside the motel office.

Close the window.

The message from her dream. Finn blinked. Was she asleep? No. She was in a motel in Washington State. Her sister, bathed in blue light, was smoothing a dollar bill against her thigh.

Close the window.

It wasn't a dream, but it didn't feel real, either. Moments later, as her ears began to ring and dust speckled her vision, she realized why. The dreams she'd been having of her sister weren't dreams at all. They were echoes.

Close the window.

Finn/Zadie watched the bird with the pinstripe wings whistle from the branch of a persimmon tree, its tiny body barely bigger than the fruit itself.

Close the window.

If she closed the window, the words would finally go away. Finn/Zadie hooked her fingers over the bottom sash, ready to pull.

Then out of the corner of her eye, she saw her mother.

Nora Wilder, back turned, frozen in the driveway.

Keys dangling at her side. The hand that held them trembled.

She bent over, unlatched her anklet. Silver links crumpled to the ground.

Finn could hear her own voice in her head calling her mom's name, begging her to stay.

But Finn/Zadie said nothing. She watched coolly as Nora climbed in her car and drove away.

Then she closed the window.

When Zadie returned, her sister was standing in the middle of the room waiting for her, an icy expression on her face. "You saw," Finn said.

She gave her sister a puzzled look. "Saw what?"

"You *watched* her leave."

Zadie's stomach lurched. She didn't need to ask who *her* was.

"You could have stopped her," Finn croaked, "but you didn't. You just let her go."

"How do you—"

"I was there, Zadie! I was *you*!" She was shaking now.

For the last five years, Zadie had dreaded this moment, but seeing the betrayal on Finn's face was worse than anything she could have imagined. "I thought she'd be back. I didn't know she'd disappear."

"But you hoped it," Finn spat.

"That's not true."

"You didn't even want to come out here in the first place. Why? Why'd you hate her so much?"

"I didn't hate her. I was angry."

"What did she do? Ground you? Make you clean your room?"

Zadie clenched her jaw. "No. Nothing like that."

"Then what was it?"

"Remember that day you lost Mom at the chili festival?"

"Sort of. Why?"

"Well, you didn't get separated. Mom left you there."

Finn shook her head vehemently. "No, she didn't."

"Yes. She did." Wounds that Zadie thought had scabbed over started reopening. They glistened in the lamplight like mulled wine. "It wasn't the first time I covered for her, either."

An angry tear escaped one of Finn's eyes and slipped down her cheek, unnoticed. "No . . ."

"I was trying to protect you."

"I don't need protecting."

"So I should have . . . what? Told my kid sister that her mom blacks out and nearly kills herself wandering off a cliff?"

"What cliff?" Finn's voice shook.

"You wanna know why I didn't stop her that day? Because she was already gone, Finn. She had been for months. You just didn't see it."

"You wouldn't let me! I could have helped."

"You were twelve."

"You didn't have to do it alone."

Zadie laughed bitterly. "What would you know about being alone?"

"What's that supposed to mean?"

"You *have* a family."

"I haven't even said yes yet!" Then, realizing she'd said too much, Finn fell silent.

"Yes to what?"

Finn hesitated for a moment, then said, "Kathy and Steve offered to adopt me."

Zadie felt like she'd had the wind knocked out of her. It was a full five seconds before she drew another breath. "When were you going to tell me?"

"I told you. I haven't decided yet."

"Well? What are you waiting for?"

"Don't act like this is easy for me."

"Isn't it? I swear, Finn, sometimes you act like Mom's the only one who left." Zadie regretted the words the moment she gave them oxygen.

A stunned silence descended on the room. Finn gaped back at her sister with a pained expression. "That's not fair."

"Finn, I didn't mean—"

"I need a minute," she said, then shouldered past her sister and opened the door. "Don't follow me."

Zadie flinched as the door slammed behind her.

Fifteen minutes passed. The pizza Zadie had ordered arrived. She tried eating a slice but discovered she no longer had an appetite. *You should eat*, the Star seemed to say (the Star got to eat only if she ate), but even the smell of the sausage made her stomach turn, so she closed the box and listened for Finn's return.

Zadie waited for her sister for another thirty minutes before she decided to go looking for her. She wrapped a piece of pizza in a napkin—a peace offering—and carried it outside. Finn was not in the parking lot. She wasn't in the car, either. Zadie walked down the road to the beach, waited for her eyes to adjust to the moonlight, and scanned the shore. If her sister was on the beach, she didn't see her. "Finn!" Zadie's voice sounded small compared to the roar of the waves. Even if Finn was somewhere in the darkness, she was unlikely to hear her.

Zadie turned around and headed back to the motel. Finn was not in the room when she returned. Pizza grease had soaked through the napkin. Zadie threw it and the slice in the trash, grabbed her keys, and ran to her car.

Twenty-four

The Day Of

(Nora Wilder's disappearance)

"She probably just went out for cigarettes," Zadie said when their mom had been missing for almost four hours. Never mind that Nora hadn't smoked in years, but now that it was starting to look like she might not come back, the words had taken on a whole new significance.

Zadie asked their neighbor, Mrs. Reyes, to watch Finn while she drove around town. She checked all of her mom's favorite haunts, the 24/7 Pancake, the laundromat down the street that sold coffee and doughnuts, the stone bridge on the river, and of course the Fro-Yodel. None of the employees had seen her that night, so she headed to the last location on her list.

It was Thursday, open mic night at Hound Dog's. Thankfully, it was still too early in the evening for anyone to be manning the door, so Zadie was able to slip in unnoticed. She looked around the room of dimly lit faces before heading to the empty stage. A sign-up sheet sat on a stool next to a large speaker. Zadie scanned the list of names but didn't see her mom's. Then she approached the bar. "Have you seen Nora Wilder today?"

"I haven't," the bartender said, then turned to his coworker at the register. "Hey, April. You seen Nora tonight?"

The woman shook her head. "Sorry."

A sickening feeling rose in Zadie's throat as she hurried back to her car. "What have I done?" she whispered to herself. She'd watched her mom leave. She'd watched her leave and had said nothing.

It was her stupid premonition's fault. It hadn't said: *Stop your mom before she leaves forever!* No, it had told her to *close the window.* And she had. She'd closed the goddamn window. *What's the point of having a psychic ability if you can't prevent bad things from happening?*

There was no point, she decided, and swore never to use her gift again.

Twenty-Five

The Sky Is Full of Birds

Zadie had turned down what felt like every street, every alley of the little seaside town, but the only sign of life her headlights caught were the glowing eyes of a raccoon glancing up from its roadside dinner of discarded hot dog. She even drove down the sand for a mile or so, looking for figures in the water, but saw no one. When she returned to the stretch of beach they had camped at the night before, she put her car into park and pulled out her phone. No missed calls. She tried Finn's number again, but it went straight to voice mail. Either the battery had died or she'd shut off her phone. "Finn, please call me back. I'm serious. You're scaring me." That was the fifth voice mail she'd left. She would have to try another tactic.

Nora's box of cassettes was still sitting in the back seat. Zadie reached back, fished out a tape, and fed it into the player. As the opening melody of "A Song About a Bird" filled the car, she closed her eyes and softly hummed along. *It worked before. It will work again,* she told herself, and waited for a message that would lead her to her sister.

But as the last bittersweet piano chord faded out, it was clear that no premonition was coming. She rewound the tape and started over, but she didn't have any luck the second time, either. By the end of the third listen, Zadie yanked the tape out of the deck, unraveled its reel until she had a nest of ribbon balled up in her fist, then hurled it out the car window.

Joel was right, she thought, dismayed. *I should have taken her home.*

Zadie opened her contacts. At the very top of the list was *Anderson, Kathy*. Her thumb hovered over the icon for a moment before she put her phone to sleep. Twenty-four hours, that's how long she would give herself to find Finn. If her sister was still missing by tomorrow evening, she would call the police.

Dawn was breaking when Zadie first saw the small fishing village nestled at the bottom of the hill. The clapboard houses, the church steeple, the boats in the harbor were all bathed in a rosy half-light. As she drove into town, a quaint wooden sign on the side of the road certified that she was in the right place:

EARNEST, WASHINGTON

Where it's important to be . . . !

Cute, she thought. If Finn were here, she'd have made them stop and take a picture with the sign. *Maybe we can take one on our way out of town.* That was, of course, assuming that Finn was here and not, as Kathy would say, "lying in a ditch somewhere."

Stay calm, she told herself, slowing her breathing. She needed to think about this logically. If Finn in fact had hitched a ride to Earnest, she would be looking for their mom. So it stood to reason that Zadie should be doing the same. Two birds, one stone.

She parked her car in a public lot and was surprised to find she was not the only person on the beach at this early hour. A group of people in rubber boots carrying buckets and shovels was milling about, occasionally bending over to dig things out of the sand. *Clam diggers*, Zadie guessed as she stepped onto the beach herself. A faint peeping pulled her attention away from the diggers to the sand dunes on her right. She turned toward the sound and caught herself right before she stepped on a nest of plover chicks. Zadie backed away so as not to scare the tiny birds and watched as their mother swooped down to their rescue. She eyed Zadie warily before turning back to her brood and feeding them from her beak. *I'd give them the clothes off my back* is an expression that is supposed to communicate selflessness, but Zadie thought *I'd give them the food right out of my mouth* had more weight to it. She would be as good a mother as this bird, she decided. When her Star, Ladybug, *child* was born, she would give it all the food and love she could provide.

Suddenly a wave of vertigo overtook her. She stumbled away from the nest and onto her knees.

The sky is full of birds.

The premonition was back. Rather than fight it, Zadie looked up. As she did, a dark blue starling flitted through her field of vision and perched on a stem of beach grass that bowed under its weight. Starlings weren't seabirds, so what it was doing so close to the ocean, Zadie wasn't sure.

The sky is full of birds.

A burst of wingbeats drew Zadie's gaze skyward again. A whole flock of starlings briefly blackened the sky before joining their cousin on the dunes. They were a noisy bunch, chittering and screeching with no regard for all the non-birds that were probably still asleep at this early hour. For some inexplicable reason, Zadie got the impression that the chittering was meant for her, that they were trying to tell her something.

The sky is full of birds.

The first bird to land was also the first to take off. The other starlings followed its lead and flocked toward the parking lot, many of them settling on the roof of Zadie's car. It was either a sign she needed to follow these birds, or merely a suggestion that she take the station wagon through a car wash.

Feeling like Tippi Hedren in *The Birds*, Zadie inched through the flock to get to her driver's-side door. Hopefully, these weren't the kind of birds that liked to peck people's eyes out. Once she was safely inside the car, she locked eyes with a starling perched on her windshield wiper. It seemed to be waiting for something.

The sky is full of birds.

"Yeah, I know. So is my car. Now what?" *Maybe they want me to follow them.* It was a ridiculous thought, but Zadie was desperate enough to try anything. When she started her engine, the birds took off in one giant indigo cloud. "This is crazy," she muttered as she threw the car into drive and took off after the flock.

The starlings lead Zadie away from town, toward the mountains, zigging and zagging across wooded roads, vanishing into the canopy only to burst forth moments later like a great winged beast. Even when she couldn't see them, their constant chittering let her know they were nearby.

As she drove, Zadie began to second-guess her decision. "What am I doing?" she admonished herself. Here she was, chasing a flock of birds when her sister was still missing. If the old Zadie had been here, she would have splashed cold water on her face and told her to "get a grip."

The sky is full of birds.

The premonition had to be important. Why else would the same words have followed her from Texas to the Pacific Coast? Finn had listened to her echoes and it had gotten them this far. Maybe it was Zadie who was supposed to finish it.

The flock disappeared once again into the trees; this time, they didn't reemerge. Zadie pulled over to the side of the road, listening for their chatter, but didn't hear a single squawk. The road was clear, so she made a U-turn and headed back in the direction from which she'd come.

Zadie drove up and down the quarter-mile stretch of road two more times before she saw it peeking through the trees: a weathered Victorian-style cottage with yellow gingerbreading, cathedral windows, and a Juliet balcony dripping with ivy. And covering the lawn, the sagging porch, and the steep slate gables were hundreds of starlings.

The driveway was so overgrown it was no wonder it had taken Zadie several passes to see it. As her car rumbled over the weeds and grasses, she felt a stab of fear in her gut. If she knocked on that door and her mom answered, what would she say? Which stage of grief would choose to speak on her behalf? Anger? Depression? Acceptance? Would she accept her mother as she is, or would she dredge up the past? Could they rebuild their relationship or—overwhelmed by the amount of work ahead of them—let the foundation sink and the walls crumble around them?

Worse yet, what if it wasn't her mom who answered, but a stranger whose breakfast she'd rudely interrupted? She suspected the grief cycle would begin all over again, starting with denial. *Mom is here. She has to be.*

Zadie climbed the steps to the porch, nudging birds out of the way with her toes as she went. Her right hand formed a fist and hovered over the front door for several seconds before she finally knocked. Moments later, she saw a shadow pass over the window and the doorknob turn.

"Hi. Can I help you?" For a split second, Zadie thought she was looking at her mom. The woman was older than her mother, early fifties, with the same long, wavy hair only dyed strawberry blond instead of auburn. But this woman had no freckles, no crimp in her left ear. Her nails were longer, unchewed.

"Hi, uhh . . . I'm looking for Nora Wilder."

"I'm sorry. I don't know any Wilders."

Zadie's heart plummeted. "Oh, okay. Sorry to bother you."

She turned and started hurrying toward the car when she heard the woman say, "I *do* have a sister named Nora, though."

The sound of her mother's name made Zadie's breath catch. She turned back around to face the woman, pulse thrumming in her ears.

"But her last name isn't Wilder. It's Vogel. How do you know this person?"

"She's my mom."

A veil of uncertainty crossed the woman's face. "What did you say your name was again?"

"I didn't. It's Zadie."

"Zadie, I'm Jenna. Hold on a minute." Jenna disappeared back into the house, closing the door behind her.

Jenna was gone for longer than a minute. As the seconds ticked by, Zadie grew more and more anxious. Could Nora have changed her last name—"Wilder" sounded like a name her mom would have picked for herself—or was it all just coincidence? For a fleeting moment, Zadie's nerves got the better of her, and she almost got in her car and drove away.

The door opened. "Hi. Sorry about that," Jenna apologized. "Your mom . . . when was the last time you saw her?"

"Five years ago."

The woman smiled nervously. "Why don't you come inside?"

In that moment, Zadie felt like she was leaving her body. She watched herself say "Okay," then follow Jenna into the foyer with its cherrywood staircase and Turkish runner.

"This was our parents' house before they retired and moved to Florida," Jenna said. The house was tidy, but its age was showing in the cracked plaster walls and missing banister spindles. Several black-and-white family photos hung on the wall. One gentleman in a pinch cap had a bird of prey perched on his forearm. Jenna noticed Zadie looking at it. "Our grandfather. He was a falconer," she said, then moved toward the hallway. "Nora's in the conservatory. This way."

Zadie wordlessly drifted behind the stranger down the dimly lit hallway with its brass sconces and antique mirrors and teal wallpaper depicting open-mouthed birds perched on flowering branches.

She could almost hear them singing; almost see their ruby throats wobble under their tangerine beaks. If this was in fact her mother's childhood home, then these birds probably knew more about Nora's life than she did. Something about their beady stares made Zadie more aware of her own quickening heartbeat.

The conservatory was bursting with plants, from long-necked dracaenas to parlor palms and ivy creeping up wooden trellises. The glass walls were cloudy and spotted with mildew, and the tile floors had broken in enough places that weeds had sprouted in the cracks. The room was so dense with greenery that it took Zadie a moment to see her, but there, seated on a garden chair, gazing up through the glass roof, was her mother.

Any doubts Zadie had as to whether she could ever forgive Nora were gone. All she felt was a profound sense of relief.

"Mom!" Zadie rushed over and buried her face in Nora's shoulder.

Nora did not hug her daughter back. In fact, she seemed barely aware that there was anyone else in the room with her.

Zadie pulled back and looked her mom in the eye. Now up close, she could clearly see the blank space where her mom used to be. It was like looking out the window of an airplane on a cloudy day. All she saw was white.

"Mom, it's me, Zadie." Nora gave no indication that she understood. She simply blinked and returned her gaze to the glass roof on which several starlings were now perched.

Jenna appeared beside Zadie. "I think we should talk for a minute." She gently pried Zadie off Nora and guided her to the other side of a decorative screen.

"So she is your mom, then?" Jenna—her aunt—said sadly.

Zadie's throat tightened as she fought back tears. "What . . . what happened to her?"

"I've been taking care of her for five years now," Jenna began quietly. "When she showed up, she was still walking and talking. Couldn't remember almost anything that had happened to her during the eighteen years since she left home, but other than that, she seemed fine. It's only been within the last year or so that she's really gone downhill. She barely recognizes me most days."

Zadie thought back to the echo Finn had shared with her. *I don't have much time.* Nora knew she was losing herself, or at least part of her did. Zadie, on some level, had known, too. She'd seen it that night on the cliff, and still, she'd let her walk away.

Zadie's breath felt shallow, strained. "Do you know what's wrong with her?"

Jenna pulled her cardigan tight across her chest. "I'm not sure. The doctors say it's early-onset Alzheimer's, but I've treated many patients with the disease and this feels different."

"Are you a doctor?"

"A registered nurse. I retired last year to take care of Nora full time."

"What makes you think it's something different?"

Jenna suddenly looked uncomfortable. "How much do you know about your mom's past?"

"Not much. She didn't like to talk about it."

Jenna sighed like people do at the beginning of a long explanation. "Did she ever act strange? Wander off without telling you where she was going?"

Zadie swallowed, nodded.

Jenna glanced at her sister through the gaps in the screen. "She used to wander off a lot as a teen. Never left a note. Eventually our parents stopped worrying because she always came back. Then one day she didn't."

"How long ago was this?"

"It was 1999. For years, we looked for her. It broke my parents' hearts."

If what Jenna was saying was true, a twenty-three-year-old Nora had run away from her hometown—from her family—to have her. But why? Why travel all the way across the country to have a baby in a strange town where she didn't know a soul? Why do it alone when she had a sister and parents who could have helped her?

Because it was never up to her, Zadie thought. Her mom was as much a victim of her circumstance as her daughters, maybe more so. She'd not only lost her family—twice—but she'd lost all the memories that make up a life. It was like she had never lived at all.

Zadie stole a glance at Nora. "My sister, Finn, is going through the same thing."

Jenna looked momentarily stunned by the realization that she had not one niece but two. "Is she losing her memory, also?"

It was a long explanation, one Zadie didn't have time for. "Sort of. She's in trouble, and I'm hoping Mom can help me."

Clearly dubious, Jenna said, "You're welcome to try."

Zadie stepped out from behind the screen and approached her mom once more. "Can she hear us right now?"

"Maybe. She isn't always able to respond, but I can tell sometimes that she's listening."

Zadie approached her mom and placed a hand gently on her freckled arm. She was frailer than Zadie remembered, more porous-looking, like one wrong move could turn her hollow bird bones to dust. "Mom, if you can hear me, I need your help. Finn's missing."

What appeared to be a small frown seeded between Nora's eyebrows.

"Keep going," Jenna said, moving in closer.

Zadie squeezed her mom's arm tighter. "Her echoes have been bad lately. The memories she's been having . . . well, they're yours."

Nora's frown deepened.

"I think whatever is happening to you is also happening to her. I need to find her before—" She didn't need to finish her thought. Finn's future was staring her in the face.

The starlings on the roof started chittering. Nora slowly flexed her fingers and took hold of Zadie's arm. "She's asking to get up," Jenna said, hurrying around to Nora's right side. "You take one arm, I'll take the other."

Zadie and Jenna pulled Nora to standing. "Where do you want to go, Nor?" Jenna asked her sister. Nora swayed in the direction of the conservatory door. "Come on," Jenna said, nodding toward the hallway.

The three women inched down the hall of birds together. Nora's steps were shambling, but she moved with purpose to the front door. "She wants to go outside." Jenna opened the door and they stepped out into the fresh air.

The hundreds of starlings parked on the roof and lawn were making a terrible racket. "Does this happen a lot?" Zadie asked, still unnerved by the enormity of the flock.

Jenna scowled. "Unfortunately, yeah. These noisy little jerks showed up the same day Nora did and never left. Don't ask me to explain it." Zadie thought she caught a brief flash of amusement in her mother's eyes, as if the birds were not some unexplained phenomenon but an elaborate prank she'd coordinated just to annoy her sister.

"Now what?" Zadie asked. Just as the words left her mouth, the sea of winged bodies began to take flight and Nora's gaze lifted with them.

Jenna watched them go. "They're heading toward the cliffs."

"I can drive," Zadie offered.

"Your car would never make it up those dirt roads." Jenna pulled out her keys and nodded toward her pickup. "We'll take mine."

TWENTY-SIX

NEST

Jenna drove while Zadie rode in the truck bed with her mom. "She likes being able to see the sky," her aunt had explained as they helped Nora over the tailgate. The road was bumpy, so Zadie kept one arm firmly around her mother's wiry shoulder as they watched the starlings fly overhead: *flap-flap-flap-glide, flap-flap-flap-glide*. The light caught their iridescent feathers and Zadie could see not only dark blues but violets and greens, too. It was like staring up into the belly of an abalone shell.

Zadie glanced at Nora out of the side of her eye. Maybe it was only because Nora couldn't talk back, but she suddenly felt the urge to get something off her chest. "Remember that big fight we had the day before you left? The one at the festival?"

Nora blinked.

"No, of course you don't. Well, I said some pretty mean stuff, stuff I shouldn't have said."

Zadie looked at Nora again to see if she was listening. If she was, it was undetectable.

"I called you a bad mom. Do you remember that?" Shame dampened her voice. "Then when you disappeared, I figured you'd decided that you thought we deserved better than you or something."

The truck bounced over a bump in the road. Zadie instinctually tightened her grip on Nora's shoulder.

"You were a good mom. I'm sorry it took so long for me to say it." She paused. "There's something else I have to tell you . . ."

Nora waited.

"I'm pregnant."

Zadie thought she saw a Mona Lisa–esque smile play across her mom's lips, but when she blinked, it was gone.

"You're the first person I've told." It was then that Zadie realized why she hadn't told anyone else about her pregnancy, not even Finn. It was because she'd always pictured telling her mom first.

"Are you seeing this?" Jenna called back to her from the cab. Zadie turned around and saw that the starlings had gotten ahead of them and had converged into one dark mass that twisted and turned like shifting sand. "A murmuration," Zadie said, awestruck. She'd seen one once before when she was young. Nora had pointed it out to her as they sat on the roof of their garage one summer eating Popsicles. She turned back to her mother. "Is this you?"

Nora neither confirmed nor denied Zadie's claim, but she watched the birds intently.

"Can you get us over there?" Zadie called to her aunt.

"I can get us close." Jenna punched the accelerator and the truck bounced over the rutted dirt road, tree branches slapping against the windshield. It wasn't long before they burst out of the cover of the trees, and the road came to an abrupt end in a grassy plain. As Jenna slammed on the brakes, the murmuration swept dramatically over their heads, then hovered over a cliff that dropped off steeply toward the ocean.

"No . . ." Zadie gasped. Another cliff. Only this time she didn't see Finn. Was she too late?

She leaped out of the truck and sprinted to the bluff's edge, skidding to a stop just before tumbling over the side. "Finn!" she screamed into the waves, but her voice was swallowed up by the sea and thrown against the rocks fifty feet below.

Then her foot nudged something in the grass: the painted rock that Luna had given them. Zadie bent down and picked it up. Hand shaking, she held it over the lip of the bluff. The gray protrusion they'd once thought of as a volcano looked identical in shape to the jagged rocks below and the painted smoke looked instead like sea spray.

Zadie's knees felt weak. Worried she might pass out, she staggered back from the cliff. *Finn.* She'd been given a chance to stop her. She'd been given more than one. *And now . . .*

The starlings overhead continued to cry, giving voice to her pain. Zadie gazed up into the shape-shifting cloud of birds and wished they would carry her far away from this place. Tears sprang to her eyes. The sky blurred.

Then as she was turning her back on the ocean, she heard a chime. A soft tinkling sound barely audible above the ocean's roar. Some feet behind Zadie, Nora, leaning on her sister's arm, was staring intently at a stand of trees to her right. The sound seemed to be coming from them.

"Do you hear that?" Zadie asked.

Jenna shook her head. "Hear what?"

"Music!" she called back and vanished into the knot of fir trees.

The sound grew louder as Zadie stumbled through the dark thicket. It reminded her of Ursula's star song: seemingly random notes that together told a story. This one was about a woman looking for her missing sister. She feared the worst, this woman, because she was always fearing the worst. It was how she protected herself. But now that she'd thought the worst had come to pass, she had nothing left to lose.

Zadie broke through a curtain of low-hanging bows into a small clearing, the sight of which made her gasp. Branches and long grasses had been lashed together with vine to form a ten-foot-high asymmetrical dome. Woven through the gaps in the branches and draped in a crisscross pattern overhead were colorful strips of torn fabric—likely old bedsheets and curtains—and artfully daubed onto the walls with mud and clay were all of nature's finest treasures: fragments of stone, shells, feathers, seedpods, and sea glass that shimmered in the sunlight pouring in from the hole in the dome's ceiling. From that hole hung a dozen or more wind chimes. Each one was playing a different melody, and yet together they created music so beautiful it rivaled any star in the sky.

It's a nest, she thought, awestruck.

She almost didn't notice it. From where she was standing, it just looked like a pile of grasses and leaves in the center of the nest, but as she drew closer, she saw one glossy black coil of hair peeking out from the debris.

"Finn!" When she reached her sister's limp body, she flipped her over and found her eyes open but lifeless.

"Finn, it's me." Zadie's voice shook. "Finn, wake up. I found Mom." When her sister did not respond, Zadie gently squeezed her shoulders. "Finn, we did it. We found her."

But Finn's face was blank. She seemed to stare over her sister's shoulder through the hole in the dome. Zadie could even see the murmuration above them reflected in her glassy eyes, like black ink was swirling inside them.

Jenna appeared by Zadie's side and placed two fingers on Finn's wrist. "I've got a pulse," she said.

Overhead, the starlings' cries surged like professional mourners hired for a funeral. *She's not dead!* Zadie screamed inside her head. *Not yet.*

Zadie cupped her sister's cheeks in her trembling hands. "Finn, I know you're in there."

The birds in her eyes continued to circle.

"Finn, I'm sorry. All that shit I said . . . I was wrong." Zadie could feel hot tears welling in her eyes. "You didn't leave me. How could you? You were a kid. I never should have put that on you." It suddenly occurred to Zadie that Finn was now the same age she was when their mom had vanished. If Finn had been in her position, she never would have made the same mistake. She would have been better than that.

"But listen to me, okay?" One of Zadie's tears landed on Finn's cheek, and it looked for a moment like they were crying together.

"You may not have left me then, but you can't leave now. Not when I just got you back. Not when we just got Mom back."

Nora had been watching her daughters from the entrance of the nest dispassionately, as one would watch the last act of a play without having seen the first four. She knew none of the characters, had no idea as to what was at stake. She just knew that she was supposed to be feeling something, something she couldn't see from the audience.

Nora stepped forward. It was the first step she had taken on her own in four months. The women kneeling on the ground were too engrossed in the scene to see her coming. It wasn't until she was practically hovering over them that they noticed.

"Nora?" The oldest of the three women jumped to her feet and offered her a hand. The younger woman, the one who had been crying, gazed up at her with round wet eyes like a child's. And in that moment, she felt *something.* What exactly, she wasn't sure.

Then her gaze landed on the woman lying on the ground. She was barely more than a child herself, a crown of curls splayed out on the green grass. There was something familiar about her. There was something familiar about all of them.

Nora lowered slowly to her knees. The sad woman said something to her, then threaded Nora's fingers through the injured girl's. They were holding hands now, her and this stranger. The sad woman cried and the starlings wailed and Nora wondered what it all meant. That is, until one word pierced through the noise: "Mom?"

Mom. The *something* inside her made a sound like birdsong.

At first Finn thought she was looking into a mirror, but when she brought her hand to her cheek and the reflection did not, the reality of what she was seeing began to dawn on her. "Mom?"

A glimmer of recognition crossed Nora's face, followed by confusion. But Finn couldn't contain herself. She pushed herself up to sitting and slung her arms around her mom's neck. Nora's body was stiff, unyielding.

"She doesn't recognize us." Zadie was kneeling next to her. Her eyes were puffy as if she'd just been crying. Finn turned back to their mother. The glimmer she'd seen a moment ago was gone. But despite the sinking feeling in her heart, she wasn't ready to give up just yet. "Mom, it's me, Finn." She grabbed her sister's hand and pulled her closer. "And this is Zadie. We're your daughters."

Nora's eyes flicked back and forth between the two faces; then a wisp of a smile graced her mouth. "You're here," she said.

Finn and Zadie clamored into her arms, and Nora buried her face into Finn's curls. "I've been looking everywhere for you two," she said softly.

Twenty-seven

Two Thousand, Two Hundred, and Eighty Miles

Their mom didn't return all at once. Zadie and Finn sat with her as she lay on the couch, propped up by tasseled pillows, watching her drip, drip, drip back into her body. Every time a new memory came to her, the flesh between her eyebrows would crease, and she would sound it out. At first her speech was slow and halting, like sleep talk, but the more she spoke, the more fluid it became. When Nora turned to Zadie with an impish grin and said, "Knock, knock," Zadie knew she was going to be okay.

By that evening, Nora was more like her spiked-punch self. She remembered her daughters' names and would break into a huge smile every time she said them out loud. When a funny story came back to her, she told it like it was the first time, and her daughters laughed because she was laughing. Zadie still had questions, but she didn't want to break the spell of that moment.

Zadie and Finn stayed with Nora all day and night. They slept in her bed. Zadie woke briefly in the middle of the night to find her sister cuddled up against Nora's right shoulder, dozing peacefully. She watched them for a few moments, their chests rising and falling in time with each other. Then Zadie felt the little Star stir inside her.

It's okay, it seemed to say.

Zadie rested one hand on her abdomen, then slipped her head under her mother's other arm.

Finn couldn't take her eyes off her. Maybe it was the way the wind was spinning her mom's hair into rope, the way her freckles looked darker in the sun, the way her toes curled as a wave washed over her feet; or maybe it was because Finn was afraid that if she looked away, Nora would vanish.

She had yet to understand why their mom had left. At first she was so happy to see Nora, so happy to be back in her own body, that she hadn't even given it a second thought. But as the initial excitement wore off, she found herself wanting to know more. She was trying to be patient. Nora's memory had completely unspooled. It was only natural that it would take time to gather it all up. Still, her curiosity had made her restless.

She watched her mother roll up her pant legs and wade into the sea until it cut her off at the knees. Finn followed. The salt water momentarily stung the abrasions on her feet, but soon they were so cold she could barely feel them. Memories were carried to her on the wind—foghorns, seals barking, children's delighted squeals—but she paid them no attention. She couldn't focus on the past right now, only the present.

After they'd toweled off and put on warm socks, the Wilders sat in the open back of Zadie's station wagon while Nora rifled through her box of cassettes. "I can't believe you kept these," she marveled.

"I figured you'd want them back eventually," Zadie answered. Finn could see her sister blushing. She didn't like anyone knowing how sentimental she actually was.

"Thank you." Nora leaned over and gave her older child a kiss on the forehead. Zadie smiled quickly, then looked away.

Their mom closed the lid of the box and pushed it aside. Then something came over her. Hot tears sprang to her eyes. "I'm so sorry, girls. I don't think I'll ever forgive myself for what I did to you."

"Will you tell us what happened?" Finn asked. She put her arm around her mother and listened with bated breath as Nora told the story of her migration.

Two thousand, two hundred, and eighty miles. That's how far Nora had traveled. It sounded far, but it was nothing compared to the 44,000 miles Arctic terns fly from Iceland to the Antarctic and back again. Every year they circumnavigate the Earth, chasing summer to ensure that the first thing their chicks glimpse of this world is the sun.

Zadie, she explained, had been born on a brilliant spring morning. The sun was still bright the following afternoon when Nora took her daughter back to her little apartment and asked herself for the hundredth time: *How did I get here?* She had no memory of most of the 2,280 miles she'd traveled from Earnest to San Antonio. She had barely any memory of her hometown at all. It was as if her life had begun the moment she crossed the Texas–New Mexico border.

And when she crossed that same border eighteen years later heading in the opposite direction, her life began all over again.

She'd stayed in Texas longer than she should have. Most birds nest for a few months, then return home, but Nora wasn't a bird. She couldn't push her child out of a tree and watch it fall, hoping that its fledgling wings would keep it aloft. She'd raised her kids for as long as she could before it was finally her, not her daughters, who was forced into flight.

When she'd arrived back in Earnest—even as she'd hugged her sister for the first time in almost twenty years—she'd felt something was missing. But it seemed the harder she tried to remember, the easier it was to forget.

Nora spent the next five years searching for anything that would make her feel whole. Many days she would wander off into the woods while Jenna was at work and weave branches together without thinking about why she was doing it or for whom. It was the only thing that distracted her from the alarming emptiness in her heart.

Nora said she could finally see how these two seemingly separate lives fit together. She could see the jagged lines where one ended and the other began, and the remaining holes in her memory began to fill in. What she saw made her want to cry.

When she was finished, Finn exhaled. Her mom's fascination with birds had taken on a whole new significance. "You *migrated?*"

Nora appeared equally bemused by the revelation. "It's the only way I know how to explain it. I felt this . . . pull. I've felt it my whole life. I just never knew what it was. I didn't say anything, because I didn't understand it myself, and I didn't want to scare you guys."

Finn had felt the same pull. It had driven her into the wilderness barefoot and to the nest their mother had built on the ocean cliffs. She'd felt something like it as she sped down the highway on the back of a motorcycle. "Is that why you got in the accident?"

"The accident?" Nora's face went blank for a moment. "Oh, yeah. The motorcycle. I was trying to get back to you guys."

"So you *did* remember us?"

"Sometimes I would get these flashes." Nora's eyes glistened like melting ice. "Most of the time, I had no idea who you were, but that night, something clicked. I knew I had only a small window before I forgot you again."

"So you tried to get home."

"I tried, but I couldn't."

"Because it hurt too much." Finn touched her ribs.

"You felt that?" Nora looked mildly stunned. "What else did you feel?"

Finn wasn't sure how to answer her mom's question. She didn't think of her echoes that way. She hadn't just felt what Nora had felt. She'd become her. Those memories were now as much a part of her experience as her mother's. "Just that you were lost and scared. I wanted to help."

Nora squeezed her youngest's shoulder. "You did."

"Zadie's the one who actually found you."

Zadie squirmed, then shrugged. "I just followed the birds."

Finn knew there was more to Zadie's story, but she didn't press her. "So, wait . . . if a migratory instinct made you return home, why didn't you come back a few months later? Isn't that how migration works? It's a cycle."

"I'm not sure," Nora said, shrugging.

"Birds migrate to nest," Zadie broke in. Finn and Nora turned to look at her. "You left for Texas when you were pregnant with me, and you stayed until . . ."

"You were grown up," Nora finished.

Zadie nodded.

The women were silent for a few moments as they considered this new theory. They could never really be sure why Nora had migrated when she did, just as they could never be sure why Finn and Zadie possessed their gifts. The world was a more extraordinary place now than it had been a month ago, before they knew about stars that sang or trees that talked with one another. It was a world where you could think you'd lost someone forever, only to be reunited years later. A *happy ending,* Finn thought, profoundly relieved that such a thing actually existed.

"Oh! I have something for you, too." Finn pulled up her pants leg, undid the silver chain around her ankle, and handed it to her mom.

"My anklet!" Nora gasped.

"I've been keeping it safe for you." Finn searched Nora's face for a sign as to whether her mom remembered dropping it in their driveway five years ago—if she'd intended it as a bread crumb for Finn to follow or if the act had simply been a side effect of her confusion—but she found no such clarity.

Nora stared down at the tiny letters in her palm. After a moment, she said, "I think you should keep it," then looped the chain around Finn's ankle and closed the clasp. "It looks better on you, anyway."

"Thanks, Mom." *Mom.* The word should have come naturally to Finn, but it felt strange on her tongue. Nora was her mom, so then why did she feel guilty? *Because Kathy and Steve are my parents, too,* she thought. She realized then that she'd made her decision.

"I'll be right back. I have to make a call."

Finn walked down the beach until she was just out of earshot, then dialed Kathy's number. "Hey, it's Finn," she said, glancing back over her shoulder. "I just wanted to let you know I'm coming home."

My girl is a woman now. The epiphany was a gut punch. The last time Nora had seen Finn, she wore braces and still needed a night-light to sleep. Now Finn was taller than she was, an adult not just in stature but in comportment and ambition. Her daughter had endured a lot of pain to find her, but by the easiness of her smile you'd never know it.

As she watched Finn from a distance, Nora mourned the time she'd lost. Five years. Over a quarter of her younger daughter's life. She owed a debt of gratitude to the couple who had raised her during that time. The Andersons must have made sure that Nora's absence didn't crush Finn's spirit. That, or Finn's spirit was too resilient to be crushed.

Zadie's scars, on the other hand, were plainer. It pained Nora to know that she had put them there, and she searched for the magic words that would help them heal. But the longer she sat with her daughter, breathing in rhythm with the waves, the more apparent it became that no such words existed. Their scars would heal, but only with time. If Zadie would have her, she would be a part of her life for as long as she wanted. Hers and her grandchild's.

"How far along are you?"

Zadie looked surprised. "Eight weeks . . . I didn't think you could actually hear me." Her daughter paused as though waiting for Nora to give her some sage piece of wisdom about motherhood that she would later pass on to her kid, but Nora didn't. Instead, she patted Zadie on the back of the hand and said, "Don't worry. You'll figure it out."

"Is it hard?"

Nora gazed out over the ocean as if the story of those eighteen years of motherhood were a boat on the horizon. "Every day you'll wonder if you're doing it right. There will be days when you know you didn't. Those are the hardest . . ." she said as her voice trailed off.

After a few moments of silence, Nora went on. "I should have told you what I was going through."

Zadie nodded, then reached out and squeezed her mother's hand.

When they returned to the house, Nora declared she needed to lie down and excused herself to her bedroom. For the first time in two days, Zadie and Finn were alone. Silence settled like dust. There was so much to talk about, but neither of them knew exactly where to begin.

"Let's take a walk," Zadie said.

Finn nodded.

Even through the thicket, they could feel the wind from the ocean. They could hear it, too, in the gentle *thwap* of the cotton drapery and the wind chimes that danced above their heads. It was midafternoon. The sun spilled in through the open roof of the nest. A garland of colored sea glass cast turquoise trapezoids on Zadie's bare arms.

"I can't believe she made all this," Finn said as she ran her fingers along the wall of woven branches. "It must have taken her years."

"Too bad she didn't make one for us when we were younger. I would have loved reading in here." Zadie glanced at her sister out of the corner of her eye. "You know, I'm still having a hard time wrapping my brain around all *this*. It doesn't feel real."

"Same." Finn sat cross-legged on the ground and looked up through the hole in the roof. "You know, my bird, Chris, used to do this thing . . . he'd hop around his loft, flap his wings like crazy, make a ton of noise. I figured he was sick or something, so I took him to the vet. She said it was normal for birds in captivity to act that way. In the spring, they get restless because they know they're supposed to be migrating, but they can't."

"I'm guessing Mom is Chris in this analogy?"

Finn continued, "I asked the vet how birds know how to migrate over such long distances. She said there are lots of different theories—magnetic fields, the position of the sun, even smell—but no one knows for sure."

"It's a mystery."

"So are we, if you think about it."

Zadie joined Finn cross-legged on the ground. "How are you feeling, by the way?"

"Honestly?" Finn smiled. "Pretty good."

The fog that had settled over her sister appeared to have been lifted, just as it had from their mother. Somehow their reunion had saved them both.

As if Finn had read Zadie's mind, she said, "When I was in her memories, I always felt like I was only half there, you know? I guess bringing us back together was enough to make her whole again."

"Sure, if you want to be corny about it," Zadie joked.

"If you've got a better explanation, I'm listening."

"Nope. Let's run with yours for now."

Finn smiled. "Okay."

Zadie angled herself toward her sister. "Hey, about the other night—"

"Don't worry about it. I said some shitty things, too."

"So we're good?"

"We're good."

The wind struck another chord on the chimes. They listened wordlessly to the music.

After a few moments, Zadie asked, "Was that Kathy you were on the phone with earlier?"

"Yeah." Finn hesitated. "She says she's booking me a ticket. My flight leaves tomorrow. I wish I could stay longer, but I've already worried them enough as it is."

Zadie nodded. She'd known this day was coming, but it still stung. "So you're taking them up on their offer, then? To adopt you?"

Finn looked surprised. "Oh! No . . . I told them I love them and that I'll always be in their lives, but that I couldn't do that to Mom . . . or to you."

A lump formed in Zadie's throat. "Really? You said that?"

"Unfortunately you're stuck with me," her sister said with a smile.

Defying every aloof instinct in her body, Zadie scooped her sister into a hug. She wanted to tell her how much it meant to her that she'd chosen them, how much *Finn* meant to her, but she'd spent all her emotional energy on the hug itself. Instead she cracked, "And to think I was so close to getting rid of you."

"Ha! You're gonna have to try harder than that."

Zadie pulled back, quickly brushing a rogue tear from her cheek.

"What about you?" Finn asked. "What are you going to do now?"

"I think I might stick around here a little longer. I have some things I need to work out."

"With Mom?"

"Yeah. Well, and there's this other thing . . ."

Finn waited.

"I'm pregnant."

"I was wondering when you were going to tell me," Finn said, her tone unexpectedly blasé.

"You knew?"

"It wasn't hard to guess. You've looked nauseated ever since we left Texas."

"Oh, I thought I was hiding it well." Zadie should have known she couldn't pull one over on her sister.

"Does Dustin know?"

"Not yet."

"What about Mom?"

"She knows."

Finn smiled, eyes bright. "I'm so excited."

"Me too."

How many lies would she tell? Zadie wondered. How many drafts of the story of this world would she write before there was one good enough for her baby? And what if her child could see into future? Then it didn't matter how many lies she told, her child would discover the truth eventually. Nora had kept secrets. Maybe she could try being honest.

EPILOGUE

TWENTY-EIGHT

A SONG ABOUT A BIRD

"She's here!"

Jenna turned away from the window toward her sister, who was bounding down the stairs two at a time. Nora's hair—which she had recently dyed a vibrant shade of purple—had been pulled into a messy bun, and her clothes, which had once hung off her too-thin frame, now clung to the muscles she'd built loading trucks at the tuna cannery. She hurried past Jenna to the window. "She looks taller. Don't you think?"

"Looks the same to me."

"Don't you think she looks taller, Zadie?"

Zadie looked up. Through the window, she could see Finn heaving a suitcase out of the trunk of her car. She didn't look taller, but she looked self-assured, happy. Most of their weekly phone conversations had revolved around her new college life: the friends she was making; the culinary merit of various dining halls; which professors asked their students to call them by their first names and which professors had sticks up their tweed-clad butts. It came as no surprise to Zadie that her sister was thriving there and, aside from an unfortunately timed echo in her dorm's laundry room, Finn's gift had given her little trouble. As far as the rest of the student body was concerned, she was just a normal eighteen-year-old.

"Maybe a little taller," Zadie answered, which was met with a playful glare from her aunt.

Moments later, Finn burst through the front door, and both she and Nora let out short squeals like two piglets getting their tails pulled. "My college girl!" Nora said as she smothered her daughter in a bear hug and then proceeded to spin her in circles. It made Zadie dizzy just looking at it.

After staggering away from her mother, the Tilt-A-Whirl, she gave Jenna a quick squeeze before saying, "Where's my baby niece?"

The little Star—now known as Wren—lay wriggling in Zadie's lap. At present, she was three months old and roughly the size of a husky cat. It wouldn't be long, Zadie thought, before she was big enough that her spunky kicks and punches would start to inflict actual pain. She would gladly take her little one's blows, however, because she'd never been more in love with anything in her life.

Finn sat down on the couch next to Zadie. "Can I hold her?"

"Yeah, of course." Zadie placed her baby in her sister's arms.

Wren peered up at Finn with watery blue eyes, a bubble of spit forming in the corner of her mouth as she flashed a gummy smile. "Hey there, Wren! I'm your aunt Finn." Finn turned back to Zadie. "Oh my god, Z. She's got to be one of the top five cutest babies ever!"

"She takes after her grandma," Nora said, sitting sidesaddle on the arm of the couch.

Zadie rolled her eyes and tried to hide a smile. "Mom tries to take credit for literally everything she does." Then to Nora, "I'm going to start writing your name on all of her diapers."

"It would be an honor," Nora said, winking at her granddaughter.

Nora did deserve some of the credit, Zadie thought. Ever since she'd moved into the old house at six months pregnant, both her mom and her aunt had gone out of their way to make her feel at home. They'd converted an office into a room for her and the baby. They'd hung watercolors and restored an old bed frame they'd found in the shed. Nora had even made a mobile out of gull feathers to hang over the crib.

When the baby came, her mother had cooked meals and changed diapers. She took Wren out in the stroller so Zadie could sleep.

Many times, Zadie had thought to herself *I couldn't have done this without her.* The truth was, she could have, but she was glad she didn't have to.

Even though Nora had improved immensely, there were still times when her memory faltered; moments when Zadie would find her standing in the front yard, unable to pull her eyes away from the flocks of geese on their way south. But this time, Zadie knew to hold her mother's hand until the feeling passed. She was her tether, her anchor. If Nora ever migrated again, they would do it together.

"Seriously, though . . ." Nora said, "Zadie's a really good mom."

Nora, Finn, and Jenna all turned to smile at her. Zadie fidgeted uncomfortably. "Okay, okay. Cut it out."

But Finn didn't break eye contact. "I'm proud of you, Sis."

"Shut up," she said, then smiled in spite of herself.

"So . . ." Finn began, her voice low. "Have you noticed anything yet?"

"She's only three months old, Finn."

"I know that. But it's different for everyone."

Zadie hadn't noticed anything unusual about her daughter. Not yet. She hoped she had at least a few years before she had to have that particular talk. If Wren did have a gift, she would try her best to embrace it, even if that meant letting her toddler play psychic pranks on her every once in a while.

"Oh, I almost forgot!" Finn reached into her purse with her free hand and handed Zadie a package tied up with ribbon.

"But you already got her a present," she protested.

"It's not from me."

Curious, Zadie ripped open the paper to find a tiny green bucket hat with flowers embroidered on it.

"It's from Joel."

"You guys have been talking?"

"Online, yeah. He lives in the Dakotas now. I don't remember which one, and I'm not sure he does, either. But he's moving to Hawaii next month."

"Will you thank him for me? Actually, no." Zadie carefully folded the little hat into a triangle. "I'll do it myself." She was excited for Joel. The Hawaii patch had been his white whale. She could just picture him now in his wolf shirt and flip-flops, spending afternoons combing the beach with a metal detector and eating fried shrimp. Whatever life he decided to lead next, she hoped he was happy.

"Aww! She's tired." Finn beamed down at the baby in her arms. Sure enough, Wren's eyelids were drooping and she opened her mouth in a silent, pink yawn.

"Naptime," Zadie said in a singsong voice as Finn passed Wren back to her.

"Want me to take her?" Nora offered.

"No, it's okay. You guys catch up. I'll be right back."

Zadie climbed the stairs to their bedroom. Birds chirped through the open window as she lowered her daughter gently into her crib. The second Wren hit the mattress, however, she started to squirm. Zadie placed a hand on her daughter's chest and began to hum. The vibration of her voice must have calmed her, because Wren quickly settled.

"Hush darling, hush
It's almost day"

They weren't the real lyrics. The real lyrics were too tragic. Their story would be a happy one.

"The birds are singing . . ."

The perfect half-moons of her baby's eyes slid shut as she melted into sleep.

"I'm here to stay."

Acknowledgments

To my agent, Andrea Somberg: I feel very fortunate to have you in my corner. Thank you for being my guide through the publishing world.

To Peter Wolverton and St. Martin's Press, for giving me the opportunity to publish for a second time when publishing just one book had already surpassed my most ambitious dreams.

To the folks at Literary Cleveland: Thank you for welcoming me into your community. In particular, I'd like to thank Matt, Jackie, Sam, Josh, and Jane for showing me what a supportive writing group looks like.

To my extended family, including its newest additions. (Four babies in one year!) And to my mom in particular, who has read the book more times than I have.

To Anigran, who would be telling me "Well done!" right about now.

To Max, for holding the baby while I locked myself away in the other room to work on revisions.

And to my son, Malcolm. I asked you to wait until I'd finished the book before you made your entrance into the world, but you had other plans. It's okay though, because I love you and I can't wait to watch you grow up. Oh, and I should also probably thank you for mostly sleeping through the night. You have no idea how grateful I am for that.